PRAISE for The Bl

"Chicago speak is such a great language and in *The Blue Circus*, Dennis Foley, a native Southsider, brings that language, the city itself and its rambunctious characters to life. Neighborhood streets, dive bars, and shady city deals waltz across the page, spread out like a deck of cards. But Foley holds some of the cards back and delivers them in a timely fashion, causing the reader to shake his head and marvel. This is a wonderful story about the City that Works, or doesn't work, and a family trying to push forward to survive, as only an insider can tell."

—*Reviewer's Bookwatch*

"This left-jab-and-a-solid-right-hook-to-the-jaw of a novel packs as powerful a literary punch as I've seen in years. That "stormy, husky, brawling" city that Sandburg described is still with us, and it comes surging to life in these pages. *The Blue Circus* is Southside Chicago down to the very marrow of its bones."

—Jack Lynch, former English Department Chair,
St. Laurence High School

"Part family saga, part murder mystery, part city worker tell all. Foley nails it."

—City Worker No. 1

"Make no bones about it, Foley, a former Streets and San worker, paints characters who could be twins with guys I have seen on the job site. Foley knows the city, he knows the city characters, and he knows how to write. Like one of the places in his earlier book, *The Streets and San Man's Guide to Chicago Eats*, I give Foley's book Four out of Four Forks.

—City Worker No. 2

Also by Dennis Foley:

THE DRUNKARD'S SON (Side Street Press, 2012)

THE STREETS AND SAN MAN'S GUIDE TO CHICAGO EATS
(Lake Claremont Press, 2004)

The

BLUE CiRcUs

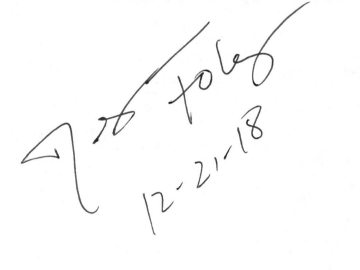

Dennis Foley

A SIDE STREET PRESS BOOK

Published by
Side Street Press Inc.
3400 West 111th Street, #412
Chicago, IL 60655

www.sidestreetpressinc.com

ISBN: 978-0-9988039-2-0

Library of Congress Control Number: 2018932109

Printed in the United States of America

First Edition: September, 2018

Cover by Nealis Keane

For my father, Jack Foley, who died far too young, and for my grandfather, Michael Roche, who said little but did much.

Contents

The

BLUE CiRcUs

Part One

The Eleven

"The subject of criminal rehabilitation was debated recently in City Hall. It's an appropriate place for this kind of discussion because the city has always employed so many ex-cons and future cons."

–Mike Royko

1. Danny Lonigan's Interview

A HERD OF CITY WORKER WANNABES dressed in jeans, flannel shirts, and work boots huddled on or around chairs and benches inside a Streets and Sanitation garage that on its best day could only be described as gray and dismal. These men awaited their opportunity to dazzle the interview panel with their knowledge of circuits, amps, and ohms in hopes of landing one of the eleven primo jobs posted for City of Chicago electricians. Ah yes, a city job—to die for. Outside, a heavy April rain beat down on the city, pelting the metallic garage roof, causing the wannabees to gaze up every now and again towards the heavens. Some found the sound soothing—Mozart keying a soft melody of sorts—while others saw it as an endless stomping of angry feet. A sliver of sunlight sliced through the few windows in the garage, supplying just enough light to compensate for the numerous burnt out bulbs overhead. Some of the hopeful read the newspaper or toyed with their phones to pass the time, while others gathered in small groups to talk about the Sox or the Cubs. It was early April, after all, the start of a new baseball season, and such chatter was certainly appropriate. And there was Danny Lonigan standing in the midst of the crew, alone and off to one side. With his long, angular frame, he looked very much at home among the other blue-collar workers. A wannabe who had just completed his interview pushed through a door near the far corner of the garage and strutted across the cement floor, followed by a secretary dressed in jeans that were far too tight.

"Daniel Lonigan," the secretary barked. Her gravelly voice surprised Danny, reminding him of his fifth-grade teacher, Mrs. Cooper, a woman who consumed cigarettes with such rapidity, her students thought smoking was her second job.

Danny stood up with a "Yo."

The secretary smiled. "This way," she announced and led Danny into the interview room.

Positioned at the back of this smallish room, Ted Flynn, one of Danny's high school classmates, and two other men sat behind an eight-foot-long, fold-up table that looked better suited for a poor man's poker game than for conducting interviews. Danny eyed the paneled walls as he entered, bare but for a White Sox poster displaying the 2005 season schedule and a few restaurant menus attached to the paneling with strips of electrical tape.

"Have a seat, please," Flynn said, his beady eyes resting like tarred BBs on his face. Danny dropped onto a metal chair across from the three men and watched as the secretary squeezed into a small grade school-style desk off to the side of the room. She scribbled something on a sheet of paper.

"Okay, Danny, you already know me," Flynn said. He tossed his right arm in the direction of the other men, "But this is Dan Cullinan and this is Mark Morgan."

Danny smiled. "Nice to meet ya." Cullinan and Morgan nodded their sizeable, balding melons at the same time and stared across the table with glazed eyes.

"Okay, let's get started," Flynn said and then cleared his throat. "On this table, as you can see, Dan, there's five different tools. I need ya to point out each individual tool and identify it for us."

Danny's face went blank. This can't be the interview, Danny thought. No way. No fuckin' way. He pushed his right hand through his shock of black hair. Danny was certainly no virgin to the interview process. He had been through plenty in his thirty-seven years, the roughest of which came with the multiple, stone-faced panels he appeared in front of before he landed the job as a prosecutor with the Cook County State's Attorney's office. But tough as those interviews were—tell us your thoughts on the death penalty, Dan; could you prosecute a father who kills the man who raped his eight-year-old daughter, Dan? how would you handle things, Dan, if a family member of yours got a drunk driving ticket and was assigned to your courtroom?—he never found them confusing.

"Is this the interview or, uh, does that come later?" Danny's eyes roamed the faces of the three men, who exchanged glances but remained mute.

Flynn finally eked out a laugh and said, "Okay, let's try this thing again, huh, Dan? Just point to each tool and identify it for us."

Danny quickly eyeballed the tools on the table and picked up the first one. "Okay. Well, this one here . . . this is a pliers." Danny set the tool down and immediately snagged another. "This one's a screwdriver."

"What kinda screwdriver?" Flynn barked.

Danny glanced at Flynn's beady eyes for a moment, before returning his focus to the screwdriver.

"This is a Phillips screwdriver. A Phillips."

Flynn nodded and smiled as if he were saying, "That's it, Danny Boy. That's the stuff. Keep going, man. You are one smart son of a bitch, and today you are demonstrating that keen intelligence of yours to the three electrical gods in this room."

Danny set the screwdriver down and tapped the next tool on the table.

"This tool here, this is a hacksaw. Ya know, the kinda saw used for cuttin' pipe." Danny fingered the next tool. "This one's a screwdriver too. But it's a flat-head screwdriver."

Silence fell upon the room as Danny eyed the last tool, a blue and yellow tool about five inches long and an inch wide on all four sides. Tapered ever-so-slightly at the top, a small metal head jutted out about a quarter-inch from its base. Danny twisted the tool between his fingers, studying it, before setting it down.

"I don't know what that tool is. No idea. Never saw it before. Never used it before."

Flynn snatched the tool and held it just inches from his face. "This is a punch tool, Danny," he said as he shook it. "It's for communication work, low voltage stuff. Ya know, wiring for phones, computers, routers, data—all that sorta shit. You punch down the wires with this thing. Can ya picture that?"

"Gottit," Danny said. "Just never did any work with that before. So I never used one."

"That's okay, Dan," said Flynn with a smile. "Four outta five ain't bad."

From her little desk, the secretary released a not-so-little belch. The four men turned their heads in unison towards her as if she were an E. F. Hutton spokesperson preparing to offer promising investment advice. The secretary ignored their eyes and continued to mark the paper on her desk. It was only then that Danny noticed she was playing tic-tac-toe against herself.

Flynn glanced at his cohorts. "Anything else?"

Cullinan and Morgan wagged their heads. Flynn climbed to his feet. Danny joined him and as he stood, he saw a small frog tinkering around on the wooden floor near the wall behind the three men. Danny did a quick double-take but his eyes had not deceived him. The frog was still there, and Danny wondered what the hell a frog was doing hanging out in this sad excuse for an interview room, let alone anywhere in Chicago. He wondered if perhaps Ted Flynn or one of the other two electrical gods had a frog terrarium in one of their offices and forgot to close the damn thing after feeding time. Danny considered saying something, but decided against it.

"All right, Dan," Flynn said, "thanks for comin' down for the interview today. We'll contact ya in about a week."

Danny's face was a confused knot. Flynn walked towards the door with Danny in tow, both men stopping just outside of the doorway. Flynn turned back.

"Ginette, go ahead and bring the next guy in."

"Sure," said the secretary, and then she wiggled herself free from her desk. Danny pawed at his chin as he waited for the secretary to walk past.

"Michael Broderick," the secretary barked into the garage, ready to start the process all over again.

"Am I okay?" Danny whispered. He looked out into the waiting area, his forehead matted with wrinkles. "I mean, there's alotta guys out here today."

"You're good to go," Flynn said. "Don't worry about the numbers."

"Okay, but what about, ya know, what about the other shit—the shit that was in all the newspapers?"

Flynn sighed. "No one here cares that you got disbarred, Dan. Big fuckin' deal." A twisted smile claimed Flynn's face. He nodded towards Morgan and Cullinan. "Hell, if anything, some of the guys around here might just hit ya up to do a will or a closing for 'em. You'll have side jobs right off the bat."

Danny's face was still a wall of wrinkles. Flynn set a hand on his shoulder. "Look, talk to your brother, okay? He'll fill ya in. Everything's gonna be fine." The men went mute as the secretary led the next wannabe past them into the interview room.

2. Hat Takes in a Movie

JIMMY "THE HAT" SCARPELLI SAT ALONE in the back row of a movie theater. A city electrician for fifteen years, Hat had long known how the system works and how to work the system. Some city workers always give a good day's work, some never give a good day's work, and some—like Hat—fell somewhere between. If this is news to you, then an appropriate salutation must now be made: WELCOME TO CHICAGO. Hat's baby blue Streets and San van slept in the parking lot beside the movie theater. From his seat, Hat watched the noon matinee unfold onscreen and laughed his ass off. He loved comedies. Sure he was fond of good shoot-'em-up, action flicks, too, but comedies— that's where Hat's heart truly sat. The eight-inch beef sandwich in his lap was half gone. Some of the juice had leaked through the butcher's paper and foil onto Hat's jeans and Sox hoodie, but that didn't faze him. Not one bit. You can always wash a pair of pants and a sweatshirt, but you don't always get a chance to munch on a Tony's Beef sandwich. Between chuckles, Hat continued to devour that beef. Once every few weeks or so, Hat rewarded himself for his hard work on the other days by taking in a movie, or he might go bowling or golfing. Today was one of those days. And the Ford City Cinema at Seventy-Sixth and Cicero was the perfect place to take in a flick. Pushed off near the far southwestern city boundary, there were never many eyes around this theater, and Hat liked that. A lot. He didn't have enough fingers and toes to count the number of flicks he'd seen at Ford City over the years: *Dances With Wolves,* when he was a kid; *Good Will Hunting,* on his top five list, and just recently he saw *The 40-Year-Old Virgin.*

Hat's cell phone, set to vibrate, went off. He wagged his head in disgust and dug into his pocket. "Dipshit," he muttered to himself when he saw the call was from his foreman, Kip Larsen. He pushed his cell back into his pocket and eyed the big screen again. A rotund actor tripped and fell while walking down a sidewalk. Hat laughed and stuffed more beef into his mouth.

3. Late Again

THOUGH THE EARLY MORNING STORM had ceased, beads of rainwater still dotted the hood of Phipps's car. An investigator with the city's Inspector General's office, he sat parked in the back of the Chicago Department of Transportation parking lot at Thirty-Fourth and Lawndale on the city's near Southwest Side. Surveillance work came easy to Phipps. He did a fair amount back when he was a cop working in the Gang Crimes Unit at Homan Square, back when he was a young buck, before he grew tired of dodging the occasional bullet and jumped ship to become an IG investigator. A file folder and a camera with a zoom lens attachment sat on the passenger seat. Phipps checked the time on his wristwatch. 12:31 p.m. Having manned his post since 8:00 a.m, he was starting to feel the effects that came with such sedentary work. Phipps stretched both legs and then rubbed his ass back and forth across the vinyl seat cushion before turning a page of the *Chicago Sun-Times.* He'd already gone through the paper three times that morning and prepared to page through it yet again when a gray Lincoln Continental entered the lot. Phipps tossed the paper to the passenger side floor, grabbed his camera, and snapped off a multitude of photos as the Continental backed into a CDOT reserved space. Jello Pellegrini, a short, portly man nearing the age of sixty, exited the car clad in polyester pants and a red, V-neck sweater. A strong easterly wind snapped the few wisps of gray hair atop Jello's head to and fro, flogging his tanned dome. Jello stood motionless for a moment, his hands pressed onto the hood of his car, smiling as he watched a garbage truck belch clouds of black smoke into the South Side air as it rumbled down Lawndale. Once the truck disappeared around a corner, Jello entered the CDOT building. Phipps set the camera on the passenger seat and made a call on his cell.

"Talk to me," Ed Gilbreath said. An assistant inspector general, the forty-year-old Gilbreath sat on a comfortable chair in his office.

"Jello just rolled in," Phipps said.

Gilbreath eyed the clock on his desk. "Well, he's twenty minutes earlier than yesterday. Maybe we should pin a medal on him."

Phipps scratched his nose as he spoke. "I'm sure he's late 'cuz he had a meetin'."

"Oh, I'm sure he had a meeting too. Important guys like him, they have all sorts of meetings." Gilbreath stood from his chair. "How many shots did you get?"

"I dunno. Fifteen or so, I guess. I wanted to get more but he seems to be waddlin' a little faster these days."

"Sounds good. Did he see you?"

"Nah, I don't think so."

A thin smile slid onto Gilbreath's face, the brightness of his teeth matching the color of his button-down shirt. "How'd you like to make Jello dance?"

"Dance?"

"Yeah. I want you to go around to his window, that big-ass picture window of his, and take a few more shots from there. Make sure he sees you, though."

"Sure ya want me to do that?"

"Sure, I'm sure. I want him to know we're watching him. I want him to have to close his blinds. Piece a shit like him doesn't deserve to have a view."

Phipps laughed. "Gottit."

4. Ronny Shares the News

AT LUNCH BREAK AT A CONSTRUCTION SITE in Des Plaines, a suburb twenty-five miles northwest of downtown Chicago, five electricians from Boulder Electric munched on footlong subs, their asses parked on the cement floor, their backs pressed against newly installed drywall. All five wore forest green, Boulder-issued T-shirts, jeans and Red Wing work boots. Ronny Monroe, whose belly indicated that he had inhaled far too many chocolate shakes with extra whip cream in his day, turned the page of the *Sun-Times* and read a bit.

"You see this shit on this city worker?" said Ronny. He jabbed a stubby index finger at the bridge of his glasses to keep them in place.

"Ya talkin' 'bout Quarters McNicholas?" one of the others said.

"Yeah." Ronny took a big bite from his sandwich and spoke while chewing. "This is quality stuff." Ronny stuffed more of his sandwich into his mouth. "This fuckin' guy goes to the shitter for two years for stealin' a boatload of money from the Tollway and now he comes out—and he gets a city job."

"You'd probably do the same shit if ya could, Ron," one of the others said.

"What, get a city job? I don't live in the city, douche bag."

"No, stuff your pockets fulla quarters if you had the chance."

"Nope," Ronny said as he shook his head. "Take too many damn quarters to make it worth my while."

"Well, if ya keep readin', you'll see that McNicholas made it worth his while," one of the others said. "Definitely. Took over $200,000 in a two-year span." The electrician laughed. "All in quarters."

"That's alotta quarters," added one of the other electricians.

Ronny set his sandwich on his expansive lap and pulled the newspaper in closer to read more. Again he jabbed a finger at his glasses to keep them in place.

5. Tom Lonigan

TOM LONIGAN'S PHONE INTERCOM beeped. "Tom, your brother's here to see you," his secretary said.

"Thanks, Marie. Send him on in."

The solid oak desk that Tom sat behind was a gift from his mother, Mary Lonigan, a gift delivered eleven years ago when Tom was first elected business manager of Local 247, the largest electricians' union in the country. A thick tree of a man in his mid-forties, to say Tom was a straight shooter was akin to saying Lake Michigan had a lot of water. Like Tom, his office décor was basic and straightforward. On the wall behind his desk hung a large framed black-and-white print of the Chicago stockyards. Off to the side, framed prints of a number of great Cubs players from the past lined the wall—guys like Ernie Banks, Billy Williams, Don Kessinger, Fergie Jenkins, Ron Santo, and Ryne Sandberg—all there in a display of love and admiration that had never been returned by their hapless organization. Next year—always next year. As Tom saw it, the real next year was always just around the corner. A pair of Everlast boxing gloves, tied together with gold laces, dangled from a nail in the wall, and a thick, dented, four-foot-long Irish shillelagh rested comfortably against the bookcase beside Tom's desk. It looked like it belonged.

Tom climbed to his feet as Danny entered his office. "Good to see ya," Tom said and then shook his brother's hand. "What's shakin'?"

"Had the interview this mornin'," Danny said. He dropped into one of the two armchairs in front of Tom's desk.

"Yeah, right. I knew it was happenin' today." Tom strummed his desktop with his right hand as he sat down. "Just didn't know, uh, know what time." He flashed his teeth. "So how'd it go?"

"Went fine." Danny's eyebrows shot up. "Wasn't much of an interview, though. No questions about any prior electrical work. None. They just had me . . . well, they had me identify some tools."

Tom feigned surprise. "Really?"

"Yep."

"So how'd ya do?"

"I hit on four outta five."

"Four outta five ain't bad." Tom laughed. "Was Ted there?"

"Yeah. He was the one doin' all the talkin'."

"Okay. Good. Glad ya got that outta the way."

Danny surveyed the room for a moment until he saw the shillelagh. "Never knew ya had Dad's old shillelagh in here."

"Yeah." Tom turned and eyed the club. "I thought it'd look good in here." He laughed. "Besides, I figure I just about own the damn thing. Most of those dents on it came from my noggin."

Danny grinned and dropped his eyes to the floor.

"Anything else? How's Kate and the kids?"

"Good, good. Everyone's good."

"All right, then." Tom climbed to his feet.

"Hey, Tom, am I . . . am I, ya know, for sure good on gettin' the job? I mean there were probably about thirty other guys there today. And then I got the other shit that—"

"Hey, Dan, stop. Stop. You're good. Don't sweat it." Tom pushed a hand through the gray-white hair atop his head. "Look, there's eleven guys goin' in, and the union has four of those slots. And you're one of those four. So you're in for sure. It's cemented in stone. It's done."

Danny leaned forward in his chair. "Good. Good. 'Cuz Ted said things would start up in about a week or ten days."

"That's right. The new guys'll start up on the next pay period, on April 18th."

"Okay. Good, 'cuz . . . well, I'm headin' back to work after I grab a quick bite, but if I'm for sure gettin' the job, I'm gonna make this my last day, then." Danny rubbed his forehead as he stood. "Probably take off a little early today. And then, ya know, take some days off before I start the new job. But I didn't wanna quit if the new job wasn't a for sure thing."

"Gottit. But no, you're good to go. You're set. And take some time off. Makes perfect sense. Take it now, 'cuz you won't get any vacation time for about half a year once ya start with the city." Tom cracked the knuckle on his right index finger. "Just do me a favor, though, okay?"

"Yeah, sure. What?"

"Give Stack a call to say thanks for keepin' ya workin'. He had ya there a long while. That's all."

"Will do. Glad to do it."

"Sounds good." Tom moved towards his door. Danny followed. "I'll talk to ya later," Tom said and then faced his brother.

"See ya, Tom. Thanks again for everything." Danny started to leave but stopped in the doorway. He turned, a shit-eating grin on his lips, and crouched into a boxing stance with his left hand in the lead, his right cocked and ready to fire. He slid to the left and then the right, dodging imaginary slow-motion punches. Tom laughed and dropped into a matching stance. And then both men, in perfect synchronization, bobbed and weaved and fired off three slow-motion punches at each other as Danny sang, "Hit 'im with the left, hit 'im with the right, punch 'im in the gut, and watch 'im fly outta sight."

6. The Three Stooges

FLYNN, CULLINAN, AND MORGAN were still holding court in the interview room. Empty Styrofoam coffee cups stood before all of them as they prepared to question Davis Winslow, the last interviewee of the day. The years had been kind to Winslow. Though thirty-five years of age, his smooth, black skin showed nary a trace of those years. You could drop him on any campus in the country, and he'd blend in with the rest of the students. There were no tools on the table for this interview. Not a one. The secretary still sat in her tiny chair in the corner doodling on scraps of paper.

"Okay. Mr. Winslow, my name's Ted Flynn." Flynn pointed to the other men. "These other guys are Dan Cullinan and Mark Morgan."

"Gentlemen," Winslow said with a smile.

Cullinan and Morgan nodded in silence. Flynn reviewed Winslow's application, circled a paragraph from the note sheet attached to the application with a red pen and slid it along the table. Cullinan took a moment to review the note and then passed the application to Morgan, who pushed it back towards Cullinan without a glance.

"Your application says you worked for Forrester Electric up until about six months ago," Flynn said.

"That's right," Winslow said.

"How long were ya there?"

"Jess about one year. A year and two months, maybe."

"Well, why'd ya get let go?"

"It was a long call." Winslow smiled. "The gift that just kept giving finally stopped giving." The three men were triplets for a moment, all of their faces bunched together in confusion. "The job ended. I went back to the Union Hall after that. Did a buncha short calls then."

Flynn leaned back in his chair and smiled. "Is that right?"

"That's right."

"Now I gotta tell ya. A buddy of mine is a foreman over at Forrester." Flynn kicked his feet up on the table. "I jingled him up the other day and asked about you. His story's a bit different than yours." Morgan and Cullinan both leaned forward.

"Oh yeah? What he say?"

"Well, according to my guy, you got shit-canned for stealin' some power tools from the job site."

Winslow chuckled. "Well, maybe he got the story wrong."

"Is that right?"

"That's right." Winslow adjusted himself in his chair. He'd had enough of these three white men. He especially had enough of Ted Flynn with his sheet-white, pasty face that looked like it should be plastered across an I HATE BLACK PEOPLE T-shirt or hiding inside a KKK hood.

"By the way," said Winslow, "what'd y'all circle on my application there?"

Flynn played dumb. "What?"

"Y'all circled somethin'. What's the big secret?"

"No big secret. I, uh, I circled the part where it says you were convicted for carryin' a gun."

Winslow tilted his head to the side and massaged his left temple. White people, he thought. They don't understand any damn thing outside of their own lily-white world. He released a half smile. "C'mon now. You gone get your shorts all in a bunch over a little ol' misdemeanor like that. Gotsta have a pistol on ya for protection. Everybody know that."

Flynn dropped his feet to the floor. "And what if ya worked here, what would ya do with that pistol then?"

"Oh, I'd leave it at home, Boss. For sure, I would."

"Leave it at home, huh?"

"That's what I jess said."

"Yeah, that's what you 'jess' said, all right."

Winslow gave Flynn the best fuck-you stare he could muster. And Flynn's eyes, those dots for pupils—Winslow could have sworn he saw ink oozing from them.

Flynn turned away, looked to Morgan and then Cullinan. "Anything else, fellas?" Morgan and Cullinan nodded their heads. "Okay, Mr. Winslow, that's it. You're all wrapped up here."

"You gotsta be kiddin' me." Winslow's eyes were still fixed on Flynn. "No questions on the kindsa work I done or the systems I put in. No questions about—"

"Nope. No other questions. None." Flynn's snatched his empty coffee cup and held it before him with both hands as if he were a priest hoisting the giant Communion wafer on the altar. "You're the last man standin' today. We're wrappin' up."

"Saved the best for last, right?" Winslow said with a smirk. "That's how it go. Ya always save the best for last."

"Sure thing," Flynn said. He scratched at the base of his nose.

Winslow rose from his seat. He did not offer a handshake, and none were offered to him. Flynn watched as Winslow marched towards the door.

"All right, Ginette, you can take off. Just hit the door on the way out."

"No problemo," the secretary said, and then she eked her way out of her chair yet again. Once she closed the interview door, Flynn started in.

"Did ya see that piece a shit's name is on the List of Eleven?"

"Yeah, I saw it," Morgan said.

Flynn paced the room, his boots beating a sorry tune into the wooden floor. "Well, I'm tellin' ya right now, that fuckin' shithead ain't comin' in here. He ain't gonna be one of the eleven. We're not gonna give a job to a gun-totin' thief. And a nigger at that." Flynn spat on the floor and rubbed the saliva in with the sole of his boot. "Now I'll gladly give him a cell to live in, but I ain't givin' him a job."

"I'm gonna give Tom a call," Morgan said.

"For what?" barked Flynn. "Winslow ain't comin' from the union."

"I know but he's—"

"Easy, gents. Easy," Cullinan said, as if he were talking to a couple of aging horses. He reviewed Winslow's application again. "This Winslow, he's, uh . . . he's one of Alderman Moffit's guys."

Flynn ran both hands through his hair. "I don't give two shits if he's one of Moffit's guys. He's a—"

"'Gun-totin' thief,'" Cullinan said. "Yeah, I know. Heard ya the first time." He locked his hands together and brought them to his lips. "Look, here's what I'm sayin'. You raise a stink on this guy and then they start pointin' fingers and lookin' at everyone's rap sheet. And if that happens, Danny Lonigan sticks out like he's got his face on an old-time milk carton."

"Yeah, I know," Flynn said, "but what I'm sayin'—"

"Ted, c'mon," Cullinan said. "Lonigan's a convicted felon. A disgraced lawyer. He's lucky he stayed outta the shitter. But if we try to muddy up the waters and bounce Winslow over a misdemeanor rap, it's gonna throw the spotlight on Danny Lonigan. And quite frankly, if we do all that, neither one of 'em gets in, and then Tom Lonigan is one pissed-off mother. And we don't want him pissed."

"You're right." Flynn said. "You're right."

Morgan released a big breath. "That man scares me." Flynn and Cullinan nodded in agreement.

"So I say we leave the list alone," Cullinan continued. "The four from the union'll be good workers, and the other seven won't know their asses from a hole in the wall, but that's okay. The eleven come in quietly, without any fanfare, and no one gives a flyin' shit."

"Fine. That's fine," Flynn said. He moved towards the door. "Just don't put that fuckin' guy in my department. One of you guys gets 'im."

"I'll take him. I'll keep an eye on him." Cullinan smiled. "Hell, I might even have him take me out to the range to gimme some shootin' lessons."

Morgan snorted out a laugh. Flynn wagged his head in disgust and walked out of the interview room with Morgan a few steps behind him. As Cullinan prepared to leave, he spotted the frog on the floor. When he knelt down, Cullinan could see that the frog was flattened and dead. He bunched his face into a frown.

"Aw, Richie D, what the hell happened to ya?" He scooped the dead frog and slid him into his shirt pocket before exiting the interview room.

7. Ziggy Returns From his Interview

CHERYL RAMIREZ LAY STRETCHED OUT on her den couch watching the History Channel on the TV. She wore a pair of her husband's sweats, the string bow-tied at the waist, and an oversized sweater. As she cast her eyes downward and rubbed her stomach, she tried to picture what her child would look like when he or she entered the world in a few months. And then she set both hands on her belly. She never thought she'd get this big. Not in a kazillion years.

Ziggy Ramirez returned from his Streets and San interview and parked his Ford Ranger in front of his Northwest Side bungalow. He entered his house and dropped his keys and sunglasses on the front hall table.

"Hey, how's my baby doin'?" Ziggy called out.

"Which one?" Cheryl hollered. Ziggy laughed and walked to

the den where he dropped onto the edge of the couch and kissed his wife.

"How you feelin', baby?"

"Feeling fine. Just bored. That's all."

"Bored?" Ziggy feigned shock. "C'mon. Sitting here all day long on this lovely couch. Watching TV, reading magazines. How could you find that boring?"

Cheryl laughed. Ziggy tugged on one of the strings dangling from the sweats Cheryl wore.

"Doubt this thing'll ever fit me again."

Cheryl shook her head and then reached for the remote. She snapped off the TV. Ziggy set his right hand gently on Cheryl's stomach.

"And how about Little Zignacio. How's he feeling? Any kicks today?"

"You don't know if it's a boy. You don't—"

"Oh yes, I do. I know."

"Okay, fine," Cheryl adjusted her body on the couch. She placed her hand atop Ziggy's. "So how'd the interview go?"

Ziggy offered a winning smile. "It went good. Real good."

"Really?"

"Well, yeah. It went as well as it could go, I guess." Ziggy softly massaged his wife's belly. Cheryl's hand moved along with his. "Weird, though. They didn't ask me any questions about my prior jobs or my prior training. They just asked me to identify different tools. Five tools. That was it. And then, well . . . there was a damn frog on the floor of the interview room."

"A frog?"

"Yeah. A frog. A fricken little frog." Ziggy twisted his face into a ball and stood up. "I sort of stepped on it by accident when I was leaving." Cheryl stared at Ziggy with concerned silence. "No one else noticed the frog." He scratched his head. "But hey, I can pick out a pliers and a screwdriver with the best of 'em, so I think I'm good on the job."

Cheryl released a nervous laugh. "I just won't feel good about all of this until we know for sure."

"I know, baby. But don't worry. Trust me. It'll be good. The union put the word in for me." Ziggy again sat beside his wife.

"And you trust those guys?"

"Yeah, I do." Ziggy smiled. "Plus, if they help out a burrito-eater like me, it makes the union guys look good too."

"I sure hope you're right."

8. A Good Book

R AINBOW BEACH ON CHICAGO'S SOUTH SIDE was the sight of a good deal of friction in the mid-1960s as black and white teens laid claim to its Seventy-Ninth Street sand. With time, as the surrounding neighborhoods changed from white to black, the whites reluctantly vacated their ties to this Lake Michigan jewel. From time to time, an occasional person of paste would still stroll across the sand or take a dip in this cozy cove. Today was one of those days.

Hat sat on a bench at Rainbow Beach, his arms stretched out to the side, resting atop the wooden backrest. Other than a man walking his dog along the shore, Hat was alone. His Streets and San van rested in the parking lot beside the beach house. The early morning rains gave way to the sun, and Hat soaked up that sun. A strong wind pushed through the area jerking the seagulls and terns across the sky as if they were kites on a string. Hat swung his right foot over his left knee, his face one of utter contentment. A cricket bounced up out of the sand onto Hat's jeans. He watched as it slowly ambled its way along the denim, stopping atop his knee. There it rubbed its elbows together and eyeballed Hat for a moment, before turning and taking in what the lake had to offer. Hat unleashed a crooked smile and reached for his book, *The Grapes of Wrath*, and opened it. With an hour to kill before he made his way back to the garage, the bookmarker took Hat to a point two-thirds through the book. The cricket stayed put and enjoyed its view as Hat turned a page, ready to get back to Tom Joad and Route 66.

9. Tires and Knives

DANNY LONIGAN STOOD BEFORE a Knaack gang box at the Des Plaines construction site, ready to snag his tools and head for home. His days with Boulder had come to an end, but as he stood there, he thought, perhaps, he shouldn't open the box. It was a fleeting thought, a baseless thought, but still—there was no denying it. After all, in a way, that storage box held two years of job memories that might just flood the coffin-sized container and spill onto the floor. Most of those memories would plant a smile on Danny's face—carrying stick after stick of one-hundred-pound pipe eight hours per day for two months in the sweltering heat last summer and not minding it one bit because his depraved partner fired off a litany of stupid jokes and wisecracks for every stick they shouldered; cold beers with his fellow electricians at various neighborhood dives around the city after work; feeling a sense of satisfaction when wrapping up at a job site and knowing that the work came in under budget and on time; the company outing to the Sox game where seventy-year-old Ed Stack, owner of Boulder Electric, got so liquored up he mooned the beer vendor when he was informed that Last Call had already taken place the inning before. There were many other job memories that would make Danny smile, but there were a few that would cause him to clench his fists.

As word spread a bit earlier in the day about Danny's imminent departure, most every electrician from Boulder Electric stopped by to offer his good-bye. A few other tradesmen wandered over to toss a joke or two Danny's way and to also offer their best wishes.

Danny stared at that locked storage box for a few moments longer. After he finally opened it, Ronny Monroe shuffled towards him and stopped about twenty feet away. "So it's really gonna happen, huh?" Ronny said. "The city's actually gonna hire you?"

Danny reached in and pulled his tool bag from the Knaack box and set it on the floor. "Yep. I start work on the eighteenth."

"Aw, c'mon, that's almost ten days away. Keep makin' money. Keep workin'. Don't quit like a pussy."

Danny stared into the emptiness of the Knaack box. He smiled as he caught sight of a used rubber lying at the bottom of the container—no doubt another warped joke from the sheet metal guys or sprinkler fitters. His smile disappeared instantly as he spoke. "Nope. Takin' some time off before I jump in there."

Danny closed the Knaack box with a bang, snatched his tool bag, and started walking towards the door. He had no intention of shaking Ronny's hand.

"Be sure to let me know if ya ever get your law license back," said Ronny with a grin. Danny stopped, his eyes fixed on the exit sign before him. "I'll let you fix my speeding tickets for me."

Danny turned around. With his tool bag hanging at his side and his long, angular body, he looked like a gunslinger ready to do battle in an old Western.

"Thanks, Ron. I'll be sure to do that. Anything for you."

Danny pushed through the door and continued down a narrow walkway before he opened yet another door, which led him into a parking lot. The sun immediately zapped Danny. Though only April, he could still feel its sting on his arms.

After heaving his tool bag into the trunk of his car, Danny slid into the driver's seat and examined himself in the rearview mirror. He didn't take notice of his brown eyes or his slightly bent nose. No, as Danny sat there, his brain focused on Ronny: Ronny slicing Danny's car tire after his first week on the job and leaving a note on his windshield saying, "No lawyers wanted. Welcome to my world. RM"; Ronny flipping an electrical circuit Danny was working on to HOT to purposely jolt him; Ronny lying to the general foreman—saying that Danny stole a missing pipe bender—to try to get him fired. There was a sense of relief on Danny's face. He saw it himself in the mirror. He released a simple smile, a smile that knew a weight had been lifted. And no matter how big or how small, it always felt good to get a weight off of your shoulders.

Danny opened the glove box and grabbed a pen and a sheet of paper. He took several minutes to scribble a note, before placing it under the windshield wiper of the pickup truck beside his car. He then pulled out a pocket knife and slammed it into the front tire on the truck's driver's side. Danny stayed put for a few seconds, and as he listened to the tire hiss and spit, a smile worked its way across his face. He then slipped back into his own car and made his getaway.

10. The Chief of Intergovernmental Affairs

*I*F EVER A MAN WERE BORN to be a *GQ* cover boy, Richard Randall was just such a man. Forty and handsome, Randall had the good cheekbones, the dimpled chin, and the bright eyes that made fashion agents drool. But Randall came from a family with roots seeded deeply in Chicago politics. So much for the aftershave commercials. As the No. 2 man to Mayor Robert Stokely, Randall's fingers were always applied to the city's pulse. When and if Mayor Stokely ever decided to hang it up or to pitch his tent in a bigger field, Randall would be ready to make his run for glory. And though Randall wasn't a male model, fashion was still very much a part of him. Whether at a press conference, a board meeting, a golf outing, or simply out walking his pudgy poodle, Richard Randall was always impeccably dressed. Always.

The official title embossed on Randall's business cards was CHIEF OF INTERGOVERNMENTAL AFFAIRS, but for those in the know, that title was a bunch of hogwash, a bunch of gobbledy-gook, a bunch of swampland in Florida. To a degree, Chicago had certainly changed with the times. It had undergone a great deal of modernization, tumbled many of its housing projects, gentrified old neighborhoods, and now sheltered many of its homeless in better facilities. Some call that progress; some don't. However, over the years, the way the city worked, the way those in power doled out jobs, the way of patronage politics—had changed little. And to those who truly knew Richard Randall, they knew him not as the Chief of Intergovernmental Affairs. Rather, they knew him by his real title, THE CITY PATRONAGE GUY. Nary a city job was given without Randall's nod or formal stamp of approval.

Randall stepped out of the mayor's office, just down the corridor from his own work space on the fifth floor at City Hall. After he entered his office, Randall closed the door and dropped into the chair behind his desk. The bright yellow tie he wore lit up the room. He grabbed his desk phone and dialed Ted Flynn.

"We've got a little problem," Randall said. "I just finished up a meeting with the Big Cheese. I have to get this one girl in. She's—"

"We already got the eleven," Flynn interrupted. "It's all done. The interviews are all over."

Randall leaned back in his chair, his eyes peering out the window, watching the sun slice the building across the street in half. "Okay, well, she was at the interview today."

"No, she wasn't. We didn't have any women at the interview today. Not a single—"

"Ted, you're not listening to me." Randall sighed. "She was there today. She interviewed. She did fantastic. Everybody loved her. Including you. Maggie Sunfield is her name." Randall paused to see if Flynn cared to interrupt him again. "She'll be one of the four coming from the union."

"But we already got four." Flynn's face was a mound of wrinkles. "Can't you get her in from one of the aldermen or from a state rep?"

"Nope. She's coming in from the union. Period."

Flynn's face went blank for a moment. "Well, how come . . . how come I ain't heard this news from Tom? How come I—"

"The Cheese just got off the phone with Tom too. He knows. He understands. It's done. It's agreed to." A silence fell over the phone for a moment as both men knew what was coming. "Look, you gotta chop one of the other four. Who are they?"

"One is Tom's own brother," Flynn barked. "One's a Mexican, one's a shithead, and the other's an Irish kid."

Randall laughed. "Sounds like the start to a joke." Flynn remained silent. "Okay, look, get rid of the black guy."

"That's a tough one. Believe me, I'd like to do that. Hell, I'd *love* to do that. But I can't. See, if I get rid of him, the short of it is, it might end up crossin' things up for Tom's own brother and blow up in all our faces."

"Okay. Bump the Irish kid, then."

"You serious?"

"I'm always serious, Ted. That's why the mayor loves me. Look, we'll have a black guy, a Mexican, a woman, and a convicted felon. We cover all the bases. Hell, we'll look like the greatest equal opportunity employer of all time." Randall smiled at his own comment. Flynn again remained silent. "And look, it's not like the Irish kid is gone for good. Let him know that he'll be first in line with the next group. Probably about six to eight months. We'll have Tom make sure he can keep shittin' on the same job site 'til then. Sound good?"

"Yeah, I guess so."

"Okay. Thanks." Randall hung up the phone and turned towards the window, his eyes fixed on the people milling about the downtown streets below.

11. The Note

THREE-THIRTY P.M. BROUGHT ABOUT THE END of yet another work day for the electricians at Boulder Electric. Ronny Monroe and four other electricians meandered across the parking lot at the Des Plaines site towards their cars and trucks, the heavy traffic from the nearby Tri-State expressway an endless buzz in their ears.

"You douche bags have a good night," Ronny barked. He strutted toward his truck.

"See ya," said one of the electricians. The others remained mute.

As Ronny neared his pickup, he saw the flat tire. "What the fuck?" He bent down to examine it. Three electricians raced off in their cars and pickups. Another noticed Ronny squatting beside his truck and circled around. He rolled down his window.

"What's wrong?" the electrician said.

"Fuckin' flat tire." Ronny cut loose a big sigh, and then spotted the note beneath his wiper blade. He snatched it. "Motherfucker," he said as he read.

"What is it?"

"'What is it?'" Ronny barked. His face hardened and he stabbed his glasses with his left index finger. "'What is it?' It's fuckin' Danny Lonigan. That's what it is. He did this shit." Ronny held the note with both hands and read it aloud.

Ron, congratulations on being a professional DICK. I needed this job and couldn't afford to get in any problems on the job site so I took your shit for almost two years. Now I'm done. I hope you like my going-away present. I find it very suitable for a mental midget like you. The tire is like your brain—FLAT. If for some reason you take exception to all of this, I'll be up at The Dubliner on Western Avenue tonight from 7-8:30 having a few beers. Have a nice life. DL

Ronny crunched the note into a ball and tossed it into a puddle of muddy water. The other electrician buried his laughter in his sleeve when Ronny looked up.

"You wanna ride?"

"No. I'll fix it. I got my spare."

"You gonna go up there tonight?"

"Damn right I'm goin' up there. He's gonna get the beatdown he deserves."

The electrician raised his eyebrows. "Now I don't know where this place, this Dubliner is, but I might just have to go and find it."

Ronny bent down again and eyed his flat tire.

12. Jello Calls the IG

JELLO PELLEGRINI HELD HIS CELLPHONE to his ear as he sat at his desk in the CDOT building. Behind him were various framed photos of Jello shaking hands with or standing beside different city and state politicians. Beside his door was a framed poster of a Hostess Twinkie with the words, "Eat Me, I'm a Twinkie" scribbled across it with a bold, black marker.

"Inspector General's Office," a pleasant young voice said. "How can I direct your call?"

"Paul Volpe, please."

"One moment, sir."

As Jello waited for his call to be connected, he stared at a framed print of the 1986 Bears Super Bowl Championship team hanging on his office wall to the right of his desk. Images of Jim McMahon slinging touchdown passes and Mike Singletary and the defense that slammed a lot of bodies to the turf flashed before him. He wondered how a team stacked like that only won one Super Bowl. He wondered how in the hell—

"Volpe here."

Jello snapped back to the present. "Hey, I had a visitor here earlier today. Some guy takin' pictures of me. Been here three or four other times too the past few weeks. I wanna know who he is."

"Well, uh . . . somethin' gonna happen to him?"

Jello laughed. "Don't worry. Nothin' bad's gonna happen. Just that, well . . . seein' how he likes to take pictures of me, I figure I should be nice like that to him. I figure I should get some pictures of him."

"You sure he's from my office?"

"Yeah, he's from your office. I saw 'im sittin' in a city car with the city M plates on my way in. He even smelled like the IG." Jello laughed. "You guys all got that same stink. Ya know . . . the smell of justice." Jello laughed again. "Anyways, he took a buncha pictures of me when I was walkin' into the building. And I'll tell ya what—if that was all he done, I'd be fine. I wouldn't bother callin' ya. See, I don't care none about someone takin' sneaky pictures of me. He can do that shit all day long. But the *manichino* came around to my office window, so's I could see him, and started takin' more pictures of me there. I had to close my drapes. And I don't like havin' to close my drapes. I like bein' able to look out and see all the riff-raff walkin' around the neighborhood. Know what I mean?"

"Gotcha."

"So just get me his info, 'kay?"

"Will do. Probably take a day or two."

"Good enough. Two days'll be fine."

Jello ended his call and looked out the window. A Streets and San dump truck from a neighboring ward yard trolled down the street while a homeless man picked through a trash can on the corner. Jello leaned back in his chair and kicked his feet up on his desk. He released a thin smile.

13. Basketball with a Side of Pasta

SWEAT. DANNY LOVED IT—THE SMELL, the taste, the feel of the drops weaving their way down your face. Sweat—your reward for hard work. He smiled as he passed a ball to his oldest son, Sam-twelve, who drained a fifteen-footer on the hoop attached to the Lonigan garage roof.

"That's it, Sammy," said Danny. "Nice shot."

Sam's forehead glistened in the sun, the beads of sweat Danny so loved bubbling across his forehead. Sam jumped back in line, behind his nine-year-old brother, Jim. The youngest Lonigan, Max, six months, slept soundly in a baby stroller beside a neighbor's garage. Alleys, Danny thought as he passed the ball to Jim, this is where basketball was meant to be played.

Jim launched his fifteen-footer but missed. Danny rebounded the ball. "Not bad, Jim," Danny said. "Shoot it again. Remember, it's all in the feet. Good feet. Step in to meet the pass. A good one-two step."

Basketball—it meant the world to Danny. In the parish where he grew up, you saw God in church on Sundays and you saw him on the courts at the park, in the alleys, or in the backyards all the other days of the week because basketball was God too. Every neighborhood kid played, filling the alleys, backyards, and parks with bouncing balls and barking lips. Call it blasphemy if you'd like, but yes, in the South Side neighborhood of Danny's youth, basketball was indeed a god. And then came high school. Danny followed Tom's footsteps to Three Blind Sinners High School, where Danny's hoop teams finished 29-3 his junior year and 28-2 his senior year. But far more than records and state rankings or wins and losses, basketball brought lessons Danny's way. He grew to understand the value of teamwork, hard work, and dedication, and though his team rarely lost, Danny also learned to lose with dignity. But far beyond that, basketball was an escape: an escape Danny needed, an escape he craved. When Danny was twelve, his father was murdered, and from that point on Danny had a ball in his hands everywhere he went—dribbling to school, dribbling to the store to bring home a gallon of milk, cranking out his Pete Maravich drills in the basement, shooting eighteen-footers in the alley, playing in the parks, spinning the ball on his finger as he watched Saturday morning cartoons or Bulls games on TV at night. Danny played or watched basketball almost 24-7. It soothed his soul.

Jimmy followed his father's directions and drained the next shot.

"Atta boy."

Kate Lonigan curbed her car in front of the Lonigan house. A teacher, she carried a satchel filled with homework papers to grade as she stepped from the car. While she walked along the gangway leading to the side-entry door to her home, Kate heard the activity in the back alley.

"Is that you, Dan?"

"Yeah, Mom," Jim yelled. He walked over to the gate and saw his mother standing in the gangway. "Dad's out here. We're all out here."

Kate followed the sidewalk that ran alongside their brick bungalow and led to the back alley. The sun fell upon her shoulder-length brown hair as her wiry body glided easily down the path. She pushed through the gate and stepped into the alley. Danny continued to rebound shots and pass the ball as he spoke.

"Hi, hon," Danny said.

Kate surveyed everything and walked towards the baby stroller. "How're the jumpers going?" She set her satchel beside the stroller and took Max into her arms.

"Good. Good. These guys are snipers. Both of 'em. Snipers."

Kate kissed Max. He stirred but continued to sleep. Kate set Max against her shoulder and chest.

"Had the interview today."

"Good."

"Tom said I'm all set. I start in about a week."

"No more Ronny, huh? I wonder if you'll be able to survive without him?" Kate flashed her perfect teeth. Danny smiled and locked his eyes on his wife. His look was one of adoration mixed with relief. And Kate could see it plain as day. She walked to Danny and set a hand on his shoulder. Danny enjoyed the warmth of his wife's touch but quickly sprang back into action, barking out orders to Jim and Sam.

"Okay, guys. Shot fake and go. All right? And don't rush the fake. Set your feet. Show it and then go. Sound good?"

The boys nodded as Danny continued to feed passes. "Oh yeah, I gotta pop up to see Hairdo at the Dubliner tonight around seven. I'll be up there for an hour, hour and a half tops. Is that cool?"

"Sure. That fine."

Max stirred a bit. Kate bounced him gently on her chest. "I'm taking the boys over to my sister's house right about then. I told her I'd come over around seven-thirty or eight. She wants to give them a gift she bought for them on vacation."

Danny passed a ball to Jim. "Cool. Well, how 'bout I pop over to your sister's when I leave the Dubliner?"

"You don't have to. But if you want to come over, sure. That'll be great."

"Good. I'll come by then."

Kate watched the boys launch a few more shots. "What do you want to do for dinner tonight?"

"I already tossed some water on the stove. It should be boilin'" about now. How's some pasta and veggies sound?"

"Sounds like a winner to me."

"Are we havin' some bread, too?" said Jim.

Danny had the basketball in his hands. He passed the ball to Sam and then glared at Jim for several seconds, freezing him.

"'Are we havin' some bread?'" Danny said, using a broken-English, Italian accent. "What kinda question is dat, huh? Of course, we're gonna have some bread. Who eats pasta and don't have no bread with it, huh, Vito?"

Danny gave Jim a playful shove, and continued with the same accent. "And I got some olive oil, and I got some Parmesan cheese, and I got some chopped garlic too. We gottit all, Vito, you unnerstand me? We gottit all. We gotta do somethin' to fatten up you little Irish hillbillies."

Everyone laughed except for Danny who continued in his role.

"You think somethin's funny? Huh, Vito? You think I'm funny? Well, ya know what I think's funny? Huh, Vito? YOU. Dat's right, YOU. You're gonna look real funny when I put my shoe up your ass."

Danny started to chase Jim, who dodged him.

"Do it, Dad," Sam yelled. "Put your shoe up his ass."

Danny chased Jim for another few seconds and stopped. He smiled, turned towards Sam and showed him his hands. Sam passed the ball and Danny fired up a twenty-footer, which missed.

"Oh, well," Danny said, "there's always tomorrow." Danny joined Kate beside the stroller. "All right, boys, I'm headin' in to get the pasta goin'. You guys got about 15 minutes."

Danny grabbed the satchel and the stroller. He followed Kate along the sidewalk towards their house.

14. The End of a Good Day

HAT EASED HIS VAN SLOWLY through the Streets and San parking lot, following a couple of other baby blue vans and white vans into the garage at 940 West Exchange, where they all parked. He stayed put in his van and continued to read *The Grapes of Wrath*. Other city electricians stood in groups by the time clock, bullshitting the last few minutes of the work day away. At 4:24 p.m., the group filed towards the time clock, and one by one, each worker swiped his ID card, officially bringing the work day to an end. Hat remained in his van, his thoughts now set on dinner. Maybe he'd stop by to visit his mom or go to see his uncle. Or maybe he'd just snag the chicken Vesuvio sandwich from Gio's and then jump into his hot tub with a few beers after eating and just chill the night away. Decisions, decisions. Hat walked to the time clock and swiped his card. The day was over, the garage strangely quiet.

15. Dress Rehearsal

MAGGIE SUNFIELD SLOWLY CREATED folds in her flannel shirtsleeves until they reached mid-forearm, her eyes fixed on the full-length mirror attached to her closet door. Just below her apartment a CTA bus barked as it bounced to a stop at the corner of Sheridan and Lunt. Though Maggie heard the bus screech, her eyes did not stray. Instead, they roamed the mirror from head to toe, giving herself a full body scan. Somewhat pleased with her look, Maggie offered a flat-lipped smile and turned towards the assorted piles of T-shirts and jeans and hoodies and flannels gathered atop her bed. She peeled off the flannel and tossed it in her *good* pile, on a chair beside her dresser. A small-caliber pistol sat on the bed, the snub-nosed barrel aimed towards Maggie, the lone witness of sorts to this one-woman fashion show. Maggie rummaged through the pile on her bed, grabbed a dark blue hoodie, and slid it on. Again she turned and preened. She nodded at her image in the mirror. Maggie stuffed the pistol into her right work boot and pulled her jeans down over her boots. A bulge appeared in her jeans at the very point where the gun stuck out of her boot. "That won't work," Maggie said as she stared at the bulge in the mirror. She removed the gun and placed it back on her bed. Maggie pulled her hoodie off, placed it in her *good* pile, and reached for a long-sleeved T.

16. If Photos Could Talk

GILBREATH CHECKED THE CLOCK on his office wall. 7:05 p.m. He rummaged slowly through the photos of Jello Pellegrini taken from earlier in the day. From the right side of his desk, Gilbreath's deceased daughter, Becca, stared at him from the photo inside a wooden, five by seven inch frame. Gilbreath slid Jello's photos into a file and grabbed the framed photo of Becca.

"I hope you're having a good day today, sweetie. I'm sure the sun is shining." Gilbreath smiled. "Maybe you should take a nice, long walk. Yeah, that sounds good. I'm sure—"

Gilbreath's head jerked when he heard a knock at his office door. Jack Wheeler, a coworker, stood there looking through the glass door. Gilbreath waved Wheeler in and set Becca's photo back in its place.

"I'm heading out, Ed," Wheeler said. "You're the last guy here so just make sure you lock the dead-bolt. Someone left it open last time. Lucky we didn't lose some shit."

"No problem, Jack. I got it. Have a good night."

"Sounds good. See ya tomorrow." Wheeler turned to leave, but stopped. "Hey Ed, I'm, uh, I'm meeting up with a buddy of mine for some late chow over at Twenty-Fourth and Oakley. Why don't you come join us?"

Gilbreath nibbled on his bottom lip for a moment.

"Nah. Thanks for the offer, though. I have a few more things to wrap up. But that sounds good. Definitely next time."

"Good enough. See ya."

Once Wheeler left the office, Gilbreath walked slowly to his second-floor window overlooking the parking lot and offering a view of downtown. He watched Wheeler pull off in his car. Gilbreath's eyes rose until he found Sears Tower. He worked his eyes across the black windows, shimmering in the setting sun. His eyes shifted and bounced until they reached the top. He thought about Becca and how she loved Sears Tower. She always said it belonged in *Star Wars* with Darth Vader living in the penthouse.

Gilbreath deserted his post at the window, removed his suit coat from his rack, and put it on. He stood by his door and turned back towards his desk.

"Sleep well, Becca. See ya tomorrow." Gilbreath snapped off his office light, ready to head for home.

17. The Dubliner

THE DUBLINER'S GREEN ENTRY DOOR STOOD like a beacon amidst the darkness in this Irish neighborhood, ready to guide those with parched throats to a stool at the bar. Situated at 109th and Western Avenue on the city's South Side, the Dubliner relished its roots along the South Side St. Patrick's Day Parade route.

Danny Lonigan sat on a stool inside the tavern, a warm, smallish place with roughly fifteen barstools and six high-backed wooden booths. A few dozen pairs of eyes were trained on assorted big screens stationed around the bar, cheering on the Blackhawks. Danny's best friend, Hairdo, an off-duty Chicago cop, sat beside him on a stool. They were joined by a couple of others. The men drank bottles of beer and watched and hoped for that next Hawks goal. The front door swung open, and Ronny Monroe entered.

"Glad ya could make it tonight," Danny chirped as Ronny

marched towards him. "Wanna buy me a drink?"

"Fuck you," Ronny barked. A number of heads swung towards Ronny. Danny climbed to his feet.

"Ooooooh. Highly intelligent comeback," Hairdo said. "Well done."

"Fuck you, too," Ronny said, his eyes set on Hairdo.

Danny laughed. "Like I told ya, Har. This guy's definite Mensa material."

"Last big thought was probably in a book report in Third grade or so, huh?" said Hairdo.

"Exactly," Danny said.

Ronny stabbed his left index finger into his glasses. "C'mon," he said. "Let's do this."

"Okay. But not right here." Danny eyed the bartender. "I don't wanna see anything get messed up in here." The bartender nodded his thanks. Danny motioned towards the rear door. "Let's step out back. That'll work best."

"We wanna come watch," Hairdo said. The others with Danny and Hairdo laughed.

"You can come, Hairdo, but that's it. If there's one thing I learned from my years in the courtroom, it's this: it's always best when there aren't too many witnesses."

Danny walked towards the back door with Ronny in tow. Hairdo lifted up his shirt, displaying the snub nose tucked into his belt, as Ronny passed.

Two Dubliner patrons stood outside smoking cigarettes and chatting when Danny pushed through the back door. Hairdo motioned for them to head inside. They nodded back, dropped their smokes to the ground, and crushed them with their shoes before returning to the bar. Hairdo wedged himself against the back door so no one else could join their private party.

The back area of the Dubliner was little more than a four-car gravel parking lot that dissolved into the alley. Danny stepped into the one open parking space, and Ronny followed. An alley light blinked episodically overhead, tossing arrows of light at Ronny and Danny.

"That was a pussy move today," Ronny said. "Slittin' my tire."

"Ya know what, Ron? For once you're right." Danny turned to face Ronny. Ten feet separated the men. "I agree with ya. It was a pussy move." Danny released a huge smile. "But it served a purpose. You're here, right?"

"Damn right, I'm here."

"And I'm glad ya are. I've been lookin' forward to this." Danny nodded. "Even dreamt about it a time or two."

Ronny was tired of listening to Danny's words. After all, he came to the Dubliner to fight. Not talk. He started things off by grunting and charging Danny, who sidestepped the bull and used his momentum to sling Ronny headfirst into one of the parked cars—a rusty, Chevy clunker, where he straightened Ronny up. Danny grabbed Ronny by his hair and slammed his head off of the roof of the Chevy. Ronny was stunned. If this were a cartoon and Danny were Popeye and Ronny were Brutus, the TV screen would no doubt be showing big *stars* above Brutus's head at this very moment.

And then Danny heard his father's voice barking in his brain. "Left hook," Jim Lonigan ordered. Danny slammed a left into Ronny's ear. "Right hook. Left uppercut." Danny slammed Ronny with two more punches, the last of which caused the big man to fold at the waist. Knees are always good things to use in alley fights, especially when a guy is bent over at the waist, and Danny was no stranger to the strategies of alley fights. He popped Ronny's face with his right knee and Ronny flattened to the ground. Jim Lonigan's laughter rattled the walls of Danny's brain, and then he was gone.

But Danny wasn't done. He grabbed Ronny by his hair, pulling his torso off the ground a bit, and slammed Ronny's face with two more big rights, opening up Ronny's cheek and bloodying his nose. Danny released Ronny's hair, and the big man fell limp to the parking lot cement, rolling onto his stomach. Danny set a knee on Ronny's back and sent a flurry of lefts and rights into Ronny's ears. After Danny stood, he finished his deed by delivering a few work boots to Ronny's ribs.

"I hope you enjoyed that as much as I did." Danny said. Ronny sucked in a big breath but barely stirred. "I'm gonna leave now,

but before I do, I got one last present for ya." Danny unzipped his
fly and pulled out his dick. "Miller Lite always makes me piss like
a racehorse."

Ronny slowly turned his head and looked up towards Danny.
A splash of urine struck him in the face. Danny circled Ronny to
make certain he soaked as much of his body as possible. When he
was completely drained, Danny returned to the pub. Hairdo stayed
put by the door, his eyes fixed on Ronny. And then he walked to
his side and stooped down. Ronny moaned and continued to
breathe heavily.

"You gonna be okay, guy?"

Ronny stirred but remained silent. Hairdo reached over and
untied one of Ronny's work boots.

"I'm takin' this boot with me." Hairdo slid the boot off of
Ronny's right foot without resistance. "Ya know, just a little
somethin'. A momento of sorts." Hairdo started back for the pub
with the boot in hand, but stopped and turned back again, staring
hard at Ronny. "You want me to call the SamBambulance for ya?"
Ronny did not answer. He turned his head slowly and looked
Hairdo's way, before he raised his left hand slightly and shot the
bird. Hairdo couldn't help but laugh. "Suit yourself, then," Hairdo
said and then returned to the pub.

18. Maggie Offers Her Thanks

A NAKED MAGGIE SUNFIELD straddled a man lying beneath
her in his Lake Shore Drive condo bedroom. Maggie glanced
outside the window at the Chicago skyline. She then turned back
and rode the man steadily, his hands on her hips.

"Oh, that feels good," the man said. "So good."

Maggie slowed to a crawl, teasing him. "I'm sure it does." She
swung her head back and set both of her hands on the man's chest.
"It's the least I could do for you."

"Glad to help, Maggie. Glad you got the job. In fact, right now,

I'm goddamn ecstatic."

Maggie continued to move slowly atop the man. "'Ecstatic.' I love that word." She began to move again, tonging her lips. "This is going to feel even better than 'ecstatic.'" Maggie increased the motion until she moved violently up and down on the man. Moans of delight filled the room.

19. The Three Amigos

NINE DAYS AFTER THE INTERVIEWS were held, ten of the eleven new city electricians gathered in a corner of the garage below Ted Flynn's office, ready to start their first day. The other workers—the veterans—climbed up the slender, wooden staircase leading to Flynn's second floor office to get their assignments for the day. If you looked at Flynn's office from the ground floor of the garage, you wouldn't think you were looking at an office so much as you were staring at an oversized shoebox standing atop eight ten-foot-long, rickety wooden posts. This raised structure, a fine example of city craftmanship and ingenuity, left storage room for communications supplies on the garage floor, beneath that box of an office. Some old-time city electricians claim a backfire from a truck taking a tight turn just outside of the garage one day nearly busted up those toothpick stilts and brought Flynn's office crashing to the cement floor.

Maggie Sunfield sat on a chair in Flynn's office filling out various work documents. Each electrician who entered the room took notice of her. Though she wore jeans and a hoodie, it was obvious to all around that she was put together. After signing her last form and turning it in to Ted Flynn, Maggie walked down the stairs into the garage.

Hat stood at the back of his van loading boxes of telephone wire. As Maggie walked towards him on her way to huddle with the other newbies, Hat stepped into her path.

"Can I ask you a question?" Hat said.

Maggie stopped and sighed. "Sure."

"Now don't take this the wrong way, cuz I'm sure you've heard it all before, but what the hell're you doin' workin' as an electrician?"

Maggie stared at Hat in silence. An image of Dick Tracy waltzed into her brain. When she was young, Maggie's father used to read old Dick Tracy comics to her, and Maggie couldn't help but think that Hat—with his square jaw and lips that slipped to the side of his face as he spoke, could be a relative of the hard-boiled, comic strip cop.

"Ah, c'mon, don't play me that way," Hat said with a smile. "Look, you gimme an hour to get a hold of some people I know, and I'll have ya workin' for a modelin' agency before lunch." Hat's head bobbed as he offered his last few words. "Swimsuit model, for sure."

"Is that right?"

"Look, I mean it."

Maggie feigned interest. "Really?"

"Hell yeah."

Maggie dropped the interested look. "Well maybe I don't want to work as a model. Maybe I already did that. Maybe I don't ever want to do that again. Maybe this is what I want to do. Maybe you should mind your own business."

Maggie blew past Hat. He watched her, but rather than checking her out, he took what she said into consideration for a moment. A brief moment. "Maybe your tits just weren't big enough," he whispered to himself as Maggie walked off towards the other newbies.

Hat grabbed another box of wire and tossed it into his van. He slammed the back door shut and looked up towards Flynn's office. He could see Flynn sitting at his desk staring into the computer, as usual. Kip Larsen, the foreman who shared the office with Flynn, sat at a matching metal desk and wrote on an assignment log, pairing workers up for the day.

"Got everyone all set?" said Flynn.

"Just about," Larsen said. "But I don't have enough guys to just go two to a van. I'll have to send some out in threes."

"Threes, fours. Whatever. Just get it set. I want 'em outta the garage. You need—"

"Okay," Larsen said as he jumped to his feet. "I got the last one. We're all set."

"Good. Let's go." Flynn slid out from his desk, and Larsen followed. The two men slowly ambled down the wooden stairs. The new workers took notice and watched as Flynn stopped a few steps from the bottom stair, with Larsen directly behind him.

"All right, everyone, gather up." As Flynn waited for the new workers to huddle around, he looked out over the garage as if he were the pope ready to shine the bright light of faith on his audience. Most of the indoor parking spots were empty, the electricians already out on the street. He surveyed the nine vans remaining in the garage and then ran his eyes across the faces of the eleven newbies standing before him.

"Okay. So this is how it is. By the end of the week, or sometime next week, all of yous guys will be given more permanent assignments. Some of yous will go to Aviation up north at O'Hare, some to communications with me here in this garage, some to Viaducts which is also here, and some to General Services at North and Throop. Until then, we're just gonna put ya in with some of our guys who've been around the block a few times so ya can get a feel for things, and because we got nothin' else for ya to do just yet, until we get those orders."

Flynn cleared his throat. "Now look, when you're out and about, do your job and don't fuck off. If ya do fuck off, I'm just lettin' ya know, you will get caught. It's just the way it is these days. This is a good job, but there's lotsa eyes watchin' ya. And they ain't our eyes, if ya know what I mean."

One of the newbies chuckled and nudged the guy beside him. Flynn zeroed in, with slits for eyes.

"You think this is funny, huh?" Flynn barked, doing his best drill sergeant impersonation. "Think I'm spoutin' shit just to spout it?" The newbie's face went blank. "Look, I'm tellin' ya the way it is. But if you think you know everything already, we'll see how long ya last." Flynn's slits for eyes stayed glued to the newbie's face. "Hell, Cammie Fleckman'll probably find you takin' a nap in your van or sittin' in a corner tavern in a couple of weeks. And then your not-so-happy face will be plastered across the ten o'clock news."

The other newbies laughed. A slight smile came to Flynn, who glanced over his shoulder at Kip Larsen, before turning back to face the newbies.

"I'm sorry," Flynn said. "You guys know me already from the interview. In case ya forgot, I'm Ted Flynn, the general foreman." He aimed a thumb over his shoulder at Larsen. "And this is Kip Larsen, the communication's foreman. He's got your assignments for the next few days, so listen up."

Larsen held his glasses in his hand. He slid past Flynn and stepped down onto the floor of the garage. Flynn stayed put behind him.

"Okay, here we go. I got seven of you guys working solo with another experienced guy and then I put some of you in pairs to work with one of our regulars. That'll take care of all eleven of you." Larsen slipped his glasses into place. "Listen up as I call out your names and assignments. When you hear your name and van number, you can head over to that van."

As Larsen called out the assignments, the newbies moved to their assigned vans, as directed. When Larsen wrapped up, Flynn pulled him aside.

"Fuck ya put Danny Lonigan with Scarpelli for?"

"I didn't think it—"

"Stop right there," Flynn said, his face an angry knot. "You're right. You just plain 'didn't think.'"

"Want me to switch him with somebody. I can—"

"Nah, leave it alone for now. I don't wanna make it look like a big deal or anything. But I'll talk to him, though."

Flynn watched as Danny stood beside a van talking to Hat and Ziggy. Larsen worked his way back up the stairs.

From his perch on the second step, Flynn called out, "Danny Lonigan."

Danny hustled over to him.

"Look, the guy you're workin' with . . . well, don't let him get you into any shit, all right?" Flynn said. "He ain't exactly the hardest worker, if you catch my drift. And he's a big-time bullshitter too. Ain't exactly someone you're wanna make a habit of hangin' around with, 'kay?

"Which guy?"

Flynn wagged his head. "Not the little Mexican guy. That's Ziggy Ramirez. He's new, too. I'm talkin' about the dago. Scarpelli's his name."

"Gottit." Danny started to walk off.

"Hey." Danny stopped. Flynn waved him in close. "His uncle is Jello Pellegrini."

"Is that right?" Flynn nodded. Danny eyed Flynn for a moment, turned and walked back to join Ziggy and Hat by the van. The men finished loading the van and drove off.

Ziggy and Danny were on their knees collecting scraps of telephone wire from the floor at the 27th Ward yard office on the city's West Side when Hat approached.

"All right, fellas," Hat said, "we're all wrapped up here so let's make like a tree and get ready to leave."

Ziggy and Danny snagged the last few pieces of wire while Hat sauntered over to the ward secretary, an older black woman.

"You're all set, Missy," said Hat, his words a mixture of charm and bravado. "The new phone line is up and runnin'."

"Already?"

"Yep. No more busy calls," Hat said. "That extra line'll get everything through for ya."

"Thank you so much."

Hat nodded. "We aim to please."

The three men walked outside to the ward yard parking lot and tossed the last few leftover strands of telephone wire and an empty box of wire into the ward Dumpster. Hat opened the rear van door.

"Grab two boxes each, okay guys?" All three men reached into the back of the van and grabbed two boxes of Cat 5 phone wire. "We gotta set these over in the basement stairwell on the side of the building. A buddy of mine from the ward needs 'em."

Ziggy and Danny, with Hat in tow, deposited the wire as directed and walked towards their van.

"So Lonigan," Hat said, "my people tell me you're goin' to night school to become a writer. Is that right?"

Hat climbed into the driver's seat. Ziggy jumped into the passenger seat. Danny didn't answer. He settled into the back of the cargo van, parking himself on a plastic milk crate. Hat started the engine and pulled off. "So do ya or don't ya, Lonigan?"

"What?"

Hat gave Ziggy a playful rap across the chest. "Jeez, these Irish guys are thick in the head, ain't they?"

Ziggy cut lose with a chuckle. Hat continued to stir the pot.

"Ya know what, Lonigan, where I come from, we don't let midget Mexicans sit in the front seat."

"Hey, fuck you, man." Ziggy's eyes were slits.

Hat laughed. This time Danny joined him.

"Easy bro," Hat barked as he took a corner. "I'm just messin' with ya." He rapped his right hand against Ziggy's shoulder. "Tell me you didn't mess with the other fucks on the job site at your last gig. C'mon, that's parta the fun, parta the game here in the circus. See I'm just skippin' the get-to-know-ya phase and jumpin' right into the shit. Unnerstand?"

Ziggy smiled. "My bad."

"That's cool," Hat said, and then he examined Danny in the rearview mirror. "So I'm still waitin' on that answer, Lonigan."

"Yeah, I do. I go two nights a week to Columbia, downtown. Workin' on my MFA."

Hat took another turn and drifted slowly down the street.

"So what sorta shit ya write?"

"Ah, ya know, a little bit of everything."

After he stopped at a red light, Hat turned back and glanced at Danny. "What sorta bullshit is that?" He laughed and imitated Danny, his tone whiny and nasally, "'A little bit of everything.'" And then he continued, "Look, man, you wanna be a writer, you gotta exaggerate. You gotta be descriptive. You gotta have *voice*. You gotta *see it. Hear it.* You gotta have *pizazz*. You gotta—"

"'Pizazz?'" Danny leaned forward on his crate. "Are you

kiddin' me? What do you know about writing?"

"I read all the time, Holmes. And I write alotta shit too, okay? Mostly poems. I write other shit too, but mostly poems."

Danny words were filled with disbelief. "You write poems?"

"Yeah, I write poems."

"I never met a guy who wrote poems before," Ziggy said. "Women, yeah. Guys, no."

"He doesn't write poetry," Danny said with a smirk. "He's fulla shit. Ted Flynn even said so."

Hat hit the brakes and curbed the van. Again, Hat imitated Danny, ratcheting up the nasally tone several degrees.

"'Ted Flynn said so.'" Hat shifted into park, his face bunched into a frown. "That's baby shit, man. Fuckin' baby shit." He turned to face Danny. "Lemme tell ya one fuckin' thing 'bout this job right now, Lonigan! Don't listen to what anyone else says 'bout someone else. Everyone's got some story, some baggage. Everyone. You of all people should know that." Hat paused to run his fingers through his hair. "And by the way, Ted Flynn's a Major League piece a shit. All he does is make Kip do his work for him so he can sit up there in his lair all day long and play card games and watch porn on his computer. And you can tell him I said so too. Fuck him."

Danny's eyes stayed on Hat for a few moments longer. Then he coughed and said, "Okay . . . so let's hear one of your poems."

Hat turned forward again. "Still don't think I write, huh?"

"No, I believe ya. I just wanna hear one."

"Me too," Ziggy said.

"Okay then. Pick yer poison, paisans," said Hat. "That's alliteration, by the way." He rubbed his hands together. "Now I got funny poems. I got sad poems. I got poems about the city. I even got poems that if you read them to your wife or girlfriend, she'd do any damn thing ya want after that. And Ziggy, they'd probably even work on your boyfriend, too."

"What the—" Ziggy said.

"Just messin, bro."

Ziggy laughed.

"But if you need help in the lady department, Ziggy, I'll get ya a poem that'll have your woman climbin' all over ya tonight. I mean it. She'll be dancin' atop—"

"My wife's six months pregnant."

"Well, when's the last time she blew ya?

"It's been—"

"All right, already," Danny said. "Let's get to the poems, huh? Let's hear one."

"Okay, Lonigan. Okay. So ya don't wanna hear about Ziggy's sex life, huh? All right. No problem. That'd probably be a short story anyways. Ya know, I jumped my wife once and now she's pregnant." Hat popped Ziggy on the shoulder again. Ziggy fought off a smile. "Okay, so this one I call, THE FIGHT IS OVER. Just so ya know, I don't think it's great. I mean it's not gonna—"

"Just read it, already," Danny barked.

"Okay. Here it goes." Hat looked at Danny and then at Ziggy. To Danny's surprise, Hat didn't read from paper. He recited from memory.

> **Walk home with me, dear friend,**
> **The fight is over.**
> **Seek refuge in my arms,**
> **Let us talk into the night.**
> **Tomorrow we shall plant flowers,**
> **The sun shall kiss your shoulders,**
> **Laughter will fill the room,**
> **And we will never let go.**
> **I promise to visit you often,**
> **I will read you words from the great ones**
> **As you rest beneath the slab**
> **With your name etched upon it.**

"That's some deep shit," Ziggy said.

"Definitely," Danny added. He turned towards Ziggy. "And he don't exactly look like the deep sort, does he?"

"Nah," Ziggy said. "Looks like the sort whose deepest thought is . . . 'Hey, Ma, is the spaghetti ready yet?'"

Danny and Ziggy busted out in laughter.

"Real nice," Hat said and then chuckled. "I open up my soul to you guys and—"

"Let's hear another one," Danny said.

"Yeah," said Ziggy. "Let me hear that Chicago one. The one you said you had about the city."

Before Hat started in, a homeless man wandered up to the driver's side of the van clad in a winter coat with a long rip on the right sleeve and pants that were far too long for him. Hat rolled down the window.

"What ya need, bro?" Hat said.

"I'm just hungry, man. Real hungry."

"How 'bout thirsty?" Hat smiled. "Ya thirsty too?"

"Truth be told," the man said with a gap-toothed smile, "I'm always bein' thirsty."

Hat pulled a few singles from his pocket and gave it to the man. "This'll take care of a bit of that thirst problem. Not much, but it's a start." Hat turned to Ziggy. "Hey Ziggy, gimme that brown bag lunch of yours."

"Hold on now. I—"

"Just gimme it. We'll go to lunch in a bit and I'm buyin'."

Ziggy handed over his lunch, and Hat passed it to the man. "Here you go, partner. This should take care of that hungry part."

"Thank ya, Sir. God bless."

Hat nodded. The three men watched the man meander slowly down the sidewalk until he disappeared around the corner.

"Ya wanna fuckin' poem about the city?" Hat said. "Well, that was *it*. Right there. Yes, indeed, that was a fuckin' poem."

"Yes, it was," Danny said. "I still wanna hear yours, though."

"Okay. Okay. Here we go. I call this one "Little Pearl." It's a shotgun poem. Hat cleared his throat, and Danny and Ziggy edged forward ever so slightly.

Little Pearl
jumps rope,
jumps rope,
jumps rope,
        while her Mamma,

smokes rope,
smokes rope,
smokes rope,
'round the corner.

Buildings fall and bangers shoot,
when can she leave this garden of soot?
Be strong, Little Pearl, shine bright,
do not become friends with the night,
Turn the pages of many books, and
you will leave this den of crooks.

There was a silence after the poem. Danny and Ziggy looked towards Hat and then gazed out the window. They were on Madison Avenue on Chicago's West Side. All around them, the storefront windows and doors along the street were either boarded over or covered with protective security bars that looked like they had grown up out of the ground after the last rusty rain. The boys let their eyes wander the streets, perhaps looking for their own Little Pearl.

"What? No feedback." Hat said.

"That was good, man. Damn good," Ziggy said. "Makes me want to clean up the streets. You should put that shit to music. Rap the hell out of it."

Danny chimed in. "Strong. Sincere. Thought provoking."

"Thanks, fellas," Hat said with sincerity. "Now how 'bout you, Lonigan. What you got for us?"

Danny laughed. "No. I got nothin' with me."

"Bullshit." Hat craned his neck and looked into the cargo area of the van. "I see your bookbag and your tool bag back there. Ten bucks says you got some of yer shit in one of those bags."

Danny laughed again and then scratched his head. "Maybe I do. But I'm not readin' any. It's kinda private stuff."

"C'mon, just read somethin'," Hat said. "Ya know, somethin' that ain't so private."

"Nope."

Hat shifted into drive and pulled the van back on the road.

"How much you weigh, Lonigan?" said Hat.

"What?" Danny narrowed his eyes.

"C'mon already. How much?"

"Two hundred twenty pounds. Why?"

Hat laughed and turned towards Ziggy. "Ziggy, did you know that we are in the presence of a fully grown and fully mature 220-pound vagina?"

"Ouch," Ziggy said.

Danny laughed. The others did as well. As the van cruised down the street, Danny eyed his bookbag.

20. Tom Pays Two Visits

TOM LONIGAN WORKED his way up the shabby wooden stairs towards Ted Flynn's office, his worn knees feeling each step he took. He stopped midway and glanced back down, wondering how this creaky staircase had survived over the years. When he walked into the office unannounced, Kip Larsen and Flynn sprang to their feet. Larsen extended his hand.

"Hi, Tom, how are ya?"

"Good, Kip. Good." The men shook hands. Tom eyed Flynn and turned back to Kip. "Can you give us a few secs?"

"No problem. Sure." Kip walked out of the office and shut the door.

"What's up?" Flynn said. Tom edged up to the window and stood in silence watching as Kip made his way down the last few stairs. He felt like taking a match to this shoebox office and locking Flynn in with the flames. As he watched Kip walk towards the far reaches of the garage, Tom pictured his left hand wrapped around Flynn's throat as he lifted him off the ground and slapped him around with his right. After Kip disappeared into a breakroom, Tom turned and walked directly in front of Flynn's desk.

"Who the fuck do ya think you are, huh? Who the fuck—"

"Tom, Tom. Easy," Flynn said, his words filled with fear. "I didn't do nothin'."

Tom's eyes bulged. "Is that right? Nothin', huh?" The color red exploded across Tom's neck and face. "Well, riddle me this, Batman. I just called up Joe Donnelly to check in with him and asked him how the job was goin' and—"

"Who the hell's Joe Donnelly?"

"'Who the hell's Joe Donnelly?'" Spittle flew from Tom's lips. He reached his monstrous left hand towards Flynn's neck but then stopped. He turned and took a few steps back before facing Flynn again. "Donnelly's the fuckin' guy you chopped outta the city job. I called all four new guys today—well, except for my own brother, to check and see how the first day on the new job was goin' and Donnelly told me that he's still workin' with Peterson Electric. He said you told him he'd be in with the next group in about six months."

The left side of Flynn's face twitched. "Tom, hold on a minute."

"Don't gimme that 'hold on' shit. Look you're—"

"Tom, Tom, I got a call on this from Randall, from Richard Randall. I swear." Flynn raised his hand as if he were taking an oath. "He told me the Mayor talked to you and there was a cunt goin' in as one of the Union's four. He said it was all set. All agreed to between you and the mayor. He told me to chop the Irish kid and that he'd go in with the next group."

"Randall said all that?"

"Yeah. I swear."

"Who is she?"

"Maggie Sunfield's her name.

Tom turned and shook his head. "Pisses me off."

"I, uh, I—"

"You shoulda called me." Tom stomped off toward the door.

"I'm sorry, Tom. How was I supposed to know? Randall said—"

Tom stopped, his hand on the knob. "That's why you shoulda called me." He turned and pushed a hand through his hair. "Look, I don't expect ya to be a mind reader, but you're a fuckin' general foreman for Christ's sake. I expect ya to use your fuckin' noggin."

Tom glared at Flynn. "You shoulda called."

"Whataya gonna do?"

"I'm gonna try and fix it."

Flynn stepped out from behind his desk. "Ya wanna use my phone. I'll leave the office if ya want."

Tom sucked in a deep breath and released it slowly. "No." He grimaced and scratched the back of his neck. "Personal visits work better in situations like this." Tom walked out the door and worked his way uneasily down the steps. Flynn fell back into his chair. He watched Tom walk slowly through the garage towards the exit door, and all the while Flynn massaged his own throat.

During the drive down to City Hall, Tom Lonigan couldn't help thinking he made a huge mistake four years ago when he backed Ted Flynn for the general foreman's position. Flynn had never shown himself to be a good decision maker. Rather, as with the current situation, he continued to demonstrate that he lacked common sense when needed most. Tom rummaged through the other candidates who were considered for the GF job. He liked several of them far better than Flynn. But Flynn's father had helped Tom get his start as an apprentice and had been good to him through the years. So Ted Flynn it was.

Tom parked in front of City Hall and put his union placard in the front window. The police officer monitoring the area gave him a wave just before Tom pushed through the revolving entry door on LaSalle Street. The lobby area bustled with people strutting across the tile floor and coming off of and going onto elevators. Lawyers clad in power suits and stoic faces, some with clients in tow, tried their best to look important as they marched across the lobby. A CPD patrolman chatted with an off-duty cop from the post he manned in the middle of the lobby. Tom boarded an elevator and exited on the fifth Floor. He headed directly to the reception area for the Mayor.

"Hello, Mr. Lonigan," the mayor's receptionist said. "How are you today?"

"I been better, Cassie. But as long as I'm still breathin' I can't complain." Tom offered a flat-lipped smile. "Is the Mayor in?"

"He is, but he's in a conference right now." Cassie glanced at her appointment book. "He should only be another minute or so."

"How 'bout the great Mr. Randall, is he in?"

Cassie laughed. "Yes, he is. Would you like me to let him know you're here?"

"Nah." Tom smiled. "I'm gonna step in and surprise him."

"I'm sure he'll enjoy that."

"I'll guaran-damn-tee he won't."

Tom banged once on the door to Randall's office and immediately walked in. Randall sat at his desk, his cell phone glued to his ear, as he looked out his window. When Tom cleared his throat, Randall swung his head towards the door and saw Tom standing there. He ended his phone call without further words and climbed to his feet. Randall walked over to Tom and extended his hand. Tom paid no attention to it.

"Who's this woman you shoved down my throat?" Randall didn't answer. "Who?"

"Easy, Tom." Randall said. "Let's try to—"

"I asked a simple question. Try answerin' it. Who the hell is she?"

Randall blinked several times before words came to his lips. "Her name's Maggie Sunfield."

Tom rolled his eyes. "I know her name already. What's she to you?"

"What do you mean?"

"You bonin' her?"

"I wish I was. Believe me, I do." Randall smiled. "She's definitely hot. Amazingly hot."

"I know who she is. I already said that."

"Well, then you know. I'm just trying to help her out. That's all."

Tom tongued his lips. "So you're not bonin' her yet. But you're hopin' to. Is that it?

"No, that's not it. I—"

"All right, forget about her for a minute, even though it seems you have a hard time doin' that. What's with the switcherooski and doin' it all behind my back?" Tom glanced at his wristwatch. "I hafta tell ya, that pisses me off to no end. You think I wouldn't find out?"

"Look, Tom. I'm sorry. This girl's been down on her luck. Her husband's a drunk, they just finished up a messy divorce. All that good stuff. And I just found out she was an electrician. So I tried to help her out. Last minute thing."

"You're bonin' her. Just admit it."

"Look, I'm not. A buddy of mine's been dating her for four or five months now. They're good together. They're happy. And she could use some happiness. So could he. She's only worked about half the year coming outta the hall so I figured I'd try to help."

Tom turned to face Randall's door and quickly turned back. "Well I got three things for ya. One. You're lyin'. You're bonin' her. Two, if you're not jumpin' her bones and this sob story about her and your buddy is true, then you shoulda called me. I'm a sucker for sob stories, but only when they're told to me directly and not after a switcherooski, and three." Tom started walking towards the door. "We're goin' to see the mayor."

Randall jumped from behind his desk, trying to slow Tom down.

"Don't go in there. He's in a meeting, Tom."

Tom continued walking at a brisk clip. They exited Randall's office and walked past the receptionist. "If he is, I'll let him know I can wait. If he's not in a meetin', hopefully we can all talk."

As the men neared the mayor's office, the door opened and Mayor Robert Stokely, a tall man of roughly fifty years, stepped out followed by two well-dressed Japanese men. The mayor eyed Tom with a smile and then shook hands, bowed and said good-bye to his visitors. Mayor Stokely then shook hands with Tom.

"Tommy, what brings you down?" Mayor Stokely said.

"I got a little problem, Mr. Mayor. I'm hopin' you can help me fix it. I just need a couple of minutes."

The mayor waved an arm towards his office. Randall opened the door and closed it after the three entered. The mayor leaned up against the edge of his desk, and Tom sat on a chair just in front of the mayor. Randall joined them, sitting on a chair beside Tom.

"Okay, here's the poop, straight and sweet," Tom said. He pointed to Randall. "Our friend Richard here jammed me good. As you know, eleven new electricians just started with the city. The union had four spots, but Richard here, unbeknownst to me until today, took one of the four spots away at the last minute and stuck some woman electrician in there and fucked the good Irish kid I slotted for that spot. Richard here was a very bad boy, very sneaky, and when he pulled this maneuver, he told my general foreman that you and me had agreed to everything. That's it." Tom's eyebrows rose. "So now I got some hot chick electrician that I didn't ask for, and who by the way I think Richard here is bonin', and I'm hopin' you can find it in your large and generous heart to maybe open up the city's checkbook so I can get the Irish kid in who was supposed to be there all along."

"I thought you said this was going to be quick."

"I lied." Tom glared at Randall. "I'm impersonating Richard."

Mayor Stokely laughed. "Ouch." He rubbed his hands together. "Richard, it looks like you've been tossed under the proverbial bus and deservedly so."

Stokely walked towards a window overlooking LaSalle Street. He stared blankly through the glass for a few seconds.

"Ya know, sometimes I just stand here, like I am now, and watch the people walk by down below, most of them hustling to wherever the hell they're goin', and you realize . . . I'm the mayor of this city, but I really don't know all that many of its citizens. Not many at all." He turned and faced Tom. "But I know you, Tom. And I trust you. And I appreciate everything you've done for me in the past. There hasn't been one time you've said *no* to me. So I won't say *no* to you now."

"Thanks, Mayor."

"Bring the kid in tomorrow and tell him he's working as a city electrician. We'll find the funds to make it work." Tom stood up and shook the mayor's hand. "I'd ask if there's anything else, but I'm afraid there might be."

Tom laughed. "No, there's nothin' else." He offered his trademark nod of sincerity. "Thanks again for your help."

As Tom let himself out, the Mayor stared at the door Tom had just closed.

"I like that man. Always have. He's definitely different. All he ever wants is what's fair and he's willing to fight for it. And it's hard to argue with or ignore the doctrine of fairness." The mayor eyed Randall. "I'd like to say I don't really care about what you did here, Richard. But that's not the truth. You used me for an endorsement, and you used Tom Lonigan for an endorsement. I don't want to know why. Just don't do it again." Stokely's eyes stayed fixed on Randall, who nodded. "And by the way, not to be a prick because I know you had to get out of here tonight for something, but the fact of the matter is you need to stay here and comb through the numbers until you can find what budget we can yank the seventy grand from to pay this new electrician. Fair enough?"

"Yes, sir."

21. Flies on the Wall

SAM AND JIM SAT BESIDE EACH OTHER at the kitchen table ready for dinner while Kate handed plates, glasses and utensils to them. Danny put the finishing touches on the sauce, stirring in a bit of oregano with a wooden spoon. He then adjusted a knob on the stove.

Sam leaned over and whispered to Jim, "We're havin' Italian again."

"Good," Jim said. "I love Italian."

"Yeah. Me too," Sam said, still whispering. He watched as his father sprinkled a bit more oregano into the sauce. "But give Dad the business anyways. Ya know." Jim nodded in affirmation.

Danny set a bowl of bow-tie pasta mixed in marinara sauce on the table. "All righty, boys, dig in."

Jimmy winced. "Pasta again?"

"What?" Danny said, a pained look on his face. "You love

pasta."

Jimmy continued his charade. "But not all the time."

Kate brought warm bread to the table and sat down. Danny sat beside her.

"It's been a week or even more than that since we last had pasta," Danny said. "I mean . . ." Danny saw Sam snickering.

"Ya know what, Vito?" Danny said, speaking in broken English, "Don't ebber complain 'bout too much pasta."

Kate set some bread on her plate. "Here we go again."

"Hey Maria, I don't like bein' interrupted when I'm talkin' man talk to my sons. Unnerstand?"

Kate didn't respond. She shrugged and drizzled some olive oil in a dish and sprinkled it with parmesan cheese.

"Now as for the both of yous, just know dis. Pasta . . . how do I say dis . . . pasta is what makes you a man. It's what—"

The boys laughed and nudged each other.

"I must say that your Italian accent is getting a little better," Kate said.

Danny dropped the broken English. "Well, I've been gettin' some good practice. One of my new partners is an Italian guy."

The Lonigans passed the bowl around and everyone spooned some pasta onto their plate and began to eat.

Kate sipped her glass of water. "Old Italian guy with an accent, huh?"

"Nah. Nah. He's about my age," Danny said. "But he's definitely old school. In reality, I don't know so much if he talks like an old school Italian guy or if it's just Bridgeportese."

"An Italian guy from Bridgeport, huh?" Kate said. "Imagine that."

"Is he a mobster, Dad?" Sam said and then shoveled some pasta into his mouth.

Danny laughed and looked at Sam with wonderment. "Where'd you pick that up?"

Sam chewed and swallowed before he spoke. "Well, in school, in social studies class, we're studying about the different neighborhoods in Chicago and how they were formed. And for Bridgeport, I know there were lots of Irish, but even more Italians in the old days. And a bunch of those guys were in the mob."

"That's cool stuff." Danny sliced a thin wedge of butter and applied it to his bread. "I wish they had a class like that when I was in grade school."

Sam continued. "And then we learned about a kid named Kenard Dotson."

"Yep. That was some bad stuff." Danny squeezed his face into a knot. "Real bad stuff. That was in the late '90s."

"Who's he?" Jim asked.

"He was a black kid, about my age," Sam said, "and he walked through Bridgeport one day and got jumped and beat bad by three or four white kids. One of 'em was a mobster's son. A couple of the witnesses ended up dead."

"That's right." Danny nodded. "And the Dotson kid himself ended up with bad head injuries from the beating he took."

"So, um, so is your new partner, ya know, is he tied in?" Kate said.

"No. I don't think so." Danny forked some noodles into his mouth. "But his uncle's definitely connected."

"Cool. Dad's workin' with a mobster's relative," Sam barked. "I can't wait to tell the kids at school. Franky Fiddler won't believe it. I'll call—"

"This is awesome," Jim said. "I'm gonna . . ."

Danny listened to his sons' words and laughed.

Cheryl Ramirez was stretched out on the den couch. Ziggy stood before her with a sheet of loose-leaf paper in his hands and a smile on his face. He stared down at his wife.

"I can't believe it." Cheryl said. "You actually wrote a poem for me. Really?"

"Yep, I put it together at work today," Ziggy said with a spark in his eye. "All by myself. I just—"

"That's not like you." She pushed herself up on an elbow. "I mean, you've never written poetry before."

"I know. I know." Ziggy smiled. "But it's somethin' that just came to me. I mean I was thinking about you laid up on the couch, carrying our wonderful child, not able to do much, and I wanted to write something special for you." Ziggy flashed his teeth again. "That's all."

"That's so sweet." Cheryl reached her left hand up. "Can I see it?"

"Is it, you know, is it okay if I read it to you? I'd rather do that."

Cheryl smiled and flattened herself into the couch again. "Please. Please do."

Ziggy ruffled the paper and began. "I call it, "Our Love." Ziggy cleared his throat.

**Our Love is what matters most.
I love you more than . . ."**

Cheryl stared at Ziggy with a smile glued to her face. She couldn't believe what he had written. She couldn't believe what she had just heard. *Oh, my God*, she thought. *Oh, my God.*

Hat stood at the bar of his favorite Bridgeport tavern, Club Pudding, a gin and tonic in hand. It was a bit after 10:00 p.m. and he'd just entered the club. The dance floor was crowded. Hat surveyed the talent and talked to the bartender.

"What's the deal here, Lenny?" Hat said. "Is this Cougar Night or somethin'?"

Lenny bunched his lips together. "Nothin' wrong with Cougars."

"Oh I'm with ya there, man. The best Cougars are the ones who have husbands with little dicks." Hat grabbed his package with his right hand. "When they get a hold of this sausage, they don't know if they wanna suck on it or chop it off to take home and put up on their mantel."

Lenny laughed. Hat continued to eyeball the crowd.

"Hey, who's that girl over there?" Hat nodded towards the left side of the crowd.

"Which one, Jimmy?"

"The one next to that tall girl with the butter face."

Lenny craned his neck.

"See her," Hat said. "Sparkly gold top. Cute face. Perky tits."

"Oh yeah, I see her. Don't know her name, though." Lenny ran a rag across the bar top. "She's been here before, though. Been in a couple times with Sherri Panico."

"Sherri, huh?"

"Yeah. I think they work together."

"A nurse, huh?"

Lenny nodded. Hat downed his drink. Lenny immediately filled it. Hat wandered over towards the girl who had caught his eye. He stopped about five feet from her and started doing a rhythmic dance, turning slowly in circles in front of her. The girl watched, as did her tall friend. Hat then set his drink on the ground, grabbed both of his ankles, and started to shake and gyrate his ass like a stripper. Hat picked up his drink and turned to face her. She laughed. Still dancing in tiny circles, Hat slipped in beside the girl, nudging the tall friend out of the way a bit.

"So ya gonna watch me dance all night or ya gonna join me?"

"I think I'll join you."

"Good. I like the way you think."

Hat and the girl moved out onto the dance floor.

"I like that gold top you're wearin'. You fill it out nice."

The girl smiled.

"So ya work with Sherri, huh?"

"You know Sherri?"

"Do I know Sherri? C'mon." Hat grabbed the girl's hand and spun her in a circle. "I chased Sherri all through high school. Sherri the Cherry." Hat squeezed her hand. "I didn't get nothin'."

The girl laughed. "Oh, I'm sure that's right. Sherri's a good girl. I love her to death. But she's definitely waiting for Mr. Right."

Hat smiled. "How 'bout you. You waitin' for Mr. Right? 'Cuz if you are, I definitely ain't him."

The girl took Hat's drink and sipped a bit before she slid the drink back into his hand. Hat moved in close and whispered in her ear.

"You should see how I dance in private."

Hat's breath massaged the girl's neck. He then tongued her ear and stepped back to gauge her response.

"Guess what?" the girl said. She waved Hat in. "I've been in this city for just over five weeks now, and I haven't been laid yet."

Hat jumped back in mock shock. "That's utterly appalling," he said, and then leaned in again. "Well, you struck gold tonight. Definitely."

Hat turned quickly, looking towards Lenny.

"C'mon with me. I wanna show you somethin'." He took the girl by the hand past assorted dancers juking and grinding, and led her to the bar.

"Can I get dem keys, Lenny?"

Lenny smiled and retrieved a set of keys from the cash register. He dropped them into Hat's right hand and watched as Hat led the girl across the dance floor, dodging bodies as they moved, to a back hallway where he unlocked a door.

The twosome headed down another hallway and stopped in front of yet another door. Hat opened the door, and the two stepped inside into darkness. Hat flipped on the light—a dark, blue mood light. They stood in the dressing area and stared out at a ten-by-ten-foot, glass-enclosed room filled from floor to thigh-height with chocolate pudding.

"Now ya know why they call this place, Club Pudding."

The girl's eyes wandered slowly across the room.

"My uncle owns this place. He came up with the idea."

The girl tongued her lips. Hat pulled her in close and kissed her. She reached a hand down and started to rub Hat's sausage through his pants. Hat stepped back to peel off his shirt. The girl did the same and they kissed again before they stripped completely. Hat led the girl into the glass-enclosed room.

"Oh my God, it's warm," the girl said, once she felt the pudding against her body.

"Damn right, it's warm. And God's got nothin' to do with it."

Hat reached down and scooped a handful of chocolate pudding. He rubbed it slowly across the girl's shoulders, breasts, and hips, taking his time, caressing each area as he moved. The girl released moans of pleasure. Hat filled his right hand with pudding again and massaged the girl's inner thighs. The moans continued until the girl pulled Hat upright and mounted him. Hat pressed her up against the glass wall where they moved rhythmically. He snapped off the mood light, leaving them in complete darkness.

"So what's your name anyways?" Hat said.

"Who cares. Just keep doing what you're doing."

Beef barley soup. Danny loved it and always had a bowl when he returned home from his night classes at Columbia College. Beef barley wasn't exactly something his mother or father dished up for dinner when Danny was a kid. Campbell's tomato soup was the usual suspect in the Lonigan pantry back then, though on occasion Mary Lonigan would let loose her wild side, and she'd come home from her trip to the Jewel with a few stray cans of chicken noodle. As best he could recall, Danny had his first bowl of beef barley soup at a funeral luncheon for one of his old undergrad teachers, Professor Jim McAfee, who up and died right in the middle of a history class one day while lecturing about the finer points of the Industrial Revolution, and that's when the beef barley love affair started. So now, one Saturday afternoon every month, Danny would brown up tiny pieces of beef in a large, well-oiled skillet, add celery, onions, carrots, and stewed tomatoes, along with a barley mix. After a bit, he'd transfer the items into a large container and add the broth and water. And then he'd douse it with pepper. Key word there—*douse*. Should you ever try to cook beef barley from scratch, just remember that no matter where you might cheat on the ingredients, don't skimp on the pepper. To Danny Lonigan, if you did that, you might as well feed your concoction to the porcelain throne.

When Danny finished cooking his monthly batch, he'd serve it to his family as the first and only course at a weekend meal. The balance of the soup was then spooned into pint-sized containers and placed in the freezer. And twice a week, when Danny returned home late from school, he'd heat up a container he left in the fridge to defrost earlier in the day, and then sit down at the kitchen table alone to slowly savor the soup. 11 p.m.—that was the usual time Danny returned from school, and Kate and the boys were fast asleep. Just Danny, his beef barley soup and his thoughts. A dangerous gathering.

On this night, as Danny slurped the last few drops of broth, he thought about heating up another bowl but instead he turned his attention to the notebook beside him, the notebook with the words *Advanced Fiction Journal* scribbled atop the front cover in bold, black marker. He had avoided looking at the journal as he ate his soup, but it was there the entire time, staring at him from its post atop the kitchen table—adjacent to the salt-and-pepper shakers, watching him dribble bits of broth on his flannel shirt, observing as he flicked his hand towards the family cat, who climbed atop the table in hopes of scoring a few drops of soup (she liked the soup too)—just staring and watching, much like a pesky little brother or sister who simply refuses to go away.

Danny opened the journal and rifled through a number of pages, stopping at several to read the first few sentences, before eventually returning to his first entry of the semester. He liked the words on this page. He had fun writing them, and "fun," to Danny, was a big part of the writing process. Sure the instructors at Columbia College often had students read parts of their journals aloud in class in search of that elusive "voice" the students were told they all had, but some instructors actually collected the journals from time to time to bring home for some quality reading. Danny occasionally found himself cracking a smile at the thought of Laurie McTeer, his advanced fiction instructor, downing her morning, heart-healthy Cheerios at her mahogany kitchen table, cup of coffee at her left flank, as she rummaged through the brilliance that was Danny's journal; or perhaps McTeer preferred to spend her quality time on the porcelain throne with Danny's journal in hand. What better way to start your day, Danny thought and then chuckled.

He pushed his empty bowl of soup to the side. The cat climbed back atop the table to take in the few drops of broth remaining in the bowl and then sat still as a sphinx, staring at Danny from a foot away. Danny grabbed his journal, climbed to his feet and read aloud to the cat.

January 26

Journals. Why? Almost every damn teacher I've had here at Columbia has required a journal for their class. I get it. I do. But I hate journals and truth be told, I've never kept one. Not before I came here. See, I want to write about what I want to write. And I want to put it to paper my way—not theirs. But hey, when you're in an advanced fiction writing class and your professor tells you a journal is mandatory, you salute your teacher like an obedient soldier, and you keep a damn journal. Now don't get me wrong. I fully understand the importance of journals. I get it like I already said. I do. Mainly, journals help you get ideas, thoughts, rants, observations, or whatever the hell else you're writing to paper—stuff you can go back to later and turn into story. But still, journaling has never been my method. When I get good ideas, I scribble key words across the palm of my left hand, or the hand of the devil as my Irish grandmother called it. On occasion, I have been known to fill up my entire palm with great one-word and two-word reminders, leaving me with no choice but to scribble away on the inside of my wrist, the part that will turn translucent and become as brittle as the skin of an apple as I grow old.

I never write on the top of my hand. It's far too boney and bumpy. Plus the words would be easily visible causing someone who sees those very words, someone like the teenage cashier at the County Fair grocery store in my neighborhood, to think I was a freak. And I can't have that happen, 'cuz, who knows . . . that cashier might just end up becoming the next queen of the South Side Saint Patrick's Day Parade, and you can't have the queen thinking you're a damn freak. So I keep my words hidden in my palm and interior wrist. And that's how I'd do it if I had it my way. SAY NO to journaling in notebooks.

The one-and two-word reminders work great when you're driving in the car and you hit a red light. You can jot a couple of good ideas onto your palm during traffic stops like that. And I must state—and I do feel almost heroic sharing this—that I NEVER write on my palm while driving. It's part of my creed. DON'T WRITE ON YOUR PALM AND DRIVE. If only the textaholics would follow suit.

There are a couple of shortcomings to my method. You've probably already guessed some of them. Hands come in contact with lots of things over the course of a day. Hands shake other hands, hands pick things up, hands swing softball bats, hands hold hotdogs with everything on 'em except ketchup, hands wear gloves, hands get sweaty. So sometimes one or more of my palm-scribbled words are flat out gone by the time I get home, before I can transfer those words onto my laptop in a file I call—MY IDEAS. Pretty damn catchy file name, huh? Anyways, that's how I work it. And sometimes those erased words never come back to you. They lounge about in THE LAND OF LOST THOUGHTS, never to return again. And I hate when that happens. I hate it almost as much as when I can't read my own damn words on my palm. Can you believe that shit? Well, it's the truth. My handwriting stinks, and there are times when I stare into my palm or wrist and all I see is "ghyuugth." Good luck figuring out what the hell that means. And who knows? Maybe, just maybe, that lost thought or idea or that illegible word would have been just what I needed to put together the next great story. Oh well, enough on that.

The other shortcoming to my method, but one I can definitely live with, is that you do catch the occasional odd look or glance from others when they see you scribbling away on your paw while you're in the driver's seat at a red light, or when you stop to get those words down when you're out walking the dog. "What's that strange man doing writing on his arm, dear," some old *blue hair has probably said to her husband when she saw me scribbling away from her nocturnal post at her apartment window. "Shouldn't he be cleaning up that massive dump his tiny dog just dropped, rather than writing on the skin of his soon-to-be translucent wrist? And come to think of it, shouldn't it be illegal for a small dog to take a dump that big?" Oh well, enough on that too. I've got my two mandatory pages done. That's it. No more wisdom. And that's good enough for me.*

Moonlight slipped through a kitchen window and landed on the cat, giving it a strange glow of sorts. Danny sat down again and grabbed a pen from atop the kitchen table. He turned the pages to the back of the journal, to the first empty page. Danny thought about scribbling some words down about today—his first day at work. And then he thought about his interview, almost ten days ago. It seemed like months ago. Hell, it seemed like a damn dream. He wrote down the date and then scribbled, "My Interview." Danny looked at his words and then crossed them off. Again his pen moved . . .

April 24 ~~My Interview~~ The Three Wise Men. Who the hell has people come to an interview to ID tools? Who does that? And who the hell has a tiny frog dancing on a wooden floor behind them during the interview and doesn't even know it? And hey, if you're going to hire a frog as your entertainment, can't you at least bust open your wallet to give the guy a top hat and a cane? Interview, my ass. What a fucking joke. But hey, I'm not here to complain. I'm ready to be taken into the

wonderful arms of the city, the City, the CITY. Yes
indeed, to the Department of Streets and Sanitation, I
say . . . I'm all yours.

22. Jim White

COLUMNIST JIM WHITE LEANED back in his chair, his size thirteens stretched across his desk. He stared into an empty legal pad on his lap, before aiming his eyes at the wall clock. It was 1:00 a.m. and White was the lone pony in the *Chicago Sun-Times* office. Every other reasonable columnist or beat writer was home fast asleep. But Jim White wasn't like every other journalist. As White flicked his hand at a fly momentarily invading his space, his desk phone rang. White glanced at it, then eyed the wall clock again. He didn't want to answer the phone. Probably some drunk calling in to ramble on about the mayor or complain about a car-sized pothole on his street. White received numerous voicemails like that during the wee hours. He eyed the caller ID—UNKNOWN CALLER—as the phone rang again. White was drawing a blank on what his next column would be about. He needed ideas. The next ring seemed even louder. White snatched the receiver.

"Jim White," he said.

"Hi ya, Mr. White," the unknown caller said. "I, uh, I didn't exactly think I'd get you this late. Thought I'd get your voicemail. Thought—"

"Well, you got me. What can I do ya for?"

"It's no big deal. Not really. But I know how you like to write stories about city workers and stuff. And I liked the last one you wrote about Quarters McNicholas. That was good stuff."

"Okay."

"Well, like I said this one's not too big a deal, but maybe you can have some fun with it." The unknown caller sneezed on the other end. "Sorry 'bout that. Bad cold going around at work."

"No problem."

"Okay, so there were two huge spools of electrical wire, copper wire, that just up and disappeared the other day from the supply room at one of the Streets and San garages."

"Which garage?"

"940 West Exchange. Ya know, over near Bridgeport."

White scribbled the address on the legal pad. "Okay. What's the value on this stuff?"

"At least fifty grand." White noted that on his pad.

"Those are good numbers. I don't know if they're front page numbers but I can probably do something with this."

"The guys in the garage are calling it "The Copper Caper." The man laughed. "It's funny shit 'cuz the garage cameras were turned off and everything. So there had to be a few guys in on this."

"And I'm guessing you don't want me to use your name on this, right?"

The caller laughed. "You read my mind."

"And what if I have some more questions. How do I get a hold of you later?"

"You don't. I'll check back with ya when I got some more info."

"Anybody at the *Trib* know about this?"

"Nope. It's all yours."

"Okay. Fair enough."

After the call ended, White continued to hold the receiver. Once he set it down, he scribbled, *COPPER CAPER*, on his notepad and circled it.

Part Two

The
Copper Caper

1. The Missing Spools

THE THREE STOOGES HUDDLED ON CHAIRS in Ted Flynn's office. To a man, all three wore worried wide eyes.

"So how much is missin'?" Flynn said.

"Two full spools' worth," Morgan said. "The big stuff. Solid copper. Thousands of pounds."

"Shit," Cullinan barked. He removed his glasses and slowly massaged the bridge of his nose with his right hand. "That's gotta . . . that's gotta be worth twenty-five, thirty grand."

"Try fifty," Morgan said. "They're twenty-five K per spool."

Flynn scratched the back of his left hand, causing flakes of scaly white skin to float towards the ground with each pass. He stopped and looked out through his window at the garage below. Various electricians shuffled about loading up their vans with equipment and supplies for the day's work while others stood beside their vans and chatted. Flynn's eyes settled in on Hat.

"I'm tellin' ya, it's gotta be him," Flynn said. "Who else would pull a stunt like that?"

"I dunno as you can say it's definitely him," Cullinan said. "I mean, just cuz—

"Look, Filcher said it was him," Flynn barked. "He said—"

"No, Filcher said he *thought* it was Scarpelli." Cullinan tossed his glasses on Flynn's desk. "That's a big difference."

"Well, he's got a key, a key to the garage," Flynn said. "I think he's still—"

"Hold on a minute," Morgan said. He stood and looked down below, his eyes searching for Hat, before turning back. "Jimmy Scarpelli has a fuckin' key to the garage? Ya shittin' me? I don't even have a key, and I'm a foreman." Morgan threw both hands up and then paced for a moment. "Who's the fuckin' Einstein who gave him a key?"

Flynn blew out a big breath. "That would be me." He twisted and stretched his neck. "Look, I gave 'im a key about a month ago to let some guys in on the weekend for overtime. He was . . . he was the senior guy that day. I forgot to get it back." He blew out another big chunk of air. "Shit."

"Well, maybe we should bring him up here," Morgan said. "Ya know, feel him out a bit."

Flynn nodded. He grabbed his desk phone and hit the intercom button. Like the great and all-powerful Oz, Flynn's voice bellowed across the speaker system in the entire garage.

"Jimmy Scarpelli, report to the general foreman's office. Jimmy Scarpelli, see the general foreman immediately."

Hat, Danny and Ziggy stopped loading half-inch pipe into their van when they heard the announcement.

"Ut oh," Ziggy said, "That's all I gotta say. Ut oh."

"Nice knowin' ya, Scarpelli," Danny added. He turned towards Ziggy. "Guess I'm movin' into the driver's seat already."

"Yeah," Ziggy said. "It'll be nice to finally get that lasagna and meatballs smell out of the van."

Hat laughed and made his way toward the staircase. Danny and Ziggy loaded a few boxes of telephone wire into the truck as Hat made his way up the wooden steps to Flynn's office. He stopped in the doorway.

"What's up?"

"You still got that key to the garage?" said Flynn.

"Yeah."

Flynn looked at Cullinan and Morgan.

"Well, how come you haven't givin' it back yet?" Flynn said.

"Cuz you haven't asked for it."

Flynn stuck his right hand out, palm up. "Well I'm askin' for it now."

Hat dug into his pocket and pulled out his key chain. He slid a key off the ring and walked it over to Flynn.

"What is this . . . the Irish Inquisition?" Hat said. "I thought the only time you three guys got together was to ask people really tough questions like, 'What kinda tool is this' and 'What kinda tool is that?'"

Cullinan swallowed a laugh. Hat dropped the key in Flynn's palm.

"We're missin' a couple of spools of copper wire from the supply room," Flynn said.

"So."

"The big spools. Solid wire. Worth over fifty grand."

"So."

"So you gotta key," Morgan said.

Hat scratched at his ear. "That's great. Just fuckin' great." His head bounced a bit on his shoulders as he spoke. "I gotta key to the garage. I ain't got no key to the damn supply room." Hat wagged his head and laughed. "You geniuses amaze me. Did you guys—"

"Quit with your bullshit already," Morgan growled. "Who you got peddlin' the shit for ya?

"'Peddlin' the shit?'" Hat stared hard at Morgan. "You watch way too many cops shows, Morgan." Hat massaged his chin. "So like I was tryin' to say before Professor Morgan interrupted me, you guys got cameras all over the damn garage. What did the footage show?"

The three men glanced at each other in silence.

"Jesus Christ. You gotta be kiddin' me. You ain't even looked at the cameras yet."

Flynn, Morgan and Cullinan dropped their eyes to the floor.

"Okay, look, this is how it's gonna shake out," said Hat. "You go take a look at that camera footage and you'll find your thief. But I'll tell ya this. I don't think anyone with balls big enough to take that load outta here is gonna be stupid enough to show his face on camera. But I might be wrong. As you three have just demonstrated, this garage ain't exactly filled with the brightest bulbs in Chicago. So maybe he shows his face. But he might be wearin' a mask or somethin'."

The three men waited on Hat's next word.

"Oh yeah, and one other thing. If the cameras don't show nothin', then we all know what that means. Someone shut 'em down. If that's the case, then it means one of your high-tech guys in that camera installation crew did the job. Or he's at least *in* on the job. And there's only five of them guys in the whole city. Even you guys should be able to track that one down."

The three men maintained their silence.

"Am I done here, or do you need me to figure somethin' else

out for you lunkheads?"

Cullinan smiled. "You're done, Jimmy. Sorry to bother ya."

"No bother. Kinda funny, actually. Almost as funny as Morgan's little dick."

"Fuck you," Morgan barked, his face a mass of angry lines.

Hat laughed and waltzed out of Flynn's office. Morgan pushed in close to the window to watch Hat walk down the stairs.

"I hate that fuckin' guy," Morgan said. "Hate 'im."

Danny and Ziggy were sitting on the rear bumper of the van when Hat returned.

"You ain't gettin' that driver's seat just yet, Lonigan," Hat said. The three smiled and climbed into their van, ready to pull out of the garage.

2. New Photos

GILBREATH MISSED IT. Flat out missed it. The blinds in his office were closed tight, allowing but a pinch of sunlight to slip through the bottom corner of the window, and that light fell squarely across the framed photo of Becca. But Gilbreath was immersed in his work, running an index finger across the type-written notes from a file. Had he been more attentive, he would have seen his daughter bathed in sunlight, staring back at him as only an angel could. Had he witnessed that, perhaps Ed Gilbreath would have taken that as a sign that his daughter was trying to contact him, trying to send a message of some sort.

Phipps, with a large, flat envelope in hand, knocked at Gilbreath's door. Gilbreath waved him in.

"We got problems, Ed," Phipps said. "Big problems." He paced the room as he spoke. "It's crazy sauce, man. Pure and lethal crazy sauce."

"What's wrong?" Gilbreath went to his window and raised the blind, giving the midafternoon sun the opportunity to invade his office.

Phipps's feet came to a halt. He cracked open the envelope and pulled out ten eight-by-ten-inch photos. He tossed them on Gilbreath's desk. Gilbreath fingered through the first few, depicting Phipps, his wife, and their four children engaged in various activities—mowing the grass, playing catch with a football, watering flowers, and all watching a baseball game on their den TV. All of the photos were taken around their home.

"He knows where I live." Phipps stared at the photo of Becca. Her impish smile did nothing to calm him. "He knows."

Gilbreath loosened his tie. "Where'd you get these?"

"They were in my mailbox. Stickin' up so I could see 'em. They were there this morning."

Gilbreath turned his focus back to the photos. He fingered through a few more, but stopped and focused on one particular photo of Phipps's kitchen.

"Jesus."

"That's right." Phipps started pacing again. "They were *inside* my house. Fuckin' inside."

3. Ziggy's Poem

HAT DROVE HIS STREETS AND SAN VAN down Western Avenue through the West Side. Ziggy manned the passenger seat, while Danny sat on his milk crate as usual. As the day closed in on noon, the streets and sidewalks along Western were clogged with activity. Hat zipped past a storefront church and eyed a black man in a white fedora, microphone in hand, preaching to a gathering of five on the sidewalk. The words, "*Love Thyself*" boomed from a speaker above the church door as the van cruised past.

"So Zigs, I forgot to ask you earlier," Hat said. "How'd it go after you read that poem I wrote for you? Did Cheryl like it? Did she pucker up and take you to the promised land?"

Ziggy turned and looked out the passenger window.

"Did she like it or not?"

Ziggy's eyes stayed fixed. "Oh well, ya know, all's not lost in love and war," he muttered, as if his mouth were full of marbles.

"What?" Hat said. He turned onto Grand Avenue, heading east. "The hell'd you just say?"

"C'mon, Jimmy," Danny said. "Let me interpret for you. I think what he's tryin' to say is . . . he didn't get a blow job."

"Well? What about it?" Hat said. Ziggy kept his eyes aimed out the window but Hat was not about to let Ziggy get the best of him. Not today. Not ever. He curbed the van and turned off the engine. "C'mon, man. Tell me."

"Look, how come when you wanna talk about stuff," Ziggy barked, "you gotta pull over to the side of the street?" Ziggy's eyes were pinched tight. "How come you can't just talk and drive at the same time like regular people? That's called multitasking, you know. That's what—"

"You ain't pushin' me off track with that shit. Did you read her my poem or not?"

Danny swallowed a smile and edged his crate up a bit closer to the action to ensure he didn't't miss a thing. And at that moment, he couldn't help but think that Ziggy and Hat belonged on a TV reality show.

"Okay, okay already," Ziggy said.

"Well?"

"No. No, I didn't," Ziggy said, his tone apologetic. "It didn't feel right, you know. So I . . . I sorta took some of your words and mixed in my own stuff."

"Ah Jeez," Danny said.

Ziggy turned toward Danny, his shoulders bunched as he spoke. "Well, it just didn't seem right. You know, me reading Jimmy's words to my own wife."

"Well, what did you read to her?" Hat said. "How'd it go?"

Ziggy took in a deep breath and released it slowly. He glanced at Hat and then Danny and then rubbed his forehead, deciding if he should share the poem he read to Cheryl. He finally pulled a slip of folded paper from his shirt pocket and held it in his hand. Hat snatched the paper and read it to himself.

"Are you shittin' me?" Hat said. He read it again, his face filled with disgust. "You ditched my words for this slop?"

"It's not that bad. It's—"

"Oh, yes, it is. It's worse than bad. It's goddamn awful. I mean I can't even get past the first two lines."

"Lemme hear it," Danny said. "C'mon, read it out loud."

Hat looked over at Ziggy, who hemmed and hawed before nodding out his affirmation. Hat cleared his throat.

"I ain't gonna read much of it," Hat said. "Not at all. Just enough to give you a taste. And that's far more than should be shared with the public." Hat's eyebrows shot up as he again eyed the poem. "Okay, the poem is entitled 'Our Love.'" He looked at Danny briefly, eyebrows still adrift, and read:

Our love is what matters most.
I love you more than a slice of BUTTERED TOAST.

Danny erupted with laughter. Hat joined him. Their laughter shook the van, causing a few passersby to gaze into the van with wide eyes. As their laughter began to cease, they looked at each other and again filled the van with laughter.

Ziggy hawked his eyes and aimed them at Hat. "It isn't that bad. It's not like—"

"Are you fuckin' kiddin' me," Hat said. His face was now caught in the crossroads between disgust and laughter. "You actually think your wife—"

Danny chimed in. "That's great. I mean, it's better than great. It's unfuckingbelievable. You love your wife more than a *slice* of *buttered toast*. I don't know if a more beautiful sentiment has ever been written, Zigs. I only wish I had thought of that line when I proposed to my wife. It's just . . ." Danny stopped as his words were again choked with laughter.

"You don't deserve pregnant woman head," Hat said. "Not now. Not ever." Hat pulled out a lighter and set the paper on fire. He started the van and pulled off, tossing the sheet of burning paper out the window as the boys drove away.

"That's to make sure no one *ever* sees that sad excuse for a poem again," Hat said, his eyes fixed on the road. "Can't believe you even had it with ya."

Ziggy started in. "Jimmy, you know it wasn't all—"

Hat turned his right hand into a stop sign. "Nope. Nope. Don't wanna hear it."

"C'mon. Look—"

"Nope. It's done. It's over."

"Buttered toast," Danny said. "Fuckin' buttered toast."

4. Tom's To Do List

MOST FOLKS MIGHT COUNT away the final few minutes before they wrap up their work day and head off for home, but Tom Lonigan still had two more items on his daily *To Do* list. He shuffled through the contents of a file folder with the name *Forberg* markered in bold ink near the top. Tom set the file in his lap and hit the intercom button on his desk phone.

"Marie, can you dig up a number for Otto Herbeck, the lawyer?"

"Sure thing. Should I dial him for you?"

"Yeah, sure. Thanks."

Tom pulled two sheets of typewritten paper from the file and studied them.

"Tom, Mr. Herbeck's on the line."

"Okay. Thanks, Marie."

Tom snagged his phone. "Hey, Otto, thanks for takin' my call."

"You got it, Tom. I'll never pass on your calls." Herbeck laughed. "The mayor, yeah. But you, no."

Tom pictured Herbeck sitting behind his desk in his tidy office on the fortieth floor of the Hancock Building staring out at Lake Michigan, watching the late afternoon waves roll in. Herbeck's clumsy feet were kicked up on his desk with one or two files resting untouched beneath his wingtips.

"Look, I'm callin' ya about the Tim Forberg case. Checkin' in on it. See the kid's been offa work about six months now with that busted shoulder. Still can't hardly lift shit. I don't know as the operation did much good. Helluva fall he took." Tom stared at the file. "Can you give me a status on the case?"

Herbeck dropped his feet to the floor. "No problem. One second, okay?"

"Yep."

Herbeck's nimble fingers keyed his laptop, and he quickly reviewed the data on his screen.

"Okay, Tom, looks like Forberg's case is coming up for a status before the Industrial Commission in three weeks. It should—"

"Look, I need ya to push this case. Push it big time. This kid needs some dough. His house fell into foreclosure, and there's already a judgment against him. I told—"

"Did he consider going to a settlement agency? They'll front him some money from the expected settlement."

"Nah, I don't have any of my guys go that route. That shit's a racket. They take way too much off the top."

"I agree, Tom, but—"

"Otto, stop right there. Look, I'm not playin' the hard ass here. I'm just statin' the truth. I send you alotta cases and I don't ask for no favors and I don't look for no cuts on the cases. But I'm askin' for help on this case now. This kid's mom works in our office. So I need you to push this case. I need this thing to either settle pronto or to go to a hearing."

"But Tom—"

"No 'buts' on this one. This thing needs to happen." Tom tightened his eyes. "Look, you been good to my guys over the years. That's why I send 'em to ya. And I'm not trying to screw ya here, but I will. This is how it breaks down. If you can't make this thing happen within six weeks, then I gotta start sendin' my guys over to Carl Haag."

"Six weeks is a bit of a stretch, Tom."

"I got faith in ya. Just get it done."

Herbeck blew out a big breath. "All right, Tom."

As the phone call ended, Herbeck still held the receiver in his hand. His glazed face seemed to be frozen in thought but it was not. The wheels were spinning but had not yet fully slipped into place. Herbeck took several deep breaths before he rapid-fire dialed a number on his desk phone.

"Bill, come on into my office, please. I need you to do something for me."

Across town, Tom scratched the name *Forberg* off of his calendar *To Do* list. He opened a drawer, pulled out a new file, and moved on to the last item.

5. Advanced Fiction Class

LAURIE McTEER RAN HER ADVANCED fiction class at Columbia College with a quiet command. Danny Lonigan and fourteen other students formed a semicircle, with McTeer at the head. One of the students finished reading her piece.

"Thanks, Sheryl," McTeer said. Her eyes wandered across the faces in the semi-circle. "Okay, what do you have?"

"I like the comedy in this part of the story," a heavily tattooed student said. "I mean, before everything was pretty serious and, today, it really starts to move. I think injecting the comedic aspect really helps."

"I agree," said another student. "The new character, Sylvia, is funny as shit. She really makes the story come alive. Makes it move."

"So we're seeing more movement now," McTeer said. "Anyone else notice anything about the movement of the story?"

"I liked the way the movement took things into the bedroom," said an older student. "Sure, we moved to the bedroom, but that also moved the story. And that sex scene was . . . well, it was hysterical. I didn't know you could do things like that with a Snickers bar."

The class broke into laughter. "Okay. Anything else?" McTeer looked around. No one offered any additional feedback. "All right, we're moving on to another piece. I'm going to pass it to someone other than the author to read. This is from a journal entry. Listen to the voice." McTeer passed the work to a young female student. "Okay, this piece is the start of something longer from what I gather. We haven't heard any of it yet in class. After we listen to it, we'll do some comment and then take a break." McTeer nodded to the student.

May 1

When I worked as an assistant state's attorney, one of my co-workers—a woman named Linda Bettis—had a son who died of leukemia when he was three. One day we were sitting in a downtown bar having a few beers after work, and that's when Linda first gave me that info. We had been office partners in the Criminal Appeals Unit for six months at that point. Looking back, I can see that Linda needed to be able to get to know me, to trust me, before she felt comfortable enough to share the story of her son's treatment and eventual death. And I get that. Makes perfect sense. But, as we all know, there are folks on the other side of the spectrum, folks who are just fine sharing their entire life story from the get-go. To them, talking about their woes comes as easily as breathing. We've all run into then—at work, a lifelong friend or two, people walking their dog at the park, the lady selling Streetwise at the corner of Clark and Adams. You know the type.

"Hi, my name's Ben. Nice to meet you," some guy standing in line waiting to put in his lunch order at Nicky's at 58th and Kedzie, says to you. Ben proceeds to grab your hand and shake it as you examine the menu board for your food options. "Did I ever tell you about the time my apartment was invaded by Pygmies, and they held me captive in the basement for two entire years and tortured me daily?" Ben says. Your eyes fall from the menu board and shift to Ben's round, mustachioed face. After all, you know what you want. You don't really need to look at the menu board. You get the same damn thing every time you come here—a Big Baby with cheese, mustard, ketchup and grilled onions with a side of dill pickle, fries and a Coke.

Ben blinks at you. "Well?" he says.

"No, you didn't tell me that," you say. "How could you? I don't even know who the hell you are."

And he says, "I'm Ben. I just told you that." Ben wags his head and barks, "You don't believe me, do you?"

You raise your eyebrows, causing Ben to think they're rocket ships ready to be launched into the clear blue sky or at least into the ceiling of Nicky's. Ben pushes up his shirt sleeve.

"See. See that," he says nodding towards the multiple cigarette burns on his arms. And you are about to say, "I didn't know Pygmies smoked," but Ben gets called *forward with a resounding, "NEXT," and he puts in his order. Ben then takes a seat and stares at you as he waits for his food. You get your order to go 'cuz you don't want to chance Ben coming over to sit with you and disturb the joy that is eating a Big Baby.*

The student reading the piece stopped and looked up.

"Okay. Comments?" McTeer said.

"The voice is strong," said a student wearing a tinfoil bracelet. "And I like how it brings Ben into the mix. Sort of like he's a foil or opposite of Linda. And I get the feeling there's more about Linda to come. I can tell."

Danny took notes as the student spoke.

"There's definitely an attitude that comes across," said another student. "You get the sense already that this guy, even though he's a state's attorney, also has some punk in him."

"I think I'm in love with Ben," said a student sitting beside the student who read the material. "If he happens to be based on a real person, let me know. Maybe we can go out some time, and I'll put my cigarettes out on his arms, if that's how he likes it."

"Okay, Cheryl," McTeer said. "Another insightful comment. The list keeps growing." McTeer released a half-smile and shook her head. "Who's next?"

"I like the grit in this piece," said a student whose boyish face suggested he was better suited for a freshman high school English class. He ran his eyes around the semicircle. "But I have to confess that I really like the fact that this guy loves Big Babys." Several students started to chuckle. "I mean, I'm a Southsider too and the Big Baby is definitely a South Side thing. But I get mine with everything—including the pickle on the burger."

The room erupted with laughter.

"All right, everyone," McTeer said. "I've been told by the powers that be here in Fictionland that anytime your students start talking about pickles and hamburgers, it's a good time to take a break. Let's meet back here in five minutes."

The students rose from their seats and dashed towards the hallway.

"Dan," McTeer called out. Danny turned around just as he got to the door. He walked over to the instructor. "Keep this going. You heard what the others said. Very good potential here."

"Will do. Probably later, though. I'm workin' on somethin else now. But it's got some of this in it too."

"Good. Get some of the new stuff to me. We'll read some in class on future dates. Keep it up." Danny nodded and made his way for the hallway.

6. Strawberry Lunch

CITY ELECTRICIAN FRANKY CONTINO SLEPT soundly in the driver's seat of his Streets and San van. A bit of a snore leaked from his lips, but it wouldn't be enough to keep his wife awake at night or to cause his dog to hide under the bed. It was lunch time after all and Franky liked to snooze during lunch whenever possible. At age sixty, he found that his body craved sleep more than it did food. The van was parked in a lakefront lot near North Avenue Beach. Maggie Sunfield sat in the passenger seat, glancing at her partner occasionally, wondering if she should straighten his toupee which had slid a bit forward during his nap. Maggie received an incoming text, smiled, and exited the van quietly, making certain she didn't cause Franky to stir.

Lake Michigan opened its arms to greet Maggie as she strolled across the sand at North Avenue Beach until she reached the water. There were no waves. A rarity, Lake Michigan was a piece of glass. Maggie removed her work boots and socks and set them in the sand. After rolling up her jeans, she walked ankle deep into the water. The cold was refreshing. She closed her eyes and raised her arms to her sides as if to say, "Here I am. Take me Lord."

"Brought something for you," a male voice said from behind

Maggie. She smiled. "Open up."

Maggie opened her mouth wide, and the man slipped a fresh strawberry between her lips. She slowly chomped on the fruit, savoring the taste, the crunch, the juice. Her face was one of joy. Maggie turned to face the man. His loafers and socks were in the sand, his cuffed pants wet from the water. Maggie laughed.

"You forgot to roll up your pants."

"I'm fine." He removed another strawberry from the container he held and slid it into Maggie's mouth.

"How's your partner doing?" he asked.

"Franky's all good," she said and then chewed the strawberry. "He'll snooze until I wake him up."

"Must be nice." The man took a strawberry for himself.

Maggie reached into the container. "Good idea, meeting up for lunch." She popped another strawberry into her mouth. "Water feels good, doesn't it?"

"It's cold, actually. Quite cold."

"But it still feels good." She snatched another strawberry and slipped it into the man's mouth. "Next Wednesday's the big night, ya know. Dinner with my parents. You ready for that?"

"Yep," the man said between bites.

"You sure?"

"Uh huh."

Maggie smiled and stuffed another strawberry into the man's mouth.

7. Bari Subs and the Hearse Parade

HAT CURBED THE VAN IN FRONT OF BARI FOODS on Grand Avenue, and the boys climbed out. City garbage trucks, CDOT vans, ComEd trucks, and a few Regular Joe straggler cars lined the street outside of Bari. If you ever find yourself in Chicago and you need to find a good lunch at a reasonable price, keep driving until you find a gathering of vehicles like this. You'll know you're in the right place then. You'll know you've hit pay dirt.

"This is the place, boys," Hat proclaimed. "The best damn Italian sub in the city."

Danny dug into his pocket and passed Hat a ten-dollar bill. "Can you get me that foot-long Italian you were talkin' about? And a bag of chips and a Coke? I'm gonna stay out here. Gotta make a call."

"Sure thing. What you want on it?"

"Everything." Danny said and then thought it over for a few seconds. "Do they have giardiniera?"

"C'mon. What sorta question is that?"

"Okay. Mild giardiniera, and some mayo too."

"Gottit."

Ziggy and Hat entered this tiny grocery. Ziggy wandered the few aisles, staring up at Italian-everything on the shelves while Hat went to the back counter to put in their sub order. Outside, Danny dropped down along the brick wall of the business next to Bari and punched his cell. Hairdo's special-needs daughter Meg answered.

"Is this my girlfriend?"

Meg released a big smile. "Hi Danny, thanks for calling me. I haven't talked with you for a while."

"Well, what you doin'?"

"My dad's reading to me. It's a good book. I like it a lot. It's called Pippy Longstockings."

"That's one of my favorites." A gray hearse zipped past on Grand. "But I have to say, I think they should change the name. Ya know, change it to . . . Megan Shortstockings."

Meg snorted with laughter. She pulled the receiver from her mouth and turned towards Hairdo, who sat beside her on their basement couch. "Danny says they should change the name of the book to Megan Shortstockings." Again she snorted out a laugh. "That's funny, Danny," she said, again talking into the phone.

"Yep. I'm a funny guy." Another hearse drifted down Grand Avenue. This one was yellow. "Hey, you said your dad's there, right?"

"Yeah, he's right here. I already told you that. Did you

forget already? He's been reading to me. He's off work today."

"He's not drunk yet is he?"

"No, no he's not drunk. He—"

"You sure? I mean, since he's off today, he probably had cereal and beer for breakfast, right?"

"No. No. He's not drunk. And he didn't have any beer for breakfast. He made blueberry pancakes for me. And he made blueberry pancakes for him, too."

"Blueberry pancakes! He doesn't need any more pancakes," Danny barked. "You know that."

Meg snorted out another laugh. "You're so funny, Danny." Meg went silent for a moment. As she spoke, her voice was soft. "Hey Danny?"

"Yeah, Meg."

"Are you still gonna marry me when I turn twenty-one?"

'Four more years, Meg. I'm countin' the days."

"But what about Kate?"

"She's fine with it. When you hit twenty-one, we're gonna move the family to Utah and become Mormons. And you're comin' with. We'll be all good then."

Wrinkles clogged Meg's forehead. She covered the phone with her hand. "Danny's moving, Dad. To Utah. Tell him not to move." She handed the phone to her father.

"What shakin', partner?" Hairdo said.

"Tell him," Meg said.

"Don't move, Dan," Hairdo barked. He then nodded and turned towards Meg. "Good news. Danny says he's not movin'." Meg's face again filled with smiling teeth.

"What's up?"

Danny froze for a moment to watch yet another hearse cruise down Grand. This one was green with yellow flames along its sides.

"You still there?"

"Yeah, sorry. Just takin' a little break for lunch, but there must be some sort of hearse convention in town. Weird. Somethin' like that. Just saw three of 'em roll past."

"Where're you at?"

"We're hittin' this sub joint called Bari Foods. One of my partners says it's the best Italian sub in the city."

"Never heard of it. Where the hell is it?"

"Up on Grand just past the expressway. About 1100 West."

"Sounds good. Bring me one home, huh?"

"Next time. They already put the order in." Danny nibbled on his lower lip. "Hey look, can you do me a favor?"

"Yeah, what do you need?"

"Okay, remember that human dildo who came into the Dubliner that one night? The guy I mixed it up with?"

"Yeah."

"I caught word from one of my guys at the old job that he's plannin' a little payback." Danny pushed a hand through his hair. "I-I just wanna know if this guy has a gun registered in his name. Ya know, it's good to know somethin' like that."

"You think he's got a gun?"

"Not sure. My buddy at Boulder said he might have one. Thought you could help me there."

"Sure. Sure. I'll run a check on him for ya. No problem." Hairdo glanced over towards Meg who now sat at a card table, crayon in hand, coloring cartoon characters in a coloring book. "I'm off for a couple of days. Want me to call it in before I go back?"

"No. No rush."

"The more I think about that moron, well . . . how about I go stop by to give him a visit. Ya know, flash my badge. Rustle him up a bit."

"Nah, I don't expect anything big."

"Okay." Hairdo grabbed a pen. "Go ahead and gimme his full name, address . . . whatever you got on this guy."

As Danny fed Hairdo the information, Hat and Ziggy strolled out of Bari with the subs. Danny flashed his right index finger their way, letting them know his call would be over shortly. Hat and Ziggy climbed into the van and unwrapped the butcher's paper surrounding their subs.

"Looks damn good," Ziggy said.

"The best," Hat said. Both men took large bites of their subs, crust flakes sprinkling the butcher's paper, and savored the taste.

The side door flew open. "Startin' without me, huh?" Danny took a seat on his crate. Ziggy handed him a bag of food.

"How is it, Zigs?"

Ziggy finished chewing and said, "Let's just say, Jimmy don't lie when it comes to subs." Ziggy took another big bite. "Man knows his shit. Definitely knows his shit."

8. The Rat King

DANNY AND HAT RARELY CRAWLED out of bed before 10 a.m. on any given Saturday, but this day was an exception. Ziggy asked the boys if they could help with a basement remodeling job. "Two hours. Tops," was how Ziggy put it. So Hat and Danny gave up some of their precious sack time. Danny also brought Hairdo along for some fun as he thought it was about time he met Hat and Ziggy. When Danny and Hairdo arrived at Ziggy's place, Hat was there already, waiting out in front, sitting in his El Camino.

Once the men entered Ziggy's house and the introductions were done, they all stood in Ziggy's kitchen.

"Where's your wife?" Hat asked. "I wanna meet her before we start workin'. Ya know, before I get all dirty."

"She's with her mom. Out buying some stuff for the baby."

Hat searched through the multitude of photos and magnets stuck to the exterior of Ziggy's fridge for pictures of Cheryl but came up empty. There wasn't a face over twelve years of age on the fridge, and all were clad in baseball hats or soccer jerseys. Hat turned towards Ziggy.

"That's too bad. I wanted her to see what a real man looks like." Hat offered a wide smile. "Even wrote a poem for her." He tapped his back pocket. "Got it right here. A nice poem. A winner. Not like that piece a shit you wrote."

Ziggy wagged his head and started down the basement stairs.

The others followed. As Ziggy neared the bottom step, he stopped abruptly and sat down. He took great measures to tuck his jeans inside his long, white socks. Hat, Danny, and Hairdo stood tall behind him.

"Thanks again for coming over. I appreciate it. I know—"

"Fuck ya doin'?" Hat said.

"Tucking my pants into my socks." Ziggy said. "What's it look like I'm doing?"

"But why?" Hat said, his eyes pinched tight.

"You never been rat hunting before, huh?"

"Rat huntin'? I thought we were comin' over here to help ya with your basement remodeling.

"Who told ya that?"

"*You* told me that."

Ziggy scratched his head. "Well, I guess we are kinda remodeling. Remodeling the basement out of rats." Ziggy smiled and then ran his eyes across the basement. "Look man, I know that peckerhead's down here somewhere. You don't want to be getting after him, and then all of a sudden he shoots up your pant leg. So you should tuck in your pants."

Danny immediately took a seat on a step and started to stuff his pants into his socks.

"Now I may be alotta things but when it comes to rats, I am one huge vagina," Hat said. "I'm out. I wouldna come over on my day off if I knew we was doin' this."

Hat sat on the steps. Ziggy and Danny finished tucking their pants into their socks and stepped onto the basement floor.

"C'mon, Jimmy," Ziggy said

"Nope." Hat set his hands on his knees. "I'll stay right here and watch you two heroes."

"I'll stay here with Jimmy too," Hairdo said. "I don't wanna clutter things up."

Danny nodded towards Hairdo and then turned towards Ziggy. "So do most Mexicans have rats in their basement?"

"Good question," Hat said. "Damn good question."

"Not all of 'em," Ziggy said. "But some do. Some even have pet rats." Ziggy smiled. "Ya know, we gotta have some filler meat for our tamales."

"Holy shit," Hat barked. "I'm never gonna eat another fricken tamale again." Hat looked around frantically, his head on a swivel. "Ya got a bucket around here? I'm feelin' sick."

"You serious?" Ziggy said.

"Hell yeah, I'm serious."

Ziggy retrieved an orange Home Depot bucket from a pile of tools and assorted junk stacked into a half-wall beside the stairs and gave it to Hat, who spread his knees and set the bucket between his legs. He cleared his throat and dropped a loogie into the bucket.

"How'd that rat get in here?" Danny said.

"All right, so picture this shit," said Ziggy. "My wife is home on bed rest, right?

"Yeah," Danny said.

"And this happens in the day, when I'm at work with you two Bozos. So she hears something down here. A noise, a crash. Something. So she pulls her big pregnant ass off the couch and waddles on down here. She thinks maybe someone's in the basement. Someone's breaking in. She gets to the bottom step and doesn't see shit." Ziggy started to laugh.

Hat set his hands atop the bucket. "That ain't even funny, man. How can you laugh at your poor pregnant wife havin' to get offa the couch? How can—"

"All right, already," Ziggy howled. "Just listen." Ziggy blew out a short burst of air before continuing. "So there she is on that bottom step and then all of a sudden, *Bam*, there he is. The rat is standing next to the stairs, and he starts gnawing on the bottom step with his big teeth, right next to my wife's big pregnant toes."

Danny's face turned a wee bit whiter. "Really?"

"Fucking A. She raced back up them stairs, slammed the basement door and jumped onto the couch again." Ziggy scratched his head and smiled. "I told her . . . I told her she shoulda just whacked him in the head with one of those sledge hammer toes of hers. That would've done him in for sure."

"That's mighty compassionate of ya, Zigs," Hat said. "Nice touch."

"So anyways, my wife said he was a monster rat. Big, big

dude." Ziggy ran his eyes slowly across the entire basement again. "Boys, we're dealing with the Rat King."

Ziggy snatched a broom from alongside the basement steps and gave it to Danny. He took a rake for himself and walked over to a commode near a corner of the basement. Danny followed.

"Take a look."

Danny leaned in slowly and stared down into the toilet.

"Whataya got a toilet sittin' in the middle of nowhere for?" Hat said.

"I ran the plumbing already and connected the toilet. I still gotta put the walls, sink, and shower in, though." Ziggy turned towards Danny. "See it?" Danny nodded.

"What is it?" Hairdo said. "What the hell is it?"

Danny turned towards Hairdo and Hat. "Footprints in the toilet. Rat footprints."

Hat winced. "Ah, Jeez."

"Yep. Peckerhead came right up outta the shitter," Ziggy said. "Probably a relative of yours, huh, Jimmy?"

"Got that right," Danny added.

"Fuck botha yous."

There was a sudden stir in the corner. Danny and Ziggy froze and went silent. The rat walked out, unafraid, from under the couch. His body was long and muscular, as though he had been pumping little rat weights for a number of years. Hat moved back a step towards Hairdo.

"Look at that thing," Hat said, his eyes stretched wide open. "Am I seeing things or is that rat fuckin' orange?"

"He's orange all right," Ziggy said. "Parts of him."

"Who the fuck ever heard of an orange fuckin' rat." Hat said.

Danny ran full bore at the rat and swung and missed with the broom. The rat screeched and darted behind the couch. Ziggy pulled the couch away from the wall and then jumped atop it. He stabbed the rake into the space between the wall and couch.

"D'you get 'im," Hat said. Ziggy shook his head. The rat slid out from the far end of the couch. Danny moved towards the rat and it skittered away, before it stopped suddenly. It turned, stood on its hind legs, and screeched at Danny, who froze.

"Look at the size of that mother," Danny said.

"He's definitely the Rat King," Ziggy said. "I mean, just—"

The rat stopped its chirping and started to run directly at the two men. Danny and Ziggy turned and ran away from the Rat King. And as Danny and Ziggy moved, Hat was no longer grossed out. He was now amused, laughing and slapping his knee as the two grown men ran from such a small creature. And Hairdo was chuckling too. After the rat chased Danny and Ziggy around a bit, it stopped again, chirping proudly, just about ten feet away from Hat, announcing to all that he was indeed the Rat King.

Danny and Ziggy crouched beside the washing machine on the far side of the basement, their faces etched in fear, when a gunshot went off.

"Holy shit," Danny barked, his eyes stretched wide open. Both men turned towards Hat, who had both arms stretched out and locked, a small caliber gun in his right hand.

"What the hell, man?" Ziggy wailed. "You coulda hurt someone. The richochet could—"

"No one's hurt." Hat smirked. "'Cept for the rat."

The men all turned instantly towards the Rat King. He lay dead on the floor with a pool of blood surrounding him.

Danny's eyes were spread wide open. "That guy's huge."

"I'm just glad my wife isn't home. She woulda dropped the baby right here and now if she heard that gunshot."

"Everything's good. Everything's cool," Hat said.

Danny poked at the rat with the broom. "Whataya gonna do with 'im?"

Ziggy looked at Hat again and winked. "I was thinking we could start making those tamales."

"Ah, for Christ's sake," Hat said. He set the gun down and grabbed the bucket again, setting it in his lap. The others laughed as Hat sucked in several deep breaths.

"I need a beer," Hat said.

"What?" Ziggy said. "Shooting rats makes you crave beer?"

Hat released a thin smile and set his bucket on the step below. "The way I see it, our remodeling, as you call it, is over and done. And now I'm thirsty cuz I worked so damn hard."

"I'm up for a few beers," Hairdo said.

"Fair enough," Ziggy said. "C'mon. There's a little place two blocks away. Up on Lawrence. We can walk there."

The foursome strolled the two blocks to the Brick and Beam Pub passing the smallish brick bungalows that lined the streets of Ziggy's neighborhood. They were all ready for a few beers and some chow. Once they settled into a booth at the bar, the boys downed several Miller Lites and made a number of toasts to the Rat King. A handful of regulars dotted the bar with drinks in front of their long faces while others huddled around the video poker machines in the far corner, ready to put their freshly cashed paychecks to use. Hat fed a bundle of singles into the jukebox so Roy Orbison, Elvis, Richie Valens, and the Neville Brothers sang their hearts out as the boys drank the afternoon away.

At one point, when the bartender delivered the food order, he stood for a moment beside the boys, scratching his head.

"Now I know it's none of my business, but I heard you guys making a bunch of toasts to the 'Rat King.'" His eyes narrowed. "Who is this . . . this Rat King guy?"

Ziggy pointed at Hat. "See this guy here." The bartender nodded. "The Rat King's a relative of his." Hat shook his head. Danny and Hairdo laughed and started in on their burgers.

"In reality," Hat said, "The Rat King's dead. And that's all that matters. That's it."

"But still," Ziggy said through a mouth full of burger, "the Rat King was a close family member to this guy here." Ziggy again pointed to Hat. "And if you ever saw him, you could tell they were related. You know, they both got those same beady eyes and they've both been able to grow mustaches since the fifth grade." Danny spat out a hunk of his burger. "Yep, the Rat King and this guy here, they were real close. So we're here to mourn his departure." Ziggy's eyes flared wide. "And that, my friend, is the story of the Rat King."

The bartender ran a hand through his gray head of hair. "Well, I still dunno who the hell the Rat King really is," he said, "but the next beer's on me."

The boys clanked their bottles together as the bartender resumed his post behind the bar.

"So Danny," Hat said between bites on his burger. "I gotta tell ya I met someone who knows ya."

"Who's that?" Danny swilled his beer.

"Ronny Monroe."

Danny set his beer down gingerly and eyed Hat. "How do ya know him?"

"He's in the same bowling league with me. He's not on my team or nothin'. Matter of fact, his team is made up of a buncha pricks who I—"

"He plays with a team of pricks, huh?" Danny's head bobbed as he spoke. "Why does that not surprise me?"

"Oh, I hear ya. You're definitely right. He's a prick."

Danny took a long slug and ran his hand across his lips. "King of the Pricks."

"Who the hell is Ronny Morgan?" Ziggy said.

"Monroe," Hairdo said. "Guy Danny used to work with. His official title is Grand Poobah of the Supreme Order of Assholes. Right Dan?"

"Got that right," said Danny.

"So anyways," Hat said, "I was havin' a few in the bowling alley bar with a couple of my guys after we wrapped up and Ronny's in there and he asks how you're doin'."

"Yeah?"

"Said you slit his tires on your last day at work and when he came to beat your ass later that night, you and a couple of guys gave him a beatdown."

Ziggy feigned disappointment. "I've lost faith in you, my brother." With sad eyes, he stared into his beer for a few seconds before smiling, snatching his beer, and taking a drink.

Danny blew out a small breath. "That guy's a trip." He wagged his head. "Fulla bullshit too. I didn't need any help. Didn't want any help."

Ziggy reached across the table and massaged Danny's shoulders. "That's more like it, champ. You tell 'im, champ."

"I was there," Hairdo said. "Monroe's fulla shit. It was a one-on-one fight."

"I figured as much," Hat said. "He *is* a big boy, though."

"So what?" Danny said.

"Well, just know this. That bonehead told me he was comin' for ya later."

"Ya know what? You're the second guy who's told me that. One of my old coworkers at Boulder called me to tell me the same shit." They all eyed Danny in silence. For a moment, Danny tried to peel the label on his beer with laser eyes. He then grabbed a bottle of ketchup, shook it and shot a mound of red onto the table. They all stared into the red.

"Let 'im come get me," Danny said. "And if he brings any of his toothless, hillbilly friends from Summit with him, I'll say HELLO to them too." He laughed and ran his eyes across everyone's face. "It'll be a mound of red just like this." He nodded towards the ketchup. "Nothin' but red."

Danny ran his right index finger through the red and shoved his finger into his mouth. He sucked it dry.

"You're weird, man," Ziggy says. "Definitely weird."

Hat smiled. "Nothing wrong with bein' weird. Beats the hell out of bein' Mexican."

"By the way, Dan," Hairdo said. I'll put that registration request in on Monroe when I go in tomorrow."

"No problem," Danny said.

Ziggy raised his glass and barked, "To The Rat King." The boys downed bottles and Ziggy signaled the bartender for a fresh round.

Hat set his empty on the table "Well, just keep your eyes open. That's all."

"I know." Danny ran his finger through the ketchup again and sucked it dry.

"This boy's a bad mother," Ziggy said.

"Yes, he is. Yes, indeed," Hairdo added.

"Even badder than Tom Lonigan," Hat said.

"Whoa, Horsey. Whoa!" Danny said. The bartender delivered the fresh beers and left. Danny shot a look at Hairdo and then took a slug. "Now I might be able to handle myself a little bit, but my brother is in a whole different league. And Hairdo can vouch for that too."

Hairdo nodded.

"I heard some stories about your bro," Hat said.

"Me too," added Ziggy. "But you never know what's true or just blown out of proportion."

"'Proportion'," Danny said with a confused look on his face. "This midget never ceases to amaze me. Yesterday he used the word *hence*, which isn't a biggie but it's still not used much these days, and he also said the word, *pachyderm*. I still haven't looked that one up yet."

"Well, you keep on standing by my side and I'll keep making you smarter. There's hope for your kind yet." Ziggy smiled. "And I'm no midget either. I'm five foot three inches."

"Any guy under five foot five is a damn midget. That's the law in Illinois."

"And he should know," Hat said. "His brain's filled with great legal knowledge like that," Hat set his eyes on Danny. "So you seen your bro in action before?"

"A few times. Not as many as you might think. You guys probably heard about how he won the Golden Gloves twice? Heavyweight division?"

"Yep. I heard that," Hat said. "I dunno who it was, but someone told me he won the last one with a broken hand."

"That's right. He broke it in the semifinal. My dad was his manager. He just taped him up real good. Told him not to use his right until he said so."

"I was at that fight too," Hairdo said. "Tom just jabbed and danced all day. Wasn't his style at all. The other guy—some even bigger Irish kid, he just kept slamming away at Tom the whole time. Then, finally, with about thirty seconds left in the last round, old man Lonigan finally gave Tom the okay."

"And that's when Tom fired a roundhouse right with that broken hand," Danny said. "Just one. And he connected with the guy's jaw. Knocked him out. *Bam.* Guy hit the canvas like a dead horse." Danny slugged his beer. "That hand never did heal up all the way after that."

"Ouch," Ziggy said.

"And my dad, ya know, he died back when I was twelve," Danny said. "Got killed, I should say. Anyways, he was a bookie for a long time, and he would use Tom as his muscle." Danny laughed. "Can you picture a fifteen, sixteen-year-old kid comin' to break your arm 'cuz you didn't pay up on your bet?

"That's funny shit," Hat said.

"Yeah, there's a bunch of other stories like that," Danny said, "but my definite favorite, is the Tom Lonigan vs. the rottweiler story."

"What?" said Ziggy with a mouth full of burger.

"He fought a fricken Rottweiler," Hairdo said.

"C'mon," Hat said.

"That's the truth," Danny said. His burger and fries were gone. He swung around and set his plate on the table in the empty booth behind him. He turned back in time to see Ziggy running his finger through the remnants of the ketchup mound on the table. He then slipped his finger into his mouth. "Ya like that?" Ziggy nodded. "Okay, so I was about eight or nine-years-old and I was in the backyard of our apartment, just playin'. Ya know, just goofin' off by myself, playin' with my Hot Wheels or somethin'. Hairdo lived across the alley but he was grounded. Set fire to a couch behind his garage one day. Got a month for that one, right, Har?"

Hairdo smiled and then slugged his beer.

"So anyways," Danny continued, "there I was in the backyard, and then all of a sudden, this dog is right there starin' at me. Right next to me. Never saw the dog before. Didn't belong to any neighbors. Big ol' rott. Must've come in from the alley. And then it starts to growl. Ya know, one of those low, snarling growls—the kind a dog gives ya right before he takes a chunk outta your ass. I was frozen. Probably shoulda just stayed frozen, but when he growled again I freaked out and took off runnin' for the back porch."

"Shit," Ziggy said, "that's what I would've done."

"So the dog chases me, and he's on me before I could even get near the porch. Starts chompin' on me. Just chompin' away. Got me in the back. Got me good. I still got the scars. They're beauties." Danny stood and lifted his shirt. Three two-inch scars scissored his back to go along with several pockmarks.

Danny sat again. "So the dog's chompin' on me and I scream. And then he chomps me again, and before I could scream again, the dog's offa me." Danny swilled his beer. "And I look up and Tom's there and he's wrestlin' the dog, rollin' around on the grass."

"How old was your Bro then?" Hat said.

"Fifteen, sixteen. It was just a little bit after he started workin' for my dad. Anyways, before you know it, Tom has the dog pinned down and just starts slammin' him in the head with a buncha rights. One after the next. And the dog starts whimperin' and Tom just keeps poundin' on him. Then, it was weird. Tom forced the dog's jaw up and held it there with one hand, and that dog's Adam's Apple was bulging out. Then Tom popped him twice in the throat with the other—right in that Adam's Apple." Danny lowered his head and went silent for a moment. "That dog didn't move after that."

"Jesus," Ziggy said.

"Oh, it ain't over yet," Danny added. "Just about but not completely. So Tom climbs to his feet and he hauls off and starts kickin' the rott in the head. Kickin' him with everything he's got. And he was wearin' steel-toed boots by that time. My dad bought him those once he started workin for 'im. And I mean he's kickin' him so hard, the rott's head is movin' a foot or more with each crack. It was like the dog was spinnin' in circles around the yard. And Tom didn't look like he had any plans on stoppin' any time soon. He had this crazed look on his face. So he boots the rott a few more times, and then I said, 'Hey Tom . . . I think he's dead already.' So Tom stopped, took a few deep breaths, and said, 'Sometimes you just gotta make sure.' And then he bent down, threw the dog over his shoulder, went out into the alley, and dumped the dog into one of our neighbor's garbage cans. And that's . . . that."

"How bad was he beat up?" Hat said.

"Sounds weird, but just a scratch or two. That's it. Me on the other hand, I earned the opportunity to go to the hospital for shots and stitches."

"That's good stuff," Ziggy said. "Remind me to always bow when your brother is in my presence."

"No doubt," Hat said.

"And he helped you get your city job too," Hairdo added, "so I guess you could say he saved your ass again."

Danny smiled and took another slug. "The only problem with this job is . . . ," Danny added, "I get stuck havin' to hang around with numbskulls all the time."

Ziggy laughed and lifted his beer. "Raise 'em up, boys. Let's have a toast to *dead rats, dead rotts, and Tom Lonigan.*

"Amen," said Danny. The four men clanked their glasses and downed their beers.

9. Probation

THE DIRKSEN FEDERAL BUILDING in downtown Chicago is a rather dull-looking, thirty-story, heap of steel and glass that sits at the intersection of Jackson and Dearborn. Glued together in 1964, the building was named after Illinois's native son, Everett Dirksen, a former US congressman and senator known as the Wizard of Ooze for his sharp, oratorical skills. While the exterior may be worthy of little more than a sigh or a cough to a passerby, the guts of this building are where stories lie. The Dirksen courtrooms have seen an abundance of infamous trials—with defendants ranging from the stoic white collar criminal to the corrupt state court judge or politician on the take to the hit man or mobster being dragged in on murder or RICO charges. It also houses various government offices like the US Probation Office. That's what brings Danny Lonigan down here once a month—to see his probation officer.

Whenever Danny made his monthly jaunt downtown to check in with his probation officer, he always stopped first at Miller's

Pub, a few blocks away from the Dirksen Building, for an order of sautéed sausage, peppers, and onions with garlic bread. Danny would sit at a little table beside the bar with a window view and take in the autographed photos stationed throughout the entire restaurant. In Miller's, he felt a connection to the past, to an earlier time in Chicago, to his father. Old man Lonigan used to hold all of the important family celebrations—birthdays, Communion meals, anniversaries, and the like—at Miller's.

And when his food arrived, Danny would let the real show begin. He'd fork a hunk of sausage or a wedge of green pepper between his teeth and gaze out the window at the comings and goings of people strutting down Wabash Avenue or at the el trains passing overhead—people and trains alike, all flashing and sparking before him. In a scaled-down form, everything Chicago had to offer passed by Danny's window on those days. His viewing made him think of the old Clint Eastwood movie, *The Good, the Bad, and the Ugly.* No two days were ever the same at Miller's, and Danny loved that. Though he despised coming to see Monique Gamble, his PO, Danny always looked forward to his time at Miller's.

A fashionable, black woman of roughly forty years, Monique Gamble had always been fair and straightforward with Danny. No, Danny didn't hate coming to see Monique. She was good at her job, a true professional, and Danny respected that. He simply hated having to report to anyone once a month. The act of reporting, having someone looking over your shoulder, monitoring your activities—it served as a permanent reminder to Danny that he was a convicted felon and would always be a convicted felon. And that was a bell that would never ring quite true in his ears or in his soul.

Danny sat across the desk from Gamble in her smallish office. She removed a file from a drawer and fished through it.

"Thanks again for meeting me this late in the day," Danny said, a look of sincerity plastered across his face.

"No problem. I understand how it's tough to ask for time off when you're still somewhat new to a job." Gamble continued to work her fingers through the file.

"I should be fine next month, though."

Gamble removed a brochure. "This is the one here." She handed a brochure to Danny. "Looks like it could be a good fit for you."

Danny examined the front of the brochure clad with young boys of all colors standing beside adult males of similar colors.

"Big Brother Program?" Danny slowly turned through the four pages.

"That's right. We've placed a few others with them in the past. It was a positive experience for everyone."

Danny set the brochure on the corner of Gamble's desk. "So how's it work?"

"Well, first off, they've already reviewed your information and the nature of your crime. They have approved you for this work. It's run by the Mercy Home for Boys."

"Over on Jackson?"

"Right. But these kids are in the Big Brother program. They don't live at the Mercy Boys Home. This program has been instrumental in helping keep kids in their own homes so they don't become wards of the state."

"Got it."

Gamble looked at Danny in silence for a moment. She wondered how a lawyer, an assistant state's attorney at that, could do something as dumb and reckless as Danny did. But she would never ask about that. Not to Danny, not to any of the defendants she oversaw. Her job was to monitor; not to delve into the circumstances surrounding each crime.

"So the deal is . . . they'll find someone for you to be a big brother to," Gamble said. "They'll match two of you together and you'll meet with your little brother every weekend and do something. Do something fun. You know, go to the park, go to a ball game, go to the zoo. Museums. Things like that."

"I see."

Danny's response wasn't exactly what Gamble expected. "We need to get you started on your community service, Mr. Lonigan. And this program beats picking up trash from the side of the interstate."

Danny leaned back in his chair for a moment and stared up at the ceiling. "Ya know what? I get this. I do." Danny faced Gamble again. "But to tell you the truth, I'd rather just pick up the trash on the side of the road."

This definitely wasn't what Gamble envisioned. After all, she took the time to find something worthwhile because Lonigan had talents. He had kids. He could relate to a twelve-year-old. He was a former attorney, for Christ sakes.

"You'd prefer to pick up garbage?" Gamble said with slivers for eyes and a look that suggested—Oh, I get it. You just don't want to help some poor black kid who desperately needs help. I get it.

"Look, my dad came out of Mercy Home. Lived there for six years when he was a kid. I love what they do to help kids. I get all that." Danny grabbed the brochure and shook it.. "And this thing, this program. I think it's great. I do. But it's something . . . it's something I should probably do on my own some time, ya know, when I'm not on probation." Danny scratched at his head. "See, maybe it sounds weird, but I view my community service as something that should be more like a punishment. And picking up trash on the highway or in some forest preserve is definitely punishment. I know that sounds weird, but the truth is, I don't want any more preferential treatment. I mean, they already transferred my probation to you guys, rather than have me go through the state system. That's one. And my brother helped me get my new job with the city. And I'm glad to have it. For sure. But that's enough, I figure. Anyways, that's how I see it. And, well, taking some kid out to go do fun things—I don't see that the same way. It's like I'm getting another shot at something because of who I am. A shot someone else probably wouldn't get."

"Very well, Mr. Lonigan," Gamble said as she aimed an arm towards Danny, "we can accommodate that."

Danny returned the brochure to Gamble. "Thanks. I appreciate that. And would it be possible to maybe do the garbage pick-up work on Sundays?"

"Saturdays or Sundays, either will work."

"Sundays are better. That way I have a built-in excuse to miss church."

"Well, if you did your community service on Saturdays and went to church on Sunday," Gamble said with a bit of a smile, "wouldn't it fit better with your notion of a punishment?"

"No, No. Sundays are way better." Danny scratched his neck and smiled. "I don't wanna punish myself too much."

Gamble smiled and nodded her approval. "Very good, Mr. Lonigan." She marked a date on Danny's folder. "I will send you an email with your community service start date. It should begin next weekend. And we'll meet the same date, same time next month . . . unless I hear differently from you."

Danny shook Monique Gamble's hand and walked out her door.

10. The Doors of Jello

#6 SO ONE OF MY NEPHEWS CALLED MY UNCLE the other day," Hat said. "Told him he was quittin' school at the end of the semester." Hat nibbled on his lower lip. "Why the fuck would ya wanna do that?"

The van rolled North on Pulaski towards the CDOT building at Thirty-Fourth and Lawndale. Danny and Ziggy nibbled on donuts and sipped milk from tiny cartons while Hat drove.

"What year is he?" Danny said.

"He's eighteen. A freshman."

"That's wild," Danny said. "I mean, I know 40-year-old men who would pay good money just to go back to college for a week."

"No doubt," Hat said.

Danny took a bite of his donut. "So what happened? Why's he wanna quit?"

"I dunno for sure." Hat pulled up to a red light at Sixty-Third and Pulaski, his eyes drifting towards the oversized cigar store Indian on the Northwest corner. Big Chief, as he was affectionately known to the locals, was the unofficial mayor of the West Lawn neighborhood—second in power only to state rep Mike Madigan—and Big Chief, now clad in spectacles, glared back at Danny from his post atop an optometrist's office building. "He said somethin' about some big Iowa farm girl. I guess she sat on my nephew. Broke a couple of his ribs."

Ziggy spat out a chunk of his glazed donut. "Good one, Jimmy," Ziggy said. "But really, what happened?"

Hat hit the gas as the light went green. "I'm not shittin' ya, man. That's the truth."

"Holy shit," Danny said. "Remind me to never send any of my sons to school in Iowa."

The three men laughed. Ziggy grabbed his hunk of donut from the dashboard and slid it back into his mouth. "So where's he going to transfer to?"

"He's not," Hat said. "My uncle's gettin' him a gig with the city."

Ziggy's face flashed with approval. "Can't go wrong with that," he said. "Eighteen years old and making some decent bank with a city job."

A wide smile came to Hat's lips. "Ya know, I still remember my first city job." He ran his right hand across his lips. "I was fifteen. Ya know, a summer job. My uncle got me that job too."

"Imagine that," said Danny.

Hat curled his right arm and flexed until a solid, potato-sized bulge stood strong and proud at his bicep. "So can you guys picture me as a lifeguard?" Hat laughed. "Which way to the beach?" Traffic slowed to a crawl as the van neared the light at Archer Avenue. Students from Curie High School filed across the street. "Yep, had my little orange shorty-shorts and my orange tank top with the word *Guard* stamped on the front." Hat laughed again. "Only lasted one day."

"One day?" Ziggy cackled. Danny joined him. "Why does that not surprise me?"

"Fuck you."

"So what the hell happened?" Danny said.

"Well, they sent me down to work at Twelfth Street Beach. Ya know, over by the planetarium."

"Yeah, I know that place," Ziggy said. "I used to go there when I was in high school."

"No shit," Danny said, his face a display of mock shock. "Thought I saw some signs posted there on the beach before, saying, "No Iowa farm girls and no MIDGET swimmers allowed. How did—"

"That ain't even funny," Ziggy snapped.

"Okay, so there I am, all skin and bones in my nice orange suit, and they put me in a rowboat and send me out to man the beach. Me and one other guard. Separate boats. And, ya know, this is all new to me and, well, I don't swim so good neither. So then—"

"Hold on. Hold on," Ziggy said, his face a confused knot. "How do you get a job as a lifeguard if ya can't swim? I mean—"

"I got one word for you, Zigs," Danny said. "JELLO."

Ziggy nodded his agreement.

"So anyways, there I am out in the water and the waves are bouncin' the rowboat all over, twistin' me this way, turnin' me that way. And I'm lookin' over at the other guard in the water, ya know, and his boat . . . well, his boat is perfectly straight and he's starin' ahead, watchin' all the little swimmers in front of him. But the thing is . . . not only do I not swim so good, but I never rowed a boat before neither, so I don't know what the hell I'm doin'." Hat laughed as he turned East on Thirty-First Street. "So I look up again and the mate is standin' there on the beach just starin' out at me with his hands on his hips. I can't see his face, but I know he's not too happy. And then he throws his arms up in the air, like he's sayin', 'What the fuck are you doin'?' and then I throw my hands up and . . . well, I probably should'na done that 'cuz that's when my oars slid off the boat. See, I forgot to put 'em in the little oar holes. And well, I jumped into the water to get the oars. To save 'em. And I did. I got 'em and I tossed 'em back into the boat. But then I tried to climb back into the boat and, well, that didn't go so good neither. I flipped the boat over and when it flipped, the edge of the boat nicked me on the head. So now I'm bleedin'. And I look back, and I'm thinkin' about tryin' to swim to shore. But I'm pretty far out now and I'm not sure I can make it. And I'm startin' to get sorta lightheaded. And then I start thinkin' about an old movie I saw before, ya know, one of those old black-and-white World War II flicks about how a captain should go down with his ship. So anyways, I just held onto the boat as best I could and floated. And then—"

"This is great," Ziggy said. "Jimmy, the lifeguard. Fucking going down with his ship. That's allegiance right there." Ziggy laughed. "Wish I could've been there to see it in person."

"So finish the story," Danny barked. "What happened next?"

"Not much after that, really," Hat said. "The mate had to get in a boat and row out to rescue me. Towed me and my boat and my oars back. And then when we got ashore, I told him I could barely swim."

"So they fired your ass, huh?" Ziggy said.

"Nah, I didn't get fired," Hat said. "That was my last day workin' on the beach as a lifeguard. But I still had a job. See they just moved me to the other side of the harbor there. Ya know, about 300 yards away, and I worked the rest of the summer at Burnham Harbor boathouse, puttin' worms on fishing poles for the little day camp kids who came down on field trips. Same pay."

"I came down on one of those trips," Danny said. "Right over by the planetarium."

"Yep, that's where we were. Just me and some other kid my age from Lincoln Park. Total La Bag. Anyways, on the days when we didn't have any day camp visitors, I got to sit in the harbor house, watch TV, and eat peanut butter and jelly sandwiches all day long."

"Fifteen, worms, TV, and PBJs," Danny said. "That's damn good livin'."

As Hat drove the van into the CDOT parking lot, two other Streets and San vans were parked near the entry door.

"Looks like we got company," Ziggy said.

Hat parked beside one of the other vans, and the men grabbed their tool bags from the rear of the truck.

"Yeah. My uncle's been tryin' to get alotta shit updated in here," Hat said. "So I know there's been some guys workin' steady here doin' all sortsa jobs."

The boys stood before the entry door and rang the bell. They were buzzed in and entered the office area where a number of workers tended to their duties in their work stations. Hat's aunt, Antonella Sorrentino, stood from her cubicle.

"Look at this nice hunk of boy," Antonella said as she approached Hat. Her big head of hair tossed a shadow across Hat's face. "Look at you." She hugged Hat and gave him a kiss. After Hat introduced Danny and Ziggy, suddenly Antonella's beaming face became one of concern. "Where's your hat, Jimmy? Where is it? How come—"

"I, I, ya know, I haven't been wearin' it lately. Ya know, I figured—"

"What. No hat?" She wagged her head in disgust. "I been givin' you a new hat every year, every year since you was nine or ten."

"Twelve actually."

"So, twelve. So what?" Antonella said. "And you been wearin' 'em since. How can you have the name HAT if you don't wear your hat?"

Ziggy smiled. "I didn't know his name was Hat."

"But we do now," Danny added. Hat rolled his eyes.

Antonella turned towards Danny and Ziggy. "Yes his name's Hat. It's been that way for about twenty-five years now. He always wears my hats. Never takes 'em off."

"Not even when he sleeps?" Ziggy said.

"Well, of course, he takes his hat off when . . ." Antonella stopped when she saw Ziggy laughing. She grabbed Hat by the arm. "Go get your hat. C'mon."

"But I don't have one with me. They're all—"

"Don't you gimme that crap. I know you got a couple in the van. Go get—"

"I don't. I cleaned the van and—"

"Go!"

Hat set his tool bag on the floor and left the CDOT building. When he returned, he sported a tweed Irishman's cap, cut into pie-shaped sections, pulled down a bit to the side.

"You buy him Irish hats?" Danny said.

"Yeah. It's the best tweed. The best. And I love Ireland. I go there almost every year. After I go to Italy first, of course."

"Of course," Danny said.

"And I always buy Hat a new hat. He's got over twenty of them now."

With all the eyes on him, Hat played it up. He turned and twisted a bit, set his hand on his square chin, preening as a male model would.

"Looks good on ya, Hat," Danny said.

"Sure does, Hat," Ziggy added.

"Of course, it does," Antonella said. "I picked it out for him."

"Okay, now that I have my hat back on, can I go see my uncle?" Hat smiled. "I mean, we do have some work to do here today."

Antonella was all business. "You wanna go the long way or the short way?"

"Let's go the long way. That way I can give these guys a bit of the lay of the land."

"Lemme kiss you good-bye now in case I don't see you when you go." Antonella gave Hat another smooch and walked back to her station. She hit a button and held it, filling the office with a deafening buzz. Danny peered over his shoulder, fully expecting to see a plane engine roaring in the corner. Hat pushed through a standard door and the buzzing stopped. Danny and Ziggy followed him out of the office where they entered a fifteen-foot wide hallway with a high ceiling and lined with cinderblocks. Hat stopped and pointed at a door on the wall covered over with red, steel jail bars.

"My uncle's office is in there." Hat stared at the door for a moment. "But no one goes in through that door, 'cept for him. And me. And my aunt if she wants to."

Danny and Ziggy looked at each other with raised eyebrows. Before them stood yet another door—an overhead garage door that was almost the width of the hallway. Hat rang the buzzer on the wall and winked up at the camera. Antonella buzzed him in. Danny crossed himself, a gesture of thanks that this buzzing sound paled in comparison to the first one. The door rose and the three men walked through. As the door closed behind them, Danny and Ziggy looked back, before turning to face yet another garage-style overhead door.

"What the hell is this place, the movie set for *Get Smart?*" Ziggy said.

Hat chuckled. "Could be." The boys moved toward the next door. "My uncle's a firm believer in protection. I guess you could say he's the sort who likes to limit movement. Put all this shit in when he took the job over here as superintendent."

"When was that?" Ziggy said.

"Just about a year ago," Hat said. "When, when he got—" Danny and Hat locked eyes before Hat continued. "—when he got outta the joint."

Hat reached over to the wall, rang yet another bell, and eyed the overhead camera. Again the boys were buzzed in. This time the garage door did not rise. Rather, a small box entry door within the overhead door opened. Hat stuck a leg through, crouched low, and pulled the rest of his body through. Danny and Ziggy did the same. The boys stood still, staring out into a warehouse with multiple side rooms and a loading dock at the far end. They could smell fresh paint from a nearby room. Danny turned back to look at the last door, which just snapped shut.

"That's some weird shit," Danny said. "I mean, weird shit."

"I dunno," Hat said. "Well, I guess I'm used to it."

Electrician Franky Contino straddled an eight-foot ladder, installing a new fluorescent light fixture. On the floor, at the foot of the ladder, Maggie Sunfield stood beside a work cart. She passed a tool to Franky.

"Hey, Franky, be careful up there," Hat barked. "I don't wanna see ya fall and mess up your hair." Hat then whispered to the boys, "Guy wears a toupee." Franky smiled and shot the finger at Hat. Maggie gave the crew a wave. The three men waved back.

"Is that guy wearin' penny loafers?" Danny said. "I mean, I've never seen an electrician wearin' loafers to work before."

"That ain't just some guy," Hat said. "That's Franky Fuckin' Contino. He can wear whatever the fuck he wants to wear."

"Who's lookin' at the guy? I'm lookin' at that fine piece of ass," Ziggy said. "I wouldn't mind bein' her partner for an hour."

"Ready to trade us in, huh?" Danny jabbed.

"Well, you wouldn't be havin' those thoughts if you just read the poem I gave ya," Hat said. "But no, ya had to read your own slop to your wife."

Ziggy knotted his face. "I gotta go to the john."

As Ziggy started to walk off, Hat said, ""Hey, don't go beatin' off in my uncle's bathroom now."

Ziggy immediately stopped and rejoined the crew. "All right," Ziggy said. "Never mind then."

Danny's eyes were still on Franky. "Is that Franky guy wearin' a Members Only jacket? I mean, take a look. That's hilarious. Loafers and a Members—"

"C'mon let's go," Hat said. "Can't stand here gawkin' at these two all afternoon."

The three men turned a corner and walked towards the edge of the building. Hat stopped and turned back to survey the area.

"I'll show ya guys around the rest of the place some other day," Hat said. "There's a bunch of cool stuff in here. Rooms on top of rooms. For now, let's go say hello to Jello. Only don't call him that, unless he tells you it's okay. Until then, just call him Mr. Pellegrini. Okay?"

Danny and Ziggy nodded and followed Hat until he stopped before two regulation-sized gray, steel doors separated by a few feet. Hat motioned towards the one closest to the outside wall.

"That one there is the phone closet. You guys might work in there some time. It's got all the switches and shit in there for the entire building. I think Dave Flynn's workin' in there today. Saw his van outside."

Hat stood before the other steel door. He didn't knock or press any buttons. Instead he set both of his palms gently on the door and looked up into the camera just above the door. The lock to the door clicked, and Hat pushed the door open. The three entered Jello's office, where Hat was greeted with a big hug.

"Hey Unc, lemme introduce you to my partners." Hat put his hand on Ziggy's shoulder. "This is Zignacio Ramirez. He goes by Ziggy."

"Good to meet you, Ziggy."

"My pleasure, Mr. Pellegrini." The two shook hands.

"And this is Daniel Lonigan," Hat said, aiming a finger at Danny. "He goes by Danny."

"Good to meet you, Danny." Danny shook his hand.

"Same here, Sir."

"Your bother is Tom Lonigan, right?"

"That's correct, Sir."

Jello's head danced a bit on his shoulders as he spoke. "He does good work. Very good work. Keeps his guys goin'. Keeps 'em workin' even in tough times."

"His heart's definitely in it, sir. He's doin' what he loves."

"And his wife died a few years back, right? Breast cancer, if I remember it."

Danny's eyes sprang open. He would never have guessed that this man knew so much about members of his family.

"That's correct, sir."

"And he didn't have no children, right?"

"That's right, sir. My sister-in-law couldn't have kids."

"And how 'bout you, Danny Lonigan? Any rug rats around the house?"

Danny laughed. "Three boys, sir. They're a load."

Jello turned towards Ziggy. "And how 'bout the Ramirez family?"

"Got one on the way, Mr. Pellegrini," Ziggy says. "It's getting close. We already know it's gonna be a boy."

"That's good. Very good." Jello wrapped his left hand around Ziggy's jaw and gave him a playful slap with the right.

"Me and Danny are just hopin' that the new baby looks more like his mother," Hat said.

Jello pinched his eyes and leaned a bit from side to side giving Ziggy the once over. "I see what ya mean." He laughed. The others joined him. "These are good guys. Both good guys. I can tell."

"Definitely," Hat said.

Jello went to a bookcase and removed a framed photo of himself in his high school basketball uniform. "I remember your team in high school, Danny. You guys had a great team. Probably the last of the great, all-white teams. None of those around any more. Least, not that are any good." He looked down at the photo and then looked up again. "You had a solid senior year."

"We were pretty damn good, for sure, sir." Danny smiled. "It always helps when you have two all-Americans like Donlon and Drewry on the squad. Made it easy for me anyway. All I had to do was rebound and toss it back to them. They weren't gonna miss two in a row. And then we had Jankowski too. That guy snatched every big rebound and scared the holy shit out of everyone who came near him. He was one bad cat."

"I remember Jankowski," Jello said. "Tough player. Hard-nosed like you. And his Dad. I remember him, too. Guy used to spin records once a week on the radio. Every Ski in the area tuned in to his show on Sundays."

"Jan the Polka man," Danny said with a smile. "Yep. I know the dad died about ten years ago but I haven't seen the son in years. Long time for sure. I heard he started workin' back some years ago as muscle for—"

Jello laughed. "I heard that too." Jello passed the framed photo to Danny. "I could handle the ball and shoot the long one." He scratched at his balding head. "Look at them short shorts, huh?"

Danny returned the framed photo to Jello. "That's great. Those old black-and-whites are the best."

Jello set the photo back on the bookcase and removed a book—*Studs Lonigan* by James Farrell. He handed it to Danny, who examined it.

"You ever read that book?"

"No. I'm familiar with it, though. I know it's a trilogy. But I've never read it."

"You keep that book. You read it. It has your name in it." Jello nodded. "That book shows what old-time Chicago was like. Tough. Tough people. Tough places. People like you, like your family."

Jello turned to face Ziggy. "Ziggy, I wanna give you a book too."

"He don't even know how to read, Unc," Hat spat. The four men laughed. Jello searched through his bookcase. "You got any books of poetry in there? He could definitely use some help in that department."

"C'mon, not this again," Ziggy said.

Jello snatched *The Collected Poems of Walt Whitman* and gave it to Ziggy. "This man's poems are powerful. His words were about America during our early times. He saw it all and wrote about it. Beautiful words." Jello cleared his throat. "The next time I see you, Ziggy, I'm gonna ask you about "Oh Captain, My Captain." It's one of my favorites. Next time, we'll talk about it."

"Thank you very much, Mr. Pellegrini. I look forward to it."

"We'll teach him how to read by then, Unc." Laughter filled the room again.

Jello exchanged handshakes with Ziggy and Danny. "You boys come see me anytime I can help you. A friend of Hat's is a friend of mine. I mean that."

"Thanks again for the book, Mr. Pellegrini," Danny said. "Nice meetin' you."

"Thanks, Unc." Hat hugged Jello and then turned towards Danny and Ziggy. "Well, we gotta install a time clock in the hallway. That'll make two in the place."

"Good, good," Jello said. "The crew won't have to wait so long in the line then, when it's time to go home." He clasped his hands together. "Oh, and Dave Flynn is already here. I let him in the phone room, this morning. All right, boys, have a good day."

The three returned to the warehouse and Jello's door clicked closed behind them. They stood motionless for a few seconds.

"Wow. That wasn't what I expected," Danny said.

"I know what you mean," said Hat. "He's uh . . . He's a diverse man. A complicated man."

"Renaissance man," Ziggy added. "I think that works best."

"Another word to add to Ziggy's list," Danny said.

Ziggy paged through his new book, lost in thought. The door to the phone closet was now open. Hat peeked in and saw Ted Flynn's cousin, Dave Flynn, working on a phone switch. Though Ted had the big job, big pay, and the title, Hat knew that the brains in the Flynn family belonged to Dave. There wasn't any communication installation or issue this guy couldn't handle.

Hat and Danny stepped into the closet. Ziggy stood just outside, still perusing the pages of Whitman. The closet was barely five feet wide but ran about twenty feet long. A phone switch and other phone equipment, along with plastic punch-down racks, hung from a wall on one side of the room.

"Fellas," Hat said, throwing an arm towards Dave, "this is Dave Flynn and this is the type of shit you'll be workin' on later." Danny shook hands with Dave, and Hat noticed that Ziggy wasn't in the room. "Hey, Zigs. C'mon in here." Ziggy entered the closet, the book at his side, and shook hands with Dave.

Dave went back to his post in front of the phone switch, a contraption that stood about two feet by three feet tall by six inches thick. Color-coded wires raced in and out of its sides. "This shit's nothin' fancy," Dave said as his eyes rummaged across the switch, "You'll get used to it soon enough." He turned to Hat. "Don't know if you've heard, but come next week, they're finally movin' folks around. You guys are probably getting' busted up."

"That right?" Hat said.

Something near the switch drew Danny's attention. He slid past Dave and walked to the punch-down area where all the wires entered the room. Dave watched Danny for a moment before turning back to Hat. Ziggy stood by the door, his face again inside the pages of Whitman.

"That's what I've been told," Dave said. "One guy'll come with me and the other'll stay with you."

"You would know," Hat said.

"And it looks like some cake shit for now too. We'll be puttin' in about sixty to eighty time clocks in a bunch of trailers for the Water Department. They got loads of work comin' up this summer and need the clocks in those trailers."

"So actually, we'll still be together, right?" Hat said.

"Oh yeah. We'll be at the same damn sites. Just driving in two trucks instead." Dave released a wide smile. "And we'll milk that job. No more than two or three clocks per day per truck. We'll get three, four weeks out of it."

"Cool."

"And bring your clubs too. One of the sites is over by the South

Shore Country Club. They'll have four to five trailers there. We can get nine holes in one day."

Danny fingered a tiny, black device hanging from the punch down area. He stared at it until his eyes become slits. "Hey, what's this thing?" Danny said.

Dave walked over beside Danny and examined the device.

"That, my friend, is a phone tap. A bug, if you will." He patted Danny on his shoulder and removed the tap. "Good eyes, brother." Dave scribbled some numbers on a slip of paper and then yanked the tap off of the punch block and flipped it to Hat. "Let's go see him." The three men slipped past Ziggy, who was still reading.

"Hey, put that down for a minute," Hat barked.

"Yeah. Yeah. Sure." Ziggy closed the book.

Dave set both palms on Jello's door and looked up at the camera. The door buzzed, and the four men entered to find Jello seated at his desk.

"What brings you back, fellas?"

Hat handed the phone tap to Jello. "This thing was hangin' on the punch lines."

"It was on the 3221 number," Dave added. "Must've just been put there in the last week." He removed a pen-shaped instrument from his pocket and ran it across Jello's desk phone. He put his hand out, and Jello gave him his cell phone. Dave checked the cell phone with the device as well. Lastly, Dave removed another device from his back pocket and walked about the room pointing the device in different areas. The device beeped about every five seconds.

"Everything else is clean. No other taps. No bugs."

Jello held the tap in his hands. He brought it near his eyes. "What about this? Is this the Feds?"

"Nah. No way," Dave said. "That's old-time shit. Real old. The Fed stuff is much more sophisticated. They don't put shit directly on the lines anymore. They tap from off-site. This is IG shit. It's gotta be over ten years old. No one uses shit like this anymore. Except for the IG. It's what their budget allows for."

"You sure on this?" said Jello.

"Positive."

"Thanks, Dave. As always I 'preciate what—"

"Don't thank me. Lonigan's the one who found it."

Jello turned and smiled at Danny. "How'd ya know? I mean you're new to this game."

Danny scratched at his neck. "Well, during my *first life* as an assistant state's attorney, I had a few cases where we used info obtained from wire taps. And I had to admit the taps into evidence. I just remember what they look like. That's all."

"Well, thanks for what you done, Danny. I 'preciate it."

"No problem, Mr. Pellegrini."

Jello threw his hands up. "No more of that. You call me Jello from now on. Unnerstand?

"Will do, Mr. Pellegrini."

"Jello."

"Right. I'm sorry . . . Jello."

"That's a good man."

The four men left the room. Jello stood, his eyes boring holes into the gray, steel door Danny and the others had just passed through. He still had an image of Danny in his mind. His altar boy face, long chin. The door clicked shut. Jello's eyes wandered every inch of its thirty-four by eighty-inch frame, absorbing, getting lost in that gray. But that didn't bother him. Not at all. Jello liked the color gray. He walked to the door and pressed both hands on the door at shoulder height. He closed his eyes and massaged the gray, absorbed the gray.

11. Steak Night

*I*N A BRIDGEPORT BUNGALOW on the southeast corner of 36th and Parnell, Ed Gilbreath, clad in a pinstripe suit, sat at a dining room table staring down at the New York strip steak in front of him. This hunk of meat was cooked to perfection, a brown-black hue over the entire steak and slightly charred on the edges, the way any lover of medium rare steaks would like it. A baked potato and a side of spinach claimed space on the plate as well. Adorned in a sundress, Maggie Sunfield sat beside Gilbreath while her parents looked on from across the table. Though Maggie's parents had lived in Chicago for a number of years, they were originally from Memphis and still carried a Southern drawl.

"Hey, here's a hot tip for ya, partner," said Maggie's father, Bill. "Starin' at it ain't gonna do much for ya."

"C'mon, Dad. Lay off," Maggie said. "He's going to eat it. Just give him a few seconds." Maggie pursed her lips. "I'm sure he's about to start eating this wonderful steak you marinated overnight and cooked especially for him."

"Ah, well," Gilbreath said, his words more of a moan.

"What is it, son?" said Maggie's mother, Dolores. "You can tell us."

"I, uh . . ."

"I thought you said this guy was a lawyer," Bill said. "He sure don't talk like any lawyers I know."

Maggie growled, "Would those be your DUI lawyers?"

"Easy, baby girl. Easy now. I may have been tried twice but not convicted. That's the key. And that's 'cuz I was innocent. And I thank the Lord for both of them victories."

"I know, Dad. I'm just messing with ya."

Bill stared at Gilbreath. He knew something wasn't right. He could see it in Gilbreath's eyes. And then it came to him. "How long y'all been datin' now?"

"I told you, Dad," Maggie said. Gilbreath's eyes were still on the steak. "We just had our fifth-month anniversary."

"Five whole months, huh?"

"That's right." Maggie turned and smiled at Gilbreath.

"So you mean to tell me you been datin' this poor man who you're currently forcin' to stare dead eyes into a steak, and who right now is probably feelin' sicker than a goat who just ate a bushel fulla cow chips, and you don't know he's a vegan?"

"What?" Maggie said.

"He's a vegan," Bill snapped. "I know that look. You should know this sorta shit by now. You been datin' long enough." Bill wagged his head. "Hell, I woulda cooked up a nice veggie shish kabob and grilled up a bit of salmon for him." Bill eyed the man. "You do eat fish, don't you, son?"

"Yes, sir. I do."

Maggie coughed out a sigh. "Well, I, I , uh . . . we don't really go out to dinner much."

"Don't fret none, baby girl." Bill stood and reached across the table for the plate. "Let me get that hunka beef out the way for ya, son."

Maggie reached for the plate. "No, Dad. I got it. It was my fault. I should've—"

"I already got my mitts on it," Bill said. Maggie tried to pull the plate from her father.

"No, Dad. I insist. It was my fault. I'll put it away." The tug of war continued until Bill finally let go. The plate snapped against Gilbreath's chest with a thud, sending the steak, potato, and spinach into his lap. Everyone froze for a moment.

"That land in your lap, son?" Bill said.

"Ninety percent of it."

"That a new suit you're wearin'?"

"Yes, sir."

"That's a nice suit. I liked it right off."

"Me, too," added Dolores.

"Thank you, ma'am. sir."

"You ain't gonna throw up now are ya?"

"Sir?"

"Well, some vegans I know say they feel like they're gonna puke just lookin' at a slice of meat. And since it's now sittin' in yer lap there, I figured if you were one of the throwin-up kind, this sure as hell would do it for you."

There was an awkward silence for a moment before Gilbreath picked the steak up by his right thumb and forefinger and dangled it for everyone to see. He snatched the rest of the food from his lap with a napkin and set it on the table. He then started playing taps, emulating a bugle sound with his lips.

As Gilbreath stood up from the table, Maggie started to laugh.

"May I?" he said, and then continued to play taps.

Dolores was thoroughly confused. "What's he fixin' to do?"

"May I?" Again he played taps.

"Sure, go ahead," Maggie said.

Bill smiled. "You go right ahead."

Gilbreath marched slowly into the kitchen holding the steak at arm's length, in search of a trash can, still belting out taps as he moved. Maggie and her parents were all now laughing. Maggie scooted around Gilbreath and raced to the far side of the kitchen where she stepped on the pedal to the trash can, opening the lid. Gilbreath followed her and deposited the steak. The four huddled around the garbage can, staring down at the steak in its new home. Maggie stepped off the pedal and the lid closed with a bang. The taps stopped.

"What's your full name again, son?" Bill said.

"Ed, sir. Edward James Gilbreath."

"Well, Edward James, how's about I make you a nice big salad with Romaine lettuce, tomatoes, cukes, celery, red pepper, and cheese?"

"That would be fantastic. Got any Balsamic Vinaigrette?"

Bill smiled. "Comin' right up."

12 Mary Lonigan

AS THE FAMILY MATRIARCH, seventy-four-year-old Mary Lonigan had always been there for her sons, Tom and Danny. And she was a good wife to her husband, Jim. Though he had been gone almost twenty-five years, Mary still visited Jim's gravesite weekly. On this day, Mary sat in the passenger seat of Tom Lonigan's Towncar as he drove down the road. Mary loved the way Tom handled his car: measured, precise, never too fast, courteous to others, though he always seemed to eventually pass those he let pull in front of him.

"Everything's gonna be all right, Ma," Tom said as he pulled up to the red light at 103rd and Kedzie. "Dr. Valek's one of the best so you're in good hands."

Mary abandoned her thoughts about Tom's driving. She stared out the passenger window at the Jewel grocery store on the corner for a moment. "I know, Tom." And then she watched a mother and her young daughter walk hand in hand along the sidewalk, as they approached the light across the street. Mary's attention was glued to the little girl, with her blond hair and bouncy stringlets falling alongside her ears. The girl's lavender dress was a perfect fit for this sunny day. The light turned green, and Mary continued to stare out the window at the space where the girl had been but was no more, perhaps looking for a ghost.

Tom found the silence in the car deafening. "You like him, don't ya?" Mary didn't answer. She continued to gaze out the window. "Ma, do you like Dr. Valek or not?"

Mary turned towards Tom. "Does anyone really like their doctor?" Her fingers dug into the car seat. "Well, let me rephrase that." Mary coughed. "Does anyone over the age of seventy really like their doctor? The answer to that is . . . NO. At my age, the only time you see a doctor is when . . . is when you have to . . . when something's wrong. So NO, I really don't like Dr. Valek." Mary took in a breath and released it like a whisper. "Though I must say he does have a rather shapely butt."

Tom laughed. "Valek told me he thought you had a nice ass too, Ma."

Mary chuckled and set her eyes on Tom. He returned the look and reached over to caress his mother's aging hand. Tom then took her hand into his own and held it for the balance of the trip.

13. A Hot Tip

FRANKY AND MAGGIE SAT ON BUCKETS as they ate lunch outside of the sign room at the CDOT building. Their Coleman mini-coolers were stretched wide open beside them.

"Those fumes are strong," Maggie said as she stared into the sign room, where hundreds of newly minted city street signs sat drying on metal racks. "Really strong."

"Yeah, I guess so," Franky said. "I been comin' here for four months now. I guess I'm gettin' immune to it." He took a bite out of his pastrami sandwich. "Just don't light a match and we'll be fine."

Maggie chuckled and then sipped her bottle of water. "Are those other guys gonna be here today?"

"Ya mean, Jimmy and his two new clowns?"

Maggie nodded.

"I ain't seen 'em yet today. But I know Jimmy said they had to go set up a tent in someone's backyard. So maybe they went to do that first."

"What do ya mean . . . set up a tent?"

"Ya know, one of those big party tents with the stripes on 'em. Looks like the fuckin' circus is comin' to town kinda tent. Anyways, some city bigwig has a graduation party or a birthday party or some other sorta bullshit party this weekend, so Jimmy said they gotta go tear down a tent from one bigwig's backyard and then go set it up in another."

"Really, but what—"

"Hey, who gives a flyin' fuck?" Franky took another bite out of his sandwich. His face turned into a knot. He opened his sandwich and examined the pastrami.

"What's wrong?"

"I dunno. Pastrami tastes a little funky." He pulled a slice off and dangled the meat before his nose. "Oh well." Franky put his sandwich back together and took another bite.

"So what's Jello like?"

"Good man. Been good to my family, anyways. He always stops by my mom's place to . . ." Franky stopped when he received a text. "Sweet," he muttered as he eyed the message and then climbed to his feet. "Hey look, I gotta go run an errand. Gonna be gone for a bit, and I'm takin' the van. You keep workin' on the little shit on the work order. Ya know, maybe replace a couple of receptacles. Shit like that." He stuffed his lunch items back into his cooler. "Now I might not make it back in time to get ya to the garage. But I could, though. If I'm not, I'll buzz ya or have somebody pick ya up."

"Everything okay?"

Franky smiled. "Everything's good. Real good."

Franky left the CDOT building and jumped into his city van. After a stop at his local bank branch, he punched the pedal until he arrived at the Hawthorne Race Track parking lot at Thirty-Fifth and Laramie. Franky checked his watch and bought a copy of the *Racing Times* on his way into the track. Once inside, he walked down near the front row where his cousin, Victor Contino—a blob of a human, lay with arms and legs splayed across several seats.

"You sure about this horse in the fifth?" Franky said once he dropped into a chair behind Victor. He slapped his copy of the *Racing Times*. "The sheet says he's a dog."

"Dog, schmog," Victor said. "Call 'im what you want but he's gonna win. It's his day. Put the bank on it. I just did."

"Okay. Good enough."

Franky sauntered up the cement steps and went inside the grandstand to a teller's window. "Fifth race, Number three horse. Three grand to win." Franky pushed the money through the window.

The teller counted the cash. "Okay, fifth race, Number three horse. Three Thousand dollars to win. Correct?"

"Yep."

The teller printed off the ticket and pushed it through the metal slot to Franky. "Good luck, sir." Franky nodded and left.

14. Killing Time

HAT STARED THROUGH THE WINDSHIELD lost in thought, as the van rolled down the street towards the garage. The boys had about an hour to kill, before they could swipe out. Danny sat on his milk crate in the back, his face hidden behind the wall that was the *Tribune,* while Ziggy paged through his Walt Whitman book.

"I'm gettin' hungry again," Hat said. "Wanna stop for a snack?"

"Where at?" Danny said, his face not straying from the paper.

"I'm thinkin' we hit the firehouse over on Throop Street. It's sorta on the way back, and a buddy of mine works in that house. It ain't lunch and it ain't dinner yet, but they usually have some chili or soup to snack on in between. And if they don't have no food ready, they gotta racquetball court in that house, so we can kill some time playin'."

Danny peeked over the top of the newspaper. "Sounds good to me."

"Good with you Zig?" Hat said. Ziggy didn't answer. He turned another page in his book. "Cheryl sucks camel dicks. Cheryl sucks camel dicks. Cheryl sucks camel dicks."

"What's that?" Ziggy finally said as he looked up, his face stitched with confusion. Danny laughed into his paper wall. "What'd you say?"

"I didn't say nothin'," Hat said and then adjusted the volume on the radio. "Just singing along with the song on the radio." Hat swayed to the music to be more convincing. "How's that book?"

"Oh man, this shit's good. All sorts of good stuff in here." Ziggy flipped through a few pages. "And that 'O Captain, My Captain' poem your uncle told me to read . . . I love it. Listen. Listen to the end of it." Ziggy cleared his throat and read:

Exult O shores, and ring O bells!
But I with mournful tread,
Walk the deck my Captain lies,
Fallen cold and dead.'

"That's beautiful. Just beautiful," Hat said. "I dunno what the hell it means, but who cares. He got any poems in there about burritos or sombreros?"

"No class, man. No class," Ziggy said and went back to his

his book.

Danny reached forward and grabbed a clipboard from the console. He eyed the work order for the week. "Three stops tomorrow, huh?" he said. "That won't be bad."

"Cake," Hat said as he hit his turn signal. "One stop is at Jello's, so we can chill there for a while."

Ziggy closed his book and set it on his lap. "You know, I was wondering . . ."

Hat turned onto Archer Avenue and then looked over at Ziggy. "Yeah, what?"

Ziggy smiled. "No biggie. Just, you know, just wondering how your uncle got his name." Danny nudged Ziggy and passed the clipboard to him.

Hat shrugged. "Whataya mean? What?"

"Jello," Ziggy barked. "How'd he get his name?"

Hat's eyes flared wide as he smiled. "Take a guess."

"No. No guessing," Ziggy shook his head. "No games. Just tell me."

"Guess."

"Nope."

"What're you guys in second grade or somethin'?" Danny laughed. His eyes fell on Hat. "Just tell him, already."

Hat maintained his stoic look. "Nope."

Danny turned towards Ziggy. "Go ahead and guess."

Ziggy knotted his face. "You guess."

"Okay, fine," Danny said. "I'll guess. It's easy . . . Jello was probably a bit on the chubby side when he was young."

"Are you sayin' my uncle was a fat kid?"

"Yeah," Danny said.

"Well, you're wrong." Hat stopped at a red light.

"Well, he's kinda fat, now," Danny said.

"I know, I know," Hat said. "But he wasn't fat when he was a kid."

"Okay," Ziggy said, "so the question still stands . . . how'd he get the name, Jello?"

"'Cuz he liked to eat Jell-O when he was a kid." Hat swung his head and looked at Danny in his rearview mirror. "Even a second-grader coulda figured that one out."

"He liked to eat Jell-O, huh?" Danny said. "Well, I guess I coulda got that nickname too. I liked Jell-O too. Still do. Any kid could get that nickname."

Hat smiled. "Let me clarify. He didn't just eat Jell-O. I mean, he put it on everything—Jell-O on his toast, Jell-O on his cornflakes, Jell-O on his baloney sandwich, Jell-O on his PBJs, Jell-O on his popcorn, Jell-O on—"

"That's gross," Ziggy said.

"You asked," Hat said. "His mom always had big bowls of Jell-O in the fridge."

Danny turned his eyes into slits and set his newspaper down. "Just tell me he didn't put Jell-O on his . . . on his pasta,"

"Hell no," Hat barked. "His mother woulda cut off his arms if he done that." The boys shared a laugh.

Hat turned onto Throop Street and saw the firehouse in his sights as they neared Twenty-Fifth Street. He curbed the van near the corner, just outside of the firehouse. The overhead doors were open, and two firemen worked together, folding a hose in the driveway. Other firemen moved about inside the house, one brooming the floor, while a couple of others lounged on a couch, watching TV. Hat brought Danny and Ziggy to the time clock near the entry door.

"All right, look," Hat said. "We'll head to the kitchen in a minute. But check this out first." Hat removed a tiny Allen wrench from his pants pocket and opened the time clock, swinging the red, twelve-inch square door open. The three men stared into the interior of the time clock.

"See," Hat said. The three continued to look at the time clock guts.

"I already seen the time clock this morning over at Jello's place," Ziggy said. "What exactly am I supposed to be getting from this?"

"Okay, look. I did the whole hook up on that one this morning." Hat said. "Just take a look so ya can see how it works." Hat tapped his right index finger on a smallish green board. "See this thing? That's the modem. The modem gets plugged into the clock itself, and then we run a phone line into this thing, and that gets plugged into the modem. And the two of those things record all the time swipes and send them to the comptroller every time someone swipes so everyone gets paid. That's how it is with every time clock in the city." Hat turned towards Danny and Hat. "And if either the modem or the phone line ain't workin', then the whole thing ain't workin."

Hat unplugged the phone cord from the modem. "Like that. See, now it ain't workin'." The three stared at the unplugged modem.

"You ain't gonna leave it like that, right?" Danny said.

"Oh yeah."

"How come?" Danny said. "People'll lose their swipes. They might not get paid."

"Wrong. This is the city. Everyone still gets paid," Hat said. "We all still do time sheets, right? It's just checks and balances. Besides firemen don't swipe in or out anyways. Not yet. The only swipers on these machines are from some guys who stop by at the end of the day to swipe out close to home."

"But why even unplug it?" Ziggy said. "I mean—"

"You guys are thick." Hat wagged his head. "When it's not workin', it shows up on the comptroller's computer, and the next day we get a trouble order to go and fix it." Hat offered a thin smile. "So that means we get to stop by here again tomorrow and have some more chili or soup or whatever the hell else they got goin'."

"So we're creating work for ourselves," Ziggy said.

"Einstein's got nothin' on you, Zigs. Nothin'," Hat said. "And if you're ever on the Kronos time clock crew in the future, sometimes the days are so slow 'cuz the clocks are all workin', so you gotta go disable a few to have some work for the next day. Follow me?"

Danny and Ziggy nodded as Hat used the Allen key to re-lock the clock. "All righty," Hat said. "Let's go see how that chili's doin'."

15. When You Least Expect It, Expect It

DANNY SCRATCHED HIS FOREHEAD as he reviewed what he had written that night in class. He did not think these would be the words that would come his way as the result of a "silly little word game," as Perry Jackson, his Columbia instructor, had called it. After all, what good or what harm could the words *Knife* and *Geometry* bring about. Those were the two words given to the students, and they were to write a story, rant, or essay incorporating both. Danny wrote most of the story start in class, befuddled at where his words led him. And then when he got home from school, he chose to forego his beef barley soup and set up shop at the kitchen table instead, where the words continued to flow. Again, Danny ran his eyes across his words, not believing that he would inject himself as much into what he had written.

Holy Cross Hospital–Day 2. They have me tied down to this bed, blinding white sheets wrapped across my body. I feel like a tortured slave, each one of my limbs bound to the bed rail. But I can't complain too much. I'm the one who suggested they tie me down. "I'll rip this thing right outta me," I screamed when I came to after the operation. They had sewed a tube into my chest, beneath my left armpit. "First chance I get, it's gone." So they put the ropes to me. Imagine that. Someone finally listened to what a fifteen-year-old had to say. Modern medicine at its finest.

I look kinda like Jesus on the cross with my arms stretched to my sides and all, cept I got a mattress beneath my back instead of a chunk of wood, and my legs are spread wide almost to a half-splits position, rather than danglin straight down like the Son of Man. But Jesus never had no tube runnin' out the side of his chest. We both know that. The tube is draining blood from my left lung. Now I know this might sound weird, but I actually like watchin my blood swim through that tube. I especially like when the chunks of phlegm-looking, bloody goobers wrestle their way through. I can see it all. The tube is made of a clear, flexible, plastic material and it's about a half-inch in diameter. Diameter-now there's a nice word. I learned all about that in geometry class this year. Talk about a class that'll put you to sleep, geometry's the one. Sometimes the fluid races through that tube, other times it drags along like a lowly snail. But everything that goes through that tube is comin' from me, from deep inside me-deep where my dreams hide.

I can't tell ya nothin 'bout my first day here. I was out cold when my buddies put me in a car and drove me in. That's why I started with Day 2. I'll tell ya this, though. My side is still killin me. In fact, my whole body is killin me. That's what a knife in the back will do to ya. But I'm out of danger now. Least, that's what the doctors are sayin. They say I'm gonna make it. Still, I have to stay in this Intensive Care Unit just in case, they say, just in case.

Danny stopped reading. He had another page and a half of material he chose not to re-read.

Danny was only twelve when the stabbing actually happened, but he fictionalized most of what he wrote in his notebook. He could rationalize things better that way. On paper, he was stabbed in an alley when he was fifteen, as the result of a big brawl with some local punks. In reality, it was his own father who stuck a steak knife in his back. But not even Kate had heard that story, the true story. It was kept under lock and key in the Lonigan family's memory banks, the family's soul by Mary, Tom, and Danny.

Danny tore the pages from his notebook and shredded them by hand, before mashing the shredded pages into a ball. Some things, he decided, were better left unwritten. He walked outside and deposited the ball into the black garbage can that stood behind his side porch, before dragging the garbage can out to the alley for pick up the following day. His next-door neighbor dragged his can out at the same time, so the two chatted in the alley for a bit, but all the while Danny couldn't stop thinking about that shredded ball in the garbage. He wondered if someone might find those scraps of paper and piece them back together again. *Knife* and *Geometry*—suddenly Danny hated those two words.

When his neighbor returned to his home, Danny walked out front and set the sprinkler atop the grass on his tiny box of a front lawn. Down the block, a car engine roared. Danny looked up to see which neighbor was heading out for a bit, perhaps going out to Western Avenue for a cold beverage or two. The car drifted down the street, and Danny, with a smile on his face, raised his right hand to wave, thinking it was indeed one of his neighbors. But as the vehicle grew closer, Danny's smile disappeared. A handgun hung out of the driver's window. Danny didn't see a face. All he saw was the brown and black, black and brown of that gun. As Danny turned to run, a single gunshot rang out. He didn't see the flash of gunfire, the orange kicking out of the barrel. No. Danny got hit and simply went down.

"Shit. Oh, shit." Danny breathed heavily. "Shit."

Part Three

Trigger Finger

1. Little Company of Mary Hospital

THE WHITE CROSS ATOP LITTLE COMPANY OF MARY
Hospital could be seen for miles. On any given night, residents
in Evergreen Park and nearby Oak Lawn, and even some in
Chicago's Beverly and Mount Greenwood neighborhoods, could
catch a glimpse of the cross glowing like an extra moon in the
South Side darkness.

Kate and Tom stood in a hospital hallway talking to the
emergency room doctor. Danny's two oldest boys stood off to the
side, ten to fifteen feet away, eavesdropping as best they could.

"It was an easy procedure," the doctor said. "He's going to be
just fine." He smiled. "In fact, he's feeling so good already, he said
he's ready to go home right now."

Tom's face was a gathering of concerned wrinkles. "But did ya
get the bullet out? I mean, you guys were only in there—"

"I didn't have to. It was a clean in-and-out shot. Basically, it
went through the very tip of his right arm. Up here." The doctor
rubbed his shoulder area with his left hand, "No damage to any
bones or major arteries. Just a bit of bleeding." Tom and Meg eyed
each other, pondering what the good doctor had just said. "I
stitched up a bit of muscle and skin and he's good as new."

Sam ambled up to the doctor. "Did you just say my dad's gonna
be okay?"

The doctor smiled. "I sure did. Would you like to come in and
see for yourself.

"Hell, yeah."

Tom, Kate, and the doctor all shared a laugh. The family
entered Danny's ER triage room, little more than an eight-by-
eight-foot cubicle wrapped with a blue curtain on three sides as
walls. The top half of Danny's bed was raised, and he sat tall and
alert with a wide smile on his face. Sam and Jim led the way
towards his bed, followed by Kate and Tom.

"What's up squirts?" Danny said. "Comin' to hear a dyin'
man's last words? If so, then you've come to the wrong place."

"Wow, Dad," Jim said. "I thought you'd have all sortsa tubes in ya and be barely breathin'."

"Sorry to disappoint ya, sport."

"Does it hurt a lot?" Sam said.

"It's a little sore, Sammy. For sure. But, it's not too bad." Danny reached over and rubbed the bandage covering the top of his right arm. "Just nicked me up in here. That's all. I'm ready to go home right now, but, uh . . . the doctor says I gotta wait a day."

Jim reached in and caressed his father's hand. "Dad, since you're all right and everything, is it okay to say what I been thinkin'?"

Danny glanced at Kate and Tom. Both shrugged their shoulders.

"Sure. Fire away."

"Well, this is actually pretty cool. I mean if you were hurt bad, it wouldn't be cool. But I bet you're the only dad in the neighborhood who's been shot before. I bet—"

"Ah, that's great." Danny laughed, easing the mood in the room. "Don't go runnin' around braggin' to all the kids about me gettin' shot. I don't—"

"But you been bit by a Rottweiler in the back, and you got stabbed in the back when you were in high school, and now you been shot in the back. That's way cool."

"Well, let me tell ya somethin'." He turned towards Sam. "And this goes for you too. I'd rather not have any of those things. None of 'em. Ya know what I mean?"

"Yeah, I know," Sam said.

Jimmy looked disappointed.

"Everything make sense, Jim?"

"Yeah, I guess so."

"Don't be such a sad sack," Danny barked. "Who knows? Maybe a few years from now, for a birthday present just for you, I'll go get hit by a car—*In The Back*, and we can all meet up here again."

Jimmy's face lit up. "That would be awesome. I mean, as long as you're not hurt too bad."

The room filled with laughter. Tom pulled his money clip from his pocket and peeled off six singles. "All right, boys. Here ya go."

Tom handed the money to Sam. "There's a lounge down the hall. Go get some snacks."

"Thanks, Uncle Tom," Sam said.

"Yeah, thanks, Uncle Tom," Jimmy added. The boys shuffled off down the hall.

Kate moved beside the bed, stroking Danny's right hand as she spoke. "You really feeling good. No BS?"

Danny grabbed a pillow with his left arm and stuffed it behind his head. "I'm feelin' fine. I mean it. And I meant it when I told the doctor I was ready to go home. I mean, if—"

Danny's voice came to a halt when he heard footsteps approaching. Hairdo entered the triage room, his face full of concern.

"You can wipe that sad look off your ugly mug," said Danny. "I'm fine. Just nicked me in the shoulder."

"Yeah?" Hairdo said.

"Yeah!"

Hairdo closed the curtain, pecked Kate on the cheek, and gave Tom a handshake.

"And Tom, like I said . . . I'll be in here tomorrow," Danny said, "but I wanna go back to work the next day. I'm not gonna—"

"Easy, Dan. Take a few days to make—"

"Nah. I wanna get back to work," Danny folded his arms across his chest. "I mean it ain't exactly like we're doing any big wire pulls or anything. We're just installing time clocks. And I could do that with my toes."

Tom laughed. He knew Danny was right. "Well, let's just wait and see what the doc says, okay?"

Danny eyed Tom but did not respond. Kate pushed her fingers slowly across Danny's forehead and then through his hair. "I know you're feeling fine—but if that bullet was just over one or two inches, things would be different. Way different." She stroked his hair again. "Who did this to you?"

Danny fidgeted in bed. He looked up at Kate but stayed mute.

"Who?" Kate said.

"C'mon, Danny," Tom said. "Let's have it."

"I don't know for sure. I mean, when that car rolled down the street, I didn't see a face. All I saw was the gun hangin' out the window. That's when I turned to run."

"Well, who do you THINK it might be?" Tom said.

Danny sucked in a deep breath and released it slowly. "My guess is . . . it's probably Ronny Monroe."

Tom's face went red. "Ronny Monroe? From Boulder Electric?"

"Yeah."

"I'll go see him tomorrow," Tom growled, his teeth showing. "For starters, I'll make sure he never sees another job through 247, and then we'll arrange for a few other nightmares to come his way."

"I know I'm gettin' this news to you a bit late, bud," Hairdo said. "But yeah, Monroe owns a gun. Owns three in fact."

"What's this about?" Kate said.

Danny fidgeted a bit more and played with the pillow behind his head.

"Uh, I, uh . . . I caught some info that Ronny said he was gonna try to get a payback on me. Ya know, that's all. And I asked Harry to check to see if he had any guns. That's it."

"A payback? For what?" Kate said. Danny eyes were fixed on Hairdo, but he could feel Kate boring a hole into the side of his face.

"Hold on a minute," Danny said. He turned towards Tom. "Does Ma know I got shot?"

"No. Of course not," Tom said. "And we'll keep it that way. No need to worry her."

"Okay, great. We're not going to worry your mother," Kate said. "That's wonderful. I'm glad that's settled. Now what was this *payback* for?"

"C'mon, Kate." Danny glanced at Hairdo and Kate caught it. "There's really nothin'—"

Kate turned towards Hairdo. "What's the big secret here, Harry?"

"Really. It's nothing," Danny said. "It's just that—"

"Nothin'?" Kate barked. She glared at her husband. "You get shot and say it's a payback, and you try to tell me it's nothin'."

"Tell her, Dan," Hairdo said.

"You tell her. You're the one who seems so anxious to do so."

"Okay. Fine. Dump it in my lap." Hairdo rubbed his hands together for a moment. "Well, truth is, it was the equivalent of a Vietnam firestorm. And the village was all torn up."

Kate and Tom looked confused.

"Tell it in English," Danny said.

"Right. Okay. So Danny beat the ever-livin' snot out of this Monroe guy and when it was over, he finished it up by—well, by takin', uh, by takin' a gigantic *whiz* all over his face and body."

"And?" Kate said.

"And . . . Monroe was a bloody, smelly, piss-soaked mess."

"Where did this all take place?" Kate said.

"It uh, it—" Danny started.

"I asked Harry," Kate barked. Danny sucked on his upper lip and ran his left hand across his forehead.

Kate faced Hairdo again. "Where?"

"At the Dubliner."

"At the Dubliner, huh?" Kate released a smile filled with disgust. "And was that about six or seven weeks ago, perhaps?"

Danny stared into his lap.

"Ah, yeah," Hairdo said. "I guess that sounds right."

"Yep, that would be it all right," Kate said. Kate eyed Danny. "That's the day Danny told me, all innocent like, that he was goin' to the Dubliner *just to have a beer or two* with you, Harry." She aimed her eyes at Danny whose eyes were still in his lap. "Remember that, Dan? All innocent like. Right?"

Danny looked up. "Right, Kate."

"And now look at you." Her eyes bounced from Danny to Hairdo to Tom and then back to Danny again. "You got shot because you just couldn't let things go. You had to get even with Ronny."

Hairdo jumped in to slow Kate down. "Well, I have a couple of detectives comin' up here first thing in the mornin' to start workin' the case up."

"That sounds good. Thanks, Hairdo," Tom said.

"That's fine. Great," said Kate. "But it doesn't change the fact that what Danny did was stupid. *Again!*"

"Hey, don't start in with that *Again* shit," Danny barked "Those were two entirely different scenarios. Don't start—"

"I'm going to check on the boys." Kate disappeared through the curtain. Silence hovered over the three men for a few moments, before Tom spoke.

"Ah, she's just scared. She knows she coulda lost ya. Don't take nothin' from it."

"Yeah, you know how women get," Hairdo added.

"No, I don't know how women get." Danny scratched at the left side of his chin. "I only know how Kate gets. Just Kate. And she's lots tougher than most guys I know."

Hairdo smiled and slapped Danny on his good shoulder. "Well, lucky you."

"Yeah. Lucky me."

"All right, like I said, I'm gonna go see Monroe tomorrow," Tom said. "I gotta take Ma to the doctor again in the morning, but I'll go have a chat with Monroe in the afternoon. That'll give Hairdo's guys the chance to see ya, and they can let us know if they think we can get anything rollin' from the criminal side of things." Tom eyed Hairdo. "If not, then we'll find another way to deal with it."

"Sounds good," Hairdo said.

Danny nodded in agreement.

A short while later, an orderly moved Danny to a regular hospital room. Once Danny dozed off, Tom, Hairdo, Kate and the kids all left. A few hours later, as Danny's eyes fluttered in his sleep, Hat and Jello entered his room and stood beside his bed. The men smiled, taking great pleasure in watching a grown man who looked so much at peace as he slept.

"How can someone who's just been shot look that that damn happy," Jello said.

"Should I wake 'im up?" Hat said.

Jello smiled. "Nah, wait a second." The men continued to observe Danny for another ten seconds. "Okay. Go ahead."

Hat gently nudged Danny on his good arm. "Hey Dan. It's me, Jimmy Scarpelli. Me and my uncle are here to see ya." Hat nudged Danny again. Danny stirred and smiled.

"Hey, good to see ya, Jimmy." He eyed Jello. "Mr. Pellegrini, thanks for comin' down."

The men exchanged handshakes. "It's Jello, remember?"

"My bad," Danny said. "Jello."

Jello smiled. "That's my boy."

Danny shuddered. "Hey, I gotta tell ya guys. Wow. I was havin' a wild-ass dream when you woke me up."

Hat chuckled. "What about?"

"Well, I was in this sun-filled field filled with flowers." Danny thought about what he just said. "Try sayin' that three times fast." Approving smiles leaked from Jello and Hat's lips. "Anyways, Maggie Sunfield was walkin' towards me and—"

"Who?" said Jello.

"Maggie," Hat said. "She's this ultra-fine electrician who just started a month or two ago with the city. And I mean ultra-fine."

"Ahhh. Gottit."

"So there I am sittin' under a big maple tree, and there she is walkin' towards me and she's naked from head to toe. And her skin is beautiful and olive-colored. Her boobs are pointin' out like cannons, and she's got chocolate-covered raisins for areolas. Her hair is shaggy and her bush is trimmed up just right and tight."

"I'm gettin a boner here," Hat said.

"Me too," said Jello."

Danny reached towards his crotch area. "Me three."

The men laughed. "So anyways, she walks right up to me, and I'm sittin' down like I said. She drops to her knees and puts one of those raisins right in my face. And I'm starin' right at it, and it's so beautiful, so inviting. And then . . ."

"And then what? What?" Hat barked.

"And then . . . that's when you woke me up."

"Damn. I'm sorry, man," Hat said. He turned towards Jello. "We shoulda come two to three minutes later, huh, Unc? Then

Danny coulda been eatin' Raisinets and pushin' bush." The three men broke out into laughter.

Jello walked to Danny's side. "Nice to see you're in good spirits. Ya feelin' okay?"

"Yeah. It was just a nick. I'm headin' home later today. At least I hope so."

"When Hat told me what happened and said he was comin' to visit you, I said, 'I'm comin' too.'" Jello reached in and rubbed Danny's arm. "You're a good boy. I don't like to see these sorts of things happen to good people."

Danny smiled. "Well, thanks again for comin' to see me. I appreciate it."

Jello walked over and closed the door. "You know who done this to ya?"

"Ninety-nine percent sure."

"Who?" Jello said.

"A guy I used to work with. Ronny Monroe's his name."

"That's what I figured," Hat said.

"Ninety-nine percent," Jello said. "That's good enough for me. Where's he live?"

"Somewhere over in Summit. I don't know exactly where."

"Ronny Monroe from Summit," Jello said as he nodded. "That's good enough. Look, somebody I know is gonna have a talk with Mr. Ronny Monroe from Summit. And I want ya to know that somethin' like this will never happen again. Never. You can rest easy. Your family can rest easy." Danny stared at Jello. "And do me a favor, okay?"

"Sure."

"I know your brother is probably wound up over this. And he should be. Don't tell him a word about what's gonna happen. Just tell 'im the cops are takin' care of it, okay?"

"Okay. And, uh . . . what exactly is gonna happen?"

Jello smiled and patted Danny's face. "Don't worry none about that. Ronny'll still be alive and kickin', but he won't be botherin' ya again." Jello stood up. "And how 'bout the cops. Do they have your story yet?"

"One of my best friends is a cop. He was here last night . . .

or earlier this morning, I guess I should say. Anyway, he said a couple of detectives are supposed to come see me in a bit."

"That's perfect. That'll work out just fine," Jello said. "Look, you tell the cops ya ain't sure who it was. Tell 'em all ya saw was the gun. No face. None. Ya know, that sorta stuff." Jello reached in and shook Danny's hand. "I don't wanna run into the detectives comin' to see you, so me and Hat better be goin'."

"Thanks again for comin'."

Jello nodded. Hat stepped up to the bed and shook Danny's hand. "See you a little later. I'm gonna stop back with Ziggy before we wrap up for the day. Give you a ride home if you're ready then."

"Sounds good," Danny said.

2. Mary and Dr. Valek

A N ANGULAR MAN COMFORTABLE IN HIS OWN SKIN, Dr. Jim Valek had always been a straight shooter. When Tom Lonigan's wife, Eileen, was first diagnosed with cancer, Dr. Valek was the man who delivered the news. And after Eileen went off to see various specialists during her three-year fight, Dr. Valek continued to check on her. He stopped by Tom's house several times to visit with Eileen, came to Tom's work to check in on Tom, and he was there when Eileen offered her last breath while in hospice care. That night, Valek sat with Tom as the two men emptied a fresh bottle of Jameson's at Tom's kitchen table. Two men, two glasses and a bottle—a worthy thing. In Tom Lonigan's eyes, the fifty-eight-year-old Dr. Valek was caring, compassionate, knowledgeable, and studious, a throwback who represented everything that a good doctor should be.

Mary Lonigan sat in a patient's room at Vista Medicine in Mount Greenwood while Tom lounged in the lobby, paging through a year-old *Popular Mechanics* magazine. Dr. Valek stepped into the lobby and motioned Tom into a separate room, where Valek closed the door.

"Tommy, I hate to say it, but the biopsy shows it's definitely cancer."

"For sure?"

Valek nodded. "I'm going to refer her to see Dr. Nearn."

"He's the same guy who worked on Eileen. Good guy, right?"

"Yep. He's definitely a good man. Talented oncologist. He'll set her up with an aggressive program."

"Okay, Jim, you know best." Tom let the news sink in a bit. "Did you tell all this to my mom?"

"Not yet. I wanted you to know first. That way, when I tell her, you're not shocked too. And she can lean on you for help."

"Gottit."

The two men walked into the room where Mary Lonigan waited. Dr. Valek closed the door and watched as Tom eased into a chair beside his mother.

"That's never a good sign," Mary said.

"What's that, Ma?"

"He closed the door." Mary licked her lips. "I said that's not a good sign. That's all."

Dr. Valek shot Mary a stoic glance. "Well, I always close the door when I talk to patients. It's a matter of privacy. I don't—"

"Okay. Sure. Fine."

"But you're right, Mary." Valek blew out a breath. "I don't have good news for you. I wish it was different."

"And what would that news be?" Mary said.

Dr. Valek cleared his throat. He looked at Mary and then at Tom.

"It's okay, Doctor. You can tell me." Mary smiled. "I'm a big girl, and I'm pretty sure I know where we're heading."

Dr. Valek adjusted his glasses and said, "The results of the biopsy show that you do have cancer, Mary. I've told Tom that I will be referring you to our top specialist, Dr. Christopher Nearn. He already reviewed the biopsy results. He's the one who copied me on the findings. He'll set up a program for you to take this on head first."

Mary stared at Dr. Valek in silence for a few seconds. "You know what? I'm not sure I want to go to another doctor. I like you, Dr. Valek." Mary flashed a wide smile. "Truth is, I don't like doctors in general. Who does when you're my age? But you've always been good to me. And you were good to Eileen" She stared into Valek's eyes. "And you have trusting eyes. So how about you stay on as the main doctor?"

"Well, I'm not a specialist, as you know. And Dr. Nearn—"

"See, I don't know as I'm gonna need a specialist." Mary massaged her forehead. "I'm no spring chicken anymore, and I don't really want to go have a bunch of chemo or radiation. That's not really how I want things to go."

Valek's hands rested in a position of prayer with both index fingers pressed to his lips. "I understand what you're saying, but those things can help knock out the cancer or at least lengthen your life."

Tom knew what Mary was planning to say. He could feel it. Tears began to slide down his face. Mary absorbed Dr. Valek's words, but she didn't back off. "At my age, I doubt I'm going to be strong enough to fight off a cancer. I just want to know how much time you think I have left."

"Well, I'm no specialist. I'd only be taking a guess."

"That's okay with me. What's your guess?"

Valek massaged his jaw as he considered Mary's question. "With the cancer being located where it is in the stomach and at its current stage—probably eight to ten months. Could be a bit longer. But if it spreads, well . . ."

Mary Lonigan released another big smile. "Dr. Valek, you've just made my day." She was beaming now. "When I came here today, I KNEW what the results were gonna show. I KNEW. But what I was afraid of was that you were going to tell me that I only had three weeks or six weeks or three months to go." She turned towards Tom, whose eyes were fixed on the tile floor. More tears slipped down his cheeks.

"Don't cry on my account, Tom." Mary continued to beam, and her smile was contagious. Dr. Valek found a smile climbing onto his face. "Eight months is good. Eight months is a lifetime."

"It's not a lifetime, Ma. It's—"

"Oh yes, it is. See Tom, I'll have time to do the things I want to do, time to say good-bye to those I want to say good-bye to. And mostly, I can spend time with you and Danny and Kate, and the grandkids, and maybe I can even bring Ellen home for a while. I'd like to have her home again, so I can take care of her." Mary's eyes worked their way across the ceiling. "See, in eight months I can take care of the things I need to take care of most. And I can plant some things in the garden. Perennials. Things that'll keep comin' back. But mostly, I want to spend time with you and Danny."

"That's a wonderful attitude, Mrs. Lonigan."

"I have two fine boys, Doctor. Two boys I love more than anything in the world. But I don't tell them that often enough. I guess maybe it's an Irish thing. Who knows? I don't think my own parents told me even once that they loved me. Well, for me and my sons, that's going to change. Every day, for each of the next eight months or so, I'll let them know that I love them. Every day, I'll let them know how special they are."

Tom was openly weeping now. Mary took him in her arms and pulled his head to her chest. "It's okay, Tommy. Everything's going to be okay. I love you, Tommy. I love you."

3. Detectives Laski and Bronson

TWO CHICAGO POLICE DETECTIVES clad in sport coats and ties stepped into Danny's hospital room. Danny didn't notice them at first as he was glued to a rugby match on ESPN. One detective cleared his throat. "So how you feelin' there, Mr. Lonigan?"

Danny eyed the man, white and midforties, as he bellied up to the foot of his bed. He sported a brown mustache and wire rim glasses. Danny put the other detective, a black man, at about thirty-five.

"Good. Good," Danny said.

"I'm Detective Laski," the white cop said as he flashed his badge, "and this is Detective Bronson. We're with CPD." Bronson offered his badge as well.

Danny clicked off the TV. "Okay, well, thanks for comin' by."

"So where'd this guy clip ya?" said Laski.

Danny pulled his hospital gown down a bit, revealing the bandage on his right shoulder. "Right here," he said "The doctor said it went right in and out. No big deal. I'm actually headin' home later today."

"That's good stuff," Laski said. He removed a small notepad from the left breast pocket of his suitcoat. "Okay, well, we just have a few questions for ya."

"Fire away."

"Okay," Bronson started. "Can you give us a description of the shooter?"

Danny sighed. "Truth is, I didn't see him at all. When the car rolled down the street, I walked towards it 'cuz I thought it was probably a neighbor and I was plannin' to say hello. But then I saw the gun hangin' out the window. I didn't get a look at what was behind the gun. I just turned and ran."

Laski licked his mustache. "So this happened out in front of your house?"

"Right."

"What's that address?"

"10240 South Bell."

"Gottit," said Laski. "And did ya catch what sort of car this guy was drivin'?"

Danny shook his head.

"Nothin' at all?" Laski said with a smirk. "Ya know, two-door, four-door. Blue, white, pink, purple. Anything?"

Danny squinted and leaned back until he stared up at the ceiling. "It was a newer car. I don't know what make, though," Danny said. "And it was a two-door. Not sure, but it could've been a VW."

"Volkswagen?" Laski said.

"I think so."

"You're not exactly paintin' a great picture for us," Laski said, his eyes on his notebook.

Danny threw up his left arm. "Well, yeah. See if I just stood there like a dumb ass and stared at the car and tried to see the face, I'd probably be dead now."

Bronson nodded. "How many shots did this guy get off?"

"Just the one, as far as I know."

"Have any idea who might want to shoot you?" Bronson said.

"Nope."

"C'mon, Mr. Lonigan. Help us out here," Laski said. "Someone's pissed off at ya. People don't just drive around shootin' at other people standin' on their front lawn for no reason. Help us out. Who do ya think it could be?"

Danny studied Laski for a moment. His face was carved from the streets he worked, a man who had been around the proverbial block a few times and then some. But Danny had a game plan and fully intended to stick to it.

"That's the funny thing. No one's pissed at me, as far as I know. I haven't had any disagreements or—"

"How 'bout fights," Laski said. "Big strappin' buck like you. Had any fights lately?"

"Just with my wife. But she doesn't own a gun. Not as I know, anyways."

Both detectives chuckled. Laski returned his notepad to his pocket. He removed his glasses and cleaned them with his tie.

"You related to Tom Lonigan?" Laski said.

"Yeah, he's my older brother."

"Thought so. I mean, Lonigan ain't exactly the biggest name in the Irish phone book. It's Irish, for sure, but there aren't as many Lonigans as O'Briens or O'Malleys." Laski set his glasses back in place. "So if you're Tom Lonigan's brother, that means you're the Lonigan who used to be an assistant state's attorney, right?"

Danny scratched at his jaw. "That'd be me."

"I didn't like the way that all shook out for ya." Laski said. "You got the shaft."

Danny sucked in a deep breath and released it with a loud burst. "It's all done and over now." An awkward silence filled the room.

"By the way, your brother, he helped out my family before,"

Laski said.

"Yeah? What'd he do?"

"When my oldest graduated from Mt. Carmel five, six years ago, he didn't have much goin' for himself. He wasn't the brightest bulb."

"Carmel'll do that to ya," Danny joked.

Laski laughed. "Anyways, your brother got him in the union. He's in his last year as an apprentice now. Graduation's just around the corner."

Danny nodded.

"All right, Mr. Lonigan," Laski said. "We're all done here. We're gonna hit the trail. If somethin' pops up or somethin' jogs your memory, gimme a shout." Laski passed his business card to Danny. "Good for you that guy wasn't too good a shot."

Danny smiled. "Tough to hit a movin' target."

"True. True," Laski said. Bronson nodded his good-bye as Laski and he left the room.

The detectives walked in silence along the corridor making their way towards the elevator. As they turned a corner, Bronson said, "That guy's hidin' somethin'."

"I know," Laski said.

"Then why'd you go so easy on him?" Bronson hawked his eyes. "I mean, you sorta pulled—"

"Look, that guy was a damn good prosecutor. He was one of us. Wearin' a white hat and shit. Put alotta bad guys behind bars. And then he tries some warped, sick fuckin' guy who raped a seven-year-old girl. And the guy gets off."

"Ooh, that's rough."

"Right." Laski adjusted his glasses. "But he didn't lose the case 'cuz of somethin' he did. That was on us. CPD screwed up the rape kit. We did. And the little girl's parents didn't want her to come to court to ID the guy without the other evidence. So the sick fuck walked." Laski sighed. "Don't you read the papers? This shit was all over the papers a couple of years ago."

"Nah. There's nothin' in there I wanna see."

"Well, you oughta try it sometime. You might learn somethin'."

The detectives arrived at the elevator. Laski pressed the down button.

"So anyways, about a month after the trial's over, Lonigan goes out and gets shitfaced one night, and then he goes and drives over to the fuckin' creep's neighborhood. He finds the guy comin' outta some corner tavern and takes a bat to him. Turned one of the sick prick's legs into mush. Probably woulda done a helluva lot more, but some folks jumped in and tackled him. Stopped him. The bad guy almost lost a leg. Lonigan got hit with an attempted murder charge."

"How'd he stay outta the shitter on that one?"

"His attorney got it knocked down to an aggravated battery and pled him out. And the judge gave him a gift, a well-deserved gift, in my opinion. Probation and time served. But the disciplinary board had to even the score. They yanked his ticket. So he's done practicing law for good."

"Wow. All that schooling down the . . . now it's useless."

"Yep." Laski pressed the down button again. "So the way I see it, Lonigan deserves a pass. He's earned it."

Bronson nodded in agreement.

"And just so you know . . . I think Lonigan knows for sure who the shooter is. I figure him and his brother are gonna take care of this their own way."

"Yeah?"

"Oh yeah!"

The elevator arrived and both men stepped onboard.

4. Becca's Story

GILBREATH'S EYES WERE FIXED ON SOME NOTES scribbled on a file over two months ago, but he really didn't see those notes. His mind was elsewhere, flashing through a slide show of sorts: food items, old friends, his ex-wife, newspaper headlines, his first car—they all drifted before him, stopping to display their wares for a moment or two before giving way to the next slide. As Gilbreath continued to stare at that file, the slide show came to an abrupt end, replaced by a gray haze that then became a showcase for those lovely imperfections of the eye—you know, those little black squiggly marks that shift a centimeter or so one way or the other each time you blink. Gilbreath shifted his eyes slowly up and down and then from side to side, watching those imperfect etchings glide across his file jacket, the manila coloring a perfect background for such a show. One was simply a dot, another a jagged horizontal line which grew thicker near one end and carried what looked like a distorted "E" beneath it. The viewing ended when Phipps knocked on Gilbreath's door.

"I got everyone out at my sister's house," Phipps said, after he entered Gilbreath's office.

"Great. Good to hear."

"Yeah, yeah. We moved 'em out there over the weekend. Ya know, play it safe. Probably shoulda done it earlier." Phipps took a chair in front of Gilbreath's desk.

"Where's your sister live?"

"Lombard. The drive to get my kids back to the neighborhood for school is gonna be a killer."

Gilbreath listened intently, his face marred with concern.

"Truth be told, if I really want to protect everyone, we should just up and move to New Hampshire or somethin'? Ya know, Live Free or Die—isn't that their motto?

"That's right. Live Free or Die." Gilbreath scratched his scalp. "I have to tell you I feel terrible about this whole thing. I mean, I'm the one who told you to go take pictures of him sitting in his office. That—"

"Nah. Stop, Ed. If it wasn't that, it'd be somethin' else. It's not you. It's him. He's the derelict. The thug." Phipps stood from the chair and stared into the wall for a moment, his blue eyes boring holes into the drywall. "I'm thinkin' about tryin' to find a way to get back at him. I think if—"

"Stop right there, bud." Gilbreath stood and walked to the window. He glanced out at an el train passing in the near distance. The wheels of the train whined as it took a tight turn. There were times when Gilbreath zoomed in on a face in a passing el and wondered who that face belonged to, where it was going, and who was waiting for it once it got home. But not today. Gilbreath turned around. "You don't want to get in any kind of a pissing match with this guy. Trust me. He's done a lot of shit over the years, and the only thing they could make stick was that syndicated gambling shit. And that was a joke. A complete fricken joke."

Phipps' forehead was knotted with wrinkles. "I wouldn't call it a joke," he said. "Jello served time on that one. Almost a year. So, no . . . I wouldn't exactly call it a joke."

"Okay. Fine. You're right. It was great to see him locked up for a while. But what I'm saying is that he's never been touched for the other shit, the shit he really does. The shit that matters." Gilbreath took his daughter's photo into his hands. "The best thing we can do is continue to monitor his every movement in this city job he has now. He's bound to screw something up. We already have him coming in late nearly every day, even though he says he's working full days on his time sheets."

"That's somethin' but I dunno how much." Phipps shrugged. "That ain't gonna get him sent away. It could get him fired, but I doubt it. He's got too many Chinamen to get the boot."

Gilbreath stood in silence for a few seconds before he sat in a chair beside Phipps. He passed Phipps the framed photo of Becca and offered a calming smile. "Did you know Jello was once an electrician?"

"No," Phipps said.

"He wasn't a 247 guy. He was a Local 19 guy. You know, the guys who fix the traffic lights and all the street lights. That sort of stuff."

Phipps nodded.

"Typical clout bullshit. He didn't have any formal training or apprenticeship. Hell, as best I can tell, the job he held just prior to taking the city job was working a hot dog cart at Kelly Park. Then, BOOM, one day he's magically an electrician. How in the hell you can go from being a hot dog vendor to an electrician in one day is beyond me." Gilbreath stood again and paced the room.

"And then our paths cross. At that point, Jello's only been on the job about a month. And there he was fixing a traffic light just two blocks from my house. Not much to it. So at that same time, my daughter decides to take our lab out for a walk." Gilbreath paused to rub the bridge of his nose. Phipps listened intently. Gilbreath had never talked to him in such detail before. "And of course, about thirty seconds after my daughter leaves the house, it starts raining. And it's more than just a drizzle, but my daughter loves the rain so she keeps on walking the dog." Gilbreath's Adam's apple shifted as he swallowed. "So, so my daughter happens to walk right up to the very traffic light where Jello's working, and the dumb ass is up in a bucket truck and didn't kill the power. He disconnected a wire and somehow, amazingly, didn't fry himself. But he left the wire hanging down on the ground. Nothing like a live wire in the rain, Ed." Gilbreath again stared out the window. When he turned back, his eyes were empty, glazed.

"And so my daughter comes up on the corner and the dog steps onto one of those metal sidewalk grates that you see around different places and the wire is on it and it's all wet from the rain and my dog gets zapped." Gilbeath reached over and eased the photo from Phipps's hands, his eyes fixed on his daughter's face. "They told me, the folks who saw it happen, they said . . . they said that my daughter saw the dog shaking and gyrating from the voltage and, and she, uh, she grabbed the dog to try and save it."

"Oh, Lord."

"And that's how my little girl, my Becca, died. She was ten. And she died at the inept hands of Jello Pellegrini. He was up in that bucket and didn't even know what was goin' on below him." Gilbreath set Becca's photo back on his desk. "Jello worked one more day after that as an electrician. Then they moved him into another city job."

"We'll get 'im, Ed. We will."

"I know. We just have to be patient. Very patient."

5. Danny and Tom

TOM LONIGAN PUSHED THROUGH THE ENTRY DOOR to Danny's hospital room, his face worn from a rough morning with his mother. He sidled up to Danny's bed.

"How ya feelin'?"

Danny smiled. "If I was any better, I'd be twins." Tom set his right hand on Danny's forehead. "What ya checkin' there for. I got shot. I don't have a fever."

"Yeah, I guess you're right." Tom yanked his massive paw away and scratched at a tiny scab on the tip of his nose. "So those detectives Hairdo talked about come by to see ya yet?"

"Yeah, they did. Two guys. I filled 'em in on everything. Told 'em I thought it was Ronny who did the shootin'."

"Uh huh. So what'd they say?"

"They said that with the gun being fired and him makin' threats, they thought everything would tie up nicely."

Tom's face brightened. "They think they got a case?"

"They sure sounded like it. They said they were gonna go see Ronny and see if they could get him to confess. Somethin' like that."

"So, what do you think?"

Danny adjusted himself in his bed. "Wouldn't exactly be the sort of case I'd be excited to try. Ya know, no eye witness. But I think they got enough to arrest 'im. So let's just leave 'em do their job. It might take a while, but I think it'll work out."

"Yeah?"

"For sure." Danny wrapped his hands behind his head, his elbows flared to the side like wings. "Oh yeah, the one detective said his son was a 247 guy. An apprentice. Last year, I think he said."

"What's the guy's name?"

"Ah, it was somethin' Polish. I don't remember the name though."

"South side guy?"

"Yeah. Said his kid went to Carmel."

Tom squinted as the names of fifth-year apprentices zipped through his brain. "Was it Laski?"

"Yeah, that's it. Good guy. Anyway, he said some nice things about how you helped his kid out, and then he said to make sure you don't try to handle anything yourself on this one. Ya know, to let them do it."

"He said that?"

"Well, yeah."

Tom clenched his fists and paced the room for a moment. "Ya know, it's gonna be hard to just let Ronny Monroe keep goin' to work and collectin' a check when I know he shot you. I'd like to pound a few lumps into him—just to let him know that I know. Ya know?"

"I know. Hell, I'd like to toss him around again too. But I think we should both just back off and let these detectives do their thing."

"Good enough." Tom laughed. "So did ya get him good the first time?"

Danny smiled. "Definitely got my money's worth."

"Did you really piss all over 'im, like Hairdo said?"

Danny started laughing. Tom joined him. "That was the best part. Like Hairdo said, he was one piss-soaked fool when it was all over."

"Ah, man, that's good stuff. Real good stuff." The brothers stared at each other. "I think Pop's probably laughin' his ass off right now, looking down at us," Tom said.

"Or lookin' up at us," Danny quipped.

"That could be true," Tom said with a raised brow. "For sure. But wherever the hell he is—I guarantee he's laughin'."

A young nurse hustled into the room carrying a clipboard. "Good news, Mr. Lonigan. Just got your discharge papers. You'll be free to go in a couple of hours, so you can sleep in your own bed tonight."

"Great. Thanks for the word."

"You betcha." The nurse handed the clipboard to Danny. "Just sign the different forms so we can get you going." Danny scratched his signature onto four different sheets.

"By the way," the nurse said. "I saw the police here earlier. Any word yet on the person who did this to you?"

"They pinned it down on one of his old girlfriends." Tom smiled. "A nurse."

"Yeah, you know how nurses are," Danny said.

"Very funny, guys. Very funny." Danny returned the clipboard to the nurse, who reviewed the forms. "Okay, I'm all done. Someone else will stop by later, Mr. Lonigan, to give you the doctor's formal orders and follow-up plan."

"Gottit. And thanks for all the help and attention," Danny said. "You've been great."

The nurse nodded and left the room. Danny examined Tom, who suddenly sucked in a few deep breaths and swallowed hard. He sat on a chair beside Danny's bed and scratched the crown of his head.

"What is it?" Danny moved to a sitting position in bed. "All of a sudden you look like you're about to have a heart attack or take a gigantic shit."

"Feels like both." Tom eyed the floor for a moment before climbing to his feet. "Ma got the results today." Tom swallowed hard. "She's got cancer, for sure."

Danny stared at him in silence.

"The really weird thing, though, is that Ma was happy when she got the news."

"Happy," Danny snapped. "What? She's ready to die?"

"No, no," Tom said. "I didn't mean that. Mom's not ready to check out. She said that she was afraid that they were gonna tell her she only had a few weeks or a month to live.

"Well, what, uh, what does she have?"

"Dr. Valek told her his best guess was . . . was about eight months." The brothers locked eyes on each other. "And that's what I was startin' to say why, ya know, why Ma was happy. She said eight months gives her the time to do the things she wants to do. She said, and I'm quoting here, 'Eight months is a lifetime.'"

Danny wagged his head. His words came slow. "Eight months is not a lifetime."

"It is to her." In silence, the brothers locked eyes once again.

6. Bull's-eye

HAT AND ZIGGY CRUISED DOWN CALIFORNIA AVENUE in their van heading towards Little Company of Mary Hospital. En route, Hat curbed the van.

"Check that shit out," Hat said, pointing out the window, "Looks like the Sheriff's been here." A collection of discarded furniture stood near the edge of the street in front of a house.

"I wouldna guessed you were a junker."

"C'mon, let's take a look." Hat parked, and the two exited the van and rummaged through the furniture, tools, clothes and other assorted junk on the curb—items that were once a part of someone's life, someone's family. Ziggy found a box spring and mattress and bounced atop them for a bit while Hat examined a few tables and cabinets. And then the boys saw what they were looking for.

"That's just what we need," Hat said. "He'll love it." They both smiled and loaded the item into the van. Within seconds they were gone, again rolling down the street towards the hospital.

When the boys arrived at Danny's room, he was already dressed and on his feet.

"C'mon, Dan, we'll drive you home," Hat said. "Don't go callin' your wife. She ain't even out of school yet."

"Yeah, Danny. We'll drive ya," Ziggy said. "And by the way, don't feel bad that you got shot and that, you know, no one is here from your family to take you home—not your wife, your brother, your kids. None of them. Don't feel bad at all about that. Not at all."

"Funny. Real funny," Danny said.

Ziggy looked around the room a bit and ran his hand along the empty windowsill. "I don't know, just seems like there should be a little more fanfare for someone getting out of the hospital after getting shot. I mean, you didn't get no flowers in here, I don't see any Get Well Soon cards, no little stuffed animals." Ziggy stopped to scratch his head. "And like I said, no one from your family's here."

"Thanks, again, Zigs," said Danny. "I appreciate your concern."

"Want me to call up a couple of hookers?" Hat said. "We'll get this place jumpin'."

Danny laughed and gave Hat a playful shove. "All right. I'm ready," Danny said as he snatched his gym bag.

"Good news, by the way," Hat said, as they exited his room. "Me and Ziggy just found out today that the three of us are gonna be together for at least another month."

"No shit, huh? I thought we were gettin' switched up."

"Well, we all did," Hat said, "but Dave Flynn told me that the switch ain't happening for a while. And he would know."

The boys walked along a corridor. "That guy's my new hero," Ziggy said.

"Got that right," Hat added.

"Why's that?" said Danny.

"Well, you were supposed to start workin' with Dave," Hat said. "But since you been sorta sidetracked for a few days, they gave him a new partner."

"Maggie," Ziggy barked. "Lucky bastard."

"Helluva upgrade for him," Hat said. "I like Dave. He's a good man, but I don't think he's too smooth with the ladies." Hat laughed. "He's probably creamin' in his pants two, three times a day now with Maggie sittin' next to him."

"I know I would," Ziggy said, as the boys turned the corner near the elevator. Ziggy then dropped to the corridor floor and lay flat, facing up with both of his hands turned palms up beside his ears. "I'd just like to be the seat cushion in her van for a half-hour. Just lie there underneath her. Just like this. And then I'd just sniff up all that she has to offer." Ziggy twisted his head a bit from side to side and released several exaggerated sniffing sounds.

"Get up, already," Danny barked. Ziggy didn't move. He just tilted his head and sniffed some more. Danny reached down with his good arm and yanked Ziggy to his feet.

"Poetry, man," Hat said. "That's all I gotta say to you. If you listened to me before, your life would be different. Very different.

And you wouldn't be lyin' on the hospital floor like some pervert Chihuahua."

Hat punched the elevator button and turned towards Danny. "By the way, we gotta little somethin' in the van for ya. Picked it up specially for you."

"Finally, a present," Danny said.

When the boys made it to the van, Hat did the honors. "You ready?"

"Hell yeah," said Danny.

Hat nodded and Ziggy cracked the side door to the van open. Gone was the milk crate Danny always sat on. In its place was an old, weathered, leather arm chair. Danny climbed aboard the van and dropped into the chair.

"This thing is awesome." Danny was all smiles. He adjusted himself in his new chair, getting the perfect feel. "I like the way it sits low to the ground. Real cozy like that."

"Yeah, well, that's 'cuz it ain't got no legs," Hat said.

"That's all right," Danny said. "It feels great."

"Glad you like your new throne." Ziggy smiled. "I picked it out just for you."

"He didn't pick shit," Hat growled. "I saw it on the side of a street with a bunch of other stuff."

Danny slid down a bit in his new chair. "Good stuff. Thanks, guys."

"In your haste to get comfy in that chair, you missed out on Ziggy's artwork," Hat said. "Guy's pretty damn talented. Probably a holdover from his taggin' days as a youth."

"What're ya talkin about?" Danny said.

Hat looked at Ziggy. They both laughed. "Turn around and take a look at the top of your throne," Hat said. "Ya know, the part where your back goes."

Danny scooted forward and turned back. A tiny shooting range target, complete with a bullseye, had been painted upon the black leather with white paint. Danny started laughing.

"How'd I miss that?"

"Welcome back, partner," Ziggy said. "Glad it was only a close call."

"Thanks again, guys. I appreciate it." Ziggy and Hat boarded the van. As Hat started the engine, Danny fell back into the chair and settled in.

7. Kate's Rules

DRESSED IN A DEAD HEAD TANK TOP and shorts, Kate lay in bed reading *Atlas Shrugged* as Danny pushed through the bedroom door and closed it tight, using a sock as a wedge. That was the best Danny could do when the door had no functioning lock.

"Can I hit the light?" Danny said.

Kate marked her book. "Sure." She set the book on an end table. Danny turned the light off and climbed in beside Kate. A full moon leaked through their south window showing Danny's bare chest and the bandage on his shoulder.

"So Jimmy and Ziggy picked up a chair for me to sit in, when I'm in the back of the van."

"Danny, do you—"

"Pretty cool, huh?"

Kate released a long sigh. Danny couldn't see her eyes in the darkness, but he could certainly feel them. "Do you actually think I want to talk about your new chair. If that's what—"

"Well, it's not exactly new," Danny said. "It's used. And it doesn't have any—"

"Stop already. Just stop."

Silence settled over the room. Danny turned towards Kate in the darkness. "Is this about Ronny?"

"Of course, it's about Ronny," Kate snapped. "What planet are you from?"

There was a knock at the bedroom door.

"C'mon in," Danny yelped. The door opened and Jim shuffled in. He stood at the foot of the bed in his Bears pajamas.

"I can't sleep."

"Sam snorin' again?" said Danny.

Jim rubbed the side of his face. "Yeah. Real loud too."

"Wanna jump in with us?" Danny said.

"Nah. I'm gettin' too old for that."

Danny's head jerked back. "What? You're never too old for that. And besides, you jumped in with us just last week."

"Yeah, I know. But Sean Burke from school said that anyone who sleeps with their parents after he turns eight is gay."

"You shouldn't use that word in that context, Jim," Kate said. "And don't believe what Sean Burke says. Just—"

"And he said anyone who does sleep in their parents' bed is still probably breast feeding too."

Kate sat up straight. "He said that too?"

Jim nodded. "Ma, did you ever breast feed me?"

"Well, sure I did, honey. From when you were born until you were almost eighteen months."

Jim turned his face into a ball. "That's just gross." He looked at the carpet. "I don't even wanna think about that."

"It's not gross, bud," Danny said. "It's a beautiful thing. It's a way to get you the essential nourishment that—"

"I'm gonna go downstairs and sleep on the couch." Jim said through a yawn. "Just wanted to let ya know."

"Ya sure?" Danny said.

"Yeah." Jim turned to leave and Danny followed him to the door.

"Night." Danny watched Jim make his way down the stairs before again using the sock to wedge the door shut.

"Thought you were going to be saved by the bell, huh?" Kate said. Danny stayed silent. "Didn't ya?"

"I coulda got him to stay if I pushed it."

"I doubt it. He's a pretty headstrong kid once he sets his mind to somethin'."

"You're right." Danny said. He laid down on the bed and kicked his right leg over his left. "But I must say I didn't exactly try as hard as I could have 'cuz—"

"'Cuz you put the sock in the door." Kate rolled to her side to face Danny. "Look, I'm fine with making love tonight. Are you okay, physically? I mean, do you feel up to it?"

Danny released another smile. "Wouldna put the sock in the door if I wasn't."

Danny reached a hand towards Kate's face. He kissed her softly and then caressed her breasts. Kate pulled back a bit.

"I thought about you beating up Ronny. I thought about it a lot after you told me that in the hospital. And you know what?"

"What?"

"I'm fine with it. I am."

"Yeah?"

"Well, yeah. I'm fine with you kicking his ass. He deserved it. The shit he pulled while you were there at Boulder. He got what he had coming to him. But I . . . I guess what really made me mad was that you did it all in secret. You know what I mean? You went up to the Dubliner and Harry was in on it, but—well, I wasn't in on it."

"I get it.'

"No, I don't think you do." Kate ran her hands across Danny's face. "See, I want to be as close to you as humanly possible. I want it to be like I'm a part of you. And you're a part of me."

"You are a part of me."

"I know. But I think there's more. Another level. I think we can be even closer, even stronger." Kate licked her lips. "So no more secrets, okay?"

"Deal." Danny slid closer to Kate. "If it's okay with you, I'd like to start working on that next level."

Kate kissed Danny and pulled him towards her.

8, Jankowski

AFTER A LONG DAY AT WORK AND A FEW BEERS at his favorite watering hole, Ronny Monroe pulled his pickup into his driveway and entered his tiny home in suburban Summit. There were no wife or children to greet him as he pranced through the door but Ronny cared little about that. He was on a roll and wanted to keep his buzz going or perhaps add to it, so he snatched an Old Style Tall Boy from the fridge and planted his beefy ass on his favorite front room EZ chair, right in front of his big screen TV. The White Sox were facing the Royals at the Cell, so Ronny toyed with his clicker until his beloved Sox appeared.

As Ronny watched third baseman Joe Crede pop out to the Royals first baseman, he thought, I'm better than that. I would at least put the ball in play. A tall, muscular man dressed in a dark suit drifted out in silence from the front hall closet and walked directly behind Ronny. Though Ronny's eyes were fixed on the Sox game, his brain drifted back in time to his high school playing days—to the days when Ronny, and Ronny only, saw himself as a star. The man maintained his silent post behind Ronny and watched as Sox catcher A.J. Pierzynski took a called third strike. He then struck Ronny across the head with a forearm-length, wooden club. Ronny lost consciousness, and in that state of mind his brain floated off into the land of strange things. He saw a huge, black hammerhead shark with a cheesy mustache—similar to his own, adorned with black glasses—also similar to his own, swimming circles around him as he floated on a white, rubber raft in his backyard pool. Ronny's shrink floated beside him in a matching raft, and every time Ronny eyeballed him, his shrink would say, "What do you think this all means?" And each time Ronny responded by saying, "Not everything that happens means something." And each time Ronny said that, the shark leapt high into the air and then slammed its tailfin against the water right beside Ronny's raft, causing the raft to shake violently and the shrink to laugh hysterically.

When Ronny awakened, his chest was duct-taped to a kitchen chair, his right hand was duct-taped behind him and his left hand was duct-taped to the surface of the kitchen table, with each finger splayed and taped. A rolled-up sock was lodged in Ronny's mouth, and part of his face had been duct-taped to keep the sock in place. Ronny's Red Wing work boots and socks had been removed and both bare feet were taped to the legs of the table. The TV had been turned off. On the kitchen table in front of Ronny sat his glasses, a hammer, a hand axe, a wooden club, and a briefcase. The large, muscular man sat across the table from Ronny, his suit tailored, his dark green tie—tight to the neck. But Ronny couldn't make out these simple details without his glasses, nor could he see the thin black gloves on the man's hands.

"Good to have you back amongst the living again, Mr. Monroe," Jankowski said. Ronny swung his head in slow circles trying to ease the pain from the earlier blow. "You know I read your eye doctor's prescription for your glasses the other day. You really have some serious problems. Have you ever considered Lasik?"

Jankowski's eyes flared wide open, as if waiting for an answer. "I'm sorry. I know it's difficult for you to talk. So here's how we're going to work it. When I ask you a question and the answer is YES, then moan once. If the answer is NO, then moan twice. Think you can manage that?"

Ronny didn't answer.

"Now, I've asked you two questions already and I haven't received an answer. Let's try it again. Have you ever considered Lasik?"

Again Ronny remained silent. Jankowski snatched the hammer and bashed the toes on Ronny's left foot. Ronny's eyes bugged wide open, and his cheeks turned crimson. The stuffed sock did its job as Ronny's screams could not be heard. Ronny breathed heavily and moaned steadily.

"I know that hurts. I'm sorry." Jankowski's words oozed with sincerity. "But it's important that you learn the rules. We can't communicate effectively unless you fully understand the rules. Remember now, to answer yes, moan once. To answer no, moan twice. Do you understand?"

Ronny moaned once.

"That was excellent, Mr. Monroe. Excellent." Jankowski leaned in towards Ronny. Though he was now closer, Ronny still saw little more than a blurred gray ball for a face. "Do you know Danny Lonigan?"

Ronny remained silent. This time Jankowski leaned forward

and hammered the toes on Ronny's right foot. Ronny writhed in pain and breathed heavily. Jankowski waited patiently for Ronny's moans to cease.

"Compose yourself, sir," Jankowski finally said with words barely above a whisper. "Okay, let's try this again. Do you know Danny Lonigan?"

Ronny moaned once.

"Thank you." Jankowski returned the hammer to the table and brought his hands together, massaging his knuckles. "Now, it's important that you answer this next question honestly. Very important. If you fail to do so, things will not remain as pleasant as they have been here. So here's the question . . . did you shoot Danny Lonigan a couple of days ago?"

Ronny moaned once.

"Thank you for your honesty, Mr. Monroe. I appreciate that." Jankowski opened his briefcase and removed several eight by ten photos. "I'm going to show you some photos now. I'd like you to identify the people in these photos. Are you clear on this?

Ronny moaned once.

"Now I know you're as blind as a bat without your glasses, Mr. Monroe, so I'm going to stand behind you and put them on for you. Do not in any way, shape or form attempt to turn back and look at me. That would not be a wise move. Are we clear on this?"

Ronny moaned once.

Jankowski grabbed the hammer and slid in behind Ronny. He set Ronny's glasses in place and flashed the first photo. "This is your niece, correct Mr. Monroe?"

Ronny moaned once.

"She's seven-years-old, right?"

Ronny moaned twice.

"My bad," Jankowski said with a laugh. "She's 8-years-old now, right?"

Ronny moaned once.

"You know, sometimes those birthdays just slip past before you even know it. Did you buy your niece a birthday present?"

Ronny moaned twice."

Jankowski whacked Ronny across the right ankle with the

hammer. Ronny screeched, but again his pain was suffocated by the sock.

"Sorry about that, Mr. Monroe." Jankowski itched his neck with the claw end of the hammer. "I know you answered truthfully. I should not have done that, but sometimes my emotions get the best of me. I mean, your niece, she's such a cute little creature and you're her uncle and you don't have a wife or any kids of your own, so it just seems wrong to me that you didn't get her a present. It almost seems . . . sacrilegious." Again Jankowski scratched his neck with the hammer. "But I do apologize. I will not let that happen again."

Jankowski set the hammer on the floor and flashed another photo in front of Ronny's face. "This is your mother, correct?"

Ronny moaned once.

"She lives at 5616 South 74th, in Summit, right?"

Ronny moaned once.

"Your niece, the one I just showed you a picture of, and your sister—they all live there with your mother in her house, right?"

Ronny moaned once.

"By the way, just because I was a tad bit bored when I was researching your family, I checked out the real estate taxes on your mother's house." Jankowski narrowed his eyes. "I have to tell you, you should have your mother do a tax appeal. Her taxes are way too high for the value of her home. And she's a senior citizen now and didn't even file for her senior exemption. That alone would knock off almost a grand in taxes for her each year. Something to think about, don't you agree?"

Ronny moaned once. Jankowski checked his wrist watch.

"Now, please listen carefully. If you ever try to do anything to Danny Lonigan again, please know that your niece and your mother will both disappear. And I'll probably toss your sister into the mix for good measure. You will be given the time to grieve their loss, and then after they're all buried, you will disappear. Do you understand these things, Mr. Monroe?"

Ronny moaned once.

"Are you certain?"

Ronny moaned once.

Jankowski flashed a photo of Danny Lonigan and his family. "Okay, Mr. Monroe, this is Danny Lonigan's family. See them all?"

Ronny moaned once.

"Take a good look at all those faces. Memorize them. See his wife, his two older boys. Even take a look at that little baby his wife is holding. Are you all good?"

Ronny moaned once.

Jankowski removed the photo. "Okay, good. Now there's no showing up on Mr. Lonigan's block again, no going to his place of work, no calling him on the phone. You are to have nothing to do ever again with a man named Daniel Lonigan. And this applies to every member of his family too. You walk into a restaurant and you see Mr. Lonigan in there eating some pulled pork, you walk out. You see his wife at the store buying some avocados, you walk out. You see one of his kids playing baseball at the park, you leave. Capiche?"

Ronny moaned once.

"Because there will be no time for explanations in the future. If you violate any of the aforesaid conditions, then bad things *will* happen. Are you clear on this?"

Ronny moaned once.

Jankowski removed Ronny's glasses and set them on the kitchen table. He returned the three photos to his briefcase.

"Now I have to say that just mentioning 'pulled pork' a few seconds ago gets me hungry. You ever been to Chuck's over on Seventy-Ninth Street in Burbank?" Ronny didn't answer. "That was a question, Mr. Monroe."

Ronny quickly moaned once.

"I figured you might have been to Chuck's before. It's not too far from here. I love their pulled pork. Absolutely love it. Quite frankly, I like all their food. Never had a bad meal in the place. Great beer list too." Jankowski set the hammer on the table and cracked a couple of knuckles on his left hand. "Oh well, enough on that. We're almost done here, Mr. Monroe. I want to get out and sneak in a quick nine before it gets too dark. So before I leave I have one last thing to do."

Ronny moaned once.

"That wasn't a question, Mr. Monroe. That was a statement. Understand the difference?"

Ronny moaned once.

"Okay, look . . . I'm supposed to make an example out of you. You know, break this bone, break that bone, cut this thing off, cut that thing off. But I don't really want to go there today, because you don't seem like such a bad guy. You're just a guy who made a mistake. So let's just say that your toes and your ankle are hurting, so that takes care of most of it. Does that sound fair?"

Ronny moaned once.

"But *I do* have to bring a momento back. Sorry about that. It's just something I have to do." Jankowski yawned. "Now, I'm going to reach over and unzip your fly and then—"

Ronny started to shake, shimmy and moan as best he could. Jankowski laughed.

"Take it easy, Mr. Monroe. Take it easy now. I was just joking. Don't worry, I'm not going to chop off your pecker."

Ronny settled down. Jankowski snatched the hand axe from the table. With his other hand he dialed a number on his cell phone. When his call was answered, he said, "Three minutes, please," and then hung up.

"Now Mr. Monroe, I'm going to leave you momentarily. So let's tidy up a few things before I go. Have any policemen been to see you yet?"

Ronny moaned twice.

"Good. But there will likely be some policeman coming to question you at some point. Just deny that you shot Mr. Lonigan. Everything will be forgotten on his end. No charges will be filed against you. But if you mention anything to the police or to another living soul about my visit today, I will find out and then each and every one of those bad things will happen. Clear?"

Ronny moaned once.

"Okay, now as for that momento, I'm going to be blunt here and tell you that I need to take off a chunk of your finger, your trigger finger. That's why your left hand is taped there to the table. Don't worry. Not a big chunk. You'll still have most of it and you'll still be able to work and all. Now, you might not be able to pick your nose so good any more with that finger, but hey, that's why God gave us two index fingers." Jankowski ran his gloved right hand across the axe blade. "So here's what I want you to do. When I say 'Time,' I want you to close your eyes tight and bite hard into that sock in your mouth. When I'm done, I'm going to leave. But before I go, I will untie your right hand. You can then use that hand to remove the rest of the tape and untie yourself. And when people ask what happened to your finger, I suggest you tell them you were doing some woodwork around the house and you sliced it off with your circular saw." Jankowski paused for a moment. "You do have a circular saw, don't you, Mr. Monroe?"

Ronny moaned once.

"Of course, you do. Who doesn't, right?"

Ronny moaned once.

"Okay, Mr. Monroe. Get ready." Ronny blinked spastically. "Here we go. Time."

Ronny closed his eyes as tight as he could. He shook and shivered as he turned his head towards his TV. He opened his eyes for a split second, his gaze set on the gray haze of the empty screen. For some strange reason Ronny wanted that TV *on*, wanted it *on* as much as he had ever wanted anything in his life. Witnesses, Ronny thought as he again shut his eyes tight. Please, God, please turn the TV on. Yes, Ronny wanted witnesses—others who could corroborate his story if and when he went to the police. But if Ronny's shrink were present, he would say, "Ronny, it's not likely that a bunch of fans at a Sox game could see through your TV and be witnesses to anything happening in your house." But Ronny didn't always see things the way his shrink suggested.

Jankowski pulled Ronny's index finger towards him as much as the duct tape would allow. "Hold them steady now. If not, I might get more than one by accident."

The fingers on Ronny's left hand were flared as wide as possible. Jankowski placed the blade of the hand axe over the index finger at the midway point between the first and second knuckle. He held the axe in place with his left hand and grabbed the hammer with his other hand.

"Bite that sock hard now."

Ronny did as ordered. Jankowski smashed the axe head with the hammer, and Ronny's finger came off easily. His barks and moans were still muffled by the sock. Jankowski slipped Ronny's finger into a plastic baggie and zipped it shut. He placed the finger, hammer, and axe into his briefcase and closed it. He unleashed Ronny's right hand, dropped a towel in his lap, and left through Ronny's side door. As Jankowski walked towards the street, a black sedan pulled up at the edge of Ronny's driveway. Jankowski stepped into the back seat, and the driver sped off.

9. Diversey Point

A BREEZY DAY ALONG THE LAKEFRONT, the waves pushed in towards the shore at Diversey Point, slapping the rocks. Maggie and her father sat on lawn chairs atop the rocks with fishing rods in hand, their lines in the water. Beside them was a bucket and two coolers, one for the fish and one for their beer. Clad in a Cubs hat and sunglasses, Bill watched a couple of motorboats and sailboats amble across the lake, fifty yards or so from the shore.

"How much longer ya wanna stay?" Bill said.

"Half hour. It'll be getting dark then."

Bill smiled. "You read my mind." He sipped his can of beer and motioned towards one of the big boats on the water. "Look at that one right there? She's a beauty, ain't she?"

Maggie reeled her line in, checked her bait and cast again. "Why do people always refer to boats as women?"

"'Cuz it's the right thing to do. 'Cuz that's the way it's always been. Even goin' back to the Moby Dick days." Bill took another slug of his beer. "Ships, boats, even little dinghies . . . they should all have ladies' names. Just 'cuz."

"Thanks for the enlightenment, Dad. I think I'm ready to go to Harvard now."

Bill offered an approving nod. "No doubt." He set his beer down and slowly reeled his line in a bit before letting it go slack. He turned towards Maggie but watched a few joggers tread along the lakefront trail before he spoke.

"I have to tell you that I like that man Ed you brought to dinner the other day. I can see a lot of good in him. He's not like that hunka shit you hitched up with the first time around. Hated him from Day One. But Ed's a plain, regular, good guy, and I like the way he treats you. Treats you right. And I can tell it ain't no act."

"Thanks, Dad." Maggie smiled, reeled her line in and recast. "Ed and I have a lot of fun together." She laughed. "I know he may not look like it, but he's really a funny guy. And lots of fun."

"That's good, baby girl. That's good. I wanna see ya happy. I wanna see you laughing." Bill's line pulled. "Got me one." He stood up and jerked his line a bit. He then let the fish run with the line for a while before he reeled it in. When he pulled the fish up out of the water, it was a good-sized lake perch. Bill removed the hook and tossed the fish into the cooler to keep company with the four other fish.

"That one's gonna be tasty, Dad."

"Yep. I might just freeze these fish until you and Ed come over again."

Maggie nodded. "We'll do that soon."

Bill set his rod down and grabbed his beer. "Good. Fish for sure next time. No more steak. Right?" Maggie laughed. Bill scratched his neck and adjusted his Cubs hat. "Can I, uh, can I tell you one thing that's on my mind about Ed, though. I'm not tryin' to pry but, but I gotta say it, ya know, 'cuz I kept my mouth shut the whole time you were married to Lance Loser. And I don't wanna see anything go wrong for you again."

Maggie tongued her upper lip and reached down for her beer. "That's okay, Dad. Go ahead." She downed some beer.

Bill emptied his can and set it down beside him. "Well, ya know how I just kinda sensed that Ed was a vegan. Ya know, I said I could just *feel* it?"

"Right."

"Well, I like the man. I already told you that. He's a good man

. . . but I, uh, I can tell that's there's some sort of heaviness on him. Ya know, some sort of sadness. It's like a big scar on his face that you can't see, but if you look hard enough, it's there. You can see it plain as day."

Bill crunched his face a bit and wondered if he had said too much. He waited for Maggie to speak but she turned and stared out at the water, her eyes fixed on a freighter passing ever-so-slowly miles away in Lake Michigan.

"You feel that?" Maggie said, her eyes still on the freighter.

"Yeah."

Maggie turned towards her father. "Well, you're right, Dad," she said and then finished her beer. "Ed hasn't said too much to me about it, but I do know that he had one child, a daughter, who died when she was about ten."

"Sorry to hear that." Bill rubbed his chin. "But that makes sense. That must be what I felt."

"He and his wife split ways shortly after that. He told me they weren't able to work through the grief together."

"Maybe he ain't done grievin' altogether himself."

Maggie eyed her father and then cast her eyes again out into the water until they got lost in the waves this time.

"Does he know what you do for work?"

"Not exactly."

"Plan on tellin' 'im anytime soon?"

"I hope to. Some day."

Bill reached into the cooler and pulled out two fresh PBRs. He snapped them both open and handed a can to Maggie, who set her pole down along the rocks.

"I think I'm all fished out," Bill said.

Maggie smiled. "Me too." She took a sip from her fresh beer.

They both continued to slurp their beers in silence, their eyes set on the boats passing in near darkness along the lake. The wind started to pick up, and the waves began to crash into the shore.

10. A Round of Mini Golf

JANKOWSKI, HIS WIFE, AND THEIR TWIN twelve-year-olds, stood, putters in hand, at the Eighteenth Hole at Hollywood Park in suburban Crestwood. Jankowski stepped up to the tee and after taking a few practice swings, sent his dark green ball straight ahead, watching as it clanked off one wall, then tapped into another before it rolled a few feet and fell into the cup for a hole in one. Jankowski raised his club over his head and did his best Michael Jackson moonwalk.

"Now, I don't want to brag on myself, but that is my third of the night and I believe that puts the *men* up by two." He high-fived his son, Shane.

"We know, Al," his wife, Libby, said. "We can count."

"Oh, I see how it is," Jankowski said with a laugh. He turned towards his kids. "Someone's not being a good sport."

"Dad's right, Mom," Shane said. "Don't be a sore loser."

"Maybe she didn't eat her Wheaties today," Jankowski added.

Libby refused to smile. She stepped up to the tee, eyed the cup, and sent the ball out. It also banked off a few walls and fell into the cup for a hole in one. Like her husband, she also did a moonwalk, only better, and then finished by playing air guitar on her putter.

"And on the second day," Libby said, "God created woman, so that we could kick man's ass in mini-putt-putt."

"Yeah, Mom," Debra barked and then high-fived her mother.

Jankowski brought his putter up to his mouth as if it were a microphone as his daughter prepared to putt. Just then the overhead lights kicked on.

"Debra Jankowski prepares to unleash her first shot on the very last hole of this epic battle of *Men* versus *Women*," Jankowski said using a British accent, "which, by the way, the Men will no doubt win unless Debra comes up *huge* on this very hole. And for the folks listening in at home, this shot is so *huge*, the lights on the course have just been turned on."

Debra paid no attention to her father. She set her feet a foot from her ball, lined up her putt, and sent it. The ball banked off the wall and made its way directly towards the hole. Debra bounded down the course, following the ball.

"C'mon, now. Baby needs new shoes. C'mon," she said. The ball stopped just in front of the cup. "Ooooh." Debra then tapped it in.

Jankowski looked at his daughter quizzically. "'Baby needs new shoes?'"

"You like that one, huh?" Debra said.

Jankowski released a big smile and pulled his daughter in for a hug. Shane then stepped to the tee. Jankowski released his daughter and turned his attention to Shane. "C'mon, partner, you got this one. All you gotta do is drop a deuce and this one's ours." Jankowski went silent.

"What? No commentary, Dad?" Debra said. "Where's the English guy?"

"What English guy?" Jankowski said, playing dumb.

Shane stroked the ball, and after it banked off the first wall, it came up about four feet short of the cup. Shane winced.

"You gottit," Jankowski said. "All day."

Shane studied the shot for a moment. He then eyed the ball and tapped it in.

"Way to go, killer," Jankowski said. Father and son hooked elbows and swung around in circles to celebrate their victory. Libby and Debra couldn't help but laugh. When Jankowski and son finally stopped, the four started to walk back to return their clubs.

"Oh, well," Debra said, "at least we won last week. And the week before that, and—"

"The week before that," Libby added.

Jankowski was beaming. "That's okay," he said. "Shane and I are on a winning streak now."

"You can't exactly call one game a winning streak, Dad," Debra barked.

"Well, I beg to differ," Jankowski said. "The way I see it . . ." Jankowski choked on his words, and his face instantly went flat, as if he had seen a ghost. His eyes floated across the putt-putt course and stopped on the first hole where Danny Lonigan and his family stood, preparing to begin a round of mini-golf.

"Here, Lib," Jankowski said, handing his club to his wife. "You guys go on ahead. I'll be there in a sec." He smiled. "I see someone from my high school days. I just want to say, Hi."

"Sounds good, Dad," Shane said. "But, uh, we're still gettin' ice cream, right?"

Jankowski's eyes did not stray from Danny. "For sure. Plush Horse, here we come."

Libby and her children walked towards the indoor facility to return their putters. Jankowski walked up behind Danny just as he and the rest of the Lonigans were preparing to start at the first hole. He snuck up and slapped Danny on the right shoulder. Danny dipped his shoulder and winced in pain.

"I'm sorry, man," Jankowski said.

Danny turned and saw Jankowski. Both men smiled.

"You okay?"

"Yeah. Yeah. I'm fine," Danny said. "Good to see ya, Al."

Jankowski eyed Danny's bandage. "What happened to you?"

"Just got a little banged up at work."

Jankowski nodded. "Well, I just finished playing a round with my family and I saw you. Just wanted to say, hello."

Danny turned towards his family. "Hey guys, this is Al Jankowski. We went to high school together. Played on the same hoop team. Four years' worth."

Kate, Jim, and Sam walked over to Jankowski and shook his hand.

"My dad told me about you," Sam said. "He said you got every tough rebound in the big games. And you always played solid defense."

"Ah, your dad's just stretching the truth." Jankowski laughed. "It was all about the team. We all had our roles." He ran his eyes across all of the Lonigans. "Well, I don't want to keep you guys from your fun. It was nice meeting everyone."

Jankowski removed his wallet and pulled out a business card. He handed it to Danny.

"Buzz me one day, and we'll toss a few back and catch up."

"Sounds good," Danny said. "Good seein' ya."

Jankowski motioned as if he were going to slap Danny on the shoulder again, but then stopped within inches of Danny's wound. Again Danny winced.

Jankowski laughed. "Gotcha." He left and made his way towards the indoor facility. With a wide smile on his face, Danny watched until Jankowski was gone from sight.

11. Jim White

JIM WHITE WAS WORKING LATE YET AGAIN. He sat at his desk in a nearly empty newsroom, putting the finishing touches on his column. He punched a couple of keys into his laptop. White's phone rang. He picked it up but his eyes were fixed on his laptop screen.

"Jim White."

"Hi ya, Mr. White. It's me again, your friendly neighborhood Streets and San Man."

White sat back in his chair. "The Copper Caper. I remember it well. Got anything else for me?"

"Wouldn't be calling if I didn't."

"Okay, then. Fire away." White punched a button on his laptop and it began to record their conversation.

"Just thought you'd like to know that these bosses at the garage where the wire was stolen, they ain't even filed a police report or even contacted the police yet. Ya know, they're afraid to let the word out 'cuz it makes them look like a buncha dumb asses."

White ran a hand across his balding scalp. "So who are the bosses over there?"

"The general foreman is a guy by the name of Ted Flynn. He's like a second or third cousin to the mayor. The other general foreman is Dan Cullinan. He's the state rep's brother. And the last guy, he's just a foreman, but he's in charge of the supply room. His name's Morgan. Mark Morgan."

White leaned back in his chair and kicked his feet up on the desk. "By the way, I'm not so great at notes anymore, so I'm recording all this. You okay with that?"

"I give a shit." The unknown caller cleared his throat. "Now look, I've been known to place a bet a time or two in my day, and being the bettin' man that I am, I'm bettin' that one of these three guys is involved with stealin' the wire."

"Why do ya say that?"

"Well, as far as I know, it's only these three guys and the superintendent who have keys to the garage. And no doors were jimmied or anything. Ya follow?"

"Yeah, I do." As White stared into space for a moment, he ran his left index finger across his lips. "Okay, I got some stuff I can look into. The fact that these guys didn't report the theft to the police is pretty strong stuff. That's something I can hit them with already. And then I can keep after it from there."

"Go for it. Who knows? Maybe when the word gets out, and the cops start sniffin' around, and the bigger bosses start puttin' pressure on these three mopes, somethin'll give. Someone might crack."

"Sounds good. Is that it for now?"

"Yep. 'Cept for the fact that I was thinkin' I'd like a little moniker. Ya know, like Deep Throat in Watergate. That way if you refer to me in the paper, I won't be just an 'unnamed source.' Ya know, I'd like a name."

"Works for me. I'm all for throwing some color into the situation. What's it going to be?"

"Ya know, I thought of a couple, like— The Billy Goat, Big Bowling Balls, Freddy Justice. But the problem with those is, uh, well, they all sound stupid. So how about—*The Secret San Man*?

White smiled. "I like it. It's a winner."

"Okay, Mr. White. I'll be in touch."

"Good enough."

Part Four

Ellen

1. The Return of the Three Stooges

"**T**HERE'S NO WAY THIS THING CAN GO any direction but bad," Ted Flynn said. "And bad ain't good."

Flynn, Cullinan and Morgan were gathered in Flynn's office. Down below, the electricians loaded their vans with supplies for the day but stole a look here and there up at Flynn's office as they moved about.

"Right. I agree," said Cullinan. "But if we get our story straight, we can keep it from goin' completely sideways on us. I mean, Toolis already got called down by the mayor. They'll be callin' on us in just a little bit."

Flynn snatched his copy of the *Chicago Sun-Times*. He looked at it again and then flipped it to his desk. The page 3 headline stated, "The Copper Caper."

"Page Three. What the fuck?" Flynn said. His face was a tangled mess of wrinkles, angry teeth, and pasty skin. "Tell me they couldn't bury this shit around Page 25. I mean almost no one gets past the first ten pages anymore. They just flip to the Sports section."

"Why would they bury it?" Cullinan said as he threw both hands up. "The idea is—"

"I know what the fuckin' idea is, Dan," Flynn barked. "I know. I'm just sayin' I wish for us it was a busy news day and maybe it woulda been nice if we landed on Page 25 instead of Page 3. That's what I'm sayin'."

"I know. All right, look, we just need to get our story set," Cullinan advised yet again. "I mean that's the big point here in the paper." Cullinan grabbed the newspaper and shook it. "He keeps askin' how come those in charge of this garage didn't report the missin' copper to the police."

"Ya know what?" Morgan said. "I wanna know who put this shit out there to the *Sun-Times*. Who's the fuckin' big mouth . . ." Morgan ripped the paper from Cullinan's hands and scanned it. "Who's this fuckin' . . . 'Secret San Man?'"

"Look. We probably got about ten minutes before Toolis calls on us," Cullinan said. "That's my guess. Let's try to—"

"I'll bet it's Scarpelli," Morgan said. His face was tight, his lips flat. "That fucker has it in for me. I'll bet—"

"C'mon, Mark." Cullinan ran his right hand through his hair. "We gotta get our story straight."

"It's Scarpelli," Morgan said. "I know it. The other day that prick—"

"STOP, ALREADY." Cullinan's words boomed across Flynn's room, out the door and down into the garage below. Several electricians jerked their heads up towards Flynn's office. "Just shut the fuck up." Cullinan took a few steps away from Flynn's desk and then turned back. "Look, when somethin' goes bad, it ain't Jimmy Scarpelli's fault all the time, okay? He can't do every fuckin' bad thing. He didn't make it rain locusts back in the days of Moses, he didn't crucify Christ, he didn't shoot JFK, he didn't steal the damn copper wire, and my guess is he probably didn't call Jim White either."

"Hey, fuck you. How do you know?" said Morgan.

"'Cuz his family ain't the sort that wants publicity," Cullinan said. "And he ain't a rat. If people start snoopin' around here, he's gotta be careful too. Ultra careful."

"You go ahead and say whatever the fuck ya want," Morgan barked. "I don't give a shit. I'm entitled to my opinion and I happen—"

"You're always tryin' to jam Scarpelli 'cuz ya think he banged your wife. Every chance—"

Morgan moved toward Cullinan with a clenched right fist. He swung once, but Cullinan stepped back and dodged the roundhouse.

Flynn jumped between the men. "Okay, okay. Stop. STOP." Cullinan and Morgan glared at each other. "How fuckin' stupid are we gonna look when we get called in and we all got cuts and bruises all over, huh?" Flynn shut the door with a bang and turned to face the others. "So what's our story?"

Cullinan's chest heaved as he sucked in a big breath. "I think . . . ," Cullinan said and then released that breath, the sound akin to air escaping on a soon-to-be-flat tire. "I think we should say that we were plannin' to go to the police but we didn't go yet because we were investigatin' on our own. We were tryin' to find out who it was on our own, internally. And we figured once the cops showed up in the building, everything would go haywire and we'd never find out who it was. So we were giving ourselves two or three weeks to see what we could come up with. If we came up empty, then we were gonna call the police."

"Ya think that's good enough?" Flynn said with slits for eyes. "I mean, I know Mark don't like Scarpelli, but maybe we should feed his name as the guy we're checkin' on."

Cullinan swung his head from side to side. "I wouldn't do that. It'll look—"

"C'mon, already," Morgan said.

"No. No. Stick to the story I just gave," said Cullinan. "No one needs to be tossed under the bus. And especially not Jimmy Scarpelli. I mean, think about it. If we give 'im Scarpelli's name, then they probably send the IG out to start followin' him and—"

"What the hell's wrong with that?" Morgan hissed. "The guy should have the IG on his ass."

"Great. Great. And when they're followin' him around and he does somethin' he's not supposed to do, who else ya figure they're gonna see, huh?" Cullinan glared at Morgan again. "Think about that. Ya want Tom Lonigan up our ass 'cuz the IG is followin' his brother around too. C'mon. Think."

"All right. Okay, let's go with Dan's story," Flynn said. "As far as Scarpelli goes, we can cut him loose from Danny Lonigan later and feed him to the IG then, if we need to."

Cullinan and Morgan eyeballed each other and nodded.

2. Commissioner Toolis

MAYOR STOKELY, RICHARD RANDALL, and James Toolis—Commissioner of the Streets and Sanitation Department, stood as still and silent as statues in a city hall elevator, staring into the backs of the heads of five other elevator occupants, an elevator that moved far too slowly for the mayor's liking. Stokely already had a full plate today, and now the Copper Caper had been added as a dessert. When the door opened at the fifth floor, the three men hustled out of the elevator to the mayor's office. Randal and Toolis immediately dropped into seats in front of the mayor's desk like obedient, well-trained dogs. Stokely ventured over to the snack station at the back of his office and poured three cups of coffee. Toolis fidgeted in his chair a bit. Sure he was the mayor's cousin, but he had never been summoned to come to city hall on such short notice. Stokely passed cups to Toolis and Randall.

"So, Jim," Stokely said and then sat in his chair, "do you think I need to put a little whiskey in this coffee or a lot of whiskey in it?"

"I don't think it's that bad," Toolis said. "I really don't. I mean, sure, we got beat up in the *Sun-Times* a little bit, but it's not anything like the Hired Truck situation from years back."

"Well, if memory serves me right, you didn't think the Hired Truck '*situation*,' as you call it, was going to be any big deal either. Remember that?" Stokely said. "Now I know I wasn't the mayor at the time, but you have to admit it became a lot more than a 'situation.' It became a SCANDAL."

Toolis was a bit stunned by the mayor's demeanor, and when stunned or scared or embarrassed, Toolis stuttered. "Well, Bob, I, I, I . . . sure I remember what happened w-with the Hired Truck situation. And you're right. I was wr-wr-wrong on that. But I-I wasn't the commissioner back then either. I was only the deputy commissioner."

Mayor Stokely stood and grabbed the *Sun-Times* from his desk. "You have to like the headline though—*The Copper Caper*. Very catchy. Has a nice ring to it." Stokely walked over towards a window and scanned the article again.

"Any idea who this '*Secret San Man*' might be?" Randall said.

"Not yet. I-I-I'm headin' over to the garage, w-where the w-wire was stolen, when I leave here. I'll see w-what those guys think."

"Ya know, in reality, I don't really care who the '*Secret San Man*' is," said Stokely. He joined the other two men. "Not at all. Quite frankly, if these dumb asses in charge of the garage did what they were supposed to do, then we wouldn't have any story at all, and there wouldn't be any 'Secret San Man.' But because these guys chose not to report the theft, now we all have a shitbar to chew on."

"How do ya w-want me to handle it?"

"I'll address this—this *Copper Caper* with the press today," Stokely said. He turned towards Randall. "What time is the press conference?"

"One-thirty."

"Okay, I'll talk to the press and tell them our commissioner is planning a thorough investigation into the theft itself and into the manner in which the reporting of the theft was mishandled. I'll also let them know that the police will be investigating the theft."

"How about the IG?" Randall said. "Are we bringing them in?"

"Not at this point," Stokely said. He eyed Toolis. "I'll say I think the police are better equipped to handle the theft investigation and that the commissioner has the other matter under control. I'll let them know that if we don't resolve this matter within two weeks, then we'll bring in the inspector general to assist. That's how we'll approach it. Sound good?"

Randall nodded.

"So w-what do ya want me to do?" Toolis said.

"Jim, you let the police handle the theft investigation, as it should be. As for the way the failure to report the theft was handled, I'll make it easy on ya. Find out which one of those foremen or general foremen fucked up the most, and we'll remove him from his job."

Toolis's eyes flared open. "Ya mean, for good or just a suspension until things blow over."

Stokely dropped into his chair again and swung his feet up on his desk. "First, don't assume it will blow over," Stokely snapped. "Sometimes the biggest pains in the asses start from little things. And then they just grow and grow and fester. I mean, the Hired Truck shit still gets dumped in my face two or three times a year, and I wasn't even the mayor back then. Second. Yeah. Whoever you pick is gonna be gone for good."

"But those are three pretty g-g-good guys over there," Toolis said. "You know 'em all. And, uh, well, and Ted's your cousin." Toolis scratched his head. " My cousin too."

"I know, Jim. They've all been good for us. They've all worked the elections and got the vote out. And yes, I do know that Ted Flynn is my cousin. I know he's your cousin. Thanks for the reminder." Stokely forced a smile. "I know these things. I get it. But that doesn't mean I'm gonna cover Ted's ass or the other guys' either." Stokely stood again and glared down at Toolis. "I want a message sent on this, Jim. A clear message. Whoever you decide on is the guy who goes. You pick the guy and deliver the news."

Toolis stared at his feet. "W-When do ya w-want me to do all this?"

Stokely laughed. "C'mon, Jim. Don't go making this sound like it's the hardest thing in the fucking world here now, okay?" He scratched at his forehead. "For Christ's sake, the three guys fucked up. They had an opportunity to do the right thing but they didn't do it. So now—the way I see it . . . one of 'em has to pay for it."

"Do you want me to tag along with the commissioner when he heads over to the garage?" Randall said.

"Thanks for the offer. But *no* on that one," Stokely said. "I don't want to set off any alarms." The mayor walked to Toolis's side. "Look, when you go over there, just go through your questions like it's no big deal. Don't come in swinging an axe or anything. Ya know, don't make it like some big inquiry. But still, try to find out who the main village idiot was. Once you gather up your information, then leave. The following day you call the main bad guy in to see you, and he gets his walking papers." Toolis's eyes were still in the floor. "Jim, you getting all this? You follow?"

Toolis's words came soft and slow. "I-I-It's just that . . . well, these guys, well . . ."

"I know. I know," Stokely said. He set his right hand on Toolis's shoulder. "These are your golfing buddies. Your steady foursome, right?" Toolis nodded. "If I could help, I would. But that's how it has to go."

Toolis had bored holes into his shoes for quite a bit of time, but sometimes such actions brought good ideas his way. And he thought this was just such a time. He looked up at Mayor Stokely, a glint of hope in his eyes. "But, what if—"

"No 'buts'," Stokely said with a stone face. "None."

"But what if—"

"None. NONE."

The dash of hope that had been present in Jim Toolis's eyes lay dead beside his shoes. Mayor Stokely stared at Toolis, who refused to lift his stare from the floor. Stokely returned to his desk and removed a sheet of looseleaf paper from his top drawer. He wrote the names, *FLYNN, CULLINAN and MORGAN* in big letters on different parts of the paper.

"Look, Jim, I'm going to make this easy for you," Stokely said. Randall eyed his boss. He usually knew exactly where the mayor was headed, which ideas he favored, what words might come out of his mouth, and so forth, but he had no clue at this point.

Randall's eyes stayed fixed on Stokely as he walked to the dartboard on the wall farthest from the windows. He used a dart to tack the sheet of paper with the names of the three stooges to the board.

"Okay, look," Stokely said. "I'm going to toss one dart at the board. I got Ted's name, Cullinan's name, and Morgan's name on the sheet. Whoever it lands on—or closest to—gets fired. Sound fair enough?"

Toolis and Randall stared at the mayor in silence as he removed another dart from the board and walked to where a piece of black electrical tape sat on the floor exactly seven feet, nine and a quarter inches from the front of the board. The mayor turned, toed the line, and prepared to fire the dart.

Toolis jumped to his feet. "All right, stop," he barked. "I'll do it. You don't have—"

Stokely faced Toolis with pinched eyes. "I'm not being a wise guy, Jim. I know it's tough for ya. I figure this way is as good as any." Stokely turned towards the board again and took aim. He unleashed the dart and then walked to the board to examine it.

"Come take a look."

Toolis and Randall both walked to the mayor. The dart was firmly lodged in the *R* on the name, *MORGAN*.

"Works for me," Randall said.

"Okay, Jim, check in with me tomorrow after you give Morgan the news."

Toolis shrugged. "Okay," he said, and then moved immediately for the door where he let himself out. Stokely stayed put and eyed the dartboard in silence for a few moments.

"Think he'll do it?" Randall said.

"I dunno." The mayor brought his hands together and massaged his fingers on his left hand. "He's the sorta guy who, if he was taking a piss and missed, he'd take a half hour to decide if he should clean it up with toilet paper, a rag, or a mop." Stokely chomped on his bottom lip as he turned towards Randall. "You'll have to be on standby for late tomorrow afternoon."

"Gottit." Both men again eyed the sheet of paper on the dartboard.

3. The news

KATE WAS IN THE MIDST OF A MATH SEGMENT with her third graders, espousing the difference between circumference and diameter, when she saw the assistant principal standing in the hallway, her bright flowered blouse framed in the door window.

"Okay, everyone. I'll be just a few seconds," Kate said to her students. "I want you guys to begin working on Problem Number 4. Okay? Problem Number 4." As the students eyed their problem, Kate moved for the door. She opened it and stepped into the hallway.

"Hi, Veronica, what's up?"

"Here, Kate." The assistant principal passed an envelope to Kate and dropped her somber eyes to the tile floor.

Kate tore open an edge to the envelope but stopped. "Is everything okay?"

"No, it's not," the assistant principal said. "Not at all. And lucky me, I get to be the bearer of bad news." She dropped a hand on Kate's shoulder. "I'm sorry, Kate, but the cuts for next year just came down today. They're releasing over one thousand teachers citywide. It's effective in a few more weeks, when we wrap up for the year. I'm really sorry." Kate found her eyes drifting slowly towards the hand that was still on her shoulder. As she stared at the slender fingers and the two bulbous rings, Kate imagined for a moment that she was staring at a spider that had lodged itself on her shoulder, a spider that was about to infect her with a venom of some sort. Finally, the assistant principal removed her hand and Kate stood in silence, her eyes now fixed on the partially opened envelope. The assistant principal took this opportunity to begin her escape.

"Hey, Veronica," Kate barked. The assistant principal halted. "Is there any way this can change? I mean, can the union file a protest or can we appeal this?"

The assistant principal shook her head. "This is what the union agreed to. They already signed off on it. The specifics are all in the letter." Her face went blank. "I'm sorry, Kate."

Kate looked through the window to her classroom. Her students were busy working on Problem No. 4. And though the assistant principal had disappeared around a corner, with each step she took, the clack of her heels against the tile floor echoed in Kate's ears.

4. Ellen

ST JOSEPH'S HOME FOR SPECIAL CHILDREN stood atop a hill in a wooded area in Glanton, Illinois, on the edge of the Wisconsin border. The special needs inhabitants of St. Joe's enjoyed long walks in those woods, as well as swimming in the small lake on the property, all done under the watchful and caring eyes of the staff.

Mary and Tom Lonigan sat in the St. Joe's common area with Ellen Lonigan, forty-two, dressed in a burgundy jogging suit. The three claimed chairs near a large window overlooking a stream that wound its way towards the lake. Other inhabitants sat on lounge chairs in front of a big screen TV or at tables where they played cards with some of the workers. Others just sat on chairs and stared off into space, like lost toys waiting to be put away. Tom set chess pieces on the board he had brought with him. Though she sat beside her brother, Ellen stared blankly out the window at the water.

"All right, Ellie Mae," Tom said, "We're just about set." Ellen turned towards the chessboard and watched as Tom put the last few pieces in place. The instant Tom set the final piece atop the board, Ellen huddled over the board and amidst a flurry of grunts and moans, she played a game against herself at breakneck speed. In roughly three minutes, the game was over.

"That was fantastic, El," Mary said with an encouraging smile. "You still got the moves."

Ellen did not speak. She again looked out the window at the stream. Tom began to set up the board again.

"Ya know El, I was thinkin' it would be good to have ya come home again," Mary said. "To come live with me. Wouldn't that be fun? We could go shoppin'. I could comb your hair the way you like. I could hug you. I could hold you."

Tom stopped, king in hand, and looked at his sister and then at his mother.

"I could be a good mom to you, El." Mary's lips shuddered. She fought off tears. "I could try . . . I could try to be the mom I never was for you. I'm sorry about that, El. I'm sorry I wasn't a good mother to you. I shouldna left you here all these years."

Tom completed his game set-up. "You're good to go, Ellie Mae." Ellen again turned towards the chessboard. She competed against herself again, and again finished the game in roughly three minutes.

"That was another good one, El," Mary said. "I think you play even better now than before."

Ellen folded her arms across her chest and again cast her eyes out the window. Tom watched his sister and wondered what thoughts, if any, were roaming through her mind. Mary let her eyes wander out the window as well. They fell into the stream and floated like a bobber out towards the lake. That's how it had always been—for the thirty-one years that Ellen has been here. Things happen for a reason, Mary thought. The stream always leads to the water. Where will Ellen lead me? Where can I lead her?

5. Lawyer Up

COMMISSIONER TOOLIS PUSHED THROUGH THE DOOR to Ted Flynn's office to find Flynn at his desk, while Morgan leaned against a wall.

"Where's Cullinan?" Toolis said.

Flynn yanked out his cell and stared at it. "I texted him earlier. Ten minutes ago. Said he'd be here in a minute." Flynn tucked his phone away.

"Okay. W-Well, w-we should probably just wait until he gets here," Toolis checked the time on his wristwatch.

Morgan cleared his throat several times and slid his feet back and forth on the floor. "So how'd it go with the Mayor today?" His eyes were now set on Toolis.

"Not good," Toolis said with the wag of his head. He then sat on a fold-up chair. "Not good at all. But we should w-wait for Dan."

Flynn walked to the window and stared down below. Cullinan's car raced into the garage. "He's back," Flynn said.

Cullinan jogged up the stairs, entered the room, and sat atop Kip's desk.

"All right, guys," Toolis started. "I'm gonna tell ya what I'm supposed to do, and then I'll tell ya what I think we should do." Morgan grabbed a fold-up chair leaning against a wall and sat. In total silence, the men watched Toolis.

"I'm supposed to come in here and ask some questions, make

it look like no big deal, get all the info on the *Copper Caper*, and then tomorrow I'm supposed to fire one of ya." Toolis stood up. "Look I don't w-wanna fire anybody. You guys know that. You're all my friends. But the mayor says it's gotta be done. And the fact of the matter is . . . I already been told who to fire." He blew out a sigh. "So I gotta do it."

"Is this firing . . . is it just a temporary thing?" Cullinan said. "Ya know, will whoever it is get his job back after a little while?"

Toolis scratched his neck. "I asked the mayor the same damn question. He said he w-wants to make an example out of this situation, ya know, to basically help prevent future fuck-ups. He's pissed. So whoever gets fired is gone for g-g-good. But, ya know, ya get your pension and retirement benefits. None of that is being yanked."

"So who is it?" Morgan said.

"Well, b-b-before I say it," Toolis said, "I w-w-wanna let you know—"

"C'mon Jimmy, who is it?" Morgan barked.

Toolis sucked in a deep breath and ran his eyes across Flynn and Cullinan before stopping on Morgan. "It's you, Mark."

"Me? Why me? How the fuck did they decide on me? I mean you ain't even asked any—"

"They picked you," Toolis said. "The mayor and Randall."

"Randall?" Flynn hissed. "Guy's a piece a shit."

Both of Morgan's hands were on the sides of his head. He ran his fingers through his scalp over and over again, and then he stopped abruptly, staring at Toolis with a blank face, a ghost's face. "So when's this gonna be effective?"

Toolis was now the one scratching his scalp. "I-I-I don't know exactly. I think w-within the next day or two."

Morgan twisted his face into a knot. "Two fuckin' days. That's it, huh? I got two more fuckin' days?" He stared hard at Toolis.

"Hold on a minute, Mark. Hold on," Toolis said. "Now I just w-wanna check on somethin' here." He stood tall in front of the men. "We're all sneakin' up on twenty to twenty-five years of service here. Anyone thinkin' about puttin' in for early retirement? Ya know, if one of ya guys is thinkin' about retirin', then maybe ya do it now and Mark can hang on."

Morgan looked at Flynn and Cullinan. They didn't say a word. Their eyes stayed fixed on Toolis.

"C'mon Ted, you were talkin' about punchin' out early just a few days ago," Morgan said. "Remember? And then you were gonna start up some sort—"

"Yeah. I'm definitely gonna hang it up—but not for a while. Ya know, four or five years from now. I mean, hell, I gotta pay for my son's college yet."

Morgan dropped his eyes on Cullinan, who shook his head. "C'mon Mark, stop it," Cullinan said. Morgan held his stare. "Stop, already. Look, you know I can't retire either. I got too much shit I gotta take care of."

Morgan threw his hands up. "And what about me? I ain't got any shit I gotta take care of. You don't think this is gonna—"

"Forget it," Toolis said "Just forget it. It w-wasn't right to bring that up. That's my fault. I-I shouldna done that."

Morgan walked over to Toolis and stood in front of him. "Can I ask ya somethin'?"

"Yeah. Sure."

"How'd they decide on me?"

Toolis turned away from Morgan for a moment but then turned back. "I dunno exactly. I w-was asked to leave the room for a minute, and w-w-when I-I came back, the mayor told me it w-was you." Toolis licked his lips and scratched his neck again. "Who knows. Maybe they w-went by seniority and kept the two general foremen and fired the regular foreman."

Morgan pulled his wallet out and removed a picture of his wife. He spoke as he stared at it. "Okay. Well, if it's okay with you guys, I'm gonna go home and tell the old lady. I doubt I'll be in tomorrow either." Morgan stared into the floor. "She's been talkin' about filin' for divorce for a while now. You guys know that. Well, I'm sure this'll kick that into gear."

Toolis' Adam's apple bobbed as he swallowed. "Before ya go, Mark, I-I got somethin' else I think ya should think about. See, my guess is that the mayor and Randall all think you're just gonna take this in the ass like a good soldier and just fade away. But I-I don't think ya should do that."

"Whataya sayin'?"

"I think ya should lawyer up. And fast. Get yourself on TV and give your opinion. Quick like. Say that you got fired 'cuz you were the head of the supply room. But should you be fired just cuz of that? You didn't turn off the cameras. You didn't steal anything. Ya follow?"

Morgan's face brightened. "Yeah. Yeah."

"The press'll love to hear your side of the story," Toolis said. "It'll sell papers and keep things interesting on the 10:00 p.m. news. Give 'em the "why me, poor me" approach. Ya know, if someone is at home and their house gets broken into, is it the homeowner's fault? Hell no. Ya know, shit like that. Your supply room got broken into. There's a thief out there. So why should you suffer because someone else committed a crime?"

Cullinan's head bobbed in agreement. "I like this. I do. Maybe it'll put the heat on and it gets Mark's job back."

"Yeah. I'm gonna do it."

"But what about the failure to report," Cullinan said. "What's he say there?"

Toolis looked at Cullinan. "Well, what were you guys plannin' to say on that, before all this shit popped up?"

"We were plannin' to say that we didn't report it 'cuz we were conductin' our own investigation," said Cullinan. "Ya know, we were tryin' to find the thief on our own, and we were gonna give it two or three weeks, because we thought once the police jumped into the mix, it would scare everyone off and we'd never be able to find out who the thief was then."

"That works," Toolis said. "Go with that."

"Okay. Well, I'm gonna head out," Morgan said.

"Who ya gonna call for your lawyer?" Flynn said.

Morgan ran his eyes across the faces of the three men for a moment. "I'm thinkin' I'd go with Carl Haag.

"Good choice," Toolis said.

"Gotta like a neighborhood guy," Flynn added.

"Yeah, plus his perfect teeth always look good on camera," Morgan said.

The others laughed. Morgan tried to crack a smile but couldn't.
"Yeah. Well, thanks. It's been a slice." Morgan shook hands with the three men and pushed through the door. The others watched him amble down the stairs.

"Poor fucker." Flynn rubbed his chin and dropped into his chair. "So how'd they really decide on Morgan?"

Toolis threw his best confused look at Flynn.

"W-Whataya mean?"

"C'mon, Jimmy," Flynn said. "You never been a good liar. I saw it in your face."

"Me too," added Cullinan.

"Okay. Okay," Toolis said and then rubbed his nose.

"Well?" said Flynn.

"Okay, so the mayor wrote all three of your names on a sheet of paper and stuck it on his dartboard. And then he threw a dart. It landed on Morgan's name."

"Holy shit," Cullinan said. The men stared at each other in silence.

6. A New Beginning

"**T**HAT WAS A NICE TRIP," Mary said. Tom nodded in silence and continued to push the pedal as his car cruised south on I-294. "I'm glad we went," added Mary, "and I'm lookin' forward to what's to come."

"I dunno, Ma. I don't know if this is such a good thing. I mean, she still doesn't talk. She can't say anything. She—"

"Stop that negative talk, Tom. I don't want to listen to it. Not at all. And she, well . . . you saw her, she can play chess."

"Yeah, she can play chess. Play chess better than anyone," Tom said as his car leaned into a curve. "Probably beat Bobby Fischer when he was in his prime. So what?"

"So what?" Mary's face tightened. "What sort of attitude is that? That's not like you." Mary turned her eyes into slivers. "I'm not goin' to my grave leavin' my daughter in that . . . in that dump. I've been a terrible mother for—"

"You're not a terrible mother" Tom said. "Stop sayin' that. And that place is no dump. They do a great job there. You know that." Tom massaged his chin. "C'mon, Ma. She needed help you couldn't give her. She needed treatment. Sending her there was the right move."

"That's not altogether true." Mary's words were soft and measured. She shifted and gazed out the car window. "I let her stay there because I didn't think I could do everything for her. Because I, uh, I didn't WANT to do it. I think it was just too easy to just send her out there. You know, out of sight, out of mind. That's why I was a bad mother. But now I want to be a better mother. To you, to Danny . . ." Mary turned towards the back seat and smiled. Ellen sat there, her eyes unblinking, staring out the window, clutching the chess set. "And to Ellen."

7. The Cards

A MAN OF ROUTINES, TOM LONIGAN EXAMINED the kitchen wall clock as he stood before the sink, clad in a T-shirt and boxer shorts. It had been a long day—going out to see Ellen. Sure, Tom loved his sister, but whenever he returned from the trip to visit her, he couldn't help feeling exhausted. Part of it was the drive to and from the Wisconsin border—the never-ending traffic battle, tolls, and construction on the Tri-State—but most of his exhaustion centered around the realization that every visit was yet another reminder that there was far more to Ellen than one could see. But no one had ever been able to find a way to unleash it. Not the doctors. Not Mary. Not Danny. Not Tom. And now Ellen was home. Even more for Tom to ponder.

Tom set a small dish in the sink. He had just finished three slices of Asiago cheese from Calabria Imports, along with a couple of crackers. To die for. It was 10:15 p.m. Tom sighed and thought,

Forty-five minutes until snooze time. As Tom stood there, he downed a banana next. He always had one just before going to bed, something he had done every day since he was fifteen, back when old man Lonigan told him that all the best boxers ate bananas. Tom poured a tall glass of orange juice and made his way to the front room, where he plopped onto a comfy chair for a game of solitaire. and his ESPN sports roundup. This was Tom's nightly pre-bed routine: Asiago cheese—always three slices with crackers, a banana, a glass of OJ, and a game of solitaire as he watched, or listened to, ESPN. Not exactly exciting stuff, but this routine was his—all his. Sure Tom's customs were disturbed periodically by late-night union meetings, a few midnight beers at the Dubliner with family or friends, or a good, old black-and-white on AMC. But tonight was not one of those nights.

Tom slurped his OJ and set up his solitaire game on a coffee table. He clicked on ESPN. He didn't so much watch the show as listen to it. The solitaire game required far more of his attention. And to say Tom Lonigan loved solitaire was to say the Chicago River was polluted. He could play it all day long, but he never allowed himself that pleasure. One solitaire game per night. Just one. You win or you lose. And that's all. But Tom loved the way each card, any old card, could be the card that turned the game in your favor. No, Tom didn't believe in fate. He believed that you controlled your own destiny. Each move or slight could bring you closer to the goal—to win, to have control—or it could leave you lying in the weeds crying over your loss, over what might have been.

The cards had a certain feel to them. They could be moved and shifted, and even the smallest alteration in the cards could lead to momentous change. Tom looked down at the coffee table and stared hard at his cards. Two aces across the rail. Not a bad way to start a game. On the screen, Scott Van Pelt chatted about the Red Sox Nation's latest woes, but Tom barely heard those words. He absorbed what the cards were telling him. He felt them. He waited and stared. And then he made his move, knowing that the tiniest of things could set everything in motion.

8. Painted Black

JELLO WAS CONVINCED THAT TODAY would be a good day. He woke up wth a boner after all, something any sixty-plusser would tell you is a great start to any day. And now he sat in his office chair talking on his cell phone, paging through a book as he spoke. Outside his window, a blue sky claimed the day. Jello turned as he heard a gentle rap on his picture window. Phipps stood outside with a paint roller attached to an extension pole. He flashed a mouthful of teeth and waved to Jello. Jello continued to talk on the phone but his lips went flat. Phipps dipped his roller into a bucket filled with a mixture of tar and black paint, and started to roll the mixture across Jello's picture window. Jello ended his call and waddled over beside the window. Only the glass separated the men. Phipps again waved at Jello and smiled. He then continued to roll the tar-paint across the window until every inch of glass was covered completely in black.

9. The Letter

KATE FORCED A THIN SMILE AND STARED INTO her own plate. "You guys can all just leave your dishes in the sink. I'll clean up."

Jim's eyebrows shot up. "Ya sure, Mom?" Danny, Kate, and the boys had just finished their dinner, and Jimmy stood before the sink, ready to wash off his plate.

"Yeah. Just leave it." Kate'e eyes were still focused on her plate. "You guys can all just leave your dishes in the sink. I'll get it."

Danny and Sam finished their meal and put the dishes in the sink. Sam left the kitchen with Jim. Danny started to rinse his plate.

"So what's up?"

"What?"

Danny narrowed his eyes. "Somethin's up" he said.

"That obvious, huh?"

Danny leaned against the kitchen counter. "Well, you were quiet all during dinner, and I don't think I ever heard ya tell the boys to just leave their plates in the sink before. So, yeah, I'd say it's obvious."

Kate grabbed her purse from the kitchen counter and pulled out the termination letter she had been given earlier in the day. She handed it to Danny who frowned as he read it.

"Is this cemented in stone? I mean is the union going to appeal this or something?" Danny set the letter on the counter.

Kate bunched her lips into a circle before speaking. "It's final. The union agreed to it."

"But you're a great teacher," Danny said. "You know it and they know it. Why don't they trim the fat by gettin' rid of the some of the mopes and ass-clowns they still got hangin' around. Now's the time to do that."

"It's all about the tenure." Kate stared into the ceiling. "And I only have two years. One of the lowest on the totem pole. That's it in a nutshell."

Danny set his arms around Kate's waist and pulled her tight for a hug. "You'll get somethin' quick. Don't worry. All of those little Catholic grade schools would be happy to have you. I bet that when—"

"Dan, stop." Kate pulled away. "I mean, thanks for saying that, but a thousand teachers will be sending their resumes out for each of those jobs."

"Well, it's gonna be okay," Danny said. "We'll always be okay."

"I know, Dan. I know. But I don't want to be just *okay*," Kate said. "And it wasn't okay two years ago when you got indicted. We would've lost the house if Tom didn't cover us. We would've lost everything. I don't want to go through that again. I don't want to do it."

Danny felt like a dart had been thrown his way, but he saw in Kate's eyes that she didn't intend that. She was simply worried.

"I know, Kate. But that's never gonna happen again. We'll be fine. Like I just said. The money I'm makin' is pretty good, and I can always get a second job too. No problem."

Kate folded her arms across her chest. "And you know what? I mean, sure it hurts, it really does. I like my job. I like the money. But those kids. My kids. I have them doing good things. Real good things. Our scores were up too. Significantly."

"I know. I know." Danny pulled Kate in for a hug again. "Don't go pushin' me away again." Kate laughed as Danny pulled her head to his shoulder.

10. Agent Tangel

A GATHERING OF SMALL CHILDREN and adults watched one lone tiger prance about the tiger exhibit at Lincoln Park Zoo, preparing to receive his dinner. Maggie sat on a wooden bench across from the exhibit, taking in the shrieks of delight offered by a gaggle of fourth-graders on a field trip. A thin man in his early forties approached and sat on the bench a few feet from Maggie. He wore a light gray suit and a baby-blue tie, a stark contrast to his ebony skin. The man watched the tiger shuffle back and forth, looking anxious, ready for his next meal.

"I got your phone message," Agent Tangel said. His eyes were still on the tiger. "And I fully understand what you're asking. But the answer is a definitive . . . *no*. I'm happy you're happy but *no*, you are not to let Gilbreath know in any way, shape, or form who you really are."

"I know what you're saying," Maggie argued, "but I think he'd be totally fine with it. He'd be protective of the information. I mean, in a way, it's like we're on the same team. He's the sort who—"

"If someone knows, then someone knows. And that's one more than should ever know." The tiger stood still, his eyes aimed in Tangel's direction. "He stays in the dark. End of discussion. End of story. Are we clear, Agent Coin?"

"Yeah. Sure."

"We got word that Pellegrini found a tap in the CDOT phone closet. It was one of the IGs. Gilbreath probably had it put in there." Agent Tangel passed Maggie a small package. "This is a new listening device. Picks up everything, and it's the size of a freckle. A virtual speck on the wall. I'd like you to place it in Pellegrini's office. Use the laser to move it to where you want it. Smooth stuff. But I suggest you give it a rest for another week or so. You know, to let Pellegrini cool off a bit after finding that tap."

"I'm not sure how much longer I'll be assigned to work there," Maggie said. "My partner, he told me that—"

Maggie halted her conversation when a young boy sat on the bench just beside her. The boy's mother bent down in front of her son, to tie his shoe. Maggie smiled at the two. The mom flashed her teeth in return and tended to her child.

"Good as new," the mom said. The boy jumped off the bench and reached for his mother's hand. Maggie watched as the mother and son strolled away. Agent Tangel continued to stare straight ahead. The tiger now had a huge hunk of raw meat in his mouth. Bystanders watched in awe as he tore into his meal, swallowing large chunks seemingly whole.

"So my partner, he told me that it looks like we'll be sent out to another spot pretty soon."

"Okay. Look for your opportunities, but don't force anything. If need be, we can always get you sent over there on some sort of a repair call. So don't push it."

"Okay."

Tangel folded his arms across his chest. "You're doing good work, Agent Coin. The intel you're getting to us is outstanding. Keep it coming. I want to know exactly how many total city workers Pellegrini has working in his little web and who they are. And by the way, I know it may not seem right, but you need to start pressing Gilbreath for info. Soften him up and—"

"I really don't want to do that." Maggie raked her fingers through her hair. "You may not want to hear this, but I love this guy. I do. And I don't want him to ever think I was using him. I just happened to meet him, and he just so happens to be an assistant inspector general. It had nothing to do with work. Nothing to do with our plans. So I don't think I should have to press him for info."

"Agent Coin. I'm happy for you. I mean that." Tangel cracked a smile but kept his eyes straight ahead. "Love is a good thing. It surely is. Sometimes I think love is about the only thing that keeps this world of ours from spinning completely out of control."

"I didn't know you had any soft spots, Agent Tangel."

"I don't." Tangel pushed a hand across his head, his hair tight to the scalp. "I knew love once, but that was a long time ago." He turned and looked directly at Maggie for the first time. "The job took over at that point. So much for love."

"So you understand then. So you're okay if I don't try to press Ed for information?"

"Let me ask you this, Agent Coin. People like you in the dating scene, you guys still talk when you're out on dates, right?"

"Right."

"I mean most young people I see out on dates now just sit across from each other at a dinner table and stare into their phones and send text messages. Is that what you do?"

Maggie chuckled. "No."

"I didn't think so. I know there's far more to you than that." Tangel's head bobbed. "But still, people who date, don't they sometimes talk about what happened at their job that day?" Tangel looked at Maggie who stayed silent. "They do, don't they, Agent Coin?"

"Yes. Yes, they do."

"Right, I thought so. So if you're talking to Gilbreath about how many electrical outlets you happened to install in a given day or how many light bulbs you screwed in, and he just so happens to talk about what he's been doing at his job, all I'm saying is keep him talking. Encourage it. Nurture it. Give it room to grow. Fair enough?"

"Yeah, fair enough."

Agent Tangel stood and eyed Maggie. "Have you ever been to the lemur exhibit before?"

"No."

"You should check it out before you leave. Very intelligent

animal. Highly inquisitive." Tangel took one last look at the tiger. He was now sprawled on his side, napping in the late afternoon sun after his meal. "I'll be in touch."

Maggie watched as Agent Tangel strolled off towards another part of the zoo.

11. Target practice

RONNY MONROE STOOD IN AN INDOOR SHOOTING range boxed in gray cinder blocks, his hands wrapped around a pistol, his left eye shut tight, his arms outstretched, and squeezed off six rapid-fire rounds at a human-shaped target fifty feet away. The old saying, "You can't teach an old dog new tricks," has loads of merit to it. But Ronny Monroe didn't think that old adage applied to him.

Ronny lowered his arms as he glared out at what might be perceived to be his victim. He wheeled his target in to get the close-up, to pinpoint where his bullets ripped through the head and heart. When he saw that only one of the shots landed in the kill zone, Ronny's face went blank. "Shit," he moaned. And then he fixed his eyes on his left hand, at the empty space where his index finger once was. Ronny missed that finger. He missed the accuracy that trigger finger gave him—that comfortable, easy squeeze of the trigger that was so gentle it was really more of a kiss than a squeeze. Learning to use his right hand had been a chore—at work, at the range, and at home, where he couldn't quite dig out his boogers with the same authority he could with his left index finger. But life marches on, and Ronny believed he could march with the best of them. Ronny was indeed an old dog but he believed he could learn this new trick. He would. With all his heart and soul, he knew that he would.

12. Juice

HAT STRADDLED A SIX-FOOT LADDER in an office at the CDOT building at Thirty-Fourth and Lawndale, his head inside the drop ceiling where a two-foot-by-four-foot panel had been removed. Danny and Ziggy stood on the floor ready to feed telephone wire.

"You ready," Hat screeched. Before either Danny or Ziggy could answer, Franky Contino approached and grabbed Hat's ankle.

"Can I see ya for a minute?"

"Right now?" Hat said, as he looked down. "Like this very second?"

"Yeah, right now," Franky said with bite. "What the fuck? Like it's an urgent matter of life and death to get that wire pulled. Ya shittin' me?"

"Easy, Franky," Hat said. "I was only messin' with ya."

Hat stepped down from the ladder and walked out into the hallway, away from the boys, with Franky at his side. The two walked down the corridor and stopped. Danny and Ziggy edged up to the doorway and watched the two men converse for a bit. Hat then reached into his pocket and passed something to Franky. Franky shook Hat's hand and walked off. When Hat returned, he climbed back atop the ladder.

"What was that all about?" Ziggy said.

"That's about a buncha nothin.'" Franky was now gone from sight, but Hat's eyes wandered out into the hallways towards the spot where they had been. "Franky dropped another load on a bad horse at the track the other day. His cousin gave him another crapper. Don't know why he keeps listenin' to that guy." He pushed a second ceiling tile to the side. "I just floated him a few bucks to hold him over to payday."

"I've seen ya givin' money to other guys, too, before," Danny said. "In the ward yards. What are ya, a fuckin' bank?"

Ziggy laughed. "Yeah, his last name's really Chase . . . or Chase-arelli."

"Funny," Hat said. Ziggy and Danny continued to eye him. "What's the big deal? I mean, sometimes people need money. And sometimes I have money they can use. That's all. Nothin' big. But that ain't exactly your business now, is it?" Hat set his hands on a grouping of wires, ready to start the pull.

"Well, it might be mine," Danny said. "And pretty damn soon too. My wife just got the word that she's gettin' let go at the end of the school year."

"That blows," said Ziggy.

Danny flashed his eyes at Hat. "So I might just be hittin' ya up for a few loans in the future. Either that, or I gotta go get a part-time job."

"For you, brother," Hat said, "I'll keep the juice to a minimum." The three men laughed and began to feed and pull the wire.

13. Haag's Conference

REPORTERS, NEWSPAPERMEN, AND CAMERAMEN clogged the law library at Carl Haag's Bridgeport office—some standing, some sitting in the five rows of chairs Haag set up in his conference room. A handsome man nearing forty with golden tufts of hair, Haag looked out at the gathering from behind a podium near the back of the room, an easy, confident smile on his face. Mark Morgan stood to his right.

"I want to thank all of you for being here today. I'll speak for a bit, and then my client, Mr. Morgan, will speak as well. After that, I'll gladly answer any questions you might have. Please note that upon my advice, my client will not be answering any questions after he speaks. But, as I indicated, I will certainly entertain your questions." Haag sipped his water bottle. "Let me begin by stating that I welcome the opportunity to represent Mark Morgan on this matter. He's been a union electrician for almost twenty-five years, twenty of which he's spent as a city electrician. Mr. Morgan has worked hard over that time period and has always taken pride in his work. He's worked his way up into a position of leadership, serving as a foreman for the past seven years. A job like that has helped him provide for his wife and three children over the years. And then to have that job yanked out from under him because the city's administration has succumbed to the pressure of '*The Copper Caper*,' it's utterly despicable. My client is nothing more than a scapegoat. His head was placed on the chopping block because the city needed a fall guy. Well, I'm here today to say that my client is no one's *fall guy*. He *will* have his day in court. We look forward to our day in court. The city wrongfully terminated Mr. Morgan, and he will be compensated for the city's wrongful actions." Haag surveyed the crowd. "That's enough from me for now. At this time, Mr. Morgan will make a statement. Thank you."

Haag slid to the side to allow Morgan to take the podium.

"Uh, I'm not used to this, so, I'm kinda nervous. But Mr. Haag told me that if I wanted to make a statement I should. And I definitely wanted to do that." Morgan's eyes danced across the faces in the audience, and then he scratched at the collar of his checkered button-down shirt. "What happened at my garage was wrong. Someone stole those big spools of copper. And it was worth every penny of $50,000. But I didn't steal anything. It wasn't me. If I did that, then I'd certainly deserve to be fired. But I didn't steal anything. I was the foreman in charge of the supply room. But still, if my house was robbed, no one would hold me accountable. The thief would be the bad guy. But here, I'm the one who they're holding responsible. I'm the one they fired. I don't think it's right. It's not like I left the supply room unlocked. I think they should find the thief. The real thief." Morgan looked over at Haag, who smiled approvingly.

"I'm not gonna say much more other than to say, I'm sorry we didn't report the theft to the police right away. But that wasn't my decision. Along with the two general foremen in my garage, we all decided to wait on notifying the police 'cuz we were investigatin' things on our own. Maybe it wasn't the right thing to do. I dunno. But it's what we decided to do. See, we figured we'd have a better chance of finding the thief or thieves on our own 'cuz once the police got called in, we figured everyone would sorta go on shut-down, and the thief or thieves would get spooked. We gave ourselves a three-week window. If we didn't find the thief in three weeks, then we were gonna report it to the police. I guess that was the wrong thing to do, lookin' back on it, but we did what we did with good intentions. Not with bad intentions. And ya know what? You'd think the city would at least look into things a bit further, or see what the police come up with, now that they're involved, before they go and fire ya." Morgan blew out a sigh. "Well, that's all I have for ya. Thanks."

Morgan stepped away and took a seat. Haag again manned the podium. He faced his client. "Thank you, Mark. I appreciate your earnest words." He turned towards the media. "I don't think you can ask for anyone to be more forthright than that. And now if you have any questions, feel free to fire away."

"Do you have any idea who this 'Secret San Man' might be?" said a *Tribune* reporter.

Haag released a thin-lipped smile and eyeballed Jim White, sitting in the third row of seats. "Well, I think you might want to check with your press brother, Mr. White, on that." Haag laughed. "He's in a better position to answer that than I."

White chuckled and nudged the reporter beside him. "This is going to be a fun ride."

"Fun and juicy," another reporter nearby said. "No doubt about that."

14. Arnie Bigs

THE 33RD WARD YARD HUGS THE NORTH BRANCH of the Chicago River and is tucked away on the corner of Belmont and Rockwell on the city's Northwest Side, just down the street from where the grand old amusement park, Riverview, once stood. Hat, Danny, and Ziggy parked their van in the 33rd Ward Yard, nuzzled between a couple of Streets and San garbage trucks. Hat stepped out. Ziggy grabbed the clipboard from the dashboard and examined the jobs for the day.

"What's up?" Ziggy barked through Hat's window. "I don't see nothing on here for the 33rd Ward."

Hat set a hand on the van and leaned in. He spoke through an open window. "Just sit tight for a minute, Zigs. I gotta say hello to someone in here. Just take a minute." He then set his eyes on Danny. "Hey, Dan, c'mon with. I think ya know this guy I gotta see." Hat started off towards the ward building. Danny exited the van and made his way towards Hat.

"Who is it?" Danny said.

Hat stopped and waited for Danny. "Listen, I shoulda said somethin' to ya earlier on this, but anyways. I gotta grab some cash off a guy in here. Guy owes me some money. Just c'mon in with me and stand at the door and look big and bad. Nothin' more than that. Sound good?"

Danny laughed. "Is this a joke or somethin'? Who's in there?"

"Ya gonna do it or not?"

Danny's face went flat. "Yeah. Sure."

The boys pushed through a door that led to a breakroom. Seven garbage men sat at a wooden table. Six of the men were black, one white. The men were laughing and eating their lunch as Hat and Danny entered. Hat stepped in front of a rotund, black man. Danny lurked back by the entry door, where he folded his arms across his chest and leaned against a wall. The room went silent until Hat spoke.

"All right men, I gotta talk to Arnie Bigs for a minute," Hat said.

The others looked to Arnie Bigs. He smiled and took a bite of his Italian sausage sandwich. Red sauce dripped onto the table.

"Arnie Bigs don't like to eat alone. He like company," one of the others said.

"Yeah. Arnie say sometimes he gets scared iffin he eats alone," said another. "Says he afraid his sandwich might call the Po-Leece on him for assault and battery." The workers all laughed and one guy slapped the table.

"Okay. Fine. You guys can stay," Hat said. "And that's a funny joke, too. I'll have to remember that one." Hat pushed up beside Arnie. "You didn't return my calls today, Arnie. And seein' how you're late on that $1200 ya owe me, and seein' how today's payday, I think ya should answer your damn phone."

Arnie stared at his sandwich. "I was busy. I was on the truck."

"Well ya ain't on the truck now. Let's wrap this up. How much ya got on ya?"

"I got plenty," Arnie said and then set his eyes on Hat. "But I ain't got nothin' for you right now." The other workers squealed with delight. "I done gotta take care of a couple . . ."

Danny left his post and ambled over to Arnie Bigs. He didn't utter a word. He ran his eyes across every man at the table before boring in on Arnie.

"And jess what the fuck you 'posta be?" Arnie started. "You look like—"

Danny reached in and snatched Arnie's right hand with both hands, twisting it into a pretzel. The big man slid off his chair and fell to the ground with a thud. Danny still had his hand in his grip.

"Ya done broke it," Arnie cried. "It's broke."

"You got exactly ten seconds to pay this man," Danny said.

Danny released Arnie Bigs's hand. Arnie fished through his pants pocket and pulled out a lump of cash. Hat snatched it all. He counted it up and kept $1400. He returned $700 and some change to Arnie.

Hat smiled. "I took an extra two hundred 'cuz you gotta bad attitude." Hat nodded to Danny. "Plus I gotta tip my muscle." Hat erased his smile and ran his eyes across every man at the break table. "Don't ever ask me for a payday advance again, Arnie Bigs. You're out. You other guys all know I been fair to ya. I gave you advances before. It ain't good to try and hose the guy who feeds your damn family. Unnerstand?"

"And by the way, your hand ain't broke," Danny said to Arnie Bigs. "The ligaments and all are just stretched out a bunch. That's all. It'll come back to normal in a couple of days. A week, tops." The men remained silent, their eyes fixed on the table like a group of schoolboys awaiting a lecture from their principal. Hat nudged Danny, and the two left the breakroom.

"Don't ask me to walk into any more closed doors with you again," Danny said as they moved towards the van.

Hat grinned. "C'mon, that wasn't so bad." He peeled two hundreds from his wad of cash and gave it to Danny. "A little somethin' for the effort. Thanks. And next time, don't go tellin' 'im his hand ain't broke. Let 'im think it's broke."

Danny pocketed the money. "Yeah. Yeah. I shoulda listened to Ted way back when." He laughed. "You're nothin' but trouble."

The two joined Ziggy in the van.

15. Ignotz

THIS BRUSCHETTA IS OUTSTANDING," Danny said after he downed a bite.

"It is. For sure," Hat said. "But how 'bout the baked clams? C'mon. That's why I come to this joint."

A number of diners nibbled away on their food at Ignotz Ristorante at Twenty-Fourth and Oakley, a quaint eatery in the Heart of Italy's historic area, while others gathered in the bar area. Danny, Jello and Hat sat at a table near the front window.

Danny spoke with his mouth half full. "For sure. The clams are good, too. No doubt."

"You never get nothin' but good food here. Always good. Top shelf." Jello ran his eyes around the place. "And to think a Polack owns the joint."

Danny laughed. "That's a good one."

"I'm not shittin' ya," said Jello. "His name's Gasiorowski.

Danny gave Jello a look that suggested he was full of BS.

"I mean it. His name's Roger Gasiorowski."

"Gasiorowski?" Danny said.

"That's right," Jello said. "And hey, as long as we're on the topic of Polack stuff, I got a good joke for you guys. Wanna hear it?"

Hat stuffed a baked clam into his mouth. "Yeah, yeah. Let's hear it." Danny nodded.

"Okay, so this guy walks into a bar and orders a drink. When the bartender brings 'im his drink back, the guy says, 'Hey, wanna hear a good Polack joke?' And the bartender says, 'Hey look, buddy. I'm Polish. And see those two big guys playin' pool, they're Polish. And see those two guys at the end of the bar, they're Polish too. You still wanna tell your "Polack" joke?' And the man replies, 'Not if I'm gonna have to explain it five fuckin' times.'"

Danny and Hat roared with laughter. "Ahh, that's a good one," Danny said. "I gotta tell ya . . . I'm bad with jokes. I can't ever remember 'em. But I'll remember that one." He slurped some of his wine and slid another clam onto his plate. "But the guy who owns this place isn't really Polish, is he? I mean, you're just bustin' my balls, right?"

"No, that's the truth," Jello said, and then crossed himself. "The Gospel truth."

"But the owner's mother is from Sicily, right, Unc?" Hat said. "I think ya told me that before."

"That's right." Jello's head bobbed as he spoke. "From Sicily."

"Well, we know which side of the family coughed up all the recipes, huh?" Hat joked.

"For sure. For sure," Jello added. He turned towards Danny. "How 'bout you, Dan. Got any good cooks in your family?" Hat rapped his uncle across his chest and laughed.

"My family? Good cooks?" Danny flashed a thin smile as he pondered the question. Jello and Hat leaned back and drank their wine. "Well, sure. Hell yeah. My wife's a helluva cook. Her specialty is—the *baked* potato. Her maiden name's O'Donnell. They're all tremendous baked potato cookers from the way back days in County Cork." Jello and Hat chuckled and filled their wine glasses. "And my mother. Holy shit. She's the *boiled* potato specialist. No one can match her in that department. Absolutely no one." Jello and Hat continued to laugh. Danny joined them.

"Ya know, Danny, the Irish may not be known for their fine cuisine," Jello said, "but there's no doubtin' the contributions your people have made to this country." Danny squinted. He wasn't sure if Jello was setting him up for a joke or if he was being sincere. "I mean that," Jello said. "I think the Irish and the Italians are a lot alike that way. Policemen, firemen, tradesmen, politicians— there's Irish and Italians all over the place. The big cities were built mostly on our backs.

"I agree with ya, Mr. Pellegrini."

"Jello."

"I agree, Jello," said Danny. "But it makes me laugh when ya think about the way it used to be. Ya know, my ma tells stories about how everything was so separate in the old days. Sure the blacks and whites were always separate, but then even within the whites, everyone had their little pockets where they all lived. The Irish, the Italians, the Polish, even the Lithuanians . . . they all had their own areas on the South Side. And I don't know it for a fact, but it was probably the same on the North side and West side too."

Jello nodded and took down a piece of bruschetta.

"Anyways, my ma told me about how one of her sisters, my aunt Peggy, how it was when she married an Italian guy in the midfifties. She said everyone at the reception sat at separate tables on separate sides of the room and everyone stayed offa the dance floor and just kept poundin' booze and starin' at each other. And then, once they were all good and liquored up, it just turned into a melee—the Irish against the Italians. My ma said anything that wasn't glued down to the floor went sailing across the room. Even my aunt started throwing shit around. It was just one huge brawl."

Jello laughed. "I think I was at that wedding." He laughed again. "But she's right. That's the way it was, for sure. Separate." Jello raised his glass to his lips but stopped before taking a drink. "But it ain't like that no more. All the blood's been watered down. We all have our roots, our traditions, but we're not so different any- more." He sipped his wine and set the glass down. He eyed Hat, who nodded. Jello pulled a small, decorative dark-velvet box from his pocket. It looked to be the sort that could hold a ring or other similar piece of small jewelry. He placed it on the table.

"I got a little somethin' here for ya, Danny," Jello said. "I thought you might 'preciate it. I guess ya can say what I'm givin' ya here, well . . . it's sorta a symbol of our Irish-Italian tie, of our bond. And Hat told me how ya helped 'im out in that ward yard. That's good stuff. This is a way of sayin' thanks for that, too."

Jello pushed the box across the table towards Danny who picked it up. "I hope this isn't an engagement ring," Danny said with a smile. "Ya know, I didn't exactly picture ya for the switch-hitter sort."

Jello and Hat laughed and sipped their wine. Danny opened the box. Staring him square in the face was Ronny Monroe's finger. Danny was unfazed. He simply gazed into the box, his eyes unblinking.

"That's from Ronny Monroe from Summit," Jello said. "It's his trigger finger. He's a lefty."

"How'd ya get it to stay like that?" Danny said. "Still looks all shiny and new."

"Varnish," Jello said.

"Varnish, huh?" Danny nodded. "Good to know."

"Don't go puttin' that on no chain or nothin', now?" Hat said. "Can't go wearin' it around like a St. Christopher medal."

"Can I show it to my probation officer?" Danny said. Jello and Hat fell into a fit of laughter. Danny joined them but closed the box quickly as the waitress returned to the table with their soups. Danny slipped the box into his pants pocket.

"Here ya go, boys," the waitress said. "Minestrone soup." She walked around the table setting the soup bowls before the three men. "Minestrone. Good for the stomach. Good for the soul."

16. Mayor Stokely

MAYOR STOKELY AND RANDALL SAT on comfortable chairs in the mayor's office, watching a tape of Haag's and Morgan's comments from the press conference.

"I gotta tell you, Richard . . . Morgan surprised the shit out of me. He came across pretty damn solid. Definitely solid. He wasn't his usual dipshit self." Stokely pushed a hand through his hair.

"Haag has balls, letting his client talk like that."

"Haag can work wonders with anyone." Randall snapped off the TV. "But notice that he wouldn't let Morgan answer any questions. He can rehearse him and get him ready to make a statement, but there's no way he would chance leaving Morgan to think on his feet to answer questions. Not at this point."

Stokely stared at the blank TV screen. "Is this coming on the news tonight?"

"Yep. Ten o'clock. I checked, and all the stations will be running something. Roughly a minute worth. You know, some footage from the Haag press conference and a couple of possible Q and As from other city workers."

The mayor nodded. "I tell you what. I want you to get a hold of Cullinan and Flynn."

"Right now?"

"No. Hell no," Stokely said. "Not tonight. Get a hold of them tomorrow morning and have them come down to see you at nine-thirty. I might just happen to stop by your office about that time too."

"Gottit."

17. Graduation Night

DRESSED IN HIS FINEST PINSTRIPE SUIT, Tom Lonigan's hands squeezed the sides of the podium atop the stage of the Local 247 Union Hall on Clevington Street, gazing out at hundreds sitting on metal fold-up chairs. Roughly the size of a small high school gym, the wooden floor and the bright green walls also added to the hall's gymnasium feel. To the side of Tom, atop the stage, other union officials, dressed like dandies, sat and looked approvingly at Tom as he spoke. The most recent class of apprentices had completed its five-year program, and this was their graduation day. Tom neared the end of his speech as he looked out into the audience of proud parents, grandparents, husbands, wives, assorted other family members and new journeymen.

"I commend each and every one of you for havin' what it takes to become Local 247 Union electricians," Tom said. "Our program is by no means an easy program. You put in your time, and you made it." Tom smiled. "Some of you may feel more like you survived it."

Laughter leaked from the crowd.

"But whatever the case may be, you are graduates now, and you have much to be proud of. It's a great feeling. I know. I've been in your exact same seat. But that was a long time ago, and so much has changed with our union since then. Our union now has one of the highest prevailing wage for electricians in the country."

The audience applauded.

"Our union has put together a pension plan where the contractors contribute on your behalf and it's not a stretch to say that if you are around 25 to 27-years-old or so, which many of you are, you'll have about $800,000 in your pension fund when you retire at the age of 65, *and* your medical will still be in place for you and your spouse."

More applause.

"This is a great day for Local 247. This is also probably the last time that all of you from your pack will ever be together at the same time. As we wrap up here today, I'd like to get all sixty-two graduates up here in front of the stage for a photo. That way we can add your pack photo to the collection of all the other pack photos that sit along the back wall of this room. Also, I'm sure many of you are headin' out to go eat and celebrate when we wrap up here, but if you'd like to hang around here for a while before you go, the beer and snacks are on us."

The new journeymen and their families applauded.

"So, worst case scenario, have a beer or two here and then head out with your families," Tom said. He then let his eyes roam the crowd one last time. "And now if the Local 247 graduates, representing our union's 108th Pack, will step forward, I will present you to the crowd."

Tom waited as the graduate electricians gathered in front of the stage. He smiled like a proud father as they formed just below him.

"To you graduates, congratulations to each and every one of you. Please make every effort to come to our union meetings in the future which are always held right here on the first Tuesday of every month. That way, you can stay involved in the union and have your say on the path the union takes. Ladies and gentlemen, and graduates—remember that all things can be accomplished through unions. Ours and others. With a union, we stand united, we carry strength, we have power. Unions are a lot like family that way. Always remember, UNION, UNION, UNION.

The group applauded. Tom aimed his right hand toward the graduates.

"And now ladies and gentlemen, I present to you Pack 108. These men and women are no longer apprentices. Ladies and gentlemen, let's hear it for our sixty-two new Union JOURNEYMAN electricians."

The room erupted in applause. The union officials rose to their feet to commend the graduates. The members of the crowd joined the officials by also rising to give a standing ovation. Once the applause died down, a photographer stationed the graduates for their pack photo. Tom and the other officials milled about the room shaking hands with family members and the graduates as they returned after their photo. Detective Laski, one of the proud parents on hand for the graduation, approached Tom as the crowd thinned out.

"Hi ya, Mr. Lonigan, I don't know if ya remember me, but my name is Jim Laski. I'm the father of—"

"Billy Laski," Tom said, beating Laski to the punch. Tom extended his hand, and the men shook.

"Billy's a good kid. Real good kid. The guys at Devon Electric had lotsa good things to say about him. Quite frankly, he impressed the hell out of 'em during his work there during his last apprenticeship year. Did real well on his journeyman's exam too. Scored in the Top ten percent

"That's great," Laski said. "Didn't know about the exam results. He didn't tell me that."

"Doesn't surprise me," Tom said. "He doesn't seem to be the

braggin' sort. I never even knew he boxed until one of the other apprentices told me."

"Yeah, he had some good fights." Laski smiled. "Well, I just wanted to say thanks for gettin' my son in the program. He loves the work and he feels like he belongs. Definitely. And what more can we ask for as parents, right?"

"Thanks, Mr. Laski. I appreciate the words."

"You bet." Laski cleared his throat. "And by the way how'd everything turn out for your brother after he got clipped? You guys get that squared away?"

Tom narrowed his eyes. "What's that?"

"Oh, I was just askin' about the guy who shot your brother. Bad timing on my part. Now's not the time to—"

"Nah, that's fine," Tom said. "My brother told me you came by to see 'im in the hospital. Were you guys able to find out who it was?"

"No. No. Your brother said he didn't see the guy. Said he didn't have any idea who might be after 'im."

"That's what he said, huh?"

"Right."

Tom bobbed his head. "So no luck findin' the guy, huh?"

"Nah."

"Well, thanks for checkin' on that. Hopefully, somethin'll pop up in the future." Tom smiled. "And have fun tonight. Ya guys headin' somewhere?"

"Yeah. Since we're down here, we're gonna go to Carson's. I love the slaw in that place."

"I love that slaw, too, but I never heard anyone mention that as the reason to go there. It's always, *ribs, ribs, ribs*."

Laski laughed. "Got that right. I'll eat a slab of those too." Laski extended his right hand, and Tom shook it. "Thanks again for all you done, Tom. My boy's in good hands. Definitely good hands."

"Thank you, Mr. Laski. We'll keep 'im workin'. You can count on that."

18. Prose Forms

DANNY AND A DOZEN OTHER STUDENTS SAT in a semi-circle in their Columbia College Prose Forms class. Professor Rick Maypole, a forty-something black man with an infectious, booming laugh and a hint of gray at the temples, spoke.

"Okay. So we just heard that piece by Orwell. He's writing about what's familiar to him—his job. Basic stuff. He's talking about what it was like to be a jail guard." The professor ran his eyes through every face in the semicircle. "Now, we all have interesting things happen at work. And some, as we heard last week, are more interesting than others." Maypole thought back to some of the in-class readings from the previous week. He started to chuckle—but in short order that chuckle turned into a thunderous roar. Every student in the semi-circle started laughing. They couldn't resist. When Professor Rick Maypole laughed, you laughed. It was the natural order of things.

As his laughter ceased, Maypole took a deep breath and released a sigh. "So just like last week, I want you to take about ten minutes to write about something work related. This is just a start. You can work more on it later. Just get the words going for now. See it happening, right there in front of you. Keep the pens moving. And if you don't have a job right now, look back to a job you held at an earlier point in time."

"Anything goes, right?" a student asked.

Maypole smiled. "Of course."

"So if I write about the time I walked in on my boss doin' an intern," another student said, "that's cool?"

A few students chuckled as they broke out their notebooks.

"Sure," Maypole said. "Sounds like a scream."

The student nodded. "Oh it was. A real screamer for sure." The entire class laughed.

The students settled in and began to write in their notebooks. After ten minutes passed, Maypole had several students read in class. The last reader was about finished.

"Yep," the student said. "You don't forget days like that. It's not too often you walk into your boss's office and see her getting long-stroked by an eighteen-year-old intern. And then to top it off, when she saw me, she fell off of her damn desk and broke her wrist."

The class broke out in laughter. "Oh man, that was straight," another student said. "Straight. Well done."

"I wish my work had shit like that going on," another student added. "Hell, I'd pay to see stuff like that at my job."

Maypole chuckled and flashed his teeth. "Okay, who's next?"

"That's a tough act to follow," Danny said, "but I'll roll mine out there."

Danny had a definite buzz going from the numerous glasses of red wine he had at Ignotz before class.

"Does this one have any food in it?" a student said. "I mean, man, I went to that beef place you talked about last week, and it was good. Loved it. Best damned beef sandwich I ever had."

"Well, yeah," Danny said. "There's food in this one too. So I guess you could say it's kind of a food story."

"Okay, Danny. Go ahead," Maypole said. "Just about a page, okay?"

Danny nodded and read aloud from his notebook.

"So picture this. A buddy of mine I work with tells me that he went to get some good Italian food the other day at Ignotz over on 24th and Oakley. "So there I am, eatin' the best linguine and clams known to man,' my buddy says, 'and I happen to look up and I saw it. It was so surreal.' 'Whataya talkin' about?' I say to him. 'Well there I am in the middle of that great chow and my wife is sittin' across from me and I'm thinkin' about how she's gonna be all over me later that night when we get home. Toss a couple of red wines into her and she gets mighty frisky, if ya know what I mean.'

'Okay,' I say, 'so where's this all goin'?' 'So like I was sayin',' my buddy says, 'I look up and a few tables over, there're three guys sittin' at a table and one of the guys gives a little black, velvet box to the guy sittin across from him. And I'm thinkin', Hey this is cool. Pretty damn cool. These gay dudes are gettin' engaged. I'm about to nudge my wife so she can watch, but before I can, the guy opens the little box, and there ain't no ring in there and there ain't no medal either. It's a fuckin' finger. A chopped off finger. I just about tossed my linguine and clams, and then that got me to thinkin', who the hell gives a chopped off piece of a finger to another guy? It made me want to investigate, made me want to call up that weird detective from NYPD, or better yet, maybe I could dial up Columbo from the way back days and have him come take a look. My dad always loved that show. And then I wondered—a guy who gives another guy a chopped off finger, is he a man or is he a monster?'"

Danny stopped and looked up. "And that's as far as I got so far."

"So if I go to this Ignotz place," a student said, "think I'll see somethin' like that?"

Danny smiled. "Could be."

"Hold on a second," another student said. "Is that for real, man? I mean, did your buddy really see that?"

"I dunno. He's been known to tell a tall tale or two, so it's hard to tell."

"Well, I guess that telling typifies, literally," Maypole said, "what it means to give someone the finger." Danny laughed along with a few other students. "Okay, who's going next?"

19. Brotherly Love

THE LOCAL 247 GRADUATION CELEBRATION was a success but Tom now had other things on his mind. He curbed his car in front of Danny's house. It was 9:45 p.m. and the streetlights wove their white-orange glow across the brick bungalows that lined the block. Tom exited the car still clad in his suit and knocked on the side door to Danny's house.

"Hi, Tom," Kate said. She pushed the door open. "C'mon in."

"Ya know what, Kate, I can't. I just hafta pass somethin' along to Danny and get movin'. Is he home?"

"Yeah, sure. His class finished early tonight. He just got in." Tom nodded. "Hold on a sec and I'll get him."

Kate walked towards the kitchen. A few seconds passed before Danny came to the door. "Hey, what's up?"

Tom looked at Danny and then at his own hands. "Just wrapped up the graduation ceremony tonight. Good stuff."

"Cool," Danny said.

"Can you come out here for a minute. I got somethin' I gotta give ya."

"Yeah, sure." Tom walked down the slender gangway separating Danny's house from the next-door neighbor's house and went into the backyard. Danny spoke as he followed.

"Ya know, we can go in the house if ya want. I mean, I ain't got no shoes on and my tootsies are gettin' a little cold."

As Danny entered the backyard, Tom pinned him up against the back wall to his house with a forearm to the throat and fired two right uppercuts directly into his stomach. Danny buckled over, gasping for air.

"Don't ever fuckin' lie to me," he said under his breath. "Don't ever fuckin' do it again."

"Jesus. Jesus Christ," Danny said," still gasping for air. He straightened himself against the wall. His breathing was still labored. "What the . . . what the hell was that for?"

"Detective Laski was at the ceremony tonight. His kid was one of our graduates. Remember Laski? He's the cop who came to see ya in the hospital. The cop you said you gave all the info about Ronny Monroe to. You said he was goin' to see Ronny to see if he would give a confession. Remember that bullshit?"

Danny still breathed heavily. "Sorry, Tom. Sorry about that. I just didn't want to get ya involved. I didn't—"

"Just stop, already," Tom growled. "I don't wanna hear this shit? I want the truth."

"Okay." Danny sucked in a deep breath and stood tall. "Here it is. Well . . . for whatever reason, Jello Pellegrini's takin' a likin' to me. He—"

"Jello Pellegrini?" Tom twisted his face into a knot. "Don't even tell me you're hangin' around with that piece a shit."

"I'm not. I'm not," Danny pleaded. "I just met him through Jimmy Scarpelli." Danny rubbed his stomach. "So anyways. Jello had somebody go over and take care of Ronny."

"What'd he do?"

"He roughed him up a bit and then . . ." Danny stopped and took a few steps over to the gangway to make sure it was clear. He turned back to Tom. "Well, see . . . he chopped off a part of Ronny's finger. His trigger finger."

Tom's eyes bugged open. "Ya shittin' me?"

"No. That's what they done."

"But how do you know?"

"'Cuz they gave it to me."

"The finger?"

"Yeah."

"Still got it?"

Danny nodded. "They just gave it to me tonight."

Tom ran his right hand through his mop of gray hair. "Go get it. I wanna see it."

Danny hustled back inside his house. Tom checked his wristwatch, thinking about his next stop. Danny returned with the dark velvet case. He handed it to Tom who opened it.

"That ain't much."

"It's enough to get the point across, I guess. And Ronny promised to stay the hell away."

Tom's eyes were still fixed on the finger. "How'd they get it to stay all shiny like that? It looks—"

"Varnish."

"Yeah?"

"Yeah."

Tom snapped the case shut and returned it to Danny. "And by the way, Ellen's back home."

"What?"

"Ma and me brought her home yesterday."

"No one told me. I thought you guys were just goin' up there to see her."

Tom tugged on the lapels of his suit coat. "Well, she's home now. It's what Ma wanted. You should go see her."

Danny smiled. "Damn right I'll go see her. I'll go right now."

"All right, then." Tom shot his eyes down the gangway and then back. "Sorry about the stomach shot. Had to get it outta me."

"Nah. I deserved it. I shoulda told ya everything."

"It's done. Forgotten." Tom dragged his right shoe back and forth along the sidewalk.

"What is it? You still mad?"

"Nah. I just think maybe Ronny Monroe deserved a little more than he got."

Danny wagged his head. "Tom, it's all good, all done. We won't be seein' any more of him." Danny laughed. "Or his gun anytime soon."

Tom set his right hand on Danny's shoulder. "Ma musta told me twenty times yesterday and today how much she loved me."

"That's weird."

"Just wait 'til she sees ya. She'll let you know, too." Tom took a deep breath and released it slowly. "Her days are tickin' so she told me she wants us to know how important we are to her. That's how she sees it, Dan. She wants us to know that she loves us. She says it's important that we know that." Tom scratched his nose.

"And ya know what? She's right. That's important shit."

Tom ran his right hand through Danny's hair. Tears slipped from his eyes. "I want you to know that you mean the world to me. You're my little brother, and I'm always gonna be there for ya. Always. Until I croak, anyways." Tom licked his lips. "I love ya, Danny. Love ya."

Danny's face was blank. He had never heard such words or seen such emotions from his brother before.

"All right, that's enough of this sausagefest," Tom said. "Just wanted you to know."

"Thanks, Tom. Thanks."

Danny watched as Tom walked down the gangway. He stood still as a statue until Tom pulled away in his car. Danny entered his house through the side door and found Kate in the kitchen, a glass of orange juice in her hand. Danny was beaming.

"What was that all about?" Kate said and then sipped her OJ. Danny didn't answer. He just stood there, still beaming. Kate smiled. "What? What is it?"

"My brother just told me he *loves* me." Danny's smile disappeared. He swallowed hard and fought off the tears welling in his eyes. "Tom told me he loves me. Can ya believe that?"

Kate remained silent. Danny rubbed a hand across his face and quickly regained his composure.

"And he said that Ellen's back with my ma."

"What?"

"She came home yesterday."

"Are you joking?" Kate's face was full of teeth.

"Nah, she's back." Danny started moving for the stairs that led to the second floor but then stopped. "I'm gonna go see her right now. Okay?"

"Sure, that's fine. That's great."

"I might stay the night. You know how Ellen is. You know what she likes. I'm her favorite toy."

Kate's smile grew. "I don't know why, but all of a sudden I feel like I already knew this. Like I knew Ellen was coming home. I guess it's one of those deja vu things. And Ellen's coming home is going to be a Godsend. I can feel it. It'll be good for your mom, for everyone."

"Sounds good to me." Danny headed towards the stairs. "Gonna change into my pajamas. Gotta be ready." Danny raced upstairs, his feet pounding the wooden steps on his way to his bedroom. Kate sipped her juice and thought of Ellen, dear, sweet Ellen. How good it will be to have her back. Her smile grew even wider.

20. The Late Visitor

TOM LONIGAN, STILL IN HIS PINSTRIPES, STOOD at the side door of Ronny Monroe's home. He rapped his large right paw on the storm door and waited. The light over the door went on, and Ronny answered.

"Mr. Lonigan, what're you doin' here?" Ronny said. He checked his watch. "It's almost ten-thirty."

"Sorry to bother ya this late, Ronny. I just heard about the problem that you and my brother had. He just now told me what happened to your hand. I want ya to know I feel awful about it." Tom stared into the ground momentarily and offered his best sympathetic face when he looked up. "Oh, I'm sorry. Sorry to be standin' here ramblin'. Are ya busy? Am I keepin' ya from somethin'?"

"No. No, I'm just watchin' some ESPN before I crash for the night. That's all. C'mon in."

Ronny pushed the storm door open. Tom stepped inside and Ronny closed the door behind him.

"So you just now talked to your brother?" Ronny said with a squint.

"Well, I talked to him before, ya know, after . . . well, after everything happened. So I know about all that. But I didn't know about what happened to you, to your hand 'til today."

"Your brother tell ya 'bout it?"

"Yeah." Tom said. "Mind if I take a look? Can I take a look at your hand?"

Ronny held up his left hand. Tom moved closer and held Ronny's hand to examine it, his face filled with mock horror. "Ah, Jeez, that ain't right. Just ain't right." Tom continued to hold and examine the hand.

"Tell me about it," Ronny said. "I was just—"

Tom yanked Ronny forward and stuffed the remainder of Ronny's left index finger into his mouth. He gnawed on the finger until he bit off what was left of the nub. Ronny recoiled, screeching in pain. Blood poured from his finger. Tom spat out the chunk of finger to the floor.

"Now we're even," Tom growled. "NOW." Ronny jammed his nub into his shirt to stop the bleeding. Tom jabbed a finger at Ronny.

"Don't fuck with my brother again. Ever. And keep your yap shut, too, about my little visit. Do that, and I might just keep ya workin'. Fuck this up, though, and I'll be back to see ya. And you'll get lots worse than this."

Ronny continued to moan. Tom glared at Ronny and then spat twice on the floor to clear his mouth before closing the door with a thunderous bang.

21. Danny and Ellen

DANNY STOOD JUST INSIDE his mother's apartment. "Thanks for calling me," Mary said. "I was about to doze off. But thanks for lettin' me know you were gonna stop over."

"Where is she?" Danny said, after pecking his mother on the cheek. He turned and looked around. "Where's Ellie Mae?"

"I'm sorry, Danny." Mary frowned. "She had a long day. She's already asleep. She dozed off right after you called," Mary walked down her hallway. "But c'mon." She waved at Danny to follow. "Come take a peek."

Danny followed his mother, and the two stopped just outside

of a bedroom door. From the hallway, they peeked through the open door and in the shadows, Danny could see a body lying in a bed.

"This is great, Ma. I'm glad she's home. I'm gonna—"

Mary pressed her shush finger to her lips, and Danny stopped his words. They returned to the kitchen.

"I'm gonna have a cup of tea," said Mary. "Want some?"

"Sure." Danny sat at the kitchen table.

Mary set the kettle on the stove. Then she sat down with Danny.

"So how ya feelin'?"

"Feel great now that Ellen's here."

"You know what I mean."

Mary reached across the table and patted Danny's hand. "Well, I don't feel anything different. Not at all. Not yet, anyways." She tapped Danny's hand again. "Who knows? Maybe these medicine men don't know everything they think they do."

"That'd be nice."

"Ya know, I told Tom, when something like this happens, it definitely kicks everything into perspective," Mary said. "If it's okay with you and Kate and the boys, I'd really like to do more with you. I'd like to see more of you guys."

"What?" Danny barked. "Sunday dinner's not good enough?"

Mary went speechless. Danny laughed. "C'mon, Ma. I'm just jokin'." He smiled. "You come over whenever ya want, and I want ya to bring Ellie Mae too. It'll be great for the boys to see you more and to get to know Ellen."

"Thanks, Dan. I want you to know that we're gonna have fun these next eight months or so. You're a special boy, Danny. I love ya so much. And I—"

"Hey, Ma, stop. Okay?"

"What?"

"I mean, hearin' ya say that is great and all, but, well, ya know, Tom told me you were gettin' all soft and sappy on him. I just want ya to know that, you just told me once. That's good enough."

"No, it's not. You need to hear those words more often."

"Trust me. I don't. Once is good enough for me. I don't wanna hear it all the time. I know how ya feel. And if I kept hearin' it, I might just turn into a big pile of blubberin' man-goo."

Mary laughed. "Okay, I'll try. I'm not promising anything, but I'll try."

The tea kettle whistled. Mary turned the stove off and filled two cups with kettle water.

"Well, let's just let that steep a bit." As Mary turned back, she saw Ellen, dressed in her pajamas, standing just outside of the kitchen staring at her.

"Well, look who's come to see you, Danny." Mary flicked a finger towards the hallway. Danny stood and moved over towards the kitchen entrance. He saw Ellen, smiled, and opened his arms.

"Ellie Mae. It's my Ellie Mae." Ellen moaned and made excited sounds which could not be interpreted. Her hands moved in awkward circles as if she were conducting a symphony while on speed. She moved towards Danny and grabbed him by his hand, pulling him, leading him back towards her room.

"I guess I'll have to get that tea in the morning."

Mary followed after Danny and Ellen, a wide smile on her lips. Ellen pulled Danny into her room, and they both lay down in her bed. Standing in the doorway, Mary stared into the darkness. Ellen lay on her side and slowly ran her hands across Danny's face. The sounds she emitted grew softer.

"Good to see ya, too, Ellie Mae."

Ellen worked her hands through Danny's hair and then wiped away the tears that slid down his cheek. Mary was filled with joy as she watched Ellen—forever a mystery at forty-two, yet still the doting big sister, always ready to take care of her baby brother. Mary thought back to when Danny was a toddler, and he would awake crying in the wee morning hours. Mary learned quickly back then that the crying ceased whenever Ellen lay down beside her little brother and caressed his face. Dear, dear, sweet Ellen. And now, even though Danny was almost forty, he would always be the little brother to Ellen, that special someone who needed to be held, cared for, and protected.

"I'm so happy." Mary whispered. "This makes me so happy. I love you both. I love—"

"Stop it, Ma. Ya promised."

Mary laughed through her own tears and continued to stare into the room at her two youngest children.

Part Five

Blackjack

1. Hot Dogs

JELLO HELD A BRAND-SPANKING NEW PAIR of white Converse low-tops in his hands. He bent the shoes back and forth and twisted them a bit from side to side to break them in. A signal appeared on his laptop. Jello eyed the screen and saw Danny standing outside his office door. He pressed the buzzer, and Danny entered.

"Hi, Jello, Hat said you wanted to see me." Danny stood near the door dressed in a flannel shirt and jeans, his tool belt wrapped around his waist.

"C'mon in, Danny. Close the door." Jello walked to Danny and the men shook hands. "Ya like hot dogs?"

"Yeah, sure. Who doesn't?"

"Right. Right." Jello turned off his desk lamp. "Who serves your favorite dog?"

"Well, that depends on where I'm at in the city. If I'm up north, I'll go hit Wolfy's up on Peterson or Byron's on Irving Park. But if I'm—"

"Look, Danny, I'm gonna cut to the chase. Hat told me 'bout your wife, 'bout her losin' her job. That's tough stuff." Jello slipped into his Cons.

"Yeah, I know." Danny shrugged. "But we'll live."

"I know you will. I do. But still, I figured you could use a dog. Eatin' a good dog always helps." Jello slapped Danny on the shoulder. "Can't never hurt, right?"

"Right."

"So anywhere you wanna go for a dog—North, South, East, West—you tell me where to go, and that's where we're goin'?"

Danny laughed. "Okay, how's Fat Johnnies sound, over on Western?"

"You gottit," Jello said with a smile. "That's one of my favorites, too."

Danny dropped off his tool belt with Hat and Ziggy over in the phone closet, and then got into Jello's Towncar. As the two rolled along the road, Jello flipped the radio on and tuned in to WGN.

The host talked to a guest about the pros and cons of wind turbines as an energy source.

"Ya know, Danny, the Chicago Public School system, it's . . . it's always been a nightmare. For years now. Always seems to be on the edge of fallin' completely apart. And that's a damn shame. Truancy, bad graduation rates, gang problems, low test scores, strikes. They got the whole package. And the good teachers, the teachers like your wife, they can't fix all that." Danny nodded. "It's sorta a study on how *not* to run a school system. But it ain't all CPS's fault neither. Hate to say it, but lotsa times, they don't have much to work with. The kids they're gettin' aren't getting' much parenting. Teachers can't fill all the voids. And the state doesn't come close to givin' 'em the money they need."

Jello turned onto Western Avenue, heading South.

"I hear what you're sayin'," Danny said. "But the sad part is . . . well, my wife was making some good headway with her kids. Good grades, good test scores. It makes . . ." Danny scratched the back of his head and then looked out the window.

"Look, I wanna help out." Jello reached into his coat pocket and retrieved an envelope. He passed it to Danny who held the envelope but didn't open it. Jello laughed. "You got fingers. Go on, open it."

Danny tore an edge off. He saw a stack of $100 bills in the envelope but didn't count it. The car drifted to a halt at a red light at Sixty-third and Western. Danny looked to the left, towards where the old St. Rita High School once stood.

"Hey, look, thanks for what you're tryin' to do, but I can't accept this." Danny turned his head towards Jello. "It's very nice of ya, but truth is . . . I'm not a charity case."

"Don't look at this like charity, Danny. Not at all. Wipe that notion outta your head." The car continued down Western. "Think of it as an advance payment. Okay?"

Danny turned his eyes into slits and set them on Jello.

"Look, Hat said you were lookin' into maybe gettin' a part-time job. Well, you got certain talents that I like, and I'm willin' to pay ya for 'em. And you can help me out too. Ya know, we help each other."

"How's that?"

"You got eyes, Danny. You see stuff."

"Yeah, well, I see stuff, but I don't ask questions about it."

"I know. And I 'preciate that." Jello, tired of the wind turbine talk, snapped the radio off. "Look, I got different guys who do different things for me. Some guys drive cars for me. Some guys take pictures. Some guys pass messages along. Some guys break an arm or a leg for me. Some guys cut off fingers so they can be given to other guys in nice, velvet boxes. Ya know what I'm sayin'?"

Danny laughed.

"I take care of my people. I pay 'em good." He turned towards Danny. "There's five grand in that envelope. It's yours, even if you say *no* to what I'm askin'. Unnerstand? Even if ya don't wanna do what I'm askin', it's still yours. That'll help ya get through the summer if your wife ain't workin'."

Jello curbed the car in front of Fat Johnnies near 73rd and Western. The men looked out at the hot dog stand, little more than a plywood shack painted layers of white with time. A city garbage truck rested on Western, just down from the hotdog stand. Three garbage men stood in line.

"Hard to believe the best dogs in the city come outta this place," Danny said.

Jello laughed. "But they do. It's like the old saying . . . Don't judge a book by its cover."

"That's for sure," Danny said. "So whataya need help with?"

"Well, to get right to it, I gotta get one thing done and pretty quick. It's about sendin' a message. Nothin' crazy. See there's this guy who's been nosy as hell. So right now, he needs a broken nose. Ya know, an eye for an eye. Or in this case—a nose for the nosy. Nothin' more than that."

"Five grand for a broken nose?" Danny said. "So who is this guy?"

"You're not supposed to ask questions like that, but since this is your first time, I got no problem answerin' it." Jello stared hard at Danny for a second, ready to gauge his reaction. "He's a guy who's sorta been followin' me around, ya know, and taking lotsa pictures of me. And I'm gonna tell ya now, I'll always tell ya the truth. This guy, he's an investigator with the IG. We tried to play it nice with the guy, to get him to back off, but then he came back the other day to my office and painted the outside of my windows black so I couldn't see out of 'em. Fuckin' *manichino*."

"No shit?"

"No shit."

"Yeah, well, I saw the graffiti guys workin' on the building, but I didn't know what happened."

"That's right. They were gettin' that sludge offa my windows. It's all good again."

"So what would I have to do?"

"I told ya already. Give the guy a broken nose. Give 'em somethin' to think about."

"Yeah, okay, but how and where? I mean—"

"Hey, don't sweat that. That's the easy part. I actually stay outta all that. I set you up with a guy, and he walks ya through everything. First-timer like you needs a little direction, a little help. You guys work out those details on your own."

Danny eyed the envelope in his hand. "Okay. And if I don't do this, this broken nose thing . . . if I don't agree to it, you're tellin' me that you still want me to keep this money?"

"Absolutely," Jello said. "And look, you can always say *no* to any job, Danny. Any. But know this—if you say you're gonna do it, and ya don't, then that puts *you* in the crapper. Ya follow?"

Danny nodded as he watched a school bus drift down the street with kids barking out the windows. His eyes stayed fixed on that bus, as it ambled south on Western. He pictured Kate standing in front of a classroom filled with those same kids from the bus. She was in control of her class, the students fully immersed in the lesson she shared.

"I'll think it over," Danny said.

"That's fine," said Jello, "but try not to think it over too long. I'd like to get this thing done."

Danny laughed. "Tryin' to push me, huh?"

"I'd like it done quick, but I'm not gonna offer it to anyone else 'til I hear back from you." Jello patted Danny on the knee. "Just don't go makin' me wait half a year, okay?"

"No problem," Danny said, offering his most sincere look.

"Good." Jello turned the engine off. "C'mon, let's go get those dogs. I'm starvin'."

2. Jolly Ranchers

FLYNN AND CULLINAN WERE STATIONED ON CHAIRS in Randall's office in front of his desk. Randall leaned back in his chair, ran a hand through his perfect hair, and stared at the men in silence. Flynn and Cullinan coughed occasionally and fidgeted nonstop. Mayor Stokely pushed through the door, carrying a large bag of Jolly Rancher candy in hand.

"Well, look what the cat dragged in," Stokely said, as he plopped himself up on a corner of Randall's desk and reached into the bag of candy. He removed an apple-flavored piece, unwrapped it, and slipped it into his mouth. He swung the bag towards Flynn and Cullinan.

"Jolly Rancher?"

"No thanks," Flynn said, his eyes fixed on the bag.

"No thank you, sir," Cullinan added.

Stokely turned towards Randall. "How about you, Richard?" He rattled the bag.

"Sure, I'll have one."

Mayor Stokely pulled a Jolly Rancher from the bag and flipped it to Randall. Stokely turned to face Flynn and Cullinan. He sucked on his Jolly Rancher before speaking. The slurping sound he made reminded Cullinan of the clam chowder he ate for lunch the day before.

"I love Jolly Ranchers," Stokely said. "I especially like the apple ones. Those are definitely my favorite. Sometimes, when it gets crazy busy around here, I don't even go out for lunch. I just eat a bunch of Jolly Ranchers." The mayor stood. "And you know what, I know this might sound strange saying this, but in a way I think Jolly Ranchers are a lot like people. See sometimes I'll pull a Jolly Rancher out of the bag and slip it into my mouth, and it just ain't right. Something's wrong with it. It tastes funky. Who knows? Maybe it came out of the candy factory with a defect. So I got no choice but to toss that candy away. It's just something you gotta do sometimes. You cut your losses. You follow me?"

Flynn and Cullinan watched intently as the mayor took a few steps away from Randall's desk. Stokely continued to move until he stood directly behind Flynn and Cullinan, who stared into the floor. Stokely bit into his hard candy again and again, busting it into tiny slivers with his teeth. Flynn and Cullinan flinched with each and every mashing of that hard candy. To them, it sounded as if bones were being broken. They continued to fidget and shift in silence.

"Now sometimes, there's more than one bad piece in a bag," Stokely said. "It's a rarity. Trust me on that one. I mean I've been a hard-core fan of Jolly Rancher for over forty years, since the way-back days when they were made in a plant in Colorado, and I can say that during all that time, I may have had one or two bags where there's been more than one bad piece. Just one or two. And in situations like those, I don't keep trying each piece." He flattened his lips. "Nope. In cases like that, I toss the whole bag. That's what you have to do sometimes. Toss the whole bag. You just hafta do it. It's almost like it sets the ultimate example to the other Jolly Ranchers. You know what I mean?"

Flynn and Cullinan continued to shift uneasily in their chairs. Flynn pulled out a hanky and dabbed the sweat forming on his forehead.

"Now regarding this 'Copper Caper,' Stokely said, "according to Mark Morgan—he says that you three guys didn't report the theft of that wire because you were giving yourselves three weeks to investigate on your own. You guys saw the news on the TV, right? You heard what he said, right?"

"Yes, sir. I did," Cullinan said. Cullinan nudged Flynn.

"I saw it too," said Flynn.

"Okay, great. Now I already have an opinion about that statement. A very strong opinion." Stokely cleared his throat. "Quite frankly, I view that statement as complete and utter BULLSHIT. And I'm asking right now for you two guys to tell me the truth. When I say Morgan's statement is bullshit, am I right or am I wrong?"

"Well, sir, I—" Cullinan started.

"Hold on. Hold on," Stokely said. "Let me clarify one thing. This is the only opportunity you men will have to answer this question truthfully. If a determination is made down the road that you lied to me, you will be fired." He stared into the backs of Flynn's and Cullinan's heads. "Now I'll take your answers."

The men sat in silence for several seconds, doing nothing more than exchanging the occasional glance.

"Well?" The mayor jingled the bag of Jolly Ranchers.

"That statement is . . . well . . . you're right," said Cullinan. "It's bullshit. I made that up. It was my idea."

"Ted?"

"That's, right. Morgan's statement was bullshit."

Stokely walked around in front of the men. "Okay, look. I'm not asking you guys to lie for me. Not at all. All I'm saying is *don't* lie for Morgan. If you get pulled in by Haag at a deposition or if you have to testify in court, you tell the truth. That's all. It's damn simple. Tell the truth. Don't cover Morgan's ass and go along with that three-week investigation period bullshit. Are we clear, men?"

"Yes, Mayor," Cullinan said.

"Yes, sir," said Flynn.

The mayor reached into his bag of candy. "This is a good batch of candy I got here. You want a piece?"

"Sure. I'll have one," said Flynn.

"Me too," added Cullinan.

The mayor flipped a piece to each of the two men. Randall walked out from his desk and opened his door.

"All right, guys, thanks for coming down to see me today," Randall barked. Flynn and Cullinan took the hint and climbed to their feet. They meandered to the door and left in silence, their candy pieces in their fists. Randall closed the door behind them.

"Think that'll work?" said Randall.

"Yep."

Randall scratched an ear. "But you didn't tell them not to say anything about this to Morgan. The element of surprise at a deposition or trial would—"

"I think they'll tell the truth. That's what I think. And that's all I want. And if they clue Morgan and Haag in on our little siesta here today, that's okay with me. That's fine. See, Morgan already made his statement. Broadcast it on the airways for all of Chicago to see and hear. If he tries to change it because these guys tell a different story, the damage is done. He loses credibility. And if he sticks to his story, the damage is done, because two other guys are telling a different story." Mayor Stokely closed his Jolly Rancher bag by running his fingers along the zip lock top. "Either way, Morgan loses."

"Gottit," Randall said.

3. The Secrets of the Ceiling

DANNY'S EYES WERE FIXED ON THE CEILING, with Kate asleep at his side. Tonight Kate's sleep was a quiet one and Danny was thankful for that. There were nights when her snoring made him wonder how such a God-awful sound could come from his wife, let alone any woman. Her snoring was the thing of trolls, goblins and other such similar nightmarish creatures, but tonight those creatures were on vacation. The moon tossed a blanket of light through the multiple bedroom windows, spreading its arms across the ceiling. Danny combed his way through the assorted cracks and chips overhead, the imperfections that made Danny's eyes flare wide open.

Danny often found himself staring into his ceiling as he lay in bed in darkness. At times his eyes lurked in the dark corners, at times in the brightest spots supplied by the moon. Sure, the ceiling could provide a strange comfort of sorts, but far more than that— the ceiling provided answers. When you stare into it long enough, your mind opens, oftentimes far more than usual, and the information you seek starts to flow. Any longtime ceiling starer will attest to that. As Danny's eyes roamed his bedroom ceiling, images and thoughts often flashed before him, an old-fashioned slide show of sorts. And that's when Danny weighed the decisions before him. The night before Danny pled guilty to pummeling that rapist with a bat, he stared into the ceiling. When Danny and Kate almost lost the house trying to survive on her salary alone, Danny stared into the ceiling many a night. When Jimmy was born severely premature, Danny found a certain peace when his eyes roamed the ceiling. And Danny often saw his father in that ceiling, standing there with a knife in his hand. But on this night, as Danny eyed the ceiling, the only image that came his way was the mailman carrying a barrage of letters—bill after bill, piling up at Danny's door. As he opened one envelope, two more appeared. And that's what it felt like when Danny was indicted. They couldn't pay the bills. Danny sighed and glanced over at Kate. She was right, Danny thought. We would've lost the house if Tom didn't help us out. Danny turned his eyes back towards the ceiling. He waited for the next slide show, but nothing came his way. And then he saw an image working its way towards him—growing as it moved closer—Jello, with a hot dog in hand, sitting at a picnic table outside of Fat Johnnies. Jello smiled and winked at Danny, who closed his eyes and waited for sleep, a sleep that would not come for hours. And during that wait, Danny simply watched Jello devour hot dog after hot dog.

4. Hat and Franky

USING A WOODEN SPOON, JELLO PUSHED the peppers, onions, tomatoes, garlic, and chopped chicken around in a pan on his stove. Hat sat at the kitchen table, a glass of red wine in his hand, watching as Jello shook the pan, covered it, and turned the flame to the lowest setting. A framed portrait of Robert DeNiro as Jake LaMotta, sweat dripping from his embattled face, stared at the men from a wall.

"You gotta talk to Franky," Jello said.

"I know. I will," said Hat.

"You will, huh?" Jello poured a glass of red for himself. "That's what you said last week, and he still ain't paid up." Jello sipped his wine and then removed the cover to the pan. He poured a bit of red from his glass into the pan and stirred the ingredients as the pan hissed. "Five grand's five grand. He can't be—"

"I know, Unc." Hat sipped a bit more wine. "I saw Franky today. I talked to him. He said he'd have it tomorrow."

Jello jabbed the spoon towards Hat as he spoke. "He better. I already gave him extra time."

"He knows that. He's grateful. For sure."

"He don't seem so grateful."

Hat turned his eyes towards the stove. "Think it's ready yet?"

Jello removed the cover and stirred the ingredients. "Another minute." He replaced the cover. "You just make sure that Franky knows I'm gonna have someone say hello to his useless self if he don't pay up tomorrow." Jello ran his left hand across his forehead. "I mean it."

"He knows that. He does."

Jello nodded and set the wooden spoon down.

The following day, Hat stopped at the bank on his way to work. At lunch, he took the van and left Ziggy and Danny at the job site and drove over to the CDOT building. Hat found Maggie and Franky sitting on buckets, installing new receptacles in an empty office area. He snuck up behind Franky and started giving him a shoulder massage.

"Ooh, that feels good. Real good."

Hat looked at Maggie. "Don't she ever give you a good shoulder rub?"

"Her?" Franky said, and then wagged his head. "Never."

"You never asked," Maggie said and flashed a smile.

"He didn't ask me neither," Hat said. "But then again—who needs to ask. Everyone loves a good shoulder rub." Hat continued to apply his magic touch. "You oughta be glad I'm so nice to you,

Franky." Hat ended the massage.

"I am." Franky turned back towards Hat.

"C'mon," he said, "Let's take a walk."

Maggie watched as the men walked out the office door. Franky and Hat continued walking until they made it to the loading dock, far away from Maggie, where Hat turned and faced Franky.

"You got it?" Hat said.

Franky knotted his face and shook his head.

"Well, when? When?"

"He's my fuckin' cousin," Franky snapped. "What, he can't wait a few more days?"

Hat looked around. "Easy. Easy now," he said before turning back. "You're already three weeks late."

Franky scratched the back of his head. "I know. Look, I cashed in six grand in an IRA. The check's on the way. Should be here on Friday."

"Yeah?'

"Yeah."

"Okay, I'll let him know." Hat started to walk off but stopped. "Make sure you see me on Friday, okay? Not him. Come see me with the money. Gottit?"

"Gottit."

Hat left the dock area and made his way towards Jello's office. He stopped enroute and entered a small office, empty as the workers were out to lunch. Hat snagged a blank envelope from atop one of the desks. He removed a wad of cash from his pocket and slid it into the envelope before sealing it.

"Here you go, Unc," Hat said after Jello buzzed him into his office. Hat held out the envelope. Jello stood from his desk.

"All here?"

Hat nodded. "Yep, five grand on the head."

"Ya know . . . I don't think we should help Franky out, no more," Jello said. "I mean, it's for his own good. He can't go blowin' dough like that all the time."

"Just gotta get 'im to stop listenin' to Victor," Hat said. "He's the main—"

"Victor?" Jello snickered. "Fuckin *manachino*. He ain't had a good horse in two years."

Hat released a small laugh. Jello sat behind his desk and slid the envelope into a drawer where it became one of a number of filled envelopes.

5. Carl Haag

AFTER TAKING DOWN CHEESEBURGERS AND FRIES at Jimmy's Woodlawn Tap on East Fifty-Fifth Street, in the heart of the University of Chicago's campus, Danny, Ziggy, and Hat took their official rest break at Sixty-Third Street Beach. The boys flopped their bodies down atop the sand, ready for a nap. Lifeguards manned the shore, and a couple of swimmers enjoyed the water. At the far edge of the beach, several fishermen stood along the breakwall, their lines in the water.

Danny looked out into Lake Michigan, the waves dancing gently towards the shore, and climbed to his feet. He ran his hands across his shirt and jeans, dusting off the sand particles, as he walked away from Hat and Ziggy. Out of earshot of the others, he called Carl Haag on his cell. Haag's secretary put the call through.

"Carl Haag here."

"You're my hero," Danny said, using a falsetto voice. "Will you represent me, you handsome hunk of man, you?"

Haag laughed. "Who is this?"

"It's me, Danny Lonigan, you big bonehead."

Haag laughed again. "Danny, good to hear from ya."

"Hey, I'm just callin' to say you looked good on the ten o'clock news the other day. Good stuff. I definitely liked it."

"Thanks, man. Hey, the way I see it, Morgan got screwed. I'm just gonna see what we can do about it."

"I thought he came across good, too." Danny's eyes wandered out into the water. "This'll shake out good for ya. Hell, after watchin' the both of ya, I was ready to give you guys my piggy bank money."

Haag leaned back in his chair and dropped his feet onto his desk. "Anything in that piggy bank?"

"Couple of quarters."

"Well, I'm hoping the city's piggy bank is a lot bigger than that. And hey, I heard you're in with the city now. How's that gig goin'?"

"Can't complain. Pretty laid back. Definitely not bustin' my hump like I was at the last place."

"Good for you. Glad to hear it."

"Well, look Carl, nothin' big here. Just hadn't talked to ya in a while and I wanted to buzz ya and say hello and congrats on getting that case. Nothin' else. Good to see things goin' good for ya. You deserve it."

"Danny, look. It's funny you called. I was actually gonna buzz ya. I got a call from this guy at a big firm downtown. He wants to get together for lunch."

Hearing the word "downtown," sent Danny's eyes in that direction. They stopped moving when they fell upon the Hancock Building. Sure the Sears Tower and the Prudential were nearby, but the Hancock Building had always been Danny's favorite. He loved the way the Xs worked their way up the building from the ground floor to the top. He admired its blackness.

"Is this about jumpin' in with his firm?"

"I'm not sure, but I think so. See, Mike Smith put it together. He already works with the guy."

"No shit, Smitty huh?" A wide smile roamed across Danny's face. "I haven't talked to him in a couple of years. Not since the three of us did that Mueller case together."

"Yeah?"

"So what firm is it?" Danny turned back towards the beach as a gull wrestled with an abandoned French fry a few feet away.

"Murphy and Naughton."

"That's big time, Carl. Good for you."

"Well, here's the deal, the guy I'm meetin' with, I researched him. He's a couple of years older than us. Just on the other side of the forty fence. But I see he went to the same college you did."

"No shit. He went to CBC, huh? Who is it?"

"Thomas Terence Lyons. Know 'im?"

Danny laughed. "Yeah, I know that guy. Hated 'im with a passion in college. He was three years older than me. And he played on the basketball team with me too."

"This guy was a hooper, huh?"

"Well, that depends." Danny kicked some sand as he moved along the beach. "I'm sure he'd say he was. Truth be told, he was soft and couldn't, or wouldn't, guard anyone. But he could shoot a little bit. Anyways, all I ever heard outta him at school was how many points he scored every game and how much money his father had. You know the sort. North Shore kid from Kenilworth. Born to be a prince."

"Gotcha."

"But Murphy and Naughton. That would be a great move."

"Gotta wait and see what happens."

"Whatever ya do, don't tell 'im ya know me. That'll knock ya outta the box. For sure."

"Yeah?"

"I mean it. See, this clown used to brag about how his mattress was filled with money. I mean who goes around sayin' shit like that."

"Filled with money?"

"Yep. That's what he said. So anyways, me and another guy actually checked it out one time, and guess what? Lyons wasn't lyin'. It was filled with money. Parts of it, anyway."

"Ya shittin' me?"

"Nope." Danny laughed. "But here's the deal. That mattress disappeared shortly after that discovery was made. And Lyons, well, he never came right out and pointed the finger at me, but he let others know he thought it was me."

"South Side guys goin' to school in Memphis are easy to point fingers at."

Danny laughed.

"So, was he right?"

"Hell yeah, he was right." Danny waved his left hand near his ear to shoo away a bug. "Remember Tom Moran?"

"Ya mean, Bugsy? The guy who liked to bust ashtrays across his forehead?"

"The one and only."

"Yeah, yeah. Good man."

"So Bugs was with me. He was down visiting that weekend. We got bombed on a Friday night and went to Lyons' house when everyone was gone off to a big bash at some frat. We stole the mattress but we didn't take his cash. See, in our infinite wisdom, we just decided to set the mattress on fire."

Haag rolled into a fit of laughter.

"That's right. We carried the mattress out into Lyons's backyard and set it on fire. And then we just stood there and laughed our asses off watchin' that mattress and all that cash just burn up. Took off when we heard the sirens comin'."

"Ah, that's good stuff, Dan."

"Well, jingle me up after ya meet this guy. Let me know how things go."

"Sounds good. I'll talk to ya. And thanks for the info."

6. Big Pete's Bat

DANNY AND KATE WERE THERE—AT THE LITTLE LEAGUE game. They saw it happen from the comfort of their Cubs-emblazoned camp chairs, stationed along the third base line. And now that Jim was on an operating table at Little Company of Mary Hospital, Danny and Kate replayed the event over and over again in their minds. For Kate, there was Jim, standing in the on-deck circle at the Minor League field at Beverly Park, the sun pouring down on his shoulders, his face giving off an angelic glow. He looked out at the field, a perfect green, a great day for baseball. Danny saw Jim, standing in the circle, eyeing the pitcher and timing his practice swings with each pitch, already seeing his hit in his mind—a smash to the right field fence, and after he circled second base, he slid into third with a triple. And then it happened. Reality. It can play such cruel tricks with parental thoughts. Big Pete Conroy took a monstrous swing at the plate, and the bat came loose from his sweaty palms. As Danny and Kate watched, the bat seemed to move in slow motion once it left Big Pete's hands. But in reality, the movement of the bat was anything but slow. The bat twisted end over end, a crazed boomerang of sorts, until it met its eventual target—Jim's forehead. And the impact was not a glance. It was a direct smash—with the end of the barrel striking the center of Jim's forehead, just above the bridge of his nose. Had this been an old Western, some tooth-rotted cowboy in a dark hat would've said, "He caught one right between the eyes."

Jim's knees buckled, and he fell to the ground. Danny raced in from the third base line with Kate right behind him. Danny expected to see blood, but there was none. Whatever damage was being done was happening on the inside. Jim looked up at his father with eyes blinking spastically. He couldn't speak. Danny grabbed his hand. "You'll be okay, Jim. You're gonna be okay."

Jim turned towards his mother, blinked a few more times and then blacked out.

It's never a good sign when, after a loved one's operation, you are met by a doctor and a priest. The pair walked into the waiting room where Danny, Kate, Tom and Hairdo sat stationed along a wall. When Tom saw Father Tom Houlihan, one of the parish priests from St. Barnabas, he stood and started to weep. Tom sensed the bad news coming. It was as clear as the white collar on Father Houlihan's black shirt.

The doctor watched as Father Houlihan walked down the corridor with his arm around Tom's shoulder.

"He's in recovery at the moment," the doctor said softly. He looked at Danny and then at Kate. "We had to open up his skull to relieve the pressure on his brain. There was a good deal of fluid in there."

"Can we see him?" Kate said.

"Sure. They'll be moving him to a room on the ICU floor in about five minutes. Once he's settled into that room, you can spend as much time there as you'd like." The doctor smiled. "In fact, I encourage you to be there as much as possible. You know—talk to him, hold his hand. Let him know you're there. Things like that go a long way in helping with recovery."

"So, everything's gonna be all right?" said Danny.

The doctor opened his mouth, ready to speak, but then stopped. He mashed his lips together and pushed out a burst of air. "It's a brain injury, Mr. Lonigan. We had to open his skull. That's never a good thing. But he's young and in good health otherwise. The next two days are crucial and there's a lot that can go wrong. But I'm an optimist so, yes, I think he stands a good chance of recovering fully."

Danny offered a half smile. "Thanks for your help, doctor." He shook the doctor's hand.

To Danny, Jim's ICU room contained so many machines that hissed, barked and beeped, it looked as if—somehow, some way— the oxygen monitor, the ventilator, the IV machine—they were all living, breathing animals with movements and gestures of their own, animals with long black tails plugged into the nearest electrical outlet.

Kate stood beside Jim, while Danny dropped into a chair beside Jim's bed. Hairdo stood beside Danny, his right hand on Danny's shoulder.

"Mommy's here, Jim," Kate said as she caressed her son's hand. "Daddy too." Danny twisted in his chair, his eyes bouncing from Jim to Kate and then back again. And then it happened. Danny started shaking his head to and fro and then jammed his face into his hands, muttering, "*No, No, No*" nonstop. He then raced out of the room.

Hairdo caught him about twenty feet from the room. "What're you doin'?" He grabbed Danny by the arm. They were in front of the nurses' station, and the three nurses there tried their best to ignore Danny's outburst.

"It ain't right." Danny sucked in a deep breath. "I know what's gonna happen. I can—"

"You don't know shit," Hairdo barked, and then looked up.

Three pairs of eyes were on him. "Sorry," Hairdo said, his words aimed at the nurses. He led Danny by the arm and walked him to the end of the corridor. "Look, it's time to buckle up."

Danny's breathing became labored. "You remember my old partner, Linda, from when I first started working for the state's attorney's office?"

Hairdo shook his head.

"My bad, I thought you met her before."

"Maybe I did. I dunno." Hairdo felt like giving him a slap and telling him to get back into Jim's room. That's where he should be. "But what about her?"

"She was my partner, ya know, in the Criminal Appeals Unit. And, uh, anyways, she lost her son to leukemia. He was only three." Danny's chest heaved up and down.

"That's got nothin' to do with this. Nothin'. Look, Jim needs you in there." Hairdo corralled Danny again and started pulling him back towards his son's room, but then Danny dug in his heels. "C'mon, we gotta get—"

"When Linda told me about her son and the treatment he received and how he died . . . well, it wasn't like she just told me. I mean, we were working together for six months at that point, and she told me about her son when we went out for a few beers after work one day. She had to get to know me, I guess, to trust me before she could tell me something like that."

"All right. Okay." Hairdo leaned against the corridor wall.

"But what keeps banging away at me the most is the story she told me about how for two years after her son had died, she would still drive over to La Rabida Hospital once or twice a week and park in the lot and just sit in her car and stare out at the Lake Michigan waves rolling in and out. She said she'd look over at the hospital too, knowing that her son had so much enjoyed staring out through his hospital room window and watching those same waves tumble in and out. Just sitting there in that lot, alone in her car, taking it all in, Linda told me that that gave her a feeling of peace. And she needed that feeling, that peace to move on."

"That's tough stuff, Dan. I get it. But that ain't what's gonna happen to Jim."

"The really weird thing, though, is that when Linda was telling me that story back then, I couldn't help but see everything in live action. Ya know, just like it was happening right in front of my nose—as if I could reach out and tap Linda's son on his shoulder as he lay in his hospital bed staring out at those waves."

Danny sucked in a few more deep breaths and spat the air back into the hospital corridor.

"And just now, when I was in Jim's room, I could see Linda again, in that same live action, like she was a character in a movie. Just sitting in her VW Bug in that La Rabida parking lot. Parked in the first row in a spot close to the lake. And cars are flying down Lake Shore Drive behind her on their way downtown, but Linda's just sittin' in that car—lookin' out at the waves and at the hospital. She could give two shits about those other cars. Her eyes are starin' holes into the water, and she keeps turning from time to time to look at the hospital. And as I saw all that happening, the air starts getting cold and I can see Linda's tiny, cold breaths start to cloud the windows of her car, each breath removing another sliver of pain from Linda's innards and replacing it with peace."

Tears rolled down Danny's face. He took in another long, stuttered breath.

"And then I couldn't see Linda so good cuz the windows were gettin' all fogged up. So I moved in closer. And when I peeked in that VW, Linda wasn't in there. But Kate was. She was the one sittin' behind the clogged windows. She was the one kickin' out the cold breaths."

7. The Pump Room

CARL HAAG, THOMAS TERENCE LYONS, and Mike Smith stabbed their forks into their desserts at the Pump Room on State Street. With their tassled shoes, pinstripe suits, and power ties, all three men were dressed as if they're ready to present a case to a jury or head off to a high-end wedding reception. A violinist moved about the room, stopping at tables to play with a look of utter wonderment on his face. He was a violinist, after all, and as every violinist knows—their music is indeed the sound of wonderment. Like most folks from blue-collar backgrounds, Haag had never eaten at the Pump Room. To call it upscale would be to call Wrigley Field old. Haag enjoyed the various courses of salad, soup, meat, and octopus, but he could do without the dessert— English cucumber cake. Though he was a Pump Room newbie, he would be back. He had already made that decision, long before the cucumber cake was set in front of him.

"Well, Carl, I appreciate you taking the time to meet with me," Lyons said. "Our firm has taken notice of the work you've been doing. Quite frankly, we've been very impressed. There may definitely be a way we can join forces."

"I'm interested" Haag said. "Definitely interested."

"I'm sure you are," said Lyons. "It's not every day someone gets the opportunity to join our firm."

"I understand."

"If you would like, I'll be glad to set up a meeting with a couple of other partners. They'll cover our compensation plan and benefits package."

"That'll work. I look forward to it." Haag watched the violinist as he stopped at the table beside theirs to play a slow-moving, sad song.

"And I think you'll enjoy our clientele as well," Lyons said. "Definitely upscale." He laughed. "A definite upgrade for you."

Haag released a thin smile. "Now what's that supposed to mean?"

"What?"

"That 'upgrade' comment."

Smith tugged on his tie and jumped on the grenade. "You know, Carl, I think what Thomas Terence was saying is—"

"Hold on, Smitty," Haag snapped. "I'd like to hear from Tommy Boy himself on this one."

"I don't go by, 'Tommy Boy'."

"I know." Haag stared a hole into Lyons. "So tell me about this 'upgrade.'"

Lyons laughed again. "Come on now, Carl. I like your spunk, but is this a great mystery or something? All I'm saying is that the clients you would have at Murphy and Naughton would be . . . well, they would be people of a better ilk."

"A better 'ilk,' huh?" Haag narrowed his eyes and laughed. "I gotta write that one down. I'm bettin' that word hasn't been used by anyone since the mid-eighteenth century."

Haag leaned across the table. "Look, I represent blue-collar people 'cuz that's who comes to me, and they come to me cuz they know my roots. I'm one of them. They trust me. My brothers, my cousins, they're all working men, tradesmen. Don't insult me or them with your 'upgrade' and 'ilk' comments. That's a fricken joke." The violinist moved toward their table. Haag froze him with his angry eyes. The violinist took the hint and moved along to another table. "If I had a glove, Thomas Terence, I'd slap ya with it right now. Isn't that how you people of 'ilk' do it?"

"Suit yourself, Carl," Lyons said. "It's your loss."

"Nah. It's not. Not really. It's yours." Haag stood and dropped $300 on the table. "That'll take care of lunch, boys." Haag smiled. That's some of your old college mattress money, Tommy Boy, courtesy of Danny Lonigan." Lyons stared at Haag quizzically. "And one last thing. If ya ever see me in the future, Tommy Boy, make sure I don't see you. 'Cuz if I do, I'm gonna rip that silver spoon outta your yakker and shove it up your pasty, white ass."

Haag moved for the exit but stopped en route to stuff a ten-spot into the violinist's shirt pocket.

8. Hospital

AFTER SEVEN DAYS IN THE ICU, Kate was convinced that the brain surgeon was not a good prognosticator. Still in an induced coma, Jim experienced very little change. Though Jim's oxygen readings were steady, the ventilator still did most of his breathing.

Neither Danny nor Kate left their post in Jim's room other than to visit the restroom or to get food. Tom brought fresh clothes each night when he came to visit. Hairdo, Ziggy, and Hat also stopped by the hospital most nights, and as Hairdo witnessed Jim's failure to improve, he started to wonder if perhaps Danny's vision was going to come true. Several of Kate's former coworkers stopped by to visit and support Kay. Sure Kate was worried sick about Jim, but she also started to grow concerned about Danny. He was slinking away into shutdown mode, something Kate had witnessed two-years before—after Danny was indicted on the aggravated battery charge. Kate had prodded and questioned Danny back then, but all he really did was offer a grunt or groan. And now those same grunts and groans were coming Kate's way, though once Danny seemed to force himself to say, "Let's see what the doctor says," after Kate riddled him with questions. How enlightening, Kate thought after Danny offered his six-word comment. And then Danny abruptly jumped to his feet and stared down at Jim, tears welling in his eyes.

"Do you know something I don't?" Kate had asked at that moment.

Danny could only stare at her with a confused look, a look that said both "what the fuck are you talking about?" and "leave me the fuck alone" at the same time.

"No. No. I don't know anything," Danny finally muttered. But Danny knew something. Kate was convinced of that.

On day eight, Dr. Battista rushed into Jim's room with the latest results from Jim's brain Cat scan.

"Can you come with me, please," Battista said, forcing a smile. Kate and Danny followed Battista into a room where assorted X-rays pulsated along the wall.

"Your son has a piece of bone lodged in his front lobe." Battista tapped the X-ray with a pencil. "Right here. It's a small piece. Extremely small. We couldn't see it before because of all the fluid in the area. But now that most of that is gone, we can see it."

"So what's this mean?" Kate said.

"I'm not exactly sure yet," Battista offered. "It could be the reason why his condition hasn't improved." Battista stuffed the pencil into his shirt pocket. "We need to remove it."

Kate looked at Danny. His eyes were still fixed on the X-ray. "What are the risks?" said Kate.

"There are always risks," Battista said.

"I understand that, Doctor," Kate said, "but I'd like to hear what they are specifically from you."

As Battista offered his list, ranging from full recovery to becoming a complete vegetable, Danny exited the room and hustled back to Jim's bedside. Again, images of Linda Bettis, her son, and the small, cold breaths in the car took hold of Danny's thoughts. He dropped to his knees beside Jim's bed and clasped his hands in prayer. His words were a whisper.

"I never asked you for anything, Dad. Never. But I'm askin' now. You gotta help Jimmy. You gotta. Put the word in. You gotta help us." He crossed himself and removed the St. Christopher's medal from his neck. Kate and Battista entered Jim's room just as Danny finished wrapping his medal around his son's right ankle.

9. Prayers

WHY IS IT THAT SOME PRAYERS ARE ANSWERED and others are not? How come some parents get to bring a child home from the hospital while others watch in agony as their child coughs out his or her last breath? Questions without answers. The list is endless. In Jim's case, he came home exactly ten days after the doctors re-opened his skull. The following day he was walking around the neighborhood with Kate, and he started his physical therapy classes shortly after that. The doctors were extremely pleased with Jim's recovery, saying that he was far ahead of schedule. Danny rarely mentioned his father in Kate's presence, but he told her that he was convinced his father had helped. "About time he did something for me," Danny joked as he cooked steaks on his back deck about a week after Jim returned home. Kate didn't know if Danny's father played a role in Jim's recovery or not, but she was damn glad to see a smile on her husband's face. Danny's St. Christopher medal was now a fixture on Jim's neck, and the only remnant of the operation was the sideways U-shaped scar on Jim's head.

When the bills started to roll in, Danny collected them and kept them from Kate. Her school year was over, her insurance coverage gone. Before Jim's accident, Kate had already declined the expensive COBRA coverage. Danny now wished that they had that coverage. Sure his insurance was taking care of a large portion, but there was still a sizeable amount due with more on the way. When Danny received the bill for the doctor's services for the first brain surgery, he grabbed his cell phone and put in a call to Jello. "Count me in," was all Danny said.

10. Kelly's Tavern

A NEIGHBORHOOD INSTITUTION AS IMPORTANT to the locals as St. Gabe's Catholic Church, Kelly's Tavern stands at Forty-Fourth and Wallace, and there, many a great Canaryville mind has spent time perched on a barstool. Jankowski always held an affinity for Kelly's. He grew up in the Canaryville neighborhood, on Chicago's Near South Side, where tarpaper shacks sprouted like weeds from the cracks in the cement, and where homeowners—some with a tooth or two missing—sat on their front stoops smoking and glaring at anyone or anything that appeared to be out of place. Legend has it that many a stray cat and wandering squirrel had been caught and pummeled to death by Canaryville's best stoop-sitters because "it just didn't belong." So should you decide to venture into these hallowed neighborhood streets, consider yourself forewarned.

That being said, the recent years have brought significant

change to Canaryville. Newer houses, including a mini-mansion or two on double or triple lots belonging to those with friends in high places, now stood beside the tarpaper shacks. Jankowski's father, a house painter who spoke broken English, raised his family in a Canaryville shack, and he took young Al to Kelly's on many an occasion. He also insisted that his son achieve all As in English on his childhood report cards or face the belt. Jankowski still speaks and writes the king's English perfectly, but even he had moved on—out to Orland Park, where some carry a notion that a neighborhood tavern is the local Applebee's. So when Jankowski called Danny Lonigan to schedule a meeting, he suggested Kelly's. It was a no-brainer, especially since Danny's workplace was less than a mile away.

Jankowski and Danny sat at the far end of the bar and enjoyed sharing stories of their high school days, bottles of beer in front of them. They especially enjoyed throwing playful darts at their former coach, a man they both respected.

"Before games, in the locker room . . . he just always looked like he had to take a gigantic dump," Jankowski said. "His face was so red, so tight. Like a balloon ready to pop. Always."

"Probably did," Danny added. "He'd disappear about ten minutes before each game started. Maybe that was his deuce time."

The men clanked their bottles. "To Chuckie—one helluva coach," Danny said. "And to Chuckie's deuce time." The men downed their beers. The bartender brought fresh bottles.

"I hear your son's doing lots better, huh?"

"Yeah, he's, uh . . . he's really making some big strides. Started shooting free-throws in the back alley over the weekend."

"Crazy shit," Jankowski said as he slurped his beer. "The bounce-backability of youth, huh?"

"Got that right."

Jankowski ran his right hand across his lips. "Okay, so Jello wants me to give you the lowdown on this IG guy."

Danny nodded.

"His name is Clark Phipps. Most everything you need to know about him is in here." Jankowski passed a large white envelope to

Danny, who started to open it.

"Not here," Jankowski said. "Check all that out at home." Again Danny nodded. "This thing's long overdue. But Jello told you he'd wait on you, and that's what he did." Jankowski tossed a peanut into his mouth. He crunched the shell.

"You eat the damn shells?"

"Oh yeah. Love it." Jankowski smiled. "It does wonders for your shits. Nice and full of fiber."

Danny downed some beer.

"Okay, look, in that envelope you'll find photos, and some other shit. His address is in there, his routine, everything you need to know, basically."

"Okay."

"Since this is your first time, I'll make a few suggestions. Okay, so take a couple of days to actually follow this guy around a bit, to confirm his routine. After you do that, I think you'll see that the best place to visit him would be at the Northwest corner of Marquette Park when he's jogging. You say hello to his nose there and when he goes down, you flip the fence and sprint around the corner to Marquette and Central Park, on the far side of the viaduct, and a car will be waiting for you, ready to take off southbound." Jankowski took a moment to examine Danny, whose eyes were fixed on the envelope. "That's how I'd do it if I were you. Doesn't mean that's the way you have to do it, though."

"How do I set things up with this car guy?"

"There's a number in there. You call it. He answers but doesn't say much of anything. You tell him a time and place to meet, and *presto*—he's there."

"This is kinda like movie shit," Danny said with a thin-lipped smile.

"It's a job, Danny. That's all. A job."

Danny nodded.

"There's also a business card in that envelope. You need to leave that with the guy. So obviously, you need to wear gloves when you look through this shit. And when you do the job. And once you're done looking things over and setting up your ride, you got to burn the contents. Understood?"

"Yep."

"So?"

"Sew buttons on your underwear," Danny said.

Jankowski wagged his head. "Lame-O."

"It's what came to me. It's what my dad used to say whenever I hit him with a 'So?'"

Jankowski took another slug. Danny did the same. "Just keep it simple, Dan. Nice and simple."

11. Tom's Garage

TOM LONIGAN'S HOUSE AT 106TH AND WHIPPLE in Mount Greenwood was a smallish raised ranch, a relative of so many other similar homes in the area. But what was atypical about Tom's property was what stood at the back of Tom's small lot—his oversized, double-decker garage. If you stood outside of this massive, brick structure on a weekend day or on a Monday or Thursday night, you'd hear grunts and groans and words that could probably best be described as barks. Perhaps you would nudge a bit closer to take a peek through the lone window in the garage to see if someone was filming a porno inside. But you would be wrong.

To the various young boxers in training from the ages of ten to eighteen, Tom Lonigan's garage served as their home away from home. Some came from Beverly and Mount Greenwood, while others hailed from all parts on the South Side. Tom's garage was where they came to work at their craft, to get what they needed to climb the ladder, to stay off the streets or to simply keep their head on straight.

A boxing ring sat in the center of the ground floor, and two heavy bag stations and two speed bag stations were spread about nearby. Upstairs were four stations—two jump rope and two bench press. Boxers manned every station. Most days, Tom's longtime friend, Denny Freyer, covered the stations upstairs, a half-smoked cigar always resting in his lips. Hairdo was also a regular at the garage—as was Billy Laski, with both men coaching-up the boxers at the speed bag and heavy bag stations whenever they were around. Tom always worked with the boxers in the ring. He checked his stopwatch and slipped a whistle in his mouth. He blew it twice and barked, "Time."

What happened next was pure precision. The boxers rotated quickly to their next station—feet sliding to the next station and gliding up and down stairs. And then the movement stopped, and each boxer stood frozen at the ready. Tom blew his whistle again. This time—once. Always once to start the station. Always twice to end the station work. The boxers all started their next station.

Tom roamed about the bottom floor barking at the boys dripping with sweat. "Okay, let's go. Let's work. Make yourself tougher. Make yourself better."

Tom believed in the benefits of hard work, and he instilled that belief in his boxers. Some entered Tom's program thinking it was okay to coast but soon came to understand that when you took things easy, you only cheated yourself. "And it ain't good to cheat anybody," Tom would bark. "Most definitely not yourself." The boys admired Tom and they all knew that behind his gruff exterior stood the soul of a softie—a man who would do anything to help any and all of them. Like Freyer and Hairdo and Laski, the boys all grew to love Tom.

12. Nose Job

BORDERED BY CALIFORNIA AVENUE ON THE EAST, Central Park on the West, Marquette Road on the north and Seventy-First Street on the south, Marquette Park measures a mile long and half a mile wide. A lagoon carves its way through the park, and on most warm days, you'll find a number of fishermen in the shade along the banks with rods in hand. And if you happen to be a duffer, Marquette Park's nine-hole golf course might just be the place for you. But beware—thanks to a huge gathering of our long-necked, flying friends, this course holds the record in the city for the largest gathering of goose pellets per square foot. There: you have been warned. A lazy, curved road winds through the park as well, manned by cars, motorcycles, power walkers, and joggers.

Just across from the park, at Seventy-First and Talman, a sad piece of Chicago history once stood—the one-time home of Chicago's Nazi Party, complete with swastikas emblazoned on the building. The Nazis brought Marquette Park into the national limelight in the mid-seventies, when they led the racial clash against a group of black marchers who dared to enter the park. As you could expect, things didn't go well and it was all right there on the tube—the marchers, the Nazis, the angry protesters, the bricks, the stones, the Niggers Go Home signs, the cops in riot gear.

The summer is never a time for hooded sweatshirts, but if you are a jogger looking to lose weight, anything goes. That's the look Danny went for. Clad in a dark hoodie with a Sox hat pulled tight over his head, Danny's eyes could barely be seen. Phipps was clockwork, easy to follow. Danny had observed him for three days. He always left his home at Sixty-Sixth Place and Lawndale at 6:50 p.m., jogged along the sidewalk outside of the park along Marquette Road, and then entered the park at Marquette and Kedzie, where he headed west along the interior park road to start off his three-mile loop. Phipps wore headphones whenever he ran, and Danny liked that. It was another distraction he found in his favor. As Phipps approached the northwest corner of the park, Danny jogged towards him with his head down. When Phipps rounded the turn to begin heading south, Danny was there to greet him, jogger turned assaulter, with a right hook to Phipps, well-developed nose, a punch that sent Phipps reeling into the grass. As blood poured from Phipps's nose, Danny dropped the business card on his back and then raced to the fence and hopped it. He sprinted through the viaduct, and when he reached Central Park, a black sedan, parked along the viaduct wall and aimed south, was waiting for him. Danny jumped into the backseat, and the car shot down the street.

"Thanks for your help," Danny said. The driver stared straight ahead and remained mute. Danny could see the black skin on his neck, his jaw, his ears. He didn't try to see any more than he should. He didn't move around to catch sight of the driver's face in the rearview mirror. About ten minutes later, the driver curbed the car at the Thirty-Fifth Street L station. To one side of the Dan Ryan expressway assorted Illinois Institute of Technology buildings stood tall while White Sox Park rose into the sky to the west. As Danny exited the car, he glanced at the driver as he passed and then turned nonchalantly as if he hadn't seen a thing. But he had. The driver was one of the electricians from his garage, a man named Davis Winslow.

After Danny boarded the Red Line train towards 95th Street, he reviewed everything that had just taken place, step by step, searching for flaws. Though not one for gloating, he felt good about how things had gone off. He did not find a single flaw. Piece of cake, Danny thought to himself. I can do this. Shit, yeah, I can do this. And Danny didn't feel bad about breaking the man's nose. Why feel bad? Danny thought. Five grand is five grand, and I've had loads worse done to me. As the train rumbled along the track, Danny reached across the aisle and grabbed a newspaper abandoned by a previous commuter. He snapped open the *Daily Southtown* to check the MLB box scores.

13. Lacrosse

MAGGIE SAT ALONE ON THE VERY TOP ROW OF LANE Tech stadium watching the home team square off against Evanston High School in a summer lacrosse game. The stands were sparsely populated. At the start of the second quarter, Agent Tangel, dressed in his customary fashionable suit and tie, joined Maggie. He held a bag of popcorn in his hand and offered some to Maggie as he took a bleacher seat.

"No, thanks," Maggie said. She turned her eyes back towards the field.

"Fantastic sport, isn't it?" Tangel said.

"I've never seen a game before, but I love it. Lots of action."

"The game was invented by Native Americans, Agent Coin." Tangel slipped some popcorn into his mouth and spoke while chewing. "They obviously played for enjoyment, but the game was also played, at times, to resolve differences amongst various tribes and to prevent wars."

A midfielder raced upfield with the ball in his stick. "Wow, I had no idea."

"You can always count on me to make you smarter." Tangel slid more popcorn into his mouth. Maggie laughed. "So what do you have for me?"

"Well, I did what you said to do," Maggie said. "I kept Ed talking at dinner, just the other day. And he told me that one of his investigators got jumped just the other day when he was jogging through Marquette Park. The investigator got his nose busted up."

"Okay. So?"

"So the investigator had been following Pellegrini around taking photos of him. And one day the investigator finds a bunch of pictures of him and his family in his own mailbox. Some of the photos were taken from inside their home."

"And let me guess . . . Gilbreath thinks it's Jello who's doing this, right?"

"Well, yeah. Sure. But also, when the investigator got his nose broke that day, the perp left a blank business card on top of him which said, basically, 'Don't be so Nosey.'"

"Don't be so Nosey?"

"That's right."

"That some ultra-clever shit." Tangel looked at Maggie. "Handwritten or typewritten?"

Maggie sucked on her bottom lip. "Not sure on that one. All I know is Ed's worried. He had the investigator's family move in with some other family members for now. And his kids are going to new schools when the school year starts."

"That's a good move. Play it safe."

"Right. I agree."

Tangel turned his eyes out towards the field as the parents in attendance hooted and hollered after an Evanston goal, knotting the game at three apiece. "Look, we're getting you transferred in to work with Scarpelli."

"They don't have four-man crews working out of one van, Agent Tangel."

Tangel smiled. "I know these things, Agent Coin. Believe me, I do." He slid some popcorn into his mouth. "Zignacio Ramirez will be transferred to O'Hare in the very near future. You will have the pleasure of taking his place. Our intel should come even faster then."

"Yes, sir."

Agent Tangel rose. He folded the popcorn bag at the top and placed the bag in Maggie's lap. "You need some popcorn, Agent Coin. Believe me, you do. It's like the modern-day Cracker Jack. There's a surprise in every box, or in this case—bag." Tangel looked out at the field. "And don't stay here too long. These two teams are solid but still—Loyola's the team, Agent Coin. Loyola. They win the state title nearly every year. And they look like champs again this year. You can bet the house on that one."

Maggie stayed put as Agent Tangel walked off. She searched through the bag and found a small velvet pouch tied at the top by a golden string. She opened it. Inside was a mock plastic wedding ring and a note. Maggie unfolded the note.

"Another prediction—Gilbreath will be shopping for one of these soon. He's a smart man." Maggie smiled, slid the ring onto her ring finger and turned back to watch more of the action.

14. Silent Cicadas

IT WAS A LONG, SUMMER DAY, the sort with the sweltering heat not usually found in late August. And though the day was near its end and the street lights lit the sky, Danny could still taste the day's heat in his throat as he entered his side porch. He held his newly purchased four-star Chicago flag in his right hand, ready to replace the American flag that hung from the porch pole. He climbed on top of the porch ledge, the Chicago flag draped over his right arm. As Danny stood on that ledge with his back to the street, he immediately sensed something wrong. It was the quiet. Far too quiet. Even the cicadas had stopped barking, perhaps ready to watch the pending show. As Danny gripped a side porch column with his left arm, and swung to the side so he could face the sidewalk and street, a gunshot rang out, the bullet crashing into Danny's porch window. Danny dove to the floor and flattened himself against the gray of his porch, with the flag of Chicago draped over him. Another shot rang out and, again, crashed through his porch window. Danny then heard the squeal of a tire. When he looked up, he saw Ronny Monroe's truck flying down the street.

15. The Twenty-Second District

ETECTIVES LASKI AND BRONSON SAT across the interview table from Danny and Kate. The foursome had been at the Twenty-Second District police station for over a half hour.

"You sure this time, Mr. Lonigan?" Laski said. He held his notepad in hand.

"Positive," said Danny.

"So it was this Monroe guy?" Laski said, and then reviewed his notes. "Ronny Monroe?"

"Yep. No doubt. Saw his face. Saw his truck pulling away."

Bronson tapped his pen on the table. "Do you think it was Monroe the first time, too?" Bronson said.

"Well, I dunno. Not for sure on that one 'cuz last time I didn't see him. Ya know?" Danny massaged his forehead. "But this time . . . I saw him."

"All right, Mr. Lonigan," Laski said. He removed his glasses and set them on the table. "We're gonna scoop this guy in the morning. Get the warrant tonight and go get him at his job site first thing."

"Sounds good to me," Danny said.

"That's an understatement," Kate added.

Laski slipped his glasses back on. "We'll need you to come back in and ID Monroe in a lineup once we do scoop him, okay?"

"Right. Right. No problem."

"Can you give me a few minutes alone with him," Kate quipped. "I'd like to remove his balls."

The detectives laughed. "All right, Mr. Lonigan," Laski said, and then he nodded towards Kate. "Mrs. Lonigan. We're all set and we'll likely call you tomorrow."

Danny shook Laski's hand. "Thanks, Detective."

Kate shook hands with both detectives. "We appreciate what you do."

On the ride home, with Kate at the wheel, Danny received a call from Tom.

"So how'd it go?"

"Good. They got all the info."

"You sure you told 'em everything this time?"

"Yeah. Everything. I told 'em everything."

"Sounds good. So what's the next step?"

Danny turned on the radio and punched the button for WXRT. "They're gonna go out to execute the warrant tomorrow. Looks like they'll pick him up at work."

"At work? You sure on that?"

"That's what they said."

"Good. Good. I like that. Very nice. See, if that goes down at the job site, that's a ready-made violation. That'll make it easy for me to keep that piece of shit from workin' steady for a good long while."

"Sounds good to me."

"And hey, Dan, ya know . . . I'm just wonderin' . . ." Tom went silent.

"What?"

"Well, just that . . . well, has Pellegrini said anything about all this?"

"I haven't talked to him."

"Okay, well, does Scarpelli know Ronny tried to shoot ya again?"

"Yeah, he knows."

Silence claimed the phone for a moment. "Okay, Dan," Tom finally said. "I'll talk to you later. Glad everything's shapin' up."

16. New Plans

MORGAN WALKED INTO CARL HAAG'S OFFICE and sat on a comfy chair in front of Haag's desk. Haag closed the door and spoke as he moved towards his chair.

"Look, I called you down here because we hafta cover some stuff. Things have changed." Haag dropped into his chair and examined Morgan in silence.

"Okay."

"Just so you know," Haag said, "when I first took this case, it was my intent that if this went to a jury trial, I'd ask for a million-plus. You know, you're fifty-fve so we would ask that you be compensated for losing seven to ten years of wages and then ask for punitive damages because the city's actions were wrongful."

"Right."

"But here's the deal. The city's corp counsel called me a couple of days ago and then sent me recorded statements from Flynn and Cullinan. In these recordings, they both told the same story but their story is different from yours. Way different." Haag ran his right hand alongside his neck. "They both said that they didn't contact the police after the wire came up missing."

"Yeah, so?" Morgan leaned forward in his chair.

"But they said it had nothing to do with trying to investigate and give them three weeks to find out who did it. They said they didn't report it because they were trying to cover the thing up, smooth it over in hopes that no one would find out."

Morgan scratched at his head. "That's what they said, huh?"

"Yep. And that, in my opinion, hurts us in a big way. Huge. With them on our side with matching stories, we can roll. But now they're sayin' something completely different from what you're saying . . . it hurts us, big time. And their depositions won't be for a while yet, but I'm guessing they'll say the same thing at their deps."

"Well, what if I change my story to match theirs?"

"That would be wrong. Dead wrong." Haag clasped his hands and dropped them on his desk. "First, I want you to tell the truth. That's what you're supposed to do. And second, if you change your story, you're like a sheet blowing in the wind, flip-flopping around. Makes you not believable as a witness."

"Maybe I should talk to those guys."

"Nah," Haag said with the wag of his head. "Wouldn't help now."

Morgan fell back into his chair. "Well, what do you think?"

"The corp counsel offered seventy-five grand to get rid of the case. He knows the game is changed now.

"Seventy-five grand?" Morgan's face was a wrinkled ball. "That's like only a year's wages."

"I know. But it's nothing to turn your nose up at. Not now." Haag stood and moved to the side of his desk. "Look, we could go to trial and get zero too. That's now a possibility. See, before, I'd say no way. But now, if a jury doesn't believe your testimony and thinks you lied before, they can decide they don't like you and jam you with nothin'." An eerie smile leaked from Haag's lips. "Juries are funny animals, man. You can't always trust them."

Morgan twisted his face a bit. "I dunno."

"I get that. See, my job is not to just fill ya up with BS. Ya know—'everything's fine, Mark. Let's go rip up the jury and bring back 1.2 mildo.'" Haag sat on the edge of his desk. "Maybe before, but not now. I think we should look hard at that offer. And quite frankly, I'll try to bump them to 150 or 200, and they'll probably come back at 125 or so. If that happens, I think we should take it."

"Yeah?"

Haag nodded.

17. The Goodbye Party

ZIGGY HELD A NEON ORANGE BOWLING BALL in his right hand and eyed the lone pin remaining in the alley. He made his approach, dancing towards his target on his tiptoes, a protégé from the Fred Flintstone school of bowling, and released the ball. "C'mon, baby," he barked. "Bring home the bacon." As the seven-pin exploded into the corner of Lane 1 at Timber Lanes on Irving Park, Ziggy screeched and bounced up and down like a kid who just got the Christmas gift he had long hoped and prayed for. Hat penciled in the spare while Danny, sitting beside him at the scorer's table, took a slug of Old Style.

"Correct me if I'm wrong," Ziggy gloated as he sidled up beside Hat, "but I believe that puts me four up on you, right?"

"For the moment," Hat said with a smile. "Still two frames left."

Danny fixed his eyes on Ziggy. "So you sure you're all good with this transfer? I mean, I'm guessin' you can always come back if you want to."

Hat stood and walked towards his ball. "Who the hell wants him back?" he said with a grin, before blowing a crisp burst of air at his right hand. "I'm gonna have Maggie sittin' next to me in the front seat rubbin' my nuts every day now. Sweet, sweet Maggie." Hat slid his fingers and thumb into his ball.

"Maggie?" Ziggy said. He took a seat beside Danny.

"That's right," said Hat.

"For sure?" Ziggy said.

"Yep," Hat said. "How's that old saying go—Outta sight, outta mind."

"That's the one," Danny said. Hat and Danny both howled with delight.

Hat shook the smile from his face, and with both hands on the ball he stood erect in the lane. After staring down the pins for a moment, he sent a fastball down the alley for a strike. He pranced over to Ziggy.

"See that shit. That's called a *strike*. Somethin' you haven't had yet today."

Ziggy grabbed his crotch. "Strike this." He laughed and took a slug of beer. "But you know what," Ziggy said, his words aimed at Danny. "Truth is . . . I don't mind the O'Hare transfer too much. I mean, it's only fifteen minutes from my house. But—"

"You gotta be careful, man," said Hat. Maggie was now emptied from his brain, and he was all about business, city business. "You're in the damn airport all day. Lotsa security. Cameras everywhere. Can't go anywhere and get lost. Lotsa eyes on ya. Can't go golfin'. Can't go bowlin' like this. Can't even go to the damn movies. It's like you're not even workin' for the city. It's like a real job." Hat wagged his head in disgust. "And the guys who work up there are a buncha stiffs. Every single one—except for Joe Gurso. You pal up with him, and you'll be okay. I told him you were comin' out there already."

Ziggy nodded his thanks. Hat's cell phone rang. He eyed the number and shook his head. "Fuckin' Kip." He pushed the phone back into his pocket. "Fuckin' ass clown."

"Aren't you going to answer it?" said Ziggy.

"Fuck him," Hat barked. "It's still lunch break."

Ziggy eyed the clock on the wall. "Not really."

Hat shrugged. "So what. Fuck 'im anyways."

"But hey, like you said, this move'll knock off a bunch of your commute time," Danny said. "So that's good. You'll get home quicker so you can hang out with Little Ziggy for longer parts of the day—before, ya know, before he starts to shit, vomit, and cry all the time."

Ziggy smiled and took another drink. "Little Zignacio don't cry. Not much anyway. And he sure as hell don't vomit. He's not like an Irish devil baby or something."

Danny dropped his hand atop the scorer's table and laughed. "How about that 'shit' part, though? Gonna tell me he don't shit?" He took a drink of his beer.

"Nah, he definitely takes care of that duty," Ziggy said. "And I'm the official diaper changer when I'm home."

"The joys of fatherhood," Hat said. He then eyed Danny. "You're up."

"Just a minute," Danny said. He didn't budge. He could see one of Ziggy's warped thoughts forming, dancing in his eyes.

"Ya know what's funny, though?" Ziggy said.

"What's that?" said Hat.

"I don't throw Little Ziggy's turds out." He shook his head slowly from side to side. "Nope. I scoop them off of the diaper with a spoon and put them into a big plastic bag."

Danny swallowed a smile as Hat's eyes turned into slits. "Now I gotta say," Hat started. "That's weird. I mean I've heard some weird shit before, but scoopin' your kid's dumpage into a garbage bag with a spoon . . . I'd say that moves you near the top of the *weird* list." Hat watched Ziggy in silence for a moment. "You're kiddin', right?"

"Nope," Ziggy said with a straight face.

Hat scratched his head. "Well, what the hell ya gonna do with a big plastic bag filled with little Mexican baby shits?"

"Just need it. That's all."

"'Need it'?" Hat's face was filled with disbelief. "For what?"

"Now that the Rat King's gone," Ziggy said, "I need some new filler to put in my tamales."

Hat's face went ghost white. "Ah geez," he said. "Not this shit again." He raced for the men's room.

Ziggy laughed. "I'm gonna miss jamming that guy." Danny cackled as well. "Hey," Ziggy said, his face now stoic. "That Ronny guy . . . I know we already talked through it all, but still. I just plain don't like it. You sure the cops are on it? I mean that's twice now. If he comes by again maybe—"

"I did. I did." Danny grimmaced. "I called the cops this time. They're on it."

Well, how come they haven't picked him up yet. I don't like that."

"They will."

"You sure about that?"

"I'm sure." Danny smiled. "How 'bout you? You sure you're okay with this transfer? I mean, I could say somethin' to my brother, and he could probably get it set to keep you here."

"Nah, nah," Ziggy said. "Thanks for offering, but I'll just go with the flow. You know, see how things turn out."

"Okay, cool. But if ya wanna come back, just let me know."

"You got it, partner." Ziggy downed some beer and then smiled in silence.

"What?"

"Look, now that I'm gonna be gone," Ziggy said, "you got to promise to mess with Hat every now and then for me to keep him on his toes. You know, to keep him from thinking he can take over the world."

"Will do."

"I mean it." Ziggy smiled again. "Look, I got a joke for you. Throw it at him in a week or two and let me know how it went. And then I'll get you another one." Danny smiled and took a drink of beer. "Okay, here it goes. How do you tell the difference between a guy from Bridgeport and a guy from Canaryville?"

Danny's eyebrows danced. "No idea."

"The guy from Canaryville takes the dishes out of the sink before he pisses in it."

Danny laughed and clanked bottles with Ziggy. They turned around as Hat made his return.

"What's so funny?" said Hat.

"Nothing," Ziggy said.

"Okay, look. No more talkin' about tamales or little Mexican shit balls, all right?" Hat said. Ziggy and Danny traded big smiles. Danny stood and grabbed his ball. "Hey, I mean it. I know you two think it's funny, but it's not to me." Hat bit his lower lip. "See, whenever someone talks about stuff like that—or somethin' like Rat King tamales—it's weird. It's like I can see that shit sittin' on a plate right in front of me and it's like I'm a little kid and my mom is makin' me eat every last scrap on that plate for dinner."

"Okay, okay already," Danny said. "Ziggy promises not to do stuff like that anymore, right, Zigs?"

Ziggy grinned. "Baby shit! Baby shit! Oooo-ey, gooo-ey,

baby shit."

"C'mon, man," Hat barked.

Danny raised his beer with his free hand. "To Ziggy and to his son, Ziggy Junior."

Hat raised his glass. "That's more like it."

Ziggy smiled, ready to let Hat have it yet again. Danny saw the glint in his eye.

"Don't," Danny barked.

Ziggy's smile widened and then he nodded in agreement. "Okay, to my son . . . Ziggy Junior . . . may he live a long, happy life, and may he be fortunate enough to meet good men—like you two."

The three men drained their beers and then Danny stepped out into the lane.

18. The 6511 Club

TOM AND DENNY FREYER LEANED UP AGAINST the ropes on the boxing ring in Tom's garage, while Billy Laski pushed a broom across the floor. The Saturday afternoon workout was over and the last of the boxers made his way towards the door.

"Go straight home now," Tom barked to Walker Dunne, a fourteen-year old with a quick jab and a big heart.

"Yeah," Freyer added, "stay outta the tavern."

Dunne shook Tom's hand and fired a shy smile Freyer's way before walking out the door.

"What a good kid," Tom said.

"Needs more work on the heavy bag," Hairdo said. "Doesn't like to go to the body much."

"I getcha. I see that too," Tom said. "But I like him as a person. As a kid. He's tough. No mom, no dad. His grandmother's raisin' 'im. Takes two busses to get here. Kid works hard and doesn't complain about nothin'. And hell . . . you saw it. He shakes my hand every time before he leaves."

"That's definitely worth something," Hairdo said.

"Worth millions," Tom said. He walked over to the garage fridge and returned with four bottles of beer. "And he sorta looks like Leon Spinks with that gap in his teeth. I like that look."

"He doesn't look like Leon Spinks," Freyer barked.

"You don't think so?" Tom said. Freyer wagged his head.

Tom turned to Laski. "Hey, punch out, already, Billy." Laski set the broom against the wall and joined the others. Tom passed the beers out, and the men all took down a nice drink and released a collective, "Ahhhh." The sun poured through the lone garage window, and the smell of sweat-soaked teenagers took hold of the air these men breathed. But they were all immune to that smell, especially when they had cold beers staring into their nostrils.

Danny pushed through the door. He snatched a beer from the fridge and pulled up a camp chair.

"Hey, who was that kid I just saw leavin'?" Danny laughed. "Looks kinda like Leon Spinks."

"See," Tom snickered, his eyes set on Freyer.

"As long as we keep bringin' up Leon Spinks's name," Freyer said, his eyes set on Tom, "why don't you tell these guys about the time he came into the 6511 Club."

"You tell 'im," Tom said.

"The 6511 Club?" Hairdo barked. "Are you shittin' or what?"

"Nope," said Freyer.

"Did any of the turkey birds in there try to break a chair across his neck?" Hairdo said.

Freyer shook his head. "Okay, so picture this," Freyer said, and then removed the cigar from his lips. "I'm in the 6511 Club on a Tuesday night in the middle of the summer with Tom, and Terry McGuire and a few other guys. This is back in the mid '80s and we took down a big lunch before we got there, so we had a good base set, and we're well on our way to enjoying a big night. All the turkey birds were in there downing their dark pints and talkin' their usual bullshit. So at 7 p.m., the open mic kicks in."

"Hold on," Danny said. "The 6511 Club had an open mic night?"

"Yeah," Freyer said. "Every Tuesday."

Danny leaned forward. "I thought that place was just a front for South Side IRA guys."

"Well, it was, in a way," Tom said, "but that doesn't mean you can't have an open mic night, too."

"Okay," Freyer said, "so a couple of off-the-boaters get up during the open mic and sing "Danny Boy" and "Four Green Fields" and some of the other turkeys are drippin' tears all over the bar. The usual shit. But at about 8 oclock, the door pops open and in walks Gym Shoes Callahan with Leon Spinks and one of the Mills Brothers. And next thing you know—"

"Sorry, I know this might sound stupid," Laski said, "but who're the Mills Brothers?"

Tom smiled and gave Laski a shove. "Billy . . . he don't listen to anything but the Red Hot Chili Peppers."

"Nothin' wrong with the Peppers," Danny said.

"So Billy," Tom said, "the Mills Brothers were a big-time, black song and dance group from like the '30s all the way up through the 90s.

"Okay, and, uh . . . who's Gym Shoes Callahan?" Laski said.

"He's big into boxing," Freyer said. "Surprised you don't know him."

Laski stared blankly at him.

"Don't worry about it, okay?" Freyer continued. "If you ever work an election someday, chances are you'll run into Gym Shoes. He'll be the guy in charge, and—"

"Of every campaign," Tom said. "And of every candidate. And every side. You never lose that way."

Billy watched as the others all eyed each other and cackled like crows. He had driven past the 6511 Club before, just two blocks from Marquette Park. The doors had been closed for as long as he could remember.

"So anyways," Freyer said, "every eye in the bar is set on Leon Spinks and the Mills brother, and the place goes silent. And I'm wonderin' if the bottles and chairs are gonna start flyin'."

"That's why I asked," Hairdo said.

"And I'm wonderin' what the hell Gym Shoes was thinkin'," Tom said.

Freyer continued. "But then Leon Spinks heads over to the microphone, snatches it from some turkey, and proceeds to recite the poem "Annabel Lee" from memory. From fuckin' memory. And when he's done, the turkeys are goin' nuts. Completely fuckin' nuts. 'Another one, Chomp,' they're all barkin' in their brogues. 'C'mon, Chomp. Another one." So Spinks bangs out another poem. Again from memory. I don't remember what that one was, but—"

"But the first one was definitely Annabel Lee," Tom said. "By Poe. You got that right."

"And then," Freyer started to speak but broke out into laughter. Tom joined him.

"C'mon, already," Danny barked. "I never heard any of this."

"Okay, okay," Freyer said, "so then the Mills brother goes up to the mic next, and he belts out a tune and is dancin and shakin' all over the place. And . . . and then everywhere I look, the turkey birds are all up on their stools or on the bar top jumpin and spinnin' around in circles, shakin' and bakin' with the Mills brother." Freyer fell into a fit of laughter. The others joined him. "Man, that seems like yesterday, but it was twenty years ago. Twenty fuckin' years ago." Freyer returned his cigar to his mouth. "I wasn't in the 6511 Club on a regular basis, but I can say this . . . that's the only time I ever saw a black guy in there."

"Hey," Hairdo said. "Not to rain on your parade, Denny, but hearing that story . . . well, I dunno why exactly, but it, uh, it reminded me that I wanted to show you guys somethin'. Only it ain't funny. Not like that. Definitely not."

Hairdo yanked out his cell from his pants pocket and pressed a series of buttons.

"What is it?" Tom said.

"I'm gettin' there," Hairdo said. He pressed a few more buttons and stopped. "Okay, so some bad shit went down in a bar on the Northwest Side Thursday night. You mighta heard about this already, but some off-duty cop got crazy. Beat the everlivin' snot outta some guy. Killed 'im. One of my buddies who knows a guy who knows a cop who was there said the guy was just some forty-year-old dad from Rogers Park. Good guy from what I've been told. No record. No nothin'. But this cop went after 'im and kept after 'im even when the guy was out cold on the ground."

Hairdo pulled up an image. "Here, take a look."

The five men crowded around Hairdo's phone, which displayed a coroner's photo of a badly beaten, bruised, and bloated face.

"Jesus," Tom moaned.

"What'd this guy do?" Danny said.

"Nothin'. Like I said."

"Nothin'?" Tom said with a pained look.

"Yeah. The cop's a punk. Complete fuckin' punk. Just lookin' for a fight. The reports all say the dead guy was threat'nin' the cop and swung first and then hit the cop a few times. But I doubt it. Cop's a loose canon."

"I didn't see anything about this on the news . . . or in the paper," Laski said.

"Me neither," added Freyer.

"Didn't make the ten o'clock news," Hairdo said. "And the papers had a paragraph on the guy."

"A paragraph for that?" Freyer said.

Hairdo took another slug from his bottle. "There's more to it too. I hear the bar owner might have a video. That's what my buddy told me. If that ever gets out, the shit'll hit the fan."

The men all shook their heads and drank their beer, Leon Spinks and the Mills Brothers long gone from their thoughts.

19. Dreamers

PARKED ALONG THE LAKE AT MONTROSE HARBOR, Danny, Maggie, and Hat gnawed on Bari subs in the van as they stared out at the water.

"So Danny," Maggie said, "Jimmy says you got some good material you been working on. Can you read some to us?"

From his throne, Danny glanced at Hat and then turned his eyes towards Maggie.

"Sorry, but I don't know anyone named 'Jimmy.'" Danny took a bite out of his sub.

Maggie laughed. "Sorry, *Hat*'s the one who said that." She smiled. "I'd really like to hear some."

"Ya know what, since you asked so nicely. Sure." Danny dug into his backpack and pulled out his journal. He paged through it a bit. "This is one about my state's attorney days. When I was a newbie. Just so ya know, I keep it sort of drab on purpose 'cuz I don't want to flower the events in the story. It's just that—"

"Just read it, already," Hat said.

Danny cleared his throat. "Okay, this is titled, 'Nameless.'"

I should remember his name, the victim. I don't remember the defendant's name either. But I do remember this: the victim was a plumber, and the defendant called him over to his apartment for repairs, and while the plumber was under the sink, the defendant whacked him across the back of his neck with the victim's own wrench, knocking him out. When the victim came to, he found it hard to breathe. A rag was stuffed into his mouth and a piece of rope circled his head holding the rag in place. The plumber was tied to a kitchen chair, and his shirt had been removed.

The defendant flipped on the TV and started watching The Three Stooges. In his confession, he said he liked The Three Stooges. Curly was his favorite. On TV, Moe hit Curly with a hammer, so the defendant hit the victim with a hammer. Again and again and again. He broke bones in places and made dents in others. When Curly threw a pair of pants onto an ironing board, the defendant followed his lead and plugged in his own iron. As the iron warmed up, Moe pulled out a cigar. The defendant decided to have a smoke too. Moe lit that big stogie and then inadvertently tossed the match over his shoulder. It landed in Larry's rather expansive hairdo. The defendant laughed as Larry grimaced and fanned himself from the heat atop his smoking head. The defendant put a match to the plumber's hair and laughed as the flames raced across the plumber's flat top, leaving a mound of singed, porcupined needles. When the plumber screamed in silence, the defendant laughed even harder. Then the iron was ready. He pressed it to the plumber's back and chest and face just as the Stooges had done on a previous episode. But the plumber was still alive. The defendant took a butcher knife and slit the plumber's belly open in two places, from hip to hip. The plumber's intestines spilled out onto the floor. He died a short while later. The Stooges had never done anything like that, the defendant said. He thought they would be proud.

At trial, the prosecution sought to enter four poster-sized photos of the victim into evidence. The defendant's attorney objected, saying these photos would prejudice the jury. Good ol' Judge Michael Blazek made the right call. He allowed the photos into evidence. All four. God bless Judge Blazek. He knew the photos were damaging, *but hey, the defendant deserved to be damaged. The photos were placed directly in front of the jury, staged on easels, as if a collection of art. Tears flowed immediately from the eyes of Jurors 2, 3, and 7. They didn't attempt to hold anything back. Almost all of the others gasped and swallowed their tears as they turned their eyes away. Juror 11 eyed the oversized photos and then stared at the defendant with hatred in his eyes. Good. We had our foreman. I should remember the plumber's name. I should. I really, really should.*

Danny looked up. Maggie aimed wounded eyes his way.

"That's sad on so many levels," Maggie said. She stared at her hands and then cracked a knuckle. "But it's a good sad. A sad that makes you think. A sad with a certain power to it."

"Thanks."

"I didn't know you were a state's attorney. Is that real?"

"Yeah. Unfortunately. This trial happened when I was in my last year of law school when I was clerking for the state's attorney's office. Workin' on that trial . . . it's what made me decide I wanted to be a state's attorney for sure."

"This is great. Just great," Hat said. "You been workin' with me for almost half a year now, and you ain't read diddily squat from your work for me . . . or for Ziggy neither. And then Maggie comes in for what—for all of three weeks now, and you get all warm and fuzzy and you read your shit to her. C'mon." Hat wagged his head.

Danny laughed. "What can I say? She's better lookin' than you?" He licked his lips. "Plus, she asked nicer."

Hat turned back towards Danny and narrowed his eyes. "Why don't you tell Maggie about the dream you had about her the one time? Got anything in that journal 'bout that?"

"Whataya talkin' about?" Danny said, feigning ignorance.

"You know what I'm talkin' about. You know. That dream you had when you was in the hospital after gettin' shot." Danny looked at Hat with dumb eyes. "When Jello and me came to see you."

Danny turned towards Maggie and spoke with an Irish brogue. "Me tinks our friend Hat, here, has been divin' into his bottle of whiskey a wee bit early today."

Hat laughed and went back to his sandwich.

Maggie eyed Hat. "So did he really have a dream about me?"

Danny shook his head furiously in the back seat. Hat caught it in the rearview mirror. "Nah, I was just throwin' some shit at him."

Maggie turned back towards Danny's throne. "Well, if you ever do have a dream about me, I'd be fine with it. I mean, you can't control your dreams. No one can. I have weird dreams all the time."

"Any sexual dreams?" Hat said. "Ya know, fantasies about me?"

"Actually . . . . you were in one of my dreams."

Hat released a huge smile. "See, now we're gettin' somewhere. For sure."

"Yep," Maggie said. "In my dream you got run over by a Streets and San garbage truck and died."

Danny busted out laughing. Hat smiled and took a huge bite out of his sub.

20. Gone fishing?

WHEN RONNY MONROE FAILED TO SHOW UP at his mother's house for the Tuesday lasagna dinner he never missed, Mrs. Monroe called her son. When Ronny did not answer, she drove over to his house. Ronny's truck was parked in the driveway, but Ronny was nowhere to be found. As Mrs. Monroe sat at Ronny's kitchen table, she called her daughter. Nothing. Ronny's sister hadn't heard from Ronny for four to five days either. The following day, Mrs. Monroe telephoned her son's work. Ronny had not made it to work on Monday or Tuesday of this week, and he had not reported this morning either.

As Mrs. Monroe pieced things together, the best she could determine was—no one had any contact with Ronny since Friday, the week before. Mrs. Monroe brain started to wander. Maybe he went fishing again and got caught in that weekend storm. Maybe he's been kidnapped. Maybe he went to Vegas. She wasn't sure where to begin. She called the Summit police.

21. The Cell

HAT AND FRANKY STOOD IN THE FIRST ROW of the left field bleachers at the Cell, baseball gloves in hand. Batting practice—whenever Hat went to a game, he always went early, way early, to catch the pre-game action, and hopefully snag a long one off the bat of a Sox slugger. Over the years, Hat caught batting practice balls from the likes of Harold Baines, Bo Jackson, Ron Kittle, Jermaine Dye, and Juan Uribe, to name a few—and had a collection of two dozen such balls boxed in protective plastic cases on display in his apartment. And Sox star, Paul Konerko, did not disappoint. Not on this day. He dropped a couple of bombs almost directly in Hat's lap. Never before had Hat snatched two BP homeruns. And to think he only had to move a hair to his right or left both times. Sure he had to nudge a little kid out of the way once, so he could bring home the Konerko gift, but such was life. All's fair in war and in the bleachers during BP at the Cell.

Hat gave one ball to Franky and kept the other for himself. After that, the two relocated to their actual seats in the back row of the left field bleachers, and dropped their mitts to their feet.

"Two in one day," Franky said. "That's a good omen."

"No doubt," Hat said. "KC doesn't stand a chance today."

"No, man," Franky said and then adjusted his Sox hat and toupee. "I'm talkin' about bigger fish than that."

"Like what?"

"Like goin' to the track after the game. Huh? We could get there by five-thirty or so and catch some good action. Whataya think?"

Hat eyed Franky in silence for a moment before flagging down a beer vendor—a tall boy for Franky and one for himself.

"Well?" said Franky.

Hat took a long sip of beer. A bit of foam clung to his upper lip as he spoke.

"Bad idea."

"C'mon. I'll give Victor a call and we'll bag a bundle."

"I'll say it again. Bad idea."

"You're like an old lady."

Hat laughed.

"I mean it. It's like—"

"Look, I just want to have some fun at the ballpark." Hat smiled. "Ya know, eat a dog, drink a beer. Then eat a brat and drink a beer, and then eat an Italian sausage and drink another beer. And watch the Sox beat up on the Royals the whole time. Can't we just do that? Ain't that enough fun for one day for ya?"

"All I'm sayin' is we can go to the track and double up on our fun."

Hat sat up straight in his seat and swung around to face Franky. Gone was his playful demeanor. "Okay, well, I wasn't plannin' on gettin' into this right off the bat, but since you keep pushin' the fuckin' envelope, I'll tell ya right now." Hat rubbed the back of his head with both hands. "I brought you here for a reason today. You gotta—"

"I know I'm here for a reason," Franky snapped. "I ain't fuckin' stupid. We ain't been to a game together for three years."

"Bullshit. We went last year."

Franky replayed last year's Sox schedule in his head. "Okay, my bad. You're right. We did go to a game last year."

"Damn straight. We saw three bombs that day. Against the A's. How do you forget shit like that?"

"I'm tryin to become as perfect as you," Franky quipped. "That's my goal."

"We both know that'll never happen." Hat tugged on Franky's

toupee. "Not with this rug on toppa your head."

Both men laughed and took a slug of beer.

"But for real now. I mean it. You gotta quit goin' to the track. I mean, think about it. You ain't had any luck there in a long time."

"C'mon. Ya jokin' or what?"

"No, I'm serious."

"But Jimmy, askin' me not to go to the track is like . . . well, I dunno, it's sorta like askin' a sixteen-year-old not to beat off."

Hat laughed. "Good one." He erased his smile with the swipe of a hand. "When's the last time you had a winner?"

"I win all the time. All the fuckin'—"

"When?"

'Well, look, I talked to Victor yesterday, and he said there's a couple of good horses at Hawthorne tonight. Dead bang winners."

"That's what I'm talkin' about," Hat said, his forehead matted with wrinkles. "First things first. Stop listening to Victor. He's terrible. Fuckin' terrible."

"But Jimmy, he's always got money."

"That's cuz his wife croaked a year ago and left him half a mil. But he ain't had a big day at the track in years."

Franky sipped his beer. A look of defeat claimed his eyes. "I know. You're right." Franky rubbed his nose. "I just like goin' to the track, ya know, to see the horses, to watch 'em run. Beautiful animals. Just beautiful."

"I get it, Franky. I do. And if that was all there was to it, that'd be great. But you always pull out your wallet and proceed to empty it." Hat pushed his right hand through his hair. "And that ain't so good."

The men stared out onto the field for a moment, watching the players frolic in the sunlight. A few fans walked along the outfield warning track, escorted by Sox staff members.

Hat slugged his beer. "Here's the deal. Straight up. Jello was ready to turn one of your kneecaps into mush last time. He was. For sure. Ya follow me?"

Franky nodded, and then fixed his eyes on his shoes.

"I don't wanna see that happen to you. You're my guy. But I can't keep bailin' ya out like that. I can't keep doin' that all the time.

"I know, Jimmy." Franky hung an arm around Hat's neck. "I appreciate your help. I do."

"I know you do. But this isn't about appreciation or respect or any shit like that. It's about you. About you being able to fuckin' walk. You're gettin' old. You can't handle a busted leg." The men stared out onto the field again in silence, but as that silence pushed its way into an uncomfortable zone, Hat put an end to it.

"C'mon," Hat said as he nudged Franky, "whataya say we go get that first dog."

"Okay," Franky climbed to his feet. "But I'm buyin'."

Hat stood and slapped Franky on the back.

22. The Ankle Breaker

AFTER THE MARQUETTE PARK JOB, Danny accepted several other jobs from Jello. Jankowski helped him work his way through the second job, a broken hand. And Jankowski reviewed everything as Danny planned out his third job on his own, another broken hand. For his fourth job, Danny planned and carried it out smoothly without review from Jankowski. That one was a broken tibia, accomplished by stomping on the man's leg. After each job, Winslow was parked nearby, and they drove off together. Danny soon found the code was this: You fail to pay up your bets or payday loans on time, a warning would be issued by someone like Hat or one of Jello's other dozen or so CDOT cronies, followed by a broken hand if you still didn't pay a week later. The broken leg went to those unfortunate enough to be repeat offenders. After one of Danny's visits, the money owed came in quick to Hat or to one of Jello's other associates.

The four city workers Danny had maimed had seen Danny's face, but he could care less. He wasn't trying to hide. Jankowski had told him that the city workers who owed money on gambling debts and payday loans weren't the sort who would run off to the police if they got roughed up. They knew a lot worse would be around the corner if they chose that route. And most of those city workers put in reports saying that they fell off of a ladder or a dock or a garbage truck and got their injuries during the course of the workday so they could put in a worker's comp claim. A number of those cases ended up in the hands of Carl Haag, though Haag never knew how the injuries actually happened.

By taking care of Phipps and the other four jobs, Danny was taking care of some of the hospital bills and putting some in the bank to help cover what Kate would've made as a CPS teacher the following year. He kept that money in a separate checking account, ready to use it when need be. And the "need be" would soon be upon him, since Kate did not get a new teaching job. Rather, she earned a minimal amount tutoring students. And then Danny got another call from Jankowski. When he said he wanted to meet to discuss something "Big," Danny knew something was different.

23. A Warning

HEY DAN, IT'S CARL, CARL HAAG." Haag stood in the corridor outside of a courtroom in the Daley Center, his cell pressed to his ear.

"What's up, Big Shooter?" Danny said. Along with Hat and Maggie, Danny sat on a bench overlooking Doggie Beach near the northern edge of Belmont Harbor. While the boys had already finished their Big as Your Head Burritos from La Pasadita, Maggie was still working on hers. They watched assorted hounds frolic on the beach and in the water. Assorted boats formed the backdrop of the beach, while cars flew along Lake Shore Drive and joggers and bikers trolled past on the inner trail behind them.

"You callin' to tell me you're takin' me to dinner with the millions you're gonna get on the Morgan case?"

Haag laughed. "Ah well, things don't always go as planned. Looks like we'll be wrapping that thing up sooner than later, but some problems came into the mix."

"Really," Danny said. "Mind if I ask what ya might settle on?"

"Looks like 135K."

"That's still plenty to take me to dinner."

Haag chuckled again. "We'll do that, once we settle. But listen, I got somethin' for ya. Somethin' I thought you'd wanna know. See, I was out golfin' with this guy I've known for years. He's with the IG and, well . . . your name came up."

Danny stood from the bench and walked quickly off into the grass behind the bench, stopping about thirty yards from Hat and Maggie.

"Who is this guy?" Danny said.

"Name's Janecki. John Janecki. Used to be a cop but jumped in with the IG a few years back. Good guy."

"Yeah? So what'd he say?"

"Are you workin' with some guy who's related to Jello Pellegrini?"

"Yeah."

"Well, what's his name?"

"Jimmy Scarpelli."

"That's him. That's the name he said." Haag nodded to an attorney he knew who passed him in the hallway. "Well, they got Jello in their sites, and from what I gather, they're keepin' an eye on Scarpelli too, which . . . well, you know."

"Yeah, I know." An awkward silence filled both phones. "Thanks, Carl. I appreciate the heads up."

"And Dan, if the IG's milling around, there could be others too."

"Right," Danny said. He turned back towards Hat and Maggie. Hat leaned against the chain-link fence that bordered Doggie Beach, petting a Weimaraner who had just stopped by to introduce himself. Danny smiled. "Next time you call, make sure it's about you buyin' me dinner, okay?"

"You gottit," Haag said.

Danny ended the call and walked over beside Hat.

"You ever see anyone take that long to eat a damn burrito?" Hat said as he glanced at Maggie.

"Forget about that," Danny said.

"What?"

"I just gotta call," Danny said. He eyed a black lab swimming back towards shore with a tennis ball in its mouth.

"Okay, what?" Hat said.

Danny turned back towards Hat. "A buddy just called me. Said he was golfin' with some guy he knows who's with the IG. An investigator. Said both our names came up."

"Big fuckin' deal," Hat said. "What're they gonna do—drag us in for sittin' on park benches for too long." Hat laughed. "Fuck them."

"Well, we been doin' a little more than that?" Danny said. "And he, uh . . . he said there could be others too."

Hat feigned interest. "Think they might be watchin' us now?"

"Could be," Danny said, his words full of sincerity.

"Like right now?"

Danny shrugged. "Yeah, I guess."

Hat unlatched his belt and pulled his jeans and boxers down. He bent over a bit and aimed his bare ass at the cars zipping along Lake Shore Drive and the pedestrians passing along the park trail.

From her post on the bench, Maggie finished her burrito. She looked up just in time to see Hat spank his bare ass with his right hand several times, and yell, "KISS MY ASS, IG. RIGHT NOW. PUCKER UP."

Maggie wadded her burrito wrapper into a ball and tossed her garbage into a nearby can as Hat and Danny made their way back towards her.

"What was that all about?" Maggie said.

"Oh, that," Hat said as he latched his belt. "That was my bare ass." He winked. "Like what ya see?"

"Not especially," Maggie said. The three walked back towards their van.

24. Corned Beef at Frank and Mary's

#6 **I** LOVE THIS SHIT," Jankowski said.

"What? Corned beef?" Danny said.

"Fucking A."

"Never met a Polack who liked corned beef."

"You have now."

Danny and Jankowski huddled on stools at the far end of the bar at Frank and Mary's Tavern on Elston munching on corned beef and cabbage. Hat first discovered this place when he and the boys were working at the nearby Thirty-Third Ward. For decades Mary had churned out quality hot lunches Monday through Friday, but the lunch rush had just ended at 1p.m., over an hour ago. The bar was now almost empty.

Danny chewed his meat and nodded approvingly. "Funny shit though, it's like the Italian beef story. You go to Italy—they don't have Italian beef there. That's just some shit some guy thought up when he came here to America. Same thing with corned beef."

"You saying I can't get corned beef in Ireland?" Jankowski smiled. "I think you're wrong on that one, Danny Boy."

"No. You can get it there," Danny said and then swilled some beer. "But it really originated here in the states as the big Irish meal. It really wasn't that big in Ireland. It was actually an English thing. See, the Irish people couldn't afford it. But then the Irish started serving it for tourism purposes. They thought that's what Irish-Americans thought they ate. So now they have it there."

"Wild." Jankowski swallowed a bit more meat and chased it with his beer. "So Jello wanted me to talk to you about . . . about the next thing."

"I didn't say I'd do it."

"He knows that. I know that. No problem. If it's something you don't want to do, then don't do it. That's not a problem. I'm just here to sort of be . . . well, to be your sounding board, I guess."

Danny slipped some cabbage between his lips and eyed Jankowski. "I gotta say, I don't have any problem bustin' up a nose or breaking a hand. That stuff doesn't bother me. Maybe it should, but it doesn't." Danny set his fork down. "But I'm not sure about what I think you're here to talk about. Not sure, for sure." Danny downed his Old Style.

"You don't even know what it is."

"I gotta pretty damn good idea." Danny's eyes clung to Jankowski. "I don't wanna assume anything, Al, but if I assumed that you've done this sort of thing before, would I be right?"

Jankowski slid a hunk of corned beef into his mouth and ground the meat between his teeth. Danny knew the answer to his question. He just wanted to hear Jankowski respond to it. "I've been at this game a long time, Dan, so yeah, you would be assuming correctly."

"And how'd that feel, ya know, the first time?"

"I'll gladly talk about stuff. Some. Jello told me to share what I thought was appropriate, but to begin, I'll just say this." Jankowski squinted. "This is a job, Danny. Like any other job. I told you that before. I mean, look, the Wonder bread delivery man, he slings loaves of bread onto the racks at the local 7-Eleven or the Jewel. And he gets paid. We break arms, legs, pull off ears, yeah— and sometimes we do more than that. It's a job." Jankowski slurped his beer. "Only we get paid lots better than most."

"But how'd you feel the first time?"

"I don't really remember the first time. All I know is this—the people we deal with, they're not saints. Not by a longshot. I mean, look at Ronny Monroe. He deserved to lose his finger for what he did."

"But did he deserve to disappear for firing a shot into my window?"

"In my opinion, *yeah*," Jankowski ran a chunk of corned beef through the clump of mustard on his plate and slid it into his mouth. He talked while chewing. "But I wouldn't know on that one. I'm not the guy who made him disappear."

Danny scratched his head and gave Jankowski an incredulous look. "But you said, you told him 'the rules.'"

"I did. But I never fulfilled the rules." Jankowski slugged his beer. "But anyways, ninety percent of these guys deserve what they got coming to them. And I'm okay with it. It's sort of a thinning of the herd."

"The guy whose nose I busted. The IG. Did he deserve that?"

"Damn right, he did. For fucking with Jello. Now if Jello told you to off the guy, then I'd say, No . . . he doesn't deserve that. But sometimes you get requests to do the other ten percent. It's something personal to somebody."

"Who's this guy Jello wants me to go see."

"His name, address, all that sort of shit," Jankowski nodded at the envelope on the bar counter beside Danny, "it's all right there."

"Yeah. But who is he? What did he do to deserve . . . well, ya know . . ."

"That's not up to me to tell you."

"Are you saying you don't know?"

"No. I'm just saying—I'm not saying. But if you really want to know, I heard there's a new thing called the internet. Google him." Jankowski checked his watch. "But if you take my advice, you won't do that. It makes it easier the less you know about somebody."

Danny stared directly ahead and found his face in the mirror behind the bar. Jankowski's face was also in that mirror, with his eyes staring back at Danny. Danny spoke to that image, that reflection. "But tell me, for real, you do remember the first time, don't you?"

Jankowski ran his right hand across his forehead. "Yeah, I do."

"Well, what about it?"

"That's in the past. The distant past."

Danny's eyes stayed fixed on Jankowski, who sighed and glared at Danny's reflection.

"You really wanna know how it feels, huh? Huh?" Danny nodded. Jankowski bunched his face into a knot and turned towards Danny. "Go ask your brother."

"What's that supposed to mean?"

"I said, 'Ask your brother.'"

Danny stared stupidly at Jankowski. "You really don't know, do ya?"

Danny's stare turned hard. He considered popping Jankowski in the jaw or, better yet, cracking him across his noggin with a bottle.

Jankowski scratched at his forehead. "Look, you know Tom worked for your dad."

"Yeah, so?"

Jankowski gave a look that suggested Danny needed to do a better job of putting the pieces together. "So he worked for your dad."

"My dad was a bookie," Danny screeched. "He wasn't out whackin' anyone."

Jankowski looked around the bar. "Easy." He looked around again. "Look, I'm not saying he was. Not at all. But he may have ventured into other areas, other than just being a bookie. And Tom may have strayed too."

"Fuck you," Danny barked. The bartender looked up from his newspaper, and a patron who had been staring into a shot glass, eyed the men as well.

"Look, Danny," Jankowski said. "We keep this down, or this chat is done."

Danny slurped his beer, his eyes again set in the mirror.

"All I'm saying is Tom might've been loaned out to some others from time to time to take care of a few things. That's how I heard it."

"And when was this?"

"When he was a kid, 18, 19, 20—somewhere in there. Before your dad died." Jankowski buttered a slice of rye bread, folded it in half, and stuffed the entire slice in his mouth. "Hell, I don't know if he ever really quit."

"C'mon, for Christ sakes," Danny barked. He downed his beer and left money on the bar counter to cover lunch. "I'm gonna roll."

"So what do I tell Jello?"

"I'll talk to you again tomorrow."

"Good enough." Once Danny left, Jankowski took Danny's plate and forked the remaining corned beef onto his own plate and dug in.

25. Kate's Letter

KATE PLACED STAMPS ON TWO UNSEALED ENVELOPES. She walked down her block towards the mailbox around the corner. Kate stopped a few yards from the box and removed the letter from one of the envelopes, again wondering if she should send it, wondering what good it would do. She read the letter again.

Dear Mayor Stokely,

My name is Kate Lonigan and for the past two and a half years, I have had the pleasure of teaching 3-4th grade at Glinser public school on Chicago's South Side. While I had several difficult students each year, I found that the overwhelming number of kids were eager learners who looked forward to coming to school. I thoroughly enjoyed my work and feel as though teaching disadvantaged children is where I was meant to be. In early May, I received my letter of termination due to funding. I am not writing to cry about my lost job or to beg to get it back. I know the city is facing difficult times and cuts were necessary, so I accept the fact that my job is gone. I guess, in a way, I am writing this because I feel certain things with the Chicago Public School system need to be addressed and perhaps my letter can help some other teacher in the future or provide some guidance on CPS as I see it.

Please know that I have addressed this letter to you (with a cc to the teacher's union) because in the grand scheme of things, as mayor of the City of Chicago, the CPS schools belong to you. And the kids who attend these schools are, in a way, your children.

There are a number of shortcomings facing teachers and students in schools in underprivileged neighbor-

hoods. CPS and the city itself have many solid teaching "concepts," but, truth be told, they're not so good in practice. For instance, for two years, my school did not have a science or social science curriculum. We simply were not provided books or materials. Teachers were expected to research, pay for, and print off supplies and materials for these classes on their own. I think we can both agree that more is expected and required of the city in this regard. And then there was the new series for our reading curriculum. Most of the general education classrooms received the books this past year—a month or two after the start of the school year, but no reading books were received for those in the special needs classrooms. Would you allow such things to happen at the schools your own children attend?

I could go on about other shortcomings, but I will not. As you are mayor of our city and a surrogate father to its students, I wish only to address you on one final matter: please re-evaluate the tenure system. A bad teacher should not be kept year after year simply because he or she has more seniority over a better teacher.

In my time working at Glinser, I have met and worked with numerous great teachers. These people have tremendous hearts, determination, a genuine love for their students, and go well above and beyond the typical teacher duties. However, I have also observed some teachers with unbecoming qualities. In some ways, my coworkers are not unlike co-workers in other fields— you have the good and the bad. But in no field other than teaching is the education of our youth entrusted. And yet in other fields, if you do not produce, you get your walking papers. But with the CPS the archaic system of tenure rules the system, and thus it keeps many who no longer care to be quality teachers gainfully employed.

I know you have a lot on your mayoral plate, but hopefully you can find the time to nibble on these matters for dessert. I also know that you are not a magician, but magic is not required. Common sense is. Our kids deserve better.

Sincerely,

Kate Lonigan

cc: Chicago Teachers Union

"Oh, what the hell," Kate blurted to herself. "Can't hurt." She stuffed the letter back into the envelope, licked it and the other envelope, and slipped them into the mailbox slot.

26. Sing

MIDNIGHT APPROACHED, AND DANNY, HAIRDO, and Tom had no intention of leaving the Dubliner to head for home.

"God's gift to stomachs," Tom said after he downed a shot of Jameson. A couple of empty pints and one full pint of Guinness staked their claim on the table, and Ronny's boot had been removed from its place of rest behind the bar. It stood tall and wet beside Tom, waiting to be filled yet again.

"So I think we should do a boot toast to Ellen," Tom said. "Have we toasted her yet?"

"Yeah, we did." Danny laughed. "But we can do it again. She's worthy of several toasts."

"Why not?" Hairdo added.

Tom emptied the pint of Guinness into Ronny's boot. He brought the leather to his lips and chugged the brew by letting the beer roll down the back of the boot into his mouth. He passed the boot to Hairdo who took down a healthy gulp before passing the boot yet again. Danny downed the balance and then went to the bar and brought back three more beers.

"Ya know, I didn't say anything about it before but . . . well, I didn't like it much when Ma brought Ellen home at first," Tom said. "I just thought it was gonna be too hard on her, ya know, with her havin' cancer and all. Thought everything would go haywire."

Danny passed out the fresh pints and filled the boot with beer. "Boy, were you wrong."

"I know. I know," Tom said. "And I'm happy to be wrong." He slurped some beer from the boot. "It's pretty damn amazing. I mean, according to Valek, the cancer's still there. But it's not movin'. Not one bit."

"Must be the magic of Ellen," Hairdo said.

"Got that right," Danny said.

"Let's drink to Ma again," Tom said. He took another slug of boot beer and then passed it to Hairdo.

"Nah, no more boot juice for me," Hairdo said. "That leather aftertaste is killin' me." Tom nodded and passed the boot to Danny, who drained the balance of the beer.

"I got one more toast to make," Tom said and then burped, "and then I'm done makin' fuckin' toasts for the night."

"About time," Hairdo said.

Tom laughed. "What's that supposed to mean?"

"It means . . . I dunno." Hairdo chuckled and scratched his head. "Well . . . why the hell do you guys toast shit all the time anyways? You guys are like the kings of the toasters. Why don't ya just drink your beer without toasts . . . like most people do?"

"I don't get what ya mean," Tom said.

"Yeah, what do ya mean, Har?" Danny added.

"You know what I mean," Hairdo said. Tom and Danny stared blankly at him. "C'mon, both of you guys are like, 'Hey, let's toast to that cockroach in the corner. That's a big one,' or 'Hey, look at that girl's nice ass, let's toast to that' or 'Man, this is the best god damn peanut-butter and jelly sandwich I ever had. Let's toast to it.'"

The brothers looked at Hairdo as if he had three heads. "C'mon, already, I mean, like in my family, we never make toasts when we get together. No one does. We just drink."

"Well, that's cuz, other than you, your entire family is made up of a bunch of brain-dead morons," Danny said. "Not one of 'em could put together a toast if you paid 'em."

Tom slapped Danny on the shoulder, and the brothers broke out in laughter.

"Personally, I've never toasted a cockroach," Tom said. "Have you?" he said as he eyed his brother. Again the brothers laughed. Harry just shook his head. "But ya know what, Har?" Tom continued, "all shittin' aside, the truth is I think I like makin' toasts 'cuz . . . well, my dad liked to make toasts. It was pretty much the only time I can remember him sayin' good stuff about people." Tom looked at Danny. "About us."

"Okay," Hairdo said. "Fair enough."

"'Fair enough,'" Tom said. He shot a sly smile at Hairdo before turning to Danny. "Guy's known us for over thirty years, and now all of a sudden he wants to start askin' tough questions." The three men laughed. "So anyways, as I was sayin' before Harry offered his enlightening dissertation on toasts, I have one last toast to make for the night." Tom raised the boot. "To Jimmy. How the hell anyone can bounce back from a bat to the head like that is beyond me."

Danny smiled as he watched his brother chug his boot beer. But then his smile disappeared, and his eyes went empty.

"Ya know, I never really asked ya before," Danny said, and then stopped to look over his shoulder. He continued after turning back. "But, ya know, with you bringing up Dad and toasting. Well, Hairdo already knows the story, but I never said anything to anyone else, not even to Kate . . ." And then Danny stopped. Silence claimed the table for several seconds.

"What?" Tom finally said. He set the boot down slowly and offered a thin smile, wondering where the hell Danny was going.

"Remember when Dad stabbed me?"

Tom's smile went missing. "Don't go there." Tom downed the remainder of the boot beer.

"I gotta know."

"Nope." Tom took the remaining pint and poured some of it in Danny's glass, before dumping the rest into the boot.

"C'mon, Tom."

Tom rummaged through his hair with his right hand. "Hold on." He took the empty shot glasses to the bar and returned with three fresh shots of Jameson. He pushed two across the table and kept one for himself.

"Okay, so does this mean we can talk now?" Danny chided.

Gone was Tom's earlier playful demeanor. "Go ahead," Tom said with disinterest. He set both hands behind his head and leaned back in the booth.

"Well, all I wanna know is . . . is why? That's all. Why'd he do it?"

Tom leaned across the table, his words coming rapid fire. "You didn't deserve it. I know that. Dad knew that. And he felt terrible afterwards."

"He never said so to me."

"Well, he did to me," Tom said. "And I'm sure he woulda said something to ya. He wanted to, but, well . . . he wasn't around much longer after that."

Danny remained silent for a moment, staring into his shot of Jameson. "But why?" he said softly.

"He said he saw you in his papers, his stuff. Okay? And he just snapped. Snapped. That's it." Tom leaned forward again and set his hands on the table. "Look, he didn't see *you*. It wasn't *you*. He just saw somebody lookin' through shit they shouldna been lookin' through. It coulda been you, me, a woman, Ma, Hairdo, a priest. Anybody. The same thing woulda happened. He just snapped."

Danny shook his head, his words a hair above a whisper. "I was just lookin' for a *Playboy*."

"But Dad never kept his Playboys in that blue shoebox. That's where he kept his . . . his other shit."

Danny's leaned in towards Tom. The brothers were almost face to face. "What other shit?"

"His other shit."

"But what?"

"This conversation's over." Tom downed his Jameson and motioned towards Ronny's boot. Danny passed it to him, and Tom finished it.

"So Dad did stuff other than just being a bookie?"

"Drink up!"

Danny narrowed his eyes. "What about you, Tom?" Danny said as he twisted the shot glass in circles on the table. "Did you ever do anything more than just break a hand or a leg?"

Tom stared at Danny with indifference. "Now I could ask ya who you been talkin' to. But I'm not. 'Cuz I don't give a rat's ass." Tom stood. "Drink up. Let's go."

Danny laughed. "Always givin' orders. Like you expect everyone to jump up and dance at every word you say."

Hairdo's eyebrows shot up. "Easy, Dan," he said.

"No, not easy." Danny backhanded his shot glass, knocking it to the floor. "Ya wanna know what I want?" Tom stayed silent, his eyes set on the fallen shot glass. "I wanna hear ya sing."

"What the fuck are you talkin' about?" said Tom.

Danny staggered to his feet, a yard away from Tom. "Sing," he barked.

Hairdo slid between the two men, both hands on Danny's shoulders. "Let's go, Dan."

Danny dropped into a boxer's stance, his left hand in the lead, his right hand back and cocked. He threw slow-motion punches as he sang.

"Hit 'im with the left, hit 'im with the right, punch 'im in the gut, and watch 'im fly outta sight."

Tom stared hard at his brother. Danny stepped back.

"C'mon. Dad's song, his boxing song. You know it. Sing it."

"I'm not singin' that stupid fuckin' song."

Hairdo eased back a bit.

"You used to sing it all the time. Remember? Both of us, we'd sing it together and throw fake punches." Danny dropped into a boxing stance again, but then stood tall when Tom turned away. "You used to sing that song all the time. Why not now?"

"'Cuz I'm not." Tom snagged the shot glass from the floor and set it on the table. "C'mon, let's go."

"Ya know, I was thinking the other day about Dad's song. And about you. And then it sorta came to me. I haven't heard you sing the words in a long time. It was just me singin' whenever we threw our fake punches. Not you. Not for a long time." Danny leaned in towards Tom. "You stopped singin' when you started workin' for Dad."

"Let's go." Tom said, his words more a threat than an order.

"Am I right?"

Tom turned and walked towards the back door.

"Am I?" Danny and Hairdo watched as Tom pushed his way through the back door, into the alley darkness.

27. Coach Lass

DURING A MORNING BREAK AT WORK the following day, Danny contacted Jankowski and declined to take the job Jello offered. Throughout the balance of the workday, Danny's mind was locked on James Lassandrello. He had gone through the photos and other intel Jankowski supplied on the man known to many as "Coach Lass." He also reviewed his background and resume on the website for De La Salle High School, where he worked. Sure, the job would have paid five times more than the normal pay but that mattered little to Danny. Busting up a hand or a leg—a guy can recover from all that, but taking that next step, there was no recovering from that.

After work, Danny drove to De La Salle High School at Thirty-Fifth and Michigan, just a fifty-yard stroll from Chicago Police Headquarters. He parked beneath the el tracks that ran along the west side of the school and walked up near the fence along the baseball field. Coach Jim Lassandrello was at the helm running a late summer baseball workout. As Danny observed practice, several trains clanked and rattled past the Thirty-Fifth Street station behind him towards points downtown and south.

From infield practice, to cut off plays, to batting practice—everything about Coach Lass's workout was measured and precise, leaving Danny no choice but to be impressed. As the practice came to a close and the players raked the infield, Danny walked up toward the dugout and approached Lassandrello.

"Can I ask you somethin', Coach?" Danny yelled.

Coach Lass looked up with a smile on his face. "Sure. Fire away." He ambled over to Danny. Only a chain link fence separated them.

"Well, my kids are big basketball guys, but they love baseball too. And my oldest kid, he's twelve. Anyways, he's got a pretty good arm, but he always seems to pitch outside against righties all the time."

Coach Lass's head nodded a bit, and he took Danny's words into consideration.

"Twelve-year-old, huh?" Coach Lass said and again smiled. "Is he gonna be a D man?"

Danny laughed. "Could be. Maybe D. Maybe Rice, maybe Carmel."

"Is he a righty or lefty?"

"Righty."

"Okay, and does he pitch lefty hitters outside too?"

Danny gave it a bit of thought, replaying Sam's delivery in his head. "No, those guys get pitched inside."

"That's good. I just asked because I wanted to make sure he wasn't afraid to hit someone with a pitch."

"Gottit," Danny said. "He's plunked plenty of guys. Doesn't seem to bother him."

Coach Lass pushed his hat up a bit on his forehead. The sun beat down on his face as he thought aloud. "So he's not afraid to pitch inside, but his ball is always pushing off the plate to the left." Coach Lass removed his hat and then slid it back in place. "Where does he put his foot on the rubber?"

Danny again replayed Sam's pitching motion in his mind. He stopped when he saw Sam's post foot on the rubber. "As he's looking in at the catcher, his foot is on the far, left side of the rubber. That's where—"

"Well, that's it. Gotta be," Coach Lass barked out as if he just solved a mathematical equation of vital importance. "Have him move his post foot to the other side of the rubber. You know, to the far, right side." Coach Lass smiled. "I'll bet that'll do it. His ball'll probably run right in over the strike zone then."

Danny extended his hand over the fence. "Thanks, Coach. I appreciate your help."

"And if that doesn't work, stop by and see me again."

"I will. For sure."

Coach Lass smiled. "Something else?"

Danny shook his head. "Nah. Nothin' else." Danny smiled again and walked off towards the parking lot.

Once he slid into the driver's seat, Danny watched as Coach Lass and the players stored the rakes and other equipment in a shed near the home dugout. He considered approaching Coach Lass yet again to tell him to be on the lookout, to let him know that someone wanted him to disappear. But Coach Lass wouldn't believe him. He'd probably laugh and then call security to come physically escort Danny off the premises. What Coach Lass needed was a few more visits from Danny. A couple of visits over the next day or two with more baseball questions and Coach Lass would get to know Danny a bit, and Danny would earn his trust.

28. The Heavy Bag

IT WAS 6 A.M. DRESSED IN GRAY SWEATPANTS and a Cubs T-shirt, Tom stood in front of the speed bag in his garage. He tapped the bag with his left and then his right and then stopped. A layer of sunshine pushed through the lone window, fanning itself across the ring. Three times per week, Tom started his day by holding his own private workout in his garage, before making the drive to the Union Hall. Again Tom tapped the bag with his left. Again he stopped. The words Danny threw at him at the Dubliner the other night bounced about his brain. *Sing*, Tom's eyes were fixed on the speed bag. *Sing*. He could see Danny and himself as young kids, smiling and laughing as they sang their father's song in unison and threw synchronized punches. *Sing. Sing. Sing.* Danny's words, his orders, kept running through his mind.

Tom walked over to the heavy bag and stuck the bag with a right hook and then a left uppercut. *SING. SING.* Danny's words were now screams. Tom unleashed a flurry of hooks, uppercuts, and crosses for over a minute. Sweat poured from Tom's forehead. *SING. SING.* Again Tom attacked the bag. Again the bag bounced, and the chain connecting it to the overhead beam rattled. Tom kept swinging, the sound of the bag, the rattling of the chain drowning out Danny's voice. And then Tom heard old man Lonigan's voice. "That's it, Tommy," Jim Lonigan said as Tom continued his assault on the heavy bag. "Let's have a good one now. Your best. Your very best. The bag is your enemy. Right?" Tom stopped and nodded. "Make it hurt." A smile claimed Tom's face. He stood up straight to catch his breath. Danny's voice was now long gone. "Ready?" Tom nodded. "Go." The room became a chamber of grunts, groans, rattlings, screeches, and screams.

A man walking his dog along the sidewalk stopped about twenty feet away, the sounds from the garage setting his ears at attention. His face quickly morphed into a twisted knot, his posture—Marine stiff. The dog barked nonstop and pulled the man towards the garage. The man yanked on the leash again and again, struggling to pull the dog away. Once he gained control, the man led the dog across the street from the garage and scampered off down an alley.

29. Headlines

CCOACH LASS'S TOMORROW NEVER CAME. After downing a bagel and a cup of coffee, he walked from his Bridgeport home along Thirty-Fifth Street on his way to De La

Salle the following morning. He never made it to work. The *Tribune* provided the news the following day with a Page 4 headline that read, "HS Baseball Coach Shot Dead." Accompanying the story was a photo of Lassandrello, his wife, and his three girls.

At work, Danny spent the early part of his day staring at his screwdriver or toying with the tape on his lineman's pliers. And then it happened. The slideshow. The faces of the various coaches Danny had played for over the years flashed before him. From Dave Macek, Danny's first little league coach, to his college basketball coach, Nate Newport, they were all there—barking out orders, offering instruction, smiling, grimacing, sweating. But then Coach Lass appeared—his face so big, as Danny saw it that day, it could have filled an old school, drive-in movie screen. And that face wouldn't leave. So Danny stopped working. He plopped himself on the floor in a phone closet, pressed his back against the wall, and didn't budge, the *Trib* in his lap.

"The fuck you doin'?" Hat said when he entered the closet.

Danny didn't say a word.

"You turn into a statue or somethin'?" Hat smiled. "That's it, huh? Statue man, right?"

Danny stared at the other wall, just five feet away, his eyes rummaging across the tiny green, orange, blue, and white wires entering the phone switch. And then he started to count the number of tiny green, orange, blue, and white wires that exited the other side of the switch.

"Dan, what's up?" Again Danny stayed mute, his eyes still trained on the wires. Hat massaged his chin but then walked off.

A short time later, Danny told Hat and Maggie that he was feeling sick and was going home. He refused Hat's offer to drive him home. He walked off the job site on the near Northwest Side and wandered into a tavern on Grand Avenue where he drank himself into a stupor. Every shot and beer he downed was done with a purpose—to rid his brain of that oversized image of Coach Lass. But it didn't work. Not even close. Coach Lass was still there. And every now and again, that image became an action scene with Coach Lass squinting into the early morning sun as he walked to work along Thirty-Fifth Street, or there was the close-up of Coach Lass lying in the alley beside the restaurant dumpster where they found him, a bullet hole in his forehead. Danny had a cab bring him home.

Later that night, Danny slipped into bed, with Kate asleep beside him. He pressed his back tight against the headboard. As he sat, he watched Kate's chest rise and fall peacefully, he watched the minutes change on the digital clock atop Kate's dresser, but mostly, Danny stared out the window at the large oak in his neighbor's yard, its huge gray limbs shaking with the wind in the darkness, aiming accusational wooden fingers Danny's way.

The next few days brought more of the same. Danny wandered down to the basement each night, once Kate fell asleep, where he dozed for a few hours on a couch. He liked the darkness and quiet offered in the basement. And then, as the days continued, Danny stopped eating. Almost entirely. Sure he would down a bowl of Cheerios each morning, but that was it for the remainder of the day. He dropped six pounds. Kate was thrown off by Danny's silence. She figured he was in a funk and just needed some time to clear his head. But Danny's head was anything but clear. The Coach Lass slideshow still ran amok along the walls of his brain. His remedy: he sought refuge in books. He was sure Hubert Selby or Tim O'Brien or John Steinbeck or Tobias Wolff had the answers he needed. They did not.

And then there was the other question that kept coming back to Danny . . . WHY? WHY? Why James Lassandrello? What did he do to deserve a premature death? Danny brought it up to Hat one day at work. He knew Hat had graduated from the same high school around the same time. Hat probably knew some of the guys in Coach Lass's crowd.

"Did you know that Lassandrello guy?" Danny said from his throne one day as Hat drove down the road with Maggie at his side. Hat gave Danny a quick look before he turned his eyes back to the road. Danny never knew if Hat got the word from Jello on Danny's doings. At first, he thought he did, but Hat never once asked him about anything to do with Jello. Maybe he knew, and that was just his way. Or maybe Jello kept him insulated from the bigger games.

"Yeah, I knew Lass," Hat said. "Good fuckin' guy. For sure."

"Are you talking about that schoolteacher? The coach that got shot?" Maggie said.

"Yep," Danny said.

"Give ya the shirt off his back," Hat said. "I went to his wake. Funeral too." Hat sucked in a deep breath and spat it out. "Place was packed. The captain of the baseball team gave the eulogy. Kid had some real cool memories to share. Real good. All the kids loved him." Hat turned onto Congress to head west. "Hope they catch the prick who got 'im."

"He was a coach at D, right?" Danny said.

"Yeah. Good baseball guy," Hat said. "Solid fundamentals. Old school shit. Jello's grandson played for him."

"No kiddin'?" Danny offered.

"Yep. Or I guess I should say he was on the team. Hardly played at all. And Jello thought his grandson was the goods." Hat pulled into a ward yard and parked. "Barely got off the bench—even in his senior year."

"How'd that go over with Jello?" Danny said.

"Not good. He'd be fumin' at games." Hat laughed. "Jello even approached Lass after a game one time and they got into it—you know two Paisans spittin' words at each other."

"When was this?"

"This last season . . . after a game in mid-May. Anyways, Coach Lass basically told Jello to fuck off. Said this was his program and he'd run it the way he saw fit." Hat smiled. "Big balls. Like I said—old school."

Danny's mouth went dry. He opened his bottle of water and took a huge drink.

"The kid, Jello's grandson . . . he was all broken up when he heard about his coach," Hat added. "Sure he didn't play, but that didn't matter. He loved the guy. Thought he was a great coach. Like I said, all the kids loved 'im."

The three stepped out of the van. Danny grabbed two sticks of electrical conduit. Maggie snatched a pipe bender and a box of wire. Hat led the way as they entered the Twenty-Seventh Ward administrative building.

30. Empty

DANNY SAT WITH WINSLOW IN A BOOTH at the Dubliner. Empty shot glasses and bottles, some of the fruits of their five-hour stay, decorated their table. The *Sun-Times* sat beneath Danny's right elbow, directly beside Danny's journal. Throughout the night, Danny had thumbed through the newspaper so many times he could recite for you, page and paragraph, the stories of yesterday. Splotches of red sauce were scattered across various pages as Danny and Winslow, true multitaskers, had used the newspaper as their dinner mat for their Fox's Pizza—the first actual dinner Danny had taken down in roughly a month. That newspaper had also been used to catch the tears that had slipped down Danny's cheek.

Kate lay in bed wide awake staring up at the ceiling. She peered at the alarm clock—1:15 a.m. She didn't want to make another trip to the Dubliner. She'd been there five times over the past three weeks. Danny had changed so much in that short time. He wouldn't talk. Barely ate. Was losing weight. Had no interest in sex. Quit school. Went into the basement when he returned from work to be alone to write in his journal. Slept on the basement couch. He didn't even check in on Jim any more. Kate gave him space at first, figuring Danny was in a funk of some sort. But whatever was eating at Danny was far more than a funk. Kate was now well aware of that. And then there was the Dubliner. Sure Kate had enjoyed many a fun night in there over the years, but too much was too much. She wanted Danny home. Now. Right now. She wanted him home so she could hold him and listen to him breathe. She would stay awake and hold him and listen to him breathe and cry—if he'd like, the way she heard him crying in the basement some nights when he came home from work the past few weeks.

Kate telephoned Hairdo. She hated dumping things in his lap, but Harry was family in Kate's eyes.

"What's up, lady?" Hairdo barked into his cell phone. He sat in the passenger seat of his squad car, a *Sports Illustrated* in his lap. He and his partner, Richie, trolled west down 111th Street towards Kedzie, as only cops can troll.

"I need a favor," Kate said, "Danny's out and about again."

"Gettin' to be a habit, huh?" Hairdo said. He closed the magazine.

"Do you think—"

"I'm on it, Kate. We'll head to the Dubliner right now." Hairdo nodded to Richie, who made a U-turn and headed towards Western.

"Sure you don't mind?"

"No problem at all." Hairdo laughed and switched gears. "Hey, how's Big Mamma feelin', by the way?"

"She's doing great," Kate said. "Dr. Valek said her cancer hasn't moved into any other areas."

"Good news."

"Yeah. She was here the other night for dinner with Ellen and Tom." Kate went silent for a moment. "Danny stayed in the basement the whole time. Didn't come up to eat."

"Really?"

"Yep."

"How'd that go over with Tom?"

"Tom went down to talk to him. He said Danny didn't say a word. He just stared into the TV."

"Did Tom give him a smack or anything?"

"No." Kate tapped the side of her cell against her cheek for a moment. "Ellen went downstairs and sat with him, too. And after a bit, I heard the two of them crying. Just crying together."

"Maybe Ellen can tell us what's goin' on in that noggin' of his."

"I know she could," Kate said. "But, uh . . . well, she can't."

"Yeah, right," Hairdo said and then cleared his throat. "Well . . . maybe I'll handcuff Danny and make him sit in the back of the squad for a while." Hairdo looked over at his partner. "Richie's a wee bit gassy tonight. Could be just what we need to coax a confession out of him."

Kate laughed. "Thanks, Harry."

"You bet."

As Kate ended her call, she set her cell phone on the kitchen counter and stroked the face of the family cat.

Hairdo entered the Dubliner alone and took a seat at the table beside Danny. Only four others were in the pub.

"You know Winslow, right?" Danny said. He flicked his right hand across the table in Winslow's direction.

Hairdo released a thin smile. "No, can't say as I do." Hairdo and Winslow shook hands.

"We work together. He's an electrician like me." Danny laughed. "He's my shrink too. He listens to me." Hairdo's eyebrows shot up.

"I'm not really his shrink," Winslow said. "I mostly jess listen to him ramble, and don't pay no attention to him. But as long as he buyin', I keep pretendin' I'm listenin." Danny and Winslow laughed.

"Ya know, Harry . . . ya know how sometimes you just drink, drink, drink until you start to drink yourself sober?" Danny said, his speech slurred.

"Yeah."

"Well, this is *not* one of those times." Danny and Winslow cackled like crows.

"Want something, Harry?" the bartender called out.

"Yeah, sure," Hairdo said. "How about a ginger ale." The bartender nodded. Hairdo ran his eyes around the bar.

"Kate call ya?" Danny said.

"Yep."

The bartender set the Ginger Ale on the table.

"I'll have another shot of Jame-Oh," Danny said. The bartender eyed Hairdo.

"Last one, right, Dan?" Hairdo said.

"Yep," Danny said. "And one for Winslow, too."

Hairdo nodded his approval to the bartender.

"Two Jameson's it is," said the bartender as he walked away.

Hairdo looked around the table. "Where's the boot? Ronny's boot?" Danny aimed a finger towards the bar. The boot stood atop the bar back. "Didn't feel like drinkin' out of it tonight, huh?"

"No, I'm classier than that."

Hairdo's eyes became slits. "Classy, huh? What, drinkin' outta the boot ain't classy?"

"Did you know Ronny Monroe disappeared?" Danny said.

"Really?" Hairdo's eyes remained slits. "When did this happen?"

"I dunno. Looks like nobody knows."

"Maybe he just moved to Florida or some other warm fuckin' place," Hairdo said. "Ya know, somewhere where he can lie in the sand like a beached whale." Harry glanced at Winslow but shifted his eyes back to Danny. "So look, I'm not gonna give ya the old 'I've known ya since first grade speech'—but I have known you since first grade. What the hell's up?"

"Did you know that when I was nine years old, I shot a robin and killed it. Shot it with a BB gun in my backyard. I can—"

"Not the goddamned bird story again," Winslow moaned.

Danny ignored him. "I remember . . . I left the bird in the back yard, left it to rot. But my mom found it and brought it inside the next day."

"Dan, I lived across the alley from ya, remember?" Hairdo said. "So, yeah, I remember the bird story."

"My ma . . . she was so disappointed in me. And just standing there lookin' at that bird, I realized what I had done. And I never felt so empty. Empty. And empty's not a good thing."

"Okay, so ya shot a bird when you were a kid," Hairdo said. "So what?"

"That's how I feel now too. Empty."

Winslow dropped his eyes to the ground. The bartender set two shots on the table. Hairdo studied his friend and wondered what he was trying to tell him. He ran the dead bird words through his brain again and again and watched as Danny took a tiny sip of his whiskey, before downing the entire shot.

"Well, ya can't be too damn empty," Hairdo finally said. "Ya probably got enough Jame-Oh and beer in ya to fill three bellies."

"Got that right," Winslow said.

Danny offered a smile. "I think . . . I think I'm gonna move to Ireland."

"How come?" Hairdo said. "They runnin' ads lookin' for new town drunks?" Danny went silent. He pushed the empty shot glass back and forth before him. "Run this past Kate or the boys?" Danny wagged his head. "Might wanna try that. Ya know, see what they think."

Danny looked up. "But then I'd have to talk to them."

Hairdo and Danny eyed each other in silence for a moment before Hairdo broke in. "I hear Sammy struck out fifteen guys his last Fall Ball game. And I shot some jumpers with Jim in the alley a couple of days ago. He's looking good again."

Danny's eyes returned to his empty shot glass. Hairdo stood and collected the empties from Danny's table. He carried them to the bar and paid Danny's bill.

"Ready?" Hairdo said when he returned.

Danny staggered to his feet.

"How 'bout you," Harry said to Winslow. "You need a ride?"

"Nah. I stay jess 'round the corner. On Artesian. I'm jess gonna stay and sip this here shot." Harry shook Winslow's hand again and then followed Danny out the back entrance to the waiting squad car.

31. A Plaster Cast

HAT WALKED ALING THE CORRIDOR at Thirty-Fourth and Lawndale on his way to say hello to Franky. As he turned a corner near the warehouse area, he saw Franky standing near the top of a six-foot ladder, his head and shoulders inside the drop ceiling. Franky's pants had been sliced into shorts on his right leg, to leave room for the pink plaster cast that ran from his toes to just below his knee.

Hat knocked on Franky's ladder as if it were a door.

"Hey," Franky said as he looked down.

"Where the fuck is your partner?"

"He ran to the john for a minute."

"Well, lemme help ya down. C'mon. You shouldn't be up on a ladder with a fuckin' cast on."

"Okay. Okay." Franky moved slowly down the rungs as Hat supplied back support. Franky eyed his cast when he made it to the floor. "You like the color? It's pink."

"This ain't fuckin' funny, Frank. Hear me. I told you. I—"

"I know." Franky stared into the concrete floor. "I'm sorry."

"You shouldn't be sorry. You didn't . . ." Hat coughed. "Do you know who it was, the guy who done this to ya?"

"Well, I know who ordered it."

Hat spun around, his face an angry, red knot. "FUCK."

"What? You didn't know?"

"Of course, I didn't fuckin' know. If I knew, I wouldna let it happen." Hat scratched his head. "Do you know who the guy was?"

"Yeah. I seen him before. He's some carpenter who works outta North and Throop. Dom somethin' or other. Don't know his full name though."

Franky's partner walked along the hallway towards the men.

"Hey, look buddy, I don't know your name," Hat said. "But I do know—"

"His name's Steve. Steve Mitchell," Franky said. "He's got some Greek in him too, so make sure ya keep him in front of you."

Mitchell laughed and offered his hand. Hat ignored it.

"Okay, Steve. Well, I want you to know somethin'. Your partner, Franky. He's a good man. He's important to me. And when I just got here, I saw him up on this ladder right here. So here's the deal, okay? He's gotta fuckin' cast on. See it?" Hat shot a finger towards the cast. "See that pink piece of shit wrapped round his right leg? See it? That's a fuckin' cast."

"Easy, Jimmy," Franky said. "Steve's a good kid. Real good kid."

Hat looked at Mitchell and then at Franky and turned away. He paced a few feet before turning back. "Okay, Franky. You're right." Hat faced Mitchell. "I'm sorry. Sorry 'bout jumpin' on ya like that." He offered his hand and Mitchell shook it. "My bad. Just make sure he's not gettin' up on any more ladders, okay?"

"No problem," Mitchell said. "I'll make sure he's either on a bucket or a chair."

Hat nodded. "Great. Thanks."

32. The Video

KILLING A BIT OF TIME AFTER LUNCH, Jim White sat at his desk engrossed in a game of Galaga on his computer, when his desk phone rang. White fired off a few more shots before picking up his phone.

"Jim White."

"Hi ya there, Mr. White."

"Who's this?"

"This is your friend, the Secret San Man."

White laughed. "Sorry about that. I didn't recognize your voice, right off."

"No problem. None at all. And good job, by the way, on the Copper Caper stuff."

"I thought you might like that."

"Sure did." The caller cleared his throat. "Now look, I gotta another somethin' for ya."

"Okay, fire away. But just know that I'm gonna record this again, okay?"

"Like I told ya before, I don't give a shit." The caller cleared his throat again. "So, well . . . this is about a city worker, only it's a little different 'cuz the guy's a cop."

"That's fine."

"Okay. So here it is in a nutshell. Did you hear about that guy who got beat to death in that bar on the Northwest Side about two months ago."

"You mean the guy who got in a fight with the off-duty cop? Victim's name was, uh, Jakocko. John Jakocko. Somethin' like that?"

"Yep, that's the one. Anyways, you may want to push a bit further on this one. It could turn into something big for ya. The reports all say somethin' different, but I know for a fact that the cop has some friends in high places. And it wasn't self-defense."

"You sure about that? Everything I saw said it was justifiable."

The caller coughed. "Cops coverin' another cop's ass. Surprise, Surprise."

"Okay. I'll look into it."

"Good. And you may want to push the city for a video. Word I got says the bar owner might still have a video. And that video holds all the answers."

"Hadn't heard anything about a video."

"Of course, not. It's an election year. But it's there. You just hafta get your hands on it."

"Gottit. Anything else?"

"This guy's family just filed a suit too. Might wanna keep an eye on that."

"Will do."

"That's it, Mr. White. Take care."

White hung up his phone and immediately went back to his computer. He shut down his Galaga game and dove into the events surrounding the beating.

33. Corner man

DANNY'S NEW WORK ROUTINE WAS THIS: dash to the liquor store at lunch three to four days a week for a pint of

Jameson's, and drive over to St. Barbara's Catholic school in Bridgeport where he'd pull up on the far side of Throop Street and park the van. So many city workers live in and around the Bridgeport area that, to everyone in the neighborhood, a city van is virtually invisible. It blends in. It belongs. No one from the school was alarmed to see that van there. And Danny would just sit there in the front seat and watch Lassandrello's youngest, Jenny—a 7th grader, play at recess as he downed his pint. Kids are so resilient, Danny thought, as he watched young Jenny run and chase other kids around the school lot on those days. At times as Danny watched Coach Lass's daughter race around the school yard, he couldn't help but smile. But once recess came to an end and Jenny disappeared through the school doors, Danny's smile would vanish.

But today, Jenny Lassadrello was a no show. At least she wasn't in the playlot. Home sick, Danny thought. He took one long, last pull on his whiskey bottle and then set the empty pint on the passenger seat. As the playlot cleared, Danny's eyes were fixed on the empty blacktop. The sun's rays banked off of the tar, sending shards of fire Danny's way. He raised his right hand for eye cover, and that's when he heard it. Clear as the bell that rang in the St. Barb's belfry to announce a funeral: *You shoulda told me, man. C'mon, why didn't you give me a heads up? I woulda been so ready. So ready.* Danny removed his hand and again stared out at the playlot, fully expecting to see Coach Jim Lassandrello staring back at him. But the lot was still empty, but for the reflection of the angry sun. So Danny started up the van and hit the pedal. He drove along Thirty-First Street to Lake Shore Drive, where he rolled down the van windows and let the warm air massage his face. He thought about cruising the Drive all the way north to Foster to see the joggers, bikers, boaters, and more along the shore. But as he passed Buckingham Fountain, he took a few turns and drove west—first on Congress and then on the Eisenhower. Danny exited the expressway at Cicero Avenue and drove through the heart of the West Side, making a turn here and another turn there, until he neared the intersection of Chicago and

Central, where a man worked the alley, just off the corner. He'd seen this man before on other job stops to a nearby city health facility. Danny pulled up beside him.

"What you sellin'?" Danny said through his open window.

"Fuck you care?" the man said.

Danny offered a half smile. "'Cuz I do,"

"What you want, cracker?"

"Already told ya. What you sellin'?"

The man approached the van and dropped both of his hands on the driver's side door. He peered into the cargo area before he spoke. "I sell the bess of the bess. It get you the highest of highs, and take you to the talless of mountains. Yes, sir." The man bobbed his head. "That's what I be sellin'. Want some, cracker?"

Danny licked his lips.

"Well?" The Corner Man removed a packet from his pants pocket and shook it in Danny's face.

"Nah. Just wanted to know what you were sellin'. Just curious.'"

"Curious, huh?"

"Yep."

"Curiosity killed the motherfuckin' cat, ya know." The Corner Man slid the packet back into his pocket. "And curiosity can kill a white boy, too." He let loose a toothy grin.

Danny forced a smile.

A customer slinked into the Corner Man's view, but held his ground in the doorway of an abandoned building.

"Okay. Time for you to mosey the fuck on outta here." The Corner Man waved an arm towards Danny as if he were trying to shoo flies away. "You scarin' off my steadies."

Danny drove off. In his sideview mirror, he watched as a man slid out from a building and approached the Corner Man to get his packet.

34. Tough Love

KATE WAS IN THE KITCHEN WITH THE KIDS: Max in his highchair shoveling handfuls of mushed peas into his mouth, Sam and Jim at the kitchen table ready to feast on a dinner of meatloaf, mashed potatoes and corn. Kate sat down. Danny's empty plate was just beside her. But Danny was in the basement. Again. Again. Again. Another meal. Another empty plate. Again.

"Dig in, guys," Kate said. Jimmy and Sam tore into their food. Kate slid a slice of meatloaf onto her plate, and then added the corn and mashed potatoes. She grabbed the spoon and ladled a bit of gravy onto her potatoes and then she added more. And then, yet more. And still more.

"What're ya doin', Ma?" Sam said.

Kate looked up. Sam and Jimmy had matching wide smiles. It was as if she was one of their own—a grade-schooler playing with his or her food at lunch while the teachers watched and shook their heads disapprovingly from a nearby table. Kate eyed her plate. It was swimming in gravy.

"Building a swamp, Ma?" Jimmy said.

Sam laughed.

Kate released a thin smile. "I'll be right back." She stood. "You guys keep eating. I'm going to see if your father would care to join us."

Sam's and Jimmy's faces went blank. Max stuffed more peas into his mouth.

Kate pulled the basement door closed behind her and moved down the stairs slowly but with purpose.

Danny sat on the couch scribbling in his journal. He turned when he heard the footsteps. He saw the plain blue running shoes first, then the gray leggings, and then the hoodie with the Loras College imprint, and then Kate's face. He went back to his journal, the pen scribbling frantically.

Kate moved gracefully towards Danny, as if she were approaching someone to request a first dance. She had given Danny plenty of space to resolve his issues. It clearly hadn't worked. She even overlooked his silence and his endless basement hours. And the boys—they no longer seemed to be a priority to Danny. Kate could deal with being ignored, but putting his own sons on the pay no mind list was just plain wrong.

"Care to join us for dinner tonight?"

Danny stayed focused on his journal, his thoughts.

"Meatloaf."

Danny's pen stopped. For a brief moment, the word *Meatloaf* bandied about his brain, elbowing it's way past the Coach Lass slideshow.

"Your favorite, right, Dan?" Kate let her eyes roam across every inch of her husband.

Danny's pen moved again.

"You need to eat something, Dan. You look like shit." Her tone was measured, precise, composed.

Danny's pen continued to move, now scribbling the words *Meatloaf* and *Shit* onto the page.

"Your boys need you, Dan."

Danny scribbled, *Sam, Max, Jimmy* in his journal.

Kate had enough. Her tolerance for silence, for space, for self-pity, for secrets, for being composed had finally reached its end. There was no more need for words.

Kate ripped the journal from Danny's hands and frisbeed it across the basement, the pages fluttering like a wounded bird before it hit the ground. She fully expected Danny to jump to his feet, to protest, to say something. He did not. He simply looked at his wife with an empty expression. Kate slapped Danny across the face. Hard. No response. She thwacked him again, this time with everything she could muster. Still no response. Kate took two steps and dove atop Danny, pressing his torso flat into the seat cushions on the couch. She clenched her right hand and fired two right hooks to Danny's face.

"Sammy needs you. Jimmy needs you," Kate barked as she swung. As best he could, Danny shifted beneath his wife—turning himself into a near-fetal ball, covering his face with his arms. Kate swung one more time. "And Max needs you too."

Danny stayed put. He didn't move or otherwise resist. It was as if he wanted to be beaten. And there were no tears, Not from him. None from Kate either. And there were no more words. Kate climbed back to her feet. She stood before Danny, her eyes taking in everything Danny had to offer at that moment, which wasn't much. He seemed to barely breath inside that protective fetal shell. Kate wanted to say more, to scream, to tell Danny to get his act together, to tell him he was a shitty father, to tell him that he was losing the boys, to tell him that he was losing her. Yes, her. And then, she wanted to say: *You said no more secrets. Remember that, Dan. No more secrets.* But Kate did not utter another word. She turned and walked slowly, gracefully up the stairs. She closed the door softly behind her and stood at the kitchen table. Jim and Sam were gone, their plates rinsed and washed in the sink. Max was gone too—no doubt carried off by his brothers, his high chair wiped clean. Kate sat and ate her gravy-soaked meal alone.

35. Ronny

THREE WORKERS FROM BOULDER ELECTRIC sat on buckets at their job site, eating lunch. One worker paged through the *Sun-Times*. When he hit Page 12, the worker saw the smiling face of Ronny Monroe—thick black glasses and all—staring back at him. Above that forgettable face was the headline, "Body Washes Up On Beach."

"Holy shit," the one worker barked.

"What?" one of the others said.

"It's Ronny Monroe." He jabbed a finger at the newspaper. "He's fuckin' dead. They found him floating in the water at Rainbow Beach."

"You fuckin' kiddin'?"

The man holding the newspaper shook his head. The three electricians huddled tightly together like kindergarten pals so each could read the story and munch on their sandwiches at the same time.

36. Shooter

AFTER WATCHING LASSANDRELLO'S DAUGHTER in the St. Barbara lot at lunch for weeks upon end, and downing his pints, Danny sat in his throne in the van as Hat and Maggie worked inside the firehouse at Irving Park and Damen. His thoughts drifted until they settled on the dealer offering his wares on the corner of Chicago and Central. He wondered what that would feel like—to plunge a syringe into a bulging vein. Danny could see the man who slinked out from that abandoned building when he drove off that day, the man who got his packet and, no doubt, the peace he needed. Danny pictured the man sitting in the shadows of an apartment gangway, the emptied syringe at his side, the juice running amok in his veins, a distant smile on his face. Danny nibbled his bottom lip and let his eyes rummage about the van for a few seconds until they stopped at his tool bag. He reached inside, removed a long, skinny flathead screwdriver, and began twisting the handle slowly between his fingers for almost a full minute. The sun pushed through the windshield and banked off of the blade, sending shards of light about the van with every twist and turn. Danny stopped and smiled as he stared at the handle. It was black and gold.

"My old team colors," Danny muttered to himself, as if he had just noticed the colors on his years-old screwdriver for the very first time. He raised the screwdriver to eye level for a moment, before placing it in his lap. He snatched a lineman's pliers from his tool bag and cut a foot-long piece of 14-gauge wire from a spool. He wrapped the wire once around his upper right forearm, twisting the ends of the wire with his fingers, until it formed a tourniquet of sorts. A mass of bulging veins stood atop Danny's right forearm. Again, Danny smiled as his eyes slowly wandered up and down his arm. But then thoughts of his father suddenly consumed him, and Danny was struck by how strange that was. He expected Coach Lass to be the center of attention, as usual, and yet here was Jim Lonigan creeping back into his life yet again.

"Your body is a temple," Old man Lonigan screeched. Danny

had heard his father utter those very words time and time again whenever he trained Tom and Danny in the ring. "Treat it like one."

Danny again twisted the screwdriver in slow circles and again shards of light flashed across the area. One shard struck a blue jay twitting in a small tree just beside the van, causing the bird to bounce about on several tiny branches before it finally stopped. It then set its eyes on Danny, or so he thought. And those eyes—they were pure black. Black limousine, black. End of the movie, Big Screen black. Danny turned away and again eyed the screwdriver. For a brief moment he ran the blade slowly along his right forearm, pressing hard against the flesh at times. The blue jay bounded from limb to limb, screeching, but its trills were silenced by the voice of Danny's father.

"Nice," old man Lonigan hissed as Danny created a web of two-and three-inch intersecting scratches, a bit of blood leaking from some of the tracings. Then Danny scratched his youngest son's name across his forearm with the head of the screwdriver and stopped.

"You done good," Jim Lonigan said. "Who the hell needs a temple anyways."

Danny's arm was on fire. He could feel the pain, and the pain felt good. In that moment, Jim Lonigan stood before his son with a steak knife in hand. And then he pushed it slowly into Danny's back. That's how Danny envisioned the stabbing when he reviewed it on this day. It was slow, gentle. Almost caring. But a stab in the back with a steak knife is never gentle, caring, or slow.

Danny leaned back in his throne to take it all in. He watched the tiny traces of blood push out from the multiple scratches he created on his right arm. The pain was steady, his arm still on fire. And then Jim Lonigan was gone and so was Coach Lass. Danny's thoughts again ran wild.

He imagined himself naked as he walked through a jungle of dandelions, the stalks a virtual wall. Either the dandelions were gigantic or Danny was small. He couldn't tell which was true. Either way, he liked his vision. As bits of blood dripped from his arm, he saw yellow pollen, thick as Beijing smog, floating down from the flower heads, turning Danny's body green. And Danny found that strange. And rightfully so. How can a yellow flower turn my skin green? Danny rubbed his arms with his hands, but the green stayed glued to his skin. He tried scratching at his arms, but the result remained unchanged. He was green. A cricket took notice of Danny as he continued to scrape his arms, and then moved on to his legs and the hair on his head, and that scratching, that scraping sound drew the cricket even closer. Danny stood still and stared into a full-length mirror he found leaning against the tallest of dandelions. He turned and examined his naked, green body, amazed that even his pecker was green. He slapped it a few times to see if the green would come off. It did not. And then Danny thought he should form a new band, and maybe he could get Winslow to play in his new band too—the Green Man Group. But then he wondered if Winslow's black skin would turn green like Danny's. Maybe Winslow's skin would turn red or orange. And then Danny saw it—the cricket, moving towards him in the mirror. He froze and the cricket started nipping at his shoulder. Danny was not so much in fear as he was fascinated with the cricket. Again, Danny thought—either that cricket is gigantic or I'm small.

Maggie entered the van in search of a box of wire. She saw the blood on Danny's arm and on the van floor, the wire band around his arm.

"What the hell." Danny didn't budge. His eyes were fixed on his screwdriver. "Dan, Dan. You okay or what?"

Danny shook to. "Yeah." He bounced to his feet and slid out the van door. "I gotta hit the John." As Danny walked off towards the firehouse, he removed his flannel shirt and wrapped it around his right arm.

"My God," Maggie said, when she saw more drops of blood on the arm of Danny's throne. Maggie turned around and examined the area before climbing inside the van and closing the door. She grabbed Danny's book bag and rifled through it, in search of any new material she had not yet read. She pulled out his journal and began to review it. She read damaging words about broken arms, a broken leg, Lassandrello, and the fine line between fiction and reality. As she read, the side door flew open.

"Where the hell's that wire?" Hat barked.

"Sorry," Maggie said. "I came out here to get it and found Danny in here. He just ran off to the john. But, uh, something's up. Something's wrong." She pointed at some of the blood.

"What the fuck." Hat's face was a worried knot.

"He had a wire wrapped around his arm. Sorta like a tourniquet. I, uh, . . . I think he cut himself."

"On purpose?" said Hat. His eyes widened.

Maggie nodded.

Hat stared at Maggie in silence for several seconds. "That's no good. I gotta cousin who's been cuttin' himself for years. Guy's a fuckin' basket case." But then his eyes became slits. "So answer me this, huh? Danny cuts himself and what do you do? You read his fuckin' journal?"

Maggie played it innocent and laughed. "He went to the bathroom. What could I do?"

"You could come tell me what the fuck's goin' on."

"I was gonna. I was. But Danny's journal was open, so I just read a little bit. And this one part here is funny. Really funny." Maggie smiled. "Here, listen." Maggie turned back a few pages to a point she had previously reviewed. "This one's about you." Maggie read:

> *So one of the guys I work with is a guy named Jimmy Scarpelli. Good man. When I first told my sons Jimmy's name, they wanted to know if he was a mobster. Funny shit. Kids are great, aren't they? Anyways, I laugh . . ."*

"Okay, stop," Hat barked. "Are you fuckin' nuts. Danny's hurt, and ya want me to stay here and listen to this shit." Hat aimed a hand at Maggie. She passed the journal to him, and Hat stuffed it back into the book bag. "That's his shit. His personal shit. We only hear what he wants us to hear. And only when he wants us to hear it."

Hat ran his eyes about the van. He saw more drops of blood on the floor. "Jesus Christ." He raced inside to find Danny.

Ellen sat on a couch in Mary Lonigan's apartment. She saw Danny running through the dandelion garden. And she saw the cricket, too, in hot pursuit. The full-length mirror lay broken on the garden floor. Beside it, the garden was dotted with blood. Danny was so tiny, and Ellen wondered how this happened. But now the cricket had Danny pinned up against a rock and started chewing on his right arm. Ellen wrapped her arms around her knees, turning herself into a virtual ball and rocked herself back and forth, moaning all the while. The cricket hissed at Danny and again started to gnaw on his arm. As the cricket pressed forward, Ellen rocked even faster and her moans grew louder.

37. Problems

JELLO BUZZED HAT INTO HIS OFFICE.

"Hey, Jimmy," Jello said, a wide smile on his face. "Good to see ya. Didn't— "

"Don't gimme that shit," Hat barked.

Jello's smile evaporated.

"I just left Danny Lonigan. He fuckin' sliced his arm up. On purpose. Ya hear me? On fuckin' purpose."

"What? You sayin' he slit his wrists?"

"No, he ain't tryin' to kill himself. He's, well . . . I dunno. I guess he's tryin' to hurt himself." Hat spat out a long breath. "I asked him why, and he wouldn't say a word. Couldn't say a word.

Jello walked away from Hat. Hat walked after him and spun him around.

"Get your hands offa me." Jello swung his arms to free himself from Hat's grip.

Hat shoved Jello. "The fuck ya do to him?"

Jello stabbed his right index finger into Hat's chest. "You need to be careful, Jimmy. You—"

"WHATCHA DO TO HIM?" Hat screamed.

Jello went quiet for a moment and sighed before speaking. "Look, he's a big boy," Jello said in a calm voice. "He said *no*. He has that right. And he used it. He said *no*."

Hat swung his head back and forth. "C'mon. You didn't?" Hat staggered away, drifting from side to side as if someone had just punched him in the stomach.

"He said, 'No.' Like I said, he didn't do it. So what's the problem?"

Hat stared hard at Jello. "You shouldna asked him to do THAT. Definitely not. THAT'S the fuckin' problem."

"But he didn't do it. So there shouldn't—"

"Stop. Just stop." Hat shook his head in disgust and walked out of Jello's office.

38. Church

AT BEST, DANNY, KATE, AND THE KIDS could be called part-timers for their attendance over the years at St. Barnabas Church, a stronghold in Chicago's Beverly neighborhood. They always made the biggies—Christmas, Ash Wednesday and Easter, and the boys had all been baptized there. And Jim and Sam made their Communions there as well. But other than that, going to church once a month was roughly the Lonigan average. If Danny were to be judged by his attendance at Sunday Mass, most would say that he was not a religious man. But that would be far from the truth. Danny certainly believed in a Divine Being—a god, if you will, and he always felt a certain closeness to him. And Danny was also a firm believer in silent nightly prayers. For him, that's what worked. That's what felt comfortable.

Over the years, Danny rarely asked for help for himself or his family in his prayers. The first time he knocked on God's door was when Jim was born severely premature, when his doctors didn't exactly paint a rosy survival picture. But after two operations, a twenty-eight-day hospital stay, and plenty of prayers—"Please, God. Please. Let me take him home"—survive he did. And the second was after Big Pete's baseball bat pegged Jim on his forehead.

Even now, Danny Lonigan still offered his nightly prayers. He did not ask God to forgive him for his most recent actions. As Danny saw it, he did not deserve forgiveness, and he would take whatever punishment God found appropriate. And though he still did not attend Mass regularly, once every week or two, Danny found himself drifting through the solid oak doors of St. Barnabas Church during lunch or immediately after work. At the other churches he attended in his youth, Danny would sit up close to the altar so he could have a good view of the statue of Jesus nailed to the cross, staring out at the flock he would no doubt one day save. But such was not the case here. The Christ above the St. Barnabas altar was more of a metallic piece of art, a sculpture complete with a see-through body and no eyes. How can you talk to a Christ with no eyes? That thought had bounced around Danny's skull on more than one occasion. He was more comfortable sitting in a pew off to the side of the church near the smallish statue of Mary. She had eyes. She looked real. And though she was not life-sized, Danny felt comfortable near her. So there Danny sat several days a month, absorbing the quiet, looking at Mary and offering his words, his prayers. He rolled up his sleeve to let Mary see the cuts, the slices on his right arm, the artwork he now created on a daily basis, the artwork that allowed him to feel alive. And he knew God could see those marks too. So there Danny sat talking to God, his right arm draped over the back of the pew in front of him. But as he whispered his words, he couldn't help wondering if God or Mary would even take the time to listen to someone like him anymore.

39. Quarters McNicholas

MAGGIE AND HAT INSTALLED A TIME CLOCK in a Water Department trailer while Danny slept on his throne in the van. Hat stood outside the trailer and fed telephone wire through a hole in the trailer wall Maggie had just drilled. A gathering of eight or so Water Department workers sat at two tables at the far end of the trailer, enjoying their morning break. The men didn't say a word to Maggie, but their eyes were on her, a free peep show, of sorts, as they feasted on their egg, sausage, and cheese sandwiches. One man removed a cell phone and discreetly set it on the table, before snapping several photos of Maggie. He then pulled his baseball hat down tight over his eyes and stared into a newspaper.

When Maggie and Hat took a break, the man who took the cell photos climbed into his car and drove off. He covered a number of miles before he parked along Lawndale, a few blocks away from the CDOT building on Thirty-Fourth and dialed Jello.

"Hey, it's me. We need to talk."

"So talk," Jello said.

"In person. I'm down the street in my car."

"'kay."

A few minutes passed before Quarters McNicholas saw Jello waddling towards him. McNicholas stepped out of his car with two botted waters in hand. He gave one to Jello, as the men turned and headed towards Thirty-First Street.

"So I was at work this morning in the trailer, over in the Ravenswood area."

"Yeah, so?"

"So I'm in the trailer, and I see your nephew there putting in a time clock. And he's paired up with this snatch."

"Yeah, with Maggie. That's one of his partners."

"Maggie Schmaggie," McNicholas said. "She's the fed."

Jello stopped. "What?"

"She's FBI."

"You sure about this?"

"Oh yeah."

Jello started walking again. He turned onto Thirty-First Street, heading West, with McNicholas alongside of him.

"How do ya know?"

"Her name's Coin. I met her a few years ago," McNicholas said with indifference and then took a swig of water. "You don't forget the faces of the people who help send you away."

"How's that?"

"She was the agent who testified about the number of bags of quarters they found in my basement after the raid."

"She see you today?"

"No. But I snapped a couple of photos of her to be sure." He pulled out his cell phone and showed Jello the pictures.

"That's Maggie, all right," Jello said. "Maggie Sunfield."

"I don't know what the hell her bullshit name is now, but like I said, her real name's Coin." Jello heard the squeal of rubber biting pavement and then a horn. He turned and saw a CTA bus stopped in the middle of Thirty-First Street. A coyote drifted out from the front of the bus, tossed a what's-yer-problem look at the bus driver, and then sauntered across the street. This bushy-tailed creature moved as though it belonged on a city street, as though it had every right to stop traffic and cross over to walk along the sidewalk. Jello watched until the coyote disappeared down an alley. The two men turned around and traced their path back towards McNicholas's car.

40. Gamble

MONIQUE GAMBLE SAT IN HER OFFICE in the Dirksen Building. It was 4:00 p.m. Had she a window to look out, she would have done so. Perhaps she would have stood at that window to watch the flow of people making their way towards their trains, buses, and cars—all scurrying and readying themselves for the rush-hour commute. But Gamble did not have a window in her office. Instead she had four, beige cinder-block walls. Her eyes were fixed on a framed piece of art on one of those walls, a black ink drawing of the scales of justice. Gamble bobbed her head and turned to review the material on her laptop screen. Then she hit the print button. She snatched the printed pages and reviewed the contents once again.

"Violation of Probation. Daniel P. Lonigan"

Gamble summarized as she reviewed the three paragraphs. Two missed monthly meetings for August and September. Three missed community service dates (August 24, 31, and September 7). Defendant has not responded to phone calls (four calls with messages), mail (two mailings), or emails (two emails).

Gamble signed the second page of the form and grabbed her phone. She punched in four digits.

"Hi, Jason, can you step in for a moment? I have a violation I'd like you to file."

"Do you want this filed today or is tomorrow okay?"

"Today, I've let this go long enough."

"Got it. Okay, I'll be by in a minute to grab it."

"Thanks." Gamble hung up the phone and again set her eyes on the scales of justice.

41. Sliced and Diced

KATE WALKED DOWN THE BASEMENT STAIRS. It was 3:00 a.m. Danny was splayed out naked on the couch, his journal in his lap. Kate grabbed the journal and tip-toed over to a basement window where the moon offered sufficient light. Danny's most recent words were sloppy and ran together, as though written in a panic, but Kate tried her best to make sense of them. Run-on sentences run amok about Jim Lonigan, paragraphs about Jello, and more words still about some man named Coach Lass. And as Kate turned the pages, she saw it. Blood. First, drops here and there on a page, then curved lines made up of dot after dot of the tiniest specks of blood one could ever muster—as though Danny was trying to form letters or symbols with his own droppings, and then—sloppy, bloody thumbprints on other pages. Kate turned towards Danny, her eyes fixed on his chest. It moved ever-so-slowly up and down. His sleep was deep. And in that moment the entire house seemed to take a huge breath and hold it in silence. Then the furnace hummed as it kicked on to provide warmth.

An empty fifth of tequila and a half-emptied pint of Jameson guarded the table beside the couch. And then Kate saw the potato peeler next to the smaller bottle. She wondered what that was all about. She knelt on the floor beside Danny and leaned over him as if she were a dermatologist preparing to give a thorough exam to a fair-haired Irishman. And there it was. Danny's right arm— reaching out from under his pillow in plain sight. How had she missed that? Kate counted the cuts, the nicks, the slices, the Xs, the Os, the carvings. Thirty-seven marks in total.

"Is Dad gonna be all right?" Jim had asked a few nights ago, when he heard his father crying in the basement.

Kate looked across the dinner table at Jim and Sam. "Sure, honey," She offered her best convincing smile. "He's just in a funk right now. But he'll be fine." And so Kate and the boys blocked out the sounds coming from the basement as best they could and went back to their stew.

But as Kate looked down at Danny on this day, she knew with certainly that she had lied to her boys just two days ago. And as her eyes ran up and down Danny's body, she also became acutely aware of three other things. One: this man sleeping on the couch was no longer the man she married. Two: this man's days were numbered. And three: Kate had to do something to help.

As Kate continued to view her husband, Danny was completely immune to her presence. His chest continued to rise and fall slowly as he slept. In his dreams, he sat at his backyard picnic table and scribbled words in his journal. A ball bounced nearby, and every now and again Danny would look up to see his boys shooting baskets and barking at each other in the alley. That brought a smile to his face. And then Danny sketched the faces of Jim and Sam and Max in his journal. Gone were Coach Lass and old man Lonigan and that damn steak knife. Danny's chest continued to rise and fall ever so slowly. His sleep was peaceful, the calm before the storm.

42. Decisions

EVERY MAN AND WOMAN REACHES A POINT where tough decisions have to be made. For some, it might simply be whether or not you should let your son borrow the car on a Friday night. You've seen his sixteen-year-old driving skills. He's nothing more than an accident waiting to happen. You know that. But you enjoy seeing his braces when he smiles, so you give him the keys anyways. And you spend those nights staring out your front room window, hoping to see your son and the car come back in one piece. And then as your son grows older, you have to decide which college to send him to and how much dough you're willing to toss into the college kitty. Sure, you can hold off on the funds and keep more for yourself to enjoy in retirement, but you really don't want to saddle your kid with $50,000 to $75,000 in student loan debt. So you do the right thing. You pony up and pay, pay, pay. At work, the finances are tight, and the big boss tells you that you're in charge of choosing who gets the three pink slips. You could just put a note or letter in their mailbox at work. You knew a high school principal in Burbank who did that to one of your teacher friends once. Talk about a ball-less move. You could go that route, and they'd know not to show up at the workplace the following day. But these folks have worked with your employer for years, one for almost fifteen years, so you call them all in—one at a time—and deliver the news. It's tough, but they appreciate the personal touch. It means something to them. But now, you're the mayor of a major city. And you have a terrible situation staring you square in the face. Months ago, a father of three was beaten to death inside a bar on the Northwest Side by an off-duty Chicago policeman, a policeman who just so happens to be the son of a very good friend of yours.

Everyone in the bar has either conveniently turned mute or they are cop friends who say the actions taken were in self-defense. So that's what all the reports say: justifiable self-defense. To the delight of your friend, the case was swept under the proverbial carpet and the police officer who unleashed that flurry of right hooks, heavy boots, and who slammed the victim's head off the side of a pool table repeatedly, has been back on the streets to serve and protect the citizens of Chicago for a number of weeks now. But there is a video from the bar owner, a video that speaks volumes. You saw it. But the media, the public—they have not seen the video. They never even knew it existed. What would they think if they knew you saw the video and did nothing? What would the masses think if they saw that video before the coming election? Would you survive? Decisions, decisions. Decisions like these define a man. A well-loved man, a respected man will be none of these if he fails to do the right thing. The good times will give way to the bad. And for a man who is not well-loved, here comes your head on a platter. But you want that next election badly so you can continue to put your stamp on the city. And you want to help your friend. So your friend pays a large sum to the bar owner for the video and then destroys it. Problem solved. But sometimes a rug gets lifted off the floor for cleaning, and the old dirt is still lying there for everyone to see. Sometimes, bar owners outsmart mayors and their friends, and make copies of videos. And then the city acquires videos like that, videos that are now known by all to exist, as evidence in a potential police hearing.

Stokely stared at the *Sun-Times* headline, "Video May Show Cop Is Killer." He reviewed Jim White's column, where he painted a gruesome picture. And then there's the quote. "We have settled this case with the victim's family," Mayor Stokely said at a news conference. "We felt it was the right thing to do. The actions taken by the police officer are under review at the current time, and charges are a possibility. This has been a difficult situation for the family, a painful situation. And in fairness to them, the city will not release the video at this point."

43. Kate and Mini-Mary

DANNY SAT IN A PEW AT ST. BARNABAS CHURCH, his right arm draped over the pew in front of him.

"What do you think you're doing?"

Danny heard the words, but then again Danny had been hearing lots of things lately. Maybe these were imagined words, too—words that were simply banging around inside his brain. He looked up and set his eyes on the statue of Mary, wondering if, perhaps, it was the Blessed Virgin who was gracing him with her syllables.

"Dan, what the hell're you doing?"

Danny turned around. Kate stood in a pew three rows behind him, her hands clawing the backrest of the pew in front of her.

He reached for his right sleeve and began to roll it down.

"You don't have to do that."

"What?"

"Cover up the marks."

"What're you talking about?"

Kate stayed silent, watching as Danny pushed his sleeves down until both forearms were completely covered.

"I know what you've been doing, Dan. I know." Kate let the silence take hold of her for a moment. "I've been coming down to the basement when you're sleeping or passed out, or whatever you call it. I've seen the marks."

Danny stood in the pew and turned to face Kate. His eyes were slits.

"And I've been following you. For three days now." A sad laugh leaked from Kate's lips. "I have a lot of time on my hands, Dan. You do know that, right?"

Danny maintained his silence.

"You don't think so, huh? Well, you're wrong. That's what I've been doing. Following you all over in my car. For three whole days. Like I said." Kate groaned. "Don't you even work anymore?"

"Keep it down," Danny said, his words barely a whisper. "This is a church."

"I know where I am, Dan. I *know* this." Kate let her eyes roam quickly across the sea of blond pews. But for an elderly couple on the far side near the choir box, the church was empty. "So, um . . . when do you plan to do your slicing today?" She scratched her head. "Can I watch?"

"Stop. Just stop." Danny dropped back into his pew, his eyes fixed on the floor. Kate walked out and around until she stood directly behind him. "I'm sorry. That was wrong to say that. I mean it. I'm sorry." Danny stayed silent. "Look, I'm going to get you some help." Danny shook his head back and forth. "I'm going to help you beat this. I mean it. I've been reading up on it, and together we—"

"No," Danny finally muttered. And then he turned and faced Kate. "Does Tom know?"

Kate's face became an angry ball. Of all the things to say. Here I am for you. Ready to help and you want to talk about your big brother. You're afraid to let him know your flaws. What about me? The kids? Where do we rate? Kate turned both hands into fists. Danny needed a pummeling. Another one. Indeed. Maybe that would open his eyes. Maybe that would stop the cutting. And Kate would feel so much better. But then a tear made an appearance. Kate watched as it slid across Danny's cheek.

Her words were soft, measured. "What difference does—"

"Does he know or not?" Danny erased the tear with his right hand.

"No, he doesn't."

Danny turned away, again staring into the floor. "Good. Keep it that way."

Kate stared at the slumped shoulders of the man she married thirteen years ago, the man she would do anything for. A multitude of questions zipped through her conscience at that moment, all the Hows, the Whys, the What the Hells—the same questions that had consumed her the past two days. She didn't have the answers. But she would help bring Danny back. She would learn his secret. She knew she could do this.

Mini-Mary, in her flowing blue robe, gazed at Kate from a few yards away. Kate met her gentle eyes with her own and brought her hands together for a moment in prayer. Yes, Mary would help bring Danny back. The two of them could handle this—whatever *this* was—together. And then Kate separated her hands and set them ever-so-gently atop those slumped shoulders. Danny sprang to his feet, as if someone had just set a torch to his soul, and raced out the back door of the church.

44. Shaking Like a Junkie

HAT AND MAGGIE TOILED AWAY INSIDE THE CITY WATER facility at Ninety-Fifth and Genoa, leaving Danny to snooze in his chair in the van. Patches of crust engulfed Danny's eyelashes, and he still smelled of last night's booze.

Maggie returned to the van to grab a time clock. Danny now sat upright on his throne, a newspaper in his hands as Maggie opened the side door.

"Hi ya, Mr. Pellegrini," Maggie said, hiding her surprise, when she saw Jello in the passenger seat. "Trying to wake up Danny Boy here?" Maggie smiled.

Jello chuckled. "Gettin' harder and harder to do," he said and then looked at Maggie in silence. Maggie grabbed the time clock and closed the door.

"Have a good day," she said through the passenger window. Jello nodded. When Maggie made it into the building, she immediately hustled for a deserted corner of the garage and dialed Agent Tangel on her cell.

"Something's going on," Maggie said. "Something big."

"I'd prefer specifics rather than generalities, Agent Coin," Tangel said.

"Jello Pellegrini is sitting in the front seat of our van, talking to Danny Lonigan. And that never happens. Never. You know that. I just—"

"I get it," Tangel said. "Jello doesn't go out to the underlings. They come to him. I get it." Agent Tangel stood in his office at Roosevelt and Leavitt. "If you could get close to that conversation, that would be great, but that's—"

"I'll give it a shot. I think I could swing—"

"No, No. On second thought, don't even chance it," Tangel said. He stared out the window at the nearby Cook County Juvenile Court complex. "You'd be possibly exposing yourself."

"You sure?"

"Positive," said Tangel. He walked to his desk and took a seat. "When you wrap up for the day, see if you can get some one-on-one time with Lonigan. Play it dumb. But probe him a bit on Jello's visit."

"Will do." Maggie ended the call.

Jello glared at Danny from the passenger seat. "I don't like to see you like this." His face was a ball of wrinkles. "You look like shit beat with a hammer." Danny didn't answer. He turned a page of his newspaper. "You ain't been returning my calls."

Danny spoke into his newspaper. "Maybe, that's 'cuz I don't want your calls." He turned another page.

Jello squinted. "Well, you need to hear this. Might just change things." Danny licked his finger and used it to turn a page yet again. "That girl, Maggie Sunfield. That ain't her real name. Her name's Margaret Coin. Agent Margaret Coin to be exact." Jello passed a photo to Danny who examined it. The photo displayed Maggie dressed in a business suit shaking hands with some FBI honcho. The official FBI seal stood behind them on a wall.

"She's the fed," Jello barked. Danny brought his newspaper to his lap and turned towards Jello. "My guess is she's got alotta shit on me. And she's probably got alotta shit on Hat and you too. Probably knows about Lassandrello." Jello eyed Danny's book bag. "Probably been readin' all your shit in that bag."

"Where'd you get this picture?"

"From a friend of a friend who works for the feds." Jello scratched his chest. "I gotta call on this the other day. Someone who saw Coin and knew her. I needed to get confirmation, so it took a couple of days to get this photo. To get confirmation."

Danny handed the photo back to Jello and returned to his newspaper. He turned another page. Jello snatched Danny's *Sun-Times* and threw it on the floor of the van. "She's gonna get us all tossed in the shitter," Jello barked. "You get that?" Danny stared hard at Jello. "Save yourself," Jello said. "Save me. Save Hat."

Danny reached for the newspaper.

Jello flashed his teeth as he sucked in a breath. "She needs to disappear. And that's not an ask this time. It's an order."

"You don't get to issue orders."

"I am now."

"I thought you could always say *no*," Danny barked.

Jello pushed the door open. Once he stepped out, he slammed it shut. From outside, he heard Danny.

"You said, you can always say *no*." Jello looked back at the van as he walked away. Danny was now screaming and his screams were bouncing off of the van walls. "That's how it goes, right? You can always say *no*." And then the van started to shake as Danny kicked at the side door with both feet. "You said I could always say *no*." Danny screamed. The van rocked again. Jello made his way towards his car. As he started the engine, he looked back towards the van again. It was still shaking like a junkie.

45. Danny and Maggie

DANNY SAW IT CLEAR AS DAY IN HIS MIND—Maggie splayed out on a chunk of grass in a forest preserve, the bullet wound to her temple still fresh. She was still clean, pretty. It would

take days before she turned a different shade, before a congre-
gation of maggots and other crawlers began to feast on her. And
no one would find her. Not here. Not for years, anyways. Danny
stooped over Maggie's body. These are the things that happen to
rats. He heard those words bellow against the walls of his brain.
Danny shook his head, rattling that image loose, and entered the
water department garage in a huff. He found Maggie.

"Where's Hat?

"I don't know," Maggie offered. "He said he was going to the
bathroom."

"To take a deuce?" Danny ran his bottom lip between his teeth,
his eyes darting about the garage.

Maggie narrowed her eyes. "I don't know. Just said he had to
go to the bathroom."

"Well, let's hope it's a deuce. His definitely take a while."

Danny shifted his head a bit, taking in his surroundings. Thirty
feet away, a man used a forklift to load supplies onto a tall metal
storage rack. Others were loading material into a truck. A third
man filled the air on a water truck tire. As Danny ran his eyes
across these workers, he wondered if they were staring at him,
whenever he turned away.

"C'mon with me," Danny said with the wave of his arm. He
walked to a vacant corner of the garage with Maggie in tow. Once
there, Danny yanked open a storage closet door. He eyed Maggie,
again making her feel uncomfortable.

"In here. C'mon." Maggie entered the storage closet followed
by Danny, and then Danny shut the door. For a moment the two
stood silently in darkness. And in that moment, Maggie wished she
hadn't entered that closet. She wished she had her gun with her.

"Look, here it is—straight up. So listen," Danny started. "Jello
knows who you are." Maggie didn't say a word. "Agent Coin.
That's what he said your name was."

Maggie's breaths spilled heavily into the darkness. She balled
her right hand into a fist ready to strike. Danny felt around on the
wall, his hand clanking into a broom stick and knocking it to the
floor, before finding the light switch. He flicked it on.

"Look, you need to get the hell outta here. Now. Simple as that.

Right fuckin' now!"

Maggie looked around frantically.

"Someone'll be comin' to get you. And soon. Whatever you do, don't go to your apartment or house or tent or wherever the hell ya live."

Danny pushed the door open and stepped out. Maggie followed. She had never been so thankful to see the overhead lights in a garage before.

"I'm sorry, Danny."

Danny released a thin smile. "No reason to be sorry. Just take the damn van and go. But ditch the van after a while. That's what I'd do. Drive to the el or some other train line and park it and get on a train so no one can call in the van you're in. So no one can follow ya."

"Who's coming to get me?"

Danny eyed Maggie. "It was supposed to be me." Maggie stared at Danny, momentarily frozen. "According to Jello, anyway." Danny nudged Maggie. "C'mon, you gotta go."

"But Jimmy's got the keys, right?"

"Nah," Danny said. "They're in the cupholder." Danny snatched Maggie by her right arm and led her towards the parking lot. She pulled herself free.

"You sure about this?" she said. "You should probably come with me."

"I'll be all right."

Maggie threw her left arm around Danny's neck and hugged him. "We can make you safe. Get you and your family protection."

"We'll be fine," Danny said. "Just go. Go." Maggie hustled out the door into the parking lot. Danny followed behind her and watched as she started up the van and rolled it out of the lot.

46. Blackjack

IT WAS A THURSDAY, AND DANNY LIKED THURSDAYS. They were always quiet when he came home from work. Kate would be gone with the baby. She'd drop him off at Mary's apartment and then head off to tutor some kid in Math from 4:30-6 p.m. With Kate gone, there would be no *How was your day? What do you think about* . . . , *For Christmas this year I'd like to* . . . , *C'mon, Danny, talk. Talk. Just TALK.*

And the boys, they were gone too—basketball practice at Ridge Park. Jimmy was back to his regular form. So Danny heard. Silence—that's what Danny craved. Danny could feel it. Silence, Danny could hear it. It filled the entire house. And in that silence Danny pictured Maggie on a train—rolling away to safety. Ah yes, Danny thought as he walked down the stairs into his basement, the world could use more Thursdays.

Danny snatched a Bruce Springsteen CD and slipped it into the player. He forwarded the selections until the song "Cadillac Ranch" came on. A Springsteen fan, Danny loved to hear Clarence on the sax. It was the lone invasion of silence he could tolerate. He dropped into a large black leather chair and let the song take hold of him. He didn't react outwardly. There was no shaking of the feet or bobbing of the head. But inwardly, his brain and heart shimmied. Danny set his eyes on his right arm, at the map of straight edge slices and scabs. He smiled and turned his attention to the music again. As he listened, a pair of dark dress shoes appeared atop the basement steps. And then those shoes moved slowly down the stairs, allowing Danny to see, at first, the dress pants above the shoes. And then there was the briefcase held by a gloved right hand, and then came the big shoulders with a head attached to them—Jankowski's head and shoulders.

Jankowski ambled slowly towards Danny's chair. Danny didn't move. No, he wasn't frozen with fear. He simply chose not to move. As Jankowski peered down at Danny, Clarence banged away on the sax. Danny wanted more sax, but Jankowski entered his ears instead.

"Stand up, Dan. Let's do this."

Danny eyes were fixed on a wall. "Do what?" His words were lifeless.

Jankowski clasped his gloved hands in front of him. "I coulda just been here waiting on you. But I didn't want to do it that way."

"You're a good man, Al," Danny said with a laugh.

"Look, I'm giving you a chance. That's the most anyone can ask for."

Danny aimed a finger at the briefcase as Jankowski set it on the cement floor. "What sort of prizes you got in there today?"

"You'll see soon enough." Jankowski rubbed his forehead. Danny stood and stared in silence at his former teammate. "Finally," Jankowski said. "I thought you—"

Danny surprised Jankowski with a left jab which landed on his cheek and opened a small cut. Jankowski wiped a bit of blood with his hand and smiled. "That's more like it." Jankowski raised his hands into a half boxer, half Tae Kwon Do position. "Fight for your life, Dan. Don't just take it in the ass."

Danny raised his hands and circled towards Jankowski's right. "Good one, Al. Nothin' like clever Polish thoughts." Jankowski grinned. Danny threw another jab, connecting again with Jankowski's face. The big man smiled again before he turned slightly towards his left and feigned a left jab. Danny snapped his head back slightly, away from where he thought the jab was going, just as Jankowski knew he would. And then Jankowski spun and unleashed a Tae Kwon Do roundhouse kick with his right foot which landed squarely on Danny's jaw. Danny's world went dark, and he crumpled to the basement floor. And in that darkness, Danny heard his father's voice.

"C'mon, already," Jim Lonigan barked. "Get up."

Jim stood in the corner of a boxing ring, his thick hands set on the ropes. The bell went off. Danny climbed to his feet and returned to his father. And that's when Danny noticed that it was his 12-year-old self in the ring, fighting for the 112-pound city boxing championship. Danny sat on a stool between rounds, his father sponging his face and neck, barking orders into his ear.

"Last round." Jim Lonigan said. "This is where you show your goods. This is where you show what you're made of." Jim ran the sponge over Danny's head. Drops of cold water rolled down Danny's face and neck. "That kid's tough. But you're tougher. Way tougher."

Danny nodded and bit his upper lip. And then he caught sight of his older self standing in the first row, dressed in a bloody shirt. Young Danny began to lose focus. The bell rang. Young Danny danced absently towards center ring. He dodged a jab followed by an uppercut. He thought about snapping off a jab but decided against it. He moved away from his opponent and looked out into the stands for his older self. But older Danny and his bloody shirt were gone. And in that split second when his eyes drifted away, young Danny's opponent clobbered him with a haymaker to end all twelve-year-old haymakers.

Danny came to. He was duct-taped to the chair he had been sitting in earlier. Mounds of gray tape circle his chest and legs. A sock was lodged in his mouth with tape holding it in place. His arms were taped to the sides of the chair.

Jankowski eyed his open briefcase. Inside were his hand axe, hammer, and a blackjack, along with two rolls of duct tape. He selected the blackjack. It was roughly eighteen inches long with a lead ball at the end, atop the spring. Danny had seen similar items before. He knew this one was homemade, lovingly wrapped in layers of black electrical tape, something Jankowski probably made while watching a Bears game one afternoon as he lounged around his den with his kids.

Jankowski wasted no time. He crashed the blackjack down on Danny's right forearm. Danny's eyes flared wide and his mouth tried to open. The sock swallowed his scream.

"You don't need that hand," Jankowski said. "You never were as good a shooter as you thought." Had Danny been in the right frame of mind, and without a sock in his mouth, he would've said: I never said I was a good shooter.

"Looks like you've been beating the shit out of that arm already anyways, huh, Dan?"

Again Danny wanted to say something, to talk about the slices and scabs covering his right arm. For the first time he was ready to talk about how the pain that came from the slicing, the cutting, the peeling, made him feel better, but he did not get an opportunity to speak. Jankowski hammered Danny's right forearm ten more times. Bones cracked and the arm flattened. Danny looked at his arm. He would never have thought an arm could ever be that flat. It reminded him of a long white pancake, with some freckles and hair growing out of it. Jankowski swung the blackjack several more times, connecting with Danny's jaw, kneecap, shoulder, and head. The blackjack snapped back each time, ready to deliver the next blow. The headshot did the most damage. Blood flowed from Danny' skull, and he blinked spastically. He was a boxer in the ring again, ready to fall to the canvas.

Jankowski slid around behind Danny and hammered away at Danny's ribs four times rapid fire. He popped him again, this time atop the crown of Danny's head. Jankowski stepped to the side and listened. Danny's head had slumped forward, his breathing labored.

"I'm almost done, Dan," Jankowski said. "Just a few more. Three more, in fact. That's it." Danny heard none of this. His brain was now on shutdown, his body in shock. Jankowski leaned over and whispered into Danny's ear. "I'm supposed to kill you, Dan. You know that. But I'm not." Danny didn't respond. Jankowski snatched Danny's hair with a gloved hand and barked. "You hear me?" Danny's eyes fluttered. Jankowski let loose Danny's hair. "It's your choice, Danny. Yours. You decide if you live or die." Jankowski removed his cell phone from his pocket and dialed. "Two minutes," he said and hung up.

"Shoulda just done it, Dan." Jankowski ran a gloved hand through his hair and thought back to his days when he and Danny played on the same high school basketball team. They lost the state championship game by one point. One stinkin' point. Jankowski saw himself pull down a big defensive rebound with five seconds left. Had he held on to the ball, the game would have been over, or he would've been fouled and brought home greater glory with his free throws. But Jankowski fired an outlet pass towards a guard. Problem was—he didn't see the opposing team's guard lurking in the shadows. That guard stepped in front of his outlet pass, took one dribble, and drained a jumper just as time expired to send the trophy to the other side. In the locker room, after the coach finished talking, it was Danny who threw his arm around Jankowski's neck. "Great season, Al," Danny said. "Couldna made it this far without you." And then Danny smiled and said, "The sun'll come up tomorrow. It will."

Jankowski hammered Danny three times across his face and head, tearing open flesh. "Good luck, Dan. Your choice. You decide if the sun comes up." He pulled the tape off of Danny's left arm and departed using the basement door.

Once Jankowski entered the alley, Winslow stood outside of a black sedan. Jankowski stepped into the back seat. Winslow yanked open the other back door.

"You drive your own self outta here."

Jankowski's eyes were slits. "What the hell are you doing?"

Winslow tossed the keys in Jankowski's lap. "I'm going in there."

"You don't even know who's in there."

"The hell I don't." Winslow walked through the back gate towards Danny's house. Jankowski watched him for a moment before he climbed out of the back seat and slipped into the driver's seat. He punched the pedal and tore off down the alley.

Winslow called Danny's name several times as he entered the house. He worked his way to the basement where he found him.

"My God," Winslow muttered as he removed the duct tape from Danny's body and laid him flat on the floor. Blood poured from a gaping wound on Danny's right forearm. Winslow removed his belt and applied it just above the wound, cutting off the flow. He then dialed 911.

"A man's been beaten. Beaten bad. Send an ambulance quick: 10240 South Bell. Hurry." Winslow ended the call and then listened for Danny's breath. He didn't hear it. He checked his left wrist. There was barely a pulse.

⚒

At her apartment, Mary rushed into Ellen's room. Ellen stood in a corner slamming her forehead against the wall and moaning. With each pound, the wall shook. Tears rushed down Ellen's face. Her moans grew louder. Mary jumped between the wall and Ellen.

"Stop that, Ellie Mae," Mary screamed. "Stop."

Ellen's moans grew even louder, but they were different. It was not the usual long, drawn-out moan. It was the same sound—repeated again and again. As Mary listened, it clicked. The same two syllables were being repeated. And then, Mary's eyes widened. She knew what Ellen was saying.

"Dahhh-naaay. Dahhh-naaay."

Mary pulled Ellen to her chest. "Danny? Is that what you're saying, Ellie. Is that it?" In Ellen's forty-two years, Mary had never heard her say anything that remotely resembled a word.

"Dahhh-naaay. Dahhh-naaay."

Part Six

The Answer

1. Maggie and the Mayor

MAGGIE ENTERED DANNY'S HOSPITAL ROOM and stood beside Kate and Hairdo. Tom and Hat were pinned against the wall on the other side of the room, speaking in whispers, while Ziggy and Winslow held their post near the door. Dr. Valek reviewed the nurses' notes from a clipboard. Normal ICU policies prohibit a large number of visitors, but those policies are often overlooked when one's time is near its end.

A mummy. Had Jim or Sam been in the room, that's likely what they would have thought their father looked like. Danny's entire head was wrapped with gauze, revealing peepholes around his eyes, and openings around his nose and mouth. A ventilator tube protruded from Danny's mouth with the machine hissing and breathing for him every few seconds. Just like Jim's surgery, the doctors had to open Danny's skull and induce a coma to allow the blood surrounding Danny's brain to drain. His right arm was wrapped so thick with gauze, it resembled more of a club than an arm. The remainder of Danny's body was encased in white sheets.

Maggie's eyes bounced from Tom's face to Kate's. Everyone wore worried wrinkled faces and wet eyes. Maggie could almost hear the silent prayers they muttered. She walked over and tapped Tom on the shoulder and motioned towards the hallway. They exited the room and walked towards the end of the hall before stopping.

"So what do ya think?"

"I don't know," Tom said. "He's strong as a bull, but it don't look like he's really fightin'. Looks like he's sittin' on the fence. Like he's decidin' or someone else is decidin'."

Maggie's Adam's apple rose as she swallowed. "I'm the reason why he's here." She pulled out her FBI badge and showed it to Tom. He eyed the badge but then turned to watch a nurse passing through the hallway. "We've been all over Jello Pellegrini. Anyway, Jello found out who I am. Danny was supposed to . . . well . . . Jello told him to kill me."

"Danny?"

Maggie nodded her head. "But he wouldn't do it. He told me that Jello knew who I was. We were at a Department of Water garage, and he told me to leave. To take off. So that's what I did. I took off in the van and well, eventually, went to my office."

She handed Tom a book bag. "This is Danny's," she said. "I'm giving it to you, but know this. His journal's in there. I read his entries. All of them." Tom stared at Maggie with a look bordering on disbelief. "About four or five pages in there need to be destroyed. Immediately. Ya know what I mean?"

"Yeah."

Maggie nodded. "And Tom, I , well . . I guess it's best to just say it. The doctors should probably give Danny some extra meds or help for, uh, for . . ." Maggie stopped and sucked in a deep breath.

"For what?" Tom's eyes were pinched tight. "What?"

Maggie slowly released her breath. "He's been cutting himself, Tom. Slicing himself. Ask Kate. I'm guessing she would know."

Tom's eyes immediately widened. He moaned as he fell back against the hallway wall, taking in what Maggie had just said. Tears welled in his eyes.

"He'll be okay, Tom," Maggie said. "He will." Tom stared a hole into the floor. Maggie set a hand on his shoulder. "He deserves a second chance. He does."

Tom's eyes remained focused on the floor. Danny. Slicing himself? Tom thought. But why? How could I miss that? As Maggie turned to leave, Tom snapped back.

"One thing," Tom said as he erased his tears with his right hand. "Two things, actually." Tom pulled Maggie in and hugged her. "Thanks," Tom said as he shook Danny's book bag. "Thanks for this." Tom released Maggie. "And second, let's just say I know a thing or two about Jello." Tom scratched his nose. "Don't go home. Not at all. He'll have someone stopping by there, for sure."

Maggie offered a thin-lipped smile and a nod of thanks before she walked off. As Tom moved towards Danny's room, his cell went off.

"Tom Lonigan."

"Tom, it's Mayor Stokely."

Tom leaned against the hallway wall again. "Hi, Mayor."

"Tried to reach you at your office," Stokely said. He stood in his office with a bottle of water in hand. "Your secretary told me about your brother. How's he doing?"

"Touch and go right now. Thanks for askin'."

"Well, I wanted to let you know my prayers are with your family and—"

"Thanks, Mayor."

"And Tom, I know this may not be the time but . . . I wanted to let you know that, well . . . the short of it is, I'm calling it quits. No re-election for me next year."

"Really?"

"Yep. I know this may not be the best time to talk about this. You got a lot on your mind, but here's the thing. I'd like to sit down with you. To talk. See . . . you're the first person I've shared this news with, other than my lovely wife, of course." Tom's eyes narrowed as he listened. "See, I want *you* to run for mayor. I want you to take over. I think you would do a helluva job."

"What about Randall?"

"Fuck Randall. I despise that man."

"What're you gonna do?"

Stokely laughed. "Me?" He bobbed his head. "I'll be straight up with you. The shit's gonna hit the mayoral fan soon. Big time. And I'm tired of cleaning shit off of my fan. And my face. I'll prep you for the time bombs around the corner. You got the moxie to handle it. You do. But, uh . . . as for me, personally . . . it's time to head down to Florida. Ya know, hang out on the beach, throw a line in the water. Tie some flies. That sorta shit."

"Gotcha."

"And you can take Randall. No doubt. The way you are— you're hard working. You're honest. You're loyal. And that counts big time with the voters. And I'll be glad to help assemble your team. A team that will help kick Randall's ass."

"Interesting."

"Well, Tom, what do ya say we meet tomorrow for lunch."

"I'd love to, Mayor. But can you give me a couple of days. I gotta few things I gotta do, and I wanna be here with Danny as much as possible."

"Of course. Of course. My bad." Stokely sipped his water. "How's Monday at noon in my office? Will that work for you?"

"Sounds good."

"Prayers to your brother, again."

"Thanks." Tom slipped his cell back into his pocket and made his way back towards Danny's room.

2. The Shillelagh

MARGARET COIN'S APARTMENT was on the second floor of an old, sixteen-unit building in the Roger's Park neighborhood. Just a block away, the roar of Lake Michigan's waves could be heard. Tom Lonigan stood in the shadows of the hallway of Maggie's apartment and made a call on his cell. He held his shillelagh in his other hand.

"I need two people. Immediately." Tom looked down the hallway. "Write it down. Send both to 6958 North Sheridan. One needs to disable the camera on the second floor. The other needs to set up as a painter and cover the camera outside the building. Pronto on this. Pronto. And any memory chips in the cameras need to be removed or destroyed on both cameras. And make sure we got a mattress guy nearby in the area, a mattress guy who can make everything crystal clean."

Tom hung up the phone. Earlier in the day, he had the area examined. There were no reports of any sightings of Jello's men or the feds. And that surprised him. He knew that if they hadn't been around yet, they'd be around soon. Maybe, Tom thought, they were focused on Jello's home, or perhaps, they were watching his every move from a nearby window.

Tom waited in the shadows at the far end of the second floor. A few minutes later a work van arrived. Two men dressed in baggy, white painter's pants exited, both with ladders, paint and tools in hand. One set up near the camera on the exterior of the building. He quickly covered the camera lens with electrical tape and then began to paint the window trim on the second floor. The other man, Billy Laski, with ladder in hand, met Tom at the end of the hallway.

"The camera's down there," Tom said with a nod. "Near the far end."

Laski set up his ladder below the second-floor camera and covered the lens with electrical tape and dislodged the memory chip. He flashed a thumbs-up to Tom. Tom nodded and waited as Laski then used a mini-screwdriver to gain entry to Maggie's apartment. Tom entered immediately and locked the door from the inside. Laski broke down his ladder and walked for the lobby door with his supplies in hand.

Jankowski arrived in his own car. Laski walked directly past Jankowski as he made his way towards the apartment. Jankowski turned and watched while Laski loaded the ladder into the van with the words *O'Brien Painting* emblazoned on the side. Jankowski moved towards the front door and eyed the other man painting the window trim on the bottom floor. Once Jankowski made his way to Maggie's apartment, he picked the lock and entered. He walked around the one-bedroom apartment a bit and then took a seat on a kitchen chair. He grabbed his cell phone and dialed. Jello answered.

"Yeah."

"She's not here," Jankowski said. "Quiet as a mouse."

"Okay. Sit tight for a minute. I'll get right back to ya."

"Good enough."

As Jankowski ended his call, Tom Lonigan cracked him across the head with his shillelagh. Jankowski went down to the floor. Tom opened Jankowski's suitcase and searched through it. He grabbed the duct tape and wrapped Jankowski's feet and arms, rendering him immobile. Tom filled a cup with water at the sink and splashed Jankowski's face. He shook to.

Jankowski crunched his jaw back and forth and looked up from the floor. "Long time, no see, Tom."

"I wanted you to be awake. So you would know."

"Know what? Know that it was you?" Jankowski laughed. "I figured I'd see you after what I done to Danny. Only I didn't think it would be this fast."

"Want somethin' in your mouth?"

"No, I won't scream."

Tom raised the shillelagh and smashed Jankowski across the shoulder, to test him. Jankowski winced but didn't make a sound.

"Is Danny gonna make it?"

Tom snarled and brought a blow to Jankowski's jaw, tearing open his mouth and cracking off a few teeth. Jankowski's jaw rattled as it moved.

"I know I shouldn't ask but I have to." Jankowski spat out a mound of blood. "My wife and kids?"

Tom bent over and looked Jankowski in the eyes. "I'm not Jello."

"Thanks." Jankowski examined Tom's shillelagh. "Nice club."

"It's a shillelagh. It was my dad's."

Jankowski spat again on the floor. "You ever wash the blood from it?"

Tom stood tall before Jankowski. "Gotta wrap up." He raised the shillelagh over his head.

"Tom, wait," Jankowski said, his words barely a whimper. Tom lowered his shillelagh. Jankowski sucked in and released two deep breaths before speaking. "Just thought . . . just thought you should know."

Tom narrowed his eyes and bent down again. Jankowski ran his tongue around his mouth, massaging his mangled teeth.

"What?"

"Well . . . Jello's the one who wanted your dad dead. He's the one who ordered it done."

"Jello?"

"Yeah. He told me the story before."

Tom walked away a bit, scratching at his head. He stopped and faced Jankowski. "Why?"

"No idea. He never spilled that part." Jankowski rolled his head in tiny circles. "Know where he is?" Tom nodded. Jankowski tried to laugh but instead winced in pain again. Blood spilled from his lips. "Of course, you do." Jankowski's chest heaved in search of air. "Be careful. He'll have three or four guys around him."

"Right."

Jankowski closed his eyes as Tom straddled him. Tom then brought the shillelagh down upon Jankowski's skull twice with all his might. Tom dropped to a kitchen chair. As he sat, he eyed the blood and brain matter splattered on the floor and wall. He dialed his cell phone.

"Okay. Get the mattress up here. Make sure it's a king size." Tom went to the window and signaled the man down below. That man carried his ladder and supplies back to the work van and loaded up. The *O'Brien* van pulled away. A few minutes later, a truck from Erickson Moving Company arrived, with Tim Forberg in the driver's seat and Joe Donnelly in the passenger seat. Tom watched from the front window. As the two men carried a king-sized mattress from the truck towards the apartment building, Donnelly saw Tom framed in the window. Donnelly offered a small wave and Tom nodded back. Tom then exited through the rear entry to the apartment.

Jello sat on a couch in the front room of his home. Two other men stood guard in the room. Jello dialed Jankowski. The phone rang several times before it went to voicemail. Jello hung up and dialed again. Again the call went to voicemail. Jello hung up and tucked the phone back into his shirt pocket, a concerned look on his face.

"No answer," Jello said. The men nodded, and then one jumped to his feet. He went to the window and looked down below. Hat stood guard in a lawn chair in front of the house.

3. Maggie's Apartment

AGENT TANGEL AND MAGGIE CURBED THEIR CAR in front of Maggie's apartment. As they exited the sedan, another car with two agents arrived. With the suits and ties everywhere, it looked like a gathering for a small funeral. As the other agents approached, Tangel watched two movers carry a king mattress towards a truck parked just in front of Agent Tangel's car. Tangel's eyes stayed fixed on the men as they raised the overhead door to the truck. Inside the truck were assorted furniture items like tables and chairs, bookshelves, a couch, and a refrigerator. Tangel turned to the men in the other car.

"Okay, let's go have a look," Tangel said. The four walked towards the apartment. One mover pulled down the overhead door while the other started the engine. As Tangel, Maggie, and the others entered the building, the moving truck pulled away.

Tangel, Maggie, and the two other men drew their weapons just before Maggie opened the door. They stepped inside with their guns at the ready.

"Nothing," said Tangel.

"I'll take a look around," said one of the other agents.

"That oughta take all of five seconds," said Tangel. "Hard to hide in a tiny apartment."

Maggie looked around. "Everything looks the same," she said.

"Okay, let's go," Tangel said. The agents left Maggie's apartment and gathered together out in front of Maggie's building.

"I'm sorry," Maggie said. "I thought someone might be here."

"No worries," said Tangel. "Maybe they'll be here later." He turned his head from side to side slowly. "Or maybe they're here already, watching us from a window somewhere." He turned towards the other two agents. "Set up a detail to mind the store here." As the two agents walked towards their cars, Tangel turned back towards the building. The sun glinted off of the fresh paint on the window trim. Tangel rushed forward, towards the window, as the three watched. He reached a lanky arm up and rubbed a finger across the trim. His finger came up with wet, white paint. He waved the others over and flashed his finger.

"Doesn't that look nice," Tangel said. All three looked at his finger and then examined the window. "Doesn't it seem strange that someone would paint two windows in an entire building?" Tangel looked around a bit more and noticed the camera. The tape was still on it.

"Agent Coin, does your landlord make a habit of taping over the security camera?" All of the agents examined the camera.

"No, sir," Maggie said, her eyes fixed on the camera. "That thing has never been taped before. Not that I'm aware of."

"Looks like Lonigan was right," Tangel said. "Someone's been here." He turned towards Maggie. "Any other cameras in the building?"

"One on each floor," Maggie said. "At least there's one on my floor, so I'm guessing there's one on the other floors too." Agent Tangel nodded to one of the other agents who made his way towards the entry door again. The three agents fixed their eyes on the painted window again and waited for the fourth agent. When he returned, he barked. "Second floor camera is taped up too."

4. A Call to Action

LATER THAT EVENING, TOM SAT BESIDE Kate in a recliner alongside Danny's hospital bed. His heavy eyes were set on his brother's face, or rather on the gauze surrounding his face. Tom leaned back in his chair, his hands pressed together, and offered continuous silent prayers for Danny's recovery. Every now and again, Kate turned towards Tom as his words slipped through the walls of silence and became groans. He would nod politely at Kate and then go back to staring at his brother and saying his silent prayers. And then it happened—something Tom hadn't expected. Sleep. Maybe it was the rhythmic purr of the ventilator that did him in, or perhaps it was just the fact that Tom's body was drained, his tank completely emptied. Whatever it was, Tom gave in to his urge to rejuvenate his body, his mind, his soul.

As Tom's eyelids fluttered, Kate examined her brother-in-law. He looked at peace, like an oversized teenager ready to put in a fourteen-hour power snooze on a Saturday. And Kate found that strange. How can you look so peaceful when your brother is here dying beside you? But that look of peace also put a hint of a smile on Kate's face. She reached into a gym bag and grabbed a hooded sweatshirt. She shaped it into a ball and slipped it behind Tom's thick neck to comfort him.

But Tom could not feel that sweatshirt pillow, and he was most certainly not at peace. Tom was a 19-year-old again. And here he was, yet again, kneeling before his father's casket—a dream Tom had so many times over the years, he stopped keeping track. And that casket, it was a dull brown, a brown that made one want to cry, and it was closed. It had to be. No one wants to kneel over a casket and stare at a head that's been reduced to mush by a baseball bat. Tom swayed a bit and muttered prayers, his eyes fixed on the gold framed eight-by-ten inch photo of a Young Jim Lonigan resting atop the casket.

"I'm sorry, Dad," Tom kept repeating. "So sorry. I shoulda been there. I shoulda."

Tom continued to stare at the photo—wishing it would say something to him, anything, hoping it could speak. But Jim Lonigan stayed mute, as always in this dream, his lips sealed inside that casket. He simply stared Tom's way with silent, gleaming teeth from his post inside the gold frame.

That dream played over and over as Tom slept. The buzz of an incoming text message shook Tom from his sleep. He eyed the text message as Kate snoozed beside him. Tom then checked his wristwatch. It was 2:00 a.m. He didn't get fourteen hours, but he got what he needed. He crossed himself slowly from forehead to chest, and left shoulder to right shoulder. He looked at Danny one last time and hustled out of the room.

5. The Great Escape

MAGGIE, GILBREATH, AND PHIPPS STOOD OUTSIDE of Tangel's office. Maggie knocked.

"Come in," Tangel bellowed. The three entered, and Gilbreath and Phipps stopped the moment they set foot inside the room. The entire wall behind Tangel's desk was a floor-to-ceiling mural of Jello Pellegrini from the shoulders up. Pinned to various parts of the wall were reports and smaller photos.

"Good God," Gilbreath said.

"Well," Tangel said as he extended his hand, "Most folks just call me Agent Tangel."

Maggie laughed.

"Quite the set up here," Gilbreath said, as he shook Tangel's hand. Phipps also exchanged a handshake.

"I asked Maggie to bring you both here today for a couple of reasons." Tangel sat on the corner of his desk. "First, I wanted Mr. Gilbreath to hear it from me—Maggie wanted to let you know who she was quite some time ago. Believe me, she did. But I would not allow it. For safety reasons. So don't go holding that against her."

"I fully understand," Gilbreath said.

"Good, because she certainly did not." Tangel's eyes bounced from Gilbreath to Phipps. "Second, I think we have some really good intel, here and we're getting close to cracking everything wide open. I know how important this is to you both. I know about Jello and your daughter, Mr. Gilbreath. Maggie told me about that." He faced Phipps directly. "And I know he invaded your home, Mr. Phipps, and snapped some photos of your family. Anyway, we have about twenty-five names of city workers who work in various capacities for Jello. There's more out there, but that's what we have right now. And I think we can tie Jello in to some degree to three murders over the past ten years and one recent disappearance."

"That's great," Gilbreath offered.

"It is. I agree. But we have a problem—and this brings me to my last point." Tangel scratched his head. "Jello's gone."

"What?" Maggie screeched.

"Disappeared. Vanished. Escaped. Call it what you want," Tangel said. "We tried to track him. Checked everything. Flights, trains, buses. Nothing. We're checking camera footage right now at various airports and train stations . . . in case he used a different name. But the reality of it all is—he's probably in a hut somewhere in South America or in a tiny village in Sicily slurping down some quality vino. He's gone, for sure. I wanted you to hear it first from me."

Tangel watched as Gilbreath stared again at the wall.

"Can I ask you," Gilbreath said, "why you . . . I mean, you know why I was investigating him . . . but how about you, Agent Tangel? Why were you on him?" Gilbreath's eyes stayed fixed on the Jello mural. "I mean, you have the guy's whole face on your wall."

"Because his file came to my desk," Tangel said. "Simple as that. And the closer I looked, the dirtier things got." Gilbreath nodded. "We'll continue to work up this file. We'll be ready to move against him in the event he brings his rotund, pasta-eating self back to visit some friends." Tangel eyed his mural and turned to Gilbreath and Phipps. "We'll let you know if we get our mitts on him."

"Thank you," Gilbreath said. He and Phipps shook Tangel's hand, and then the three moved for the door.

"Oh, Maggie," Tangel barked before they left, "anything in Danny Lonigan's book bag?"

"No."

"Nothing?"

"Just a bunch of journal entries and a few typed papers. Stuff for his class. Nothing that would help us. I returned it to his brother already."

Tangel ran his right hand along his scalp. "How's he doing?"

"He's still in limbo," Maggie said.

6. The Answer

TOM, HAIRDO, AND DENNY FREYER FLEW ACROSS the waters of Lake Michigan on a twenty-five-foot boat with plenty of seats and ample storage space. The weather had delivered yet another perfect fall day, a day perfect to be one with the water.

The boat took off from Skipper's Marina in South Suburban Riverdale but not before Tom and his two comrades downed a few ice-cold beverages at the marina bar. It was Hairdo's suggestion. "A breakfast beer is always a good way to start your day," he had said. So they each downed a beer and a salami-and-egg sandwich to jump start their systems. After pulling out of the marina, with Freyer at the helm, they motored a mere one hundred yards, give or take, before arriving at the lock station, connecting the Cal-Sag River to Lake Michigan. Fifteen minutes later, the boat inscribed with the name, *The Answer*, was racing across the water.

Once the men were roughly ten miles out into Lake Michigan, Freyer brought the boat to a stop. A windless day, even ten miles out, the water like glass. Tom looked about as the boat drifted. No other boats were within sight, and the Illinois-Indiana shore was but a distant, hazy memory. Freyer dragged a one-hundred pound kettlebell to the edge of the boat with a gloved hand, chewing all the while on the unlit cigar in his mouth.

"You got two of those, right?" Tom said, as he slipped on a pair of gloves.

"Yep," Freyer said. He carried the second kettlebell and set it beside the first. Now clad in black gloves, Hairdo removed a blue tarp wrapped with rope, revealing two mattresses stacked atop one another. The three men pushed and shimmied the first mattress to the starboard side of the boat, beside the kettlebells.

"And no screw-ups this time," Tom said. "I don't want no one to come floatin' back to civilization like our fat, four-fingered friend did."

The three men eyed each other. "Not to worry," Freyer said as he yanked two heavy-duty ankle chains from a gym bag. "Much better quality this time." Tom shook his head from side to side. Freyer and Hairdo grinned as they glanced at each other.

Quickly, the men went to work. Tom pulled a muscular leg covered in dark pants and a black dress shoe out a bit from the interior of the hollowed mattress. Freyer locked the chain around that ankle and attached the other end to the kettlebell. The three then rolled the body out of the mattress into Lake Michigan. The large body of Al Jankowski floated momentarily before the weight of the kettlebell pulled him under. Tom crossed himself slowly.

The men shoved the empty mattress aside and then pulled, dragged, and pushed the second mattress forward. Tom again yanked an ankle free from the hollow mattress interior. Freyer attached the ankle chain just above a white Converse gym shoe. The kettlebell was attached in seconds, and the men dumped that body into the water. They all watched as Jello Pellegrini stared face up, a bullet hole in his forehead.

"Kind of a fat fuck, huh?" Freyer said.

"Too much pasta'll do that to ya," Hairdo said with a smile.

Tom remained silent, his eyes fixed on Jello. Even after Jello sank and disappeared into the water, Tom's eyes stayed fixed on the spot where Jello had been. And in that moment, Tom thought of his father. Again, Tom crossed himself slowly.

"Ready, Tom?" Freyer said, now standing beside his perch at the steering wheel.

"Yeah, sure." Tom took a seat. Freyer started the engine and pointed the boat in a northwesterly direction to begin the return journey. Hairdo re-wrapped the two mattresses in the tarp again as the boat moved. He then sat across from Tom.

The boat zipped along the lake for a good deal of time. The only living, breathing visitors were the few gulls who floated past the boat. Tom's thoughts rolled back to Danny. He pulled out his cell and dialed Kate, but the call did not go through. A bit more time, Tom thought. A bit closer.

Tom could see Danny in his mind again, though. He imagined him in the alley behind his house shooting baskets with his sons. Danny's face had several scars on it, but he still looked handsome. His lower right arm was gone now, replaced by what Tom would call a robot arm. But Danny was at peace. He felt comfortable with his robotic arm. He couldn't slice or scalp his arm ever again, and he didn't feel the need to slice it anymore either. God decided that Danny should live but lose his arm as his immediate punishment, his penance for failing to warn Lassandrello, and Danny was just fine with that. The balance of that punishment, if any, would be delivered in time. Danny rebounded missed shots, holding the ball with both his good arm and his robot arm, and passed the ball back to his sons each time. "The next time you hit two in a row," Danny chided, "will be the first time you hit two in a row." Sam and Jim laughed. Danny passed the ball to Sam and snapped his robotic fingers at him.

Tom's cell rang. He answered it.

"Hi, Kate, how's he doing?"

"He's bouncing back." There was silence for a moment. "Where are you?"

"I'll be there in a little bit. Sorry. Had to take care of a minor emergency. Ya know, union stuff."

"I thought we were going to lose him earlier today, and I called you a bunch of times, but the calls wouldn't go through."

"Sorry about that."

"Tom, I gotta tell you, his oxygen numbers were bad. The doctors and nurses were all over him. Checking, prodding. Like I said, I thought we were gonna lose him." Kate stopped to suck in a deep breath. "And then—it was the strangest thing. Your mom brought Ellen to the hospital. She climbed right up into the bed with Danny and hugged him and held him. The nurses wanted to get her out of there, but we told them, 'No way.'" Kate began to cry but talked through her tears. "If Danny was going to die, I'd want him to be in Ellen's arms. It was beautiful." Kate tried to continue but choked on her words.

"It's okay, Kate. Take your time."

"So she's holding him and hugging him, and then all of a sudden Ellen starts crying and then she starts bawling. And then it happened. I saw one tear leak out of Danny's eyes. Just one. It was so strange. Like that tear had a life of its own. It just sat there in the corner of Danny's right eye before it finally slid away into the gauze. And that's when Danny opened his eyes and looked at me and your mom and Ellen, and he smiled. He actually winked and smiled. You could see it plain as day. His teeth showing all around that tube in his mouth. I hadn't seen a smile like that in months, Tom. It felt so good to see it, and that's when I knew he was gonna make it. And then both he and Ellen fell into a deep sleep with Ellen holding him tight." Kate paused for a moment. "Since then his oxygen numbers have been improving, and his head is doing loads better. The doctors said they'd like to take him off of the ventilator too. Most likely tomorrow for that."

"Great. Great news."

"Yeah, but Tom, when you get here—just so you know . . . they said they have to remove his right arm. Ya know . . . from the elbow down. As soon as he comes off the ventilator, they're going to do it. Said it was a necessity."

"It's just an arm, Kate. Small price to pay to be able to live."

"You're right. You're right." Kate nibbled on her bottom lip. "See you in a bit."

Tom started to return his phone to his pocket, but another call came through. He took a breath and blew it out slowly, before answering.

"Hey, it's me, Jimmy Scarpelli. Is it done?"

"Yeah, Jimmy. It's done. I owe ya."

"You don't owe me nothin'." Hat coughed. "How's Danny?"

"I'm on my way there now. But I just got off the phone with Kate. He's gonna make it. She says he's improving, big time. He's gonna make it."

"Good. Good. I'll see you over there in a little bit."

"You gottit."

Tom returned his phone to his pocket and sat back in his seat. He enjoyed the sound of the boat slicing across the water. He found it soothing, quiet. He looked at Denny Freyer at the wheel, mashing that cigar between his lips, and then at Hairdo, staring out at the water. Tom smiled. It was good to have friends like these men.

"Hey, Hairdo," Tom bellowed, "can you take over the controls for a few minutes?"

"No problem."

Freyer stepped aside to allow Hairdo to take the helm. Tom waved Freyer over.

"You got that phone on ya?" Tom said.

"Yeah."

"Well, give 'im a call and let him know that Jello Pellegrini is on the run." Freyer nodded. "Ya know, tell him he caught wind that the feds were after him and he left town. Probably in South America or Italy or Guam by now. Ya know, somethin' like that."

"That it?"

Tom nodded. Freyer dialed a number and paced as he waited for his call to be answered.

"Jim White here."

"Hi ya, Mr. White," Freyer said. "It's your friend, the Secret San Man callin'."

White perked up and sat upright at his desk.

"Good stuff on that guy that got beat up by the cop," Freyer said.

"Thanks for bringing that my way," White said. "That video . . . wow. I'm glad it's in the public eye now."

"I hear ya." Freyer gnawed on his cigar. "Look, I got somethin' else for ya. Somethin' on another city worker. Thought you might be interested."

"Always. Always." White turned on his recorder. "Fire away."

"Okay, well, it's about Jello Pellegrini. You know a bit about him, right?"

White smiled. "Sure do."

"Okay, so it seems Jello caught wind that the Feds were getting' ready to drop the hammer on him. So bein' the sorry sack of shit that he is, Jello decides that . . ."

Tom ignored the balance of Freyer's conversation and instead stared out at where he knew the shoreline would first appear. Now it was empty and gray. But Tom's eyes stayed focused, staring out into that emptiness, that gray. He waited patiently as the boat zipped along. He could already see the headline in tomorrow's *Sun-Times*: "City Worker On Run From Feds." As Tom well knew, every card has a role, a purpose. And that headline would be there for all of Chicago to see, including the mayor. That ought to keep Stokely from having a change of heart, Tom thought, as the boat drew closer to the city's boundaries. Soon Tom would see the assorted structures that marked his entry into Chicago. First would be the factory and mill smokestacks, jutting up into the far South Side sky, belching a steady flow of smog into the air near Hege-wisch, then a bit farther north, tiny houses pushed tightly beside each other for warmth and strength would dot the streets near the shore, and then Tom would see the downtown skyscrapers standing tall and strong in the late morning sky. And Tom looked forward to seeing the city, the city that would one day be his. But far more important than that, soon Tom would be with his brother. And he would stand beside him and tell him that he loved him and that he would always be there for him. Always. Until he croaked, anyway.

THE END

Acknowledgements

Writing this book has been a wonderful journey, a journey much like the one I thoroughly enjoyed during my seven-year stint as an employee in the city's Department of Streets and Sanitation. I have long been a huge fan of the City of Chicago. It has so much to offer. And sure it has its shortcomings, but, hey, we're all works in progress, right? And working for Streets and San gave me the opportunity to discover so much of the city that I had not yet seen. I came across side streets, eateries, ward yards, camouflaged garages, crematoriums, corner taverns, and other assorted strange places tucked into a neighborhood nook here or cranny there—places I never knew existed. And to say I met many an interesting, strange or odd city worker during my Streets and San days would be a supreme understatement. Most of these men and women were hard-working humans, something we should all strive to be. Yet still others caused me to shake my head and mutter to myself, *Did that guy really just do that?* The places and characters I stumbled across during my seven years as a city electrician supplied material that, over time, simply had to find its way to the page. And so, it has. In a way, *The Blue Circus* is my admittedly strange love song to Chicago, a place that will always hold space in my heart. So, thanks to the city and to the Department of Streets and San for giving me the opportunity to be your humble servant, thanks for providing material worthy of the pen, and thanks for helping me to grow as a writer.

To Joe Mueller, Jen Greene, Denny Freyer, Christine Snyder, Ryan Smith, Jack Lynch, City Worker No. 1, Chris Nearn, Terry McGuire, and City No. 2, thanks for reading these pages and for offering thoughtful suggestions. Your time and insight are truly appreciated. Thanks to Linda Naslund for combing through the material with her red pen. Thanks to my comrades in the Department of Streets and San. I thoroughly enjoyed my days as a city electrician but continue to enjoy the friendships I made even more. Lastly, to my bride, Sue—thanks for being the person you are and for working as hard as you do to give me the time to write. Teamwork with a capital T.

BOOKS BY SIDE STREET PRESS

The Drunkard's Son by Dennis Foley

Echoes from a Lost Mind by Carl Richards

We Speak Chicagoese—stories and poems by Chicago writers, Edited by Bill Donlon, et al

And These Are The Good Times by Patricia Ann McNair

Model Child by R.C. Goodwin

About the Author

A life-long Chicagoan, Dennis Foley is the author of the award-winning guidebook—*The Streets and San Man's Guide to Chicago Eats*, and a memoir—*The Drunkard's Son*. His short fiction and memoir pieces have also appeared in a number of journals. *The Blue Circus* is his first novel.

Dennis holds an MFA in Creative Writing from Columbia College-Chicago, and a JD from The John Marshall Law School. He is also a proud graduate of Christian Brothers University in Memphis. When he's not writing, Dennis runs a lacrosse program for Southside kids and uses his legal skills to keep his friends out of jail.

To reach Dennis, feel free to contact the publisher at:
info@sidestreetpressinc.com
or Dennis directly at:
foleydennis2@gmail.com